THE
SEVENTH
GIRL

ALSO BY ANDY MASLEN

Detective Ford:

Shallow Ground
Land Rites
Plain Dead

DI Stella Cole:

Hit and Run
Hit Back Harder
Hit and Done
Let the Bones Be Charred
Weep, Willow, Weep
A Beautiful Breed of Evil
Death Wears a Golden Cloak
See the Dead Birds Fly

Gabriel Wolfe Thrillers:

Trigger Point
Reversal of Fortune
Blind Impact
Condor
First Casualty
Fury
Rattlesnake
Minefield

No Further
Torpedo
Three Kingdoms
Ivory Nation
Crooked Shadow
Brass Vows
Seven Seconds

Other Fiction:

Blood Loss – A Vampire Story
Purity Kills
You're Always With Me
Green-Eyed Mobster

THE SEVENTH GIRL

A DETECTIVE KAT BALLANTYNE THRILLER

ANDY MASLEN

THOMAS & MERCER

Published by Thomas & Mercer, Seattle

www.apub.com

Amazon, the Amazon logo, and Thomas & Mercer are trademarks of Amazon.com, Inc., or its affiliates.

ISBN-13: 9781662511011
eISBN: 9781662511028

Cover photography and design by Dominic Forbes

Printed in the United States of America

For my sons, Rory and Jacob

PROLOGUE

Summer 2008

Nineteen-year-old Sally Robb feels her stomach squirming, but it's a kind of giddy excitement.

He's older than her, and out of uniform she can see he's actually pretty buff. He must work out. She smiles at the memory of her date's shy invitation.

'I thought we could go for a walk in Brearley Woods,' he said.

'Isn't that where he's dumping them?' she asked.

He grinned. 'You're not scared, are you?'

She wasn't then. Isn't now.

As they enter the woods, she looks around. They have the place to themselves. It's magical. Every shade of green you could imagine. Sunlight coming down in bright stripes like through the blinds at home. Mum loves her Venetians. Says curtains make the place look old-fashioned. Whatever.

A loud crack somewhere to their right makes her jump.

'Oh my God!' she says. 'What was that?'

He laughs. 'Jumpy, aren't we? It's probably just a deer.'

She slips her arm through his. God, his muscles are rock-hard. He turns and grins at her, looking ridiculously happy.

Another crack, to their left this time. She tries to imagine a little brown deer nosing about for acorns, or whatever it is that deer eat. And not a weirdo with a massive knife, stalking them.

'Are you sure it's just a deer?' she asks.

'It might be a rabbit, I suppose.'

She scratches the back of her neck, flipping her long brown hair out of the way. She looks over her shoulder, but they're alone. She relaxes again.

A third crack makes her jump. Literally.

'Maybe we should go back,' she says, holding his arm tighter.

'But we're nearly there,' he says. 'Look, I'll prove it's nothing.'

He strides off through the ferns, leaving her alone on the path.

There's a loud rustle and more cracking. Her pulse races. Her nerves are alight, only now it's not excitement. It's fear.

And then she laughs out of sheer relief. It really is a deer: a little brown thing with creamy spots on its back. The creature strolls on to the path in front of her on these adorable spindly legs. It stands completely still for a second, gazing at her with long-lashed eyes.

'Hey,' she coos. 'You're so pretty.'

It blinks once, turns and bounds away, white tail flashing through the ferns.

But where is *he*? Surely he should have come straight out after the deer?

She calls his name. No answer. She calls out again. Louder this time. Trying not to panic.

Because she's shouting, she doesn't hear the footsteps behind her.

'Hi, Sally,' he murmurs in her ear.

Just before she dies, she catches the smell of lavender.

CHAPTER ONE

Fifteen years later

Crouching beside the girl's lavender-scented body, Detective Sergeant Kat Ballantyne fought the sudden urge to turn and run.

It wasn't that she was squeamish. She'd seen worse. Her very first murder had involved a shotgun. Now *there* was a sight you didn't want to encounter after a full English breakfast.

Nor was she easily scared. Maybe because she still felt like a woman in a man's world, but she'd run towards danger every time, rather than waiting for backup. It had got her into trouble more than once with the brass.

Her DI in Middlehampton's Major Crimes Unit, Stuart Carver – 'Carve-up', they called him behind his back – made no secret of his dislike for her. He'd once yelled at her in front of the whole team for what he'd called her 'intensely reckless grandstanding', which she thought was a pretty fancy turn of phrase for Carve-up, quite honestly.

No. The reason she was clenching her jaw so tightly it cracked was the cause of death. Which she knew. Right here, right now. No expert colleague needed.

She knew that the bow-tied pathologist, Dr Joshua Feldman, would have to come out from Middlehampton General Hospital – MGH, everyone called it. He'd hem and haw before intoning that he couldn't say anything for certain without performing his post-mortem.

She knew that the CSIs, under the close eye of forensic coordinator Darcy Clements, would be here soon to squat beside the corpse and inspect and photograph and take samples. They'd need to run tests, perform analyses, consult databases. The lab director would refuse to be drawn until all the results were in, cross-checked, double-checked and tabulated.

But there was a difference between protocol and stone-cold certainty.

The girl was barely out of her teens. Her face was smooth and her jawline was softened to a gentle curve by a hint of residual puppy fat. From her nostrils and her perfect, plump pink lips there spilled a waterfall of tiny, hard ovals. The CSI tasked with collecting evidence from the body might wonder what, exactly, those little granules were. They'd tweeze a couple into a debris pot, screw the lid on tight and label it. But Kat could save them the trouble.

They were grains of wheat. Soaked in lavender oil.

Kat's nose was stuffy from a cold she'd only just shaken off, but she could still smell that cloying herbal aroma.

Struggling to keep her fear at bay, she told herself 2 a.m. call-outs always made her edgy. Especially when fuelled, as she was now, by strong black coffee. Trouble was, that was a lie.

Her colleagues bitched royally whenever it was their turn as duty DS. She, on the other hand, new to the unit and only recently promoted, loved it. Normally.

Yes, there was that disorientating tug from the depths of sleep when her phone rang in the small hours. But five minutes later, caffeine shooting round her system like a liquid 'WAKE UP!' call, and she was ready to go. This was what motivated her. Catching killers. Delivering justice, and closure, for those left behind.

Normally.

4

But this *wasn't* normal, was it? This was very, very far from normal.

Apart from the crudely cropped dark brown hair and the grains spilling from her mouth and nose, the girl might have been sleeping. No blood. No visible wounds. None of the signs of that vicious kind of male anger directed at women that she and her colleagues saw almost every day of their working lives. Because this *was* a man. She knew it. And she knew who he was.

There was one more piece of evidence she needed.

After pulling on a pair of purple nitrile gloves, Kat gently lifted the dead girl's scoop-necked top and peered at her chest. An expertly inked orange and pink butterfly fluttered in the hollow of her right collarbone.

The cold clench of fear squeezed harder. It was there, below the tattoo. Where she'd known it would be. Tucked into the left bra cup like a love note.

A pink origami heart.

Kat shuddered as she pulled the folded paper free and slipped it into an evidence bag. The same MO. The same victim type. The same signature.

He was back. Not a copycat. Not a disciple. *Him*. She could feel it.

Killing girls again, after a fifteen-year absence.

His last victim had been Kat's best friend, murdered a couple of weeks after her eighteenth birthday.

And it had all been Kat's fault.

CHAPTER TWO

Back in '08, Kat had believed she had no right to be alive.

She'd blown Liv off for their drink in a wine bar because she'd just been dumped. Left her best mate alone, drunk, probably staggering home with just a bag of chips for company. And he'd emerged from the dark and snatched her out of the world.

A week had gone by, then two; one month, three. The killings stopped. The case got shunted off the front pages and the news reports. Downgraded by the police. One year. Five. Ten. The case was colder than ice. Colder than the South Pole. Colder than outer space.

People forgot. People *wanted* to forget. Everybody except Kat. How could she, when Liv's death haunted her? It was why she'd dropped out of university to travel instead. On the way, meeting a nice guy from Glasgow called Ivan Ballantyne, and marrying him a couple of years later when she fell pregnant.

The nightmares had eventually stopped. For the most part.

But there were still times when Ivan had to rock her in his arms at 3 a.m. while she whimpered. Still struggling to escape the images sticking to the backs of her eyeballs like chewing gum on a well-trodden pavement.

Someone tapped Kat on the shoulder. Sniffing back a tear, she turned to see PC Abby Greene. A friend.

'CSIs are here, Kat, and the pathologist's on his way.' Abby hesitated. 'You all right?'

'Yeah, I'm fine, just chasing the last of my cold away.' She stood, clearing her throat. 'Where are the witnesses?'

Abby turned and pointed to a Mini with white stripes on the bonnet and a Union Jack on the roof, the colours transmuted to shades of grey by the flashing blue lights that strobed across the scene. Kat could make out two figures lit a sickly yellow by the interior light.

'That's them. I think they came up here for a shag.'

'In that?'

Abby grinned. 'Where there's a will. Mind you, they're a bit old for that sort of thing. Unless they're dedicated doggers.'

'Abby!'

Shaking her head, both at her mate's bawdy sense of humour and to disperse the ghosts of the past, Kat made her way out from under the flapping crime scene tape. She nodded to the white-suited figures trudging out of the gloom towards her.

She tapped on the driver's-side window then knelt beside the car so she'd be eye to eye with the occupants.

The glass hummed down to reveal a woman in late middle age, brassy blonde hair all over the place, though she'd clearly made an effort to rearrange it. Her low-cut leopard-skin top revealed an impressive, if crêpey, cleavage. Beside her, an older man – balding, thick red-plastic glasses perched on a nose too small for his face. He wore a tweed jacket and looked like a cross between Kat's old maths teacher and a retired kids' TV presenter.

'I'm Detective Sergeant Ballantyne,' Kat said, showing them her warrant card. 'I understand you found the body.'

The woman opened her mouth but the man leaned around her, cutting her off.

'That's right. My name is Brian Clamper, I'm sixty-seven, my address—'

Kat smiled. 'That's OK, sir. I'm sure my colleagues have already taken a note of your details.'

'Yes, of course, but they were just uniforms. You're a detective, aren't you? You'll want to start at the beginning, build up your own picture of events, won't you?'

'Well, they aren't "just" anything, sir. They're police constables, the same as me. But anyway, can you tell me what happened?'

The woman elbowed her consort, none too kindly, in the chest. 'Get off me, Brian, for goodness' sake! I could hardly breathe in this bloody Wonderbra in the first place without you squashing me.'

The gesture and the fact she'd used the guy's first name went a long way to allaying Kat's suspicions about the nature of their relationship. The woman smiled.

'I'm Jenny, love. Jenny Stagg. We were having a little bit of a kiss and cuddle and I was just, you know, adjusting my position. I have a bad back and it's easier if I'm on top.'

'Jenny, for God's sake!' Brian interjected. 'I'm sure DS Ballantyne doesn't need every sordid little detail.'

'Don't worry, sir,' Kat said, giving Jenny a knowing look, 'this is all confidential, and believe me, I've heard it all before.' *I've seen it, too.*

'Anyway,' Jenny continued, 'that's when I saw her.'

'The dead girl?'

'Yes. Poor love. She can't be much older than twenty.'

'Did you see anyone else while you were cuddling? Before you noticed the body, I mean?'

'To be honest, I was concentrating on what was going on in here, if you get my drift?'

'I didn't see anyone either,' the man said. 'But if it helps, I did catch a faint whiff of lavender when I had a look at her.'

Alarm bells sounded for Kat. The last thing she needed was witnesses contaminating the scene, let alone the body; a crime scene in its own right.

'Sorry, Brian, when you said you "had a look at her", can you be more specific for me?'

'Death holds no terrors for me, DS Ballantyne,' he said in a tone he presumably thought sounded worldly wise. What was he? Ex-forces. A fireman? An undertaker? 'I was a hospital porter for years. You see everything at MGH. I went over to check she was dead. Girls these days, they drink too much or take pills, whatever – and they lose control, don't they? I thought she might be sleeping.'

Kat hated the assumptions he was making about 'girls', but the trouble was, he had a point. And no, that didn't excuse any man who took advantage, whether it was unwanted advances or cold-blooded murder.

'Did you touch her, Brian?'

He bridled. 'Of course I didn't! I watch all the shows on TV; I know the drill. I could see she was dead, so I came back to Jenny and told her and then I dialled 999,' he gabbled. 'Well, not dialled. I mean, who does that these days? But I tapped it. Gave the details, the location and so on. Clear and concise, that's what they need, isn't it?'

He was sweating, and the muscle below his right eye had starting twitching. Shock. He was wound so tight he was only managing to control it by the constant talking. Kat tried to calm him down.

'You did the right thing. We're lucky you were here. We'll need to take a DNA sample from you, just for elimination purposes,' she said. 'I'll have one of my colleagues come over if you're happy to do it now?'

'Oh, yes. Anything to help the boys – er, and girls, I mean women – in blue.'

'Thanks. We'll get that sorted and then you're free to go. Just one thing, please. A request to both of you.'

'Yes, love? What is it?' Jenny said.

'Please don't mention the smell to anyone. Not the press, not on social media, not even close friends or family.'

Brian tapped the side of his nose. 'Keeping back a key detail. Smart girl! – I mean, woman.'

'Of course,' Jenny said. 'Mum's the word, eh?'

Kat nodded. She was already mapping out the case. The lines of enquiry she'd need to establish, the interviews, the wrangling over budget, the media and community relations. But part of her was looking back. Afraid yet unable to resist peering into the darkness that lay in her past. Where a killer lurked.

The police had failed to catch him last time.

This time, she vowed, would be different.

CHAPTER THREE

Kat got home at 5.15 a.m. She knew she should at least try to rest. But the small, dark room at the end of the upstairs hall was calling to her.

She unlocked the door and stepped inside.

The *Echo* had devoted tens of thousands of words to the original Origami Killer case back then. As a result, everyone in the town knew that he'd taken souvenirs – hair – from his victims. What nobody apart from Ivan Ballantyne knew was that Kat had kept souvenirs, too. In her case, that meant a murder wall in the spare bedroom of her otherwise unremarkable semi.

When she and Ivan had returned from Thailand and set up home together, she'd fetched all the newspaper clippings from her bedroom at her parents' house. Then once she'd joined the police, and gained access to the files, she'd begun researching the case obsessively. All the murders mattered, but Liv's was the one she focused on. Little by little she'd amassed a duplicate set of case files, which she returned to whenever she had some spare time.

The official murder wall had been taken down years ago, but Kat maintained hers as proof that the case wasn't dead, at least for her. The most significant articles from the *Echo* she'd photocopied and stuck to the wall. Crime-scene photos likewise. Which was why

Riley, her twelve-year-old son, was forbidden from ever entering the room.

She pulled Liv's file towards her and started reading, once again, from the very beginning.

'Just half an hour,' she murmured.

Her own snore woke her up. She checked the time – 6.17 a.m. After a quick shower and a change of clothes, she was downstairs, pushing a plate of toast at Riley, who was rubbing his eyes and groaning about 'double physics'.

'Eat!' she commanded. 'Breakfast is the most—'

'—important meal of the day. Newsflash! It isn't. It was made up by some cereal company in America so people shoved more crap down their throats.'

'Riley Ballantyne, language!'

He rolled his eyes as only boys on the cusp of their teenage years could.

'Like you and Dad never swear. It's eff-this and eff-that all the time.'

'That's enough,' she squawked, more in embarrassment than genuine anger.

After all, Riley was correct. Oh, they'd tried to rein it in, but that just made things worse. All the gosh-gollying reduced them to tears of laughter. Kat looked at Ivan for support, but he just echoed his son's eye-roll.

Riley grunted and stuffed half the piece of toast into his mouth in one go. He mumbled something through the champing.

'Swallow first, mate,' Ivan said.

Riley complied. 'I said, I need you to take me to football practice tonight.'

'I thought Bishal's dad took you on Wednesdays,' Ivan said.

'He's at some meeting or other. Work.'

Ivan looked at Kat. 'Can you take him, love?'

'You do know where I was half the night, Van? We just got a new murder investigation. It's all going to kick off in about an hour's time.'

'Yes, but if you check the family calendar, which you thought would be such a great way of coordinating all our diaries, you'd see that I'm on site over at TFG Electronics in Hertford for two days. I won't be here.'

'Mum, don't do this to me again, please,' Riley said. 'I nearly got dropped from the team last year for missing practices. Coach said I've run out of lives. I *have* to be there!'

She forced a smile on to her face, past the sharp reply she wanted to aim at her husband. 'Of course I won't, darling. What time do you need to be there?'

'Seven. At school. The field.'

'Right. Seven.' She pulled her phone out and checked the calendar. 'Oh, yes. Just like Dad said. Well, I'm going to put a reminder on top of that one so we'll be in plenty of time, yes?'

Riley nodded, swallowed the rest of his toast, slurped half a glass of orange juice, dodging back so the spillage missed his tie, and headed out of the kitchen. 'Going to miss the bus. Laters!'

'Hey!' she called after him. 'Aren't we forgetting something?'

His shoulders slumped. 'But I'm nearly thirteen.'

'I don't care. Come here or I'll have to arrest you.'

'Fine.'

He ambled back to her so she could throw her arms around him theatrically and kiss the top of his head.

'Love you, Ri-Ri.'

He jerked away as if scalded. 'Mum! For God's sake! You're the worst.'

'You love it!' she called after his retreating form.

The front door slammed.

She looked at Ivan. 'What did I do?'

13

Ivan finished his coffee. Beckoned her over and pushed his chair back from the table.

'Come and sit on my lap.'

She plonked herself down, possibly with less concern for where her bum landed than was kind. Ivan winced.

'He's right, Kat. He's not a baby.'

'Did I say he was?'

'No, but maybe ease off on all the smoochy stuff. He knows you love him. But he's embarrassed.'

She scratched the side of her nose. 'Really? You think I embarrass him? Genuine question.'

Ivan shrugged. 'Not like you mean. But he's growing up. He even talks about girls now.'

Kat felt a flash of something sad. Not grief. But a sort of mourning. Van was right. *Riley* was right. Her little boy wasn't little anymore. The time of him sitting on her lap and unselfconscious kisses at bedtime was at an end. If she was brutally honest with herself, it had been for a while. She'd just been resisting.

'OK. I get it. I *do*,' she said as Ivan raised his eyebrows. 'I'll give him more space. It's just, I can still remember giving birth to him. My baby. *Our* baby.'

Ivan smiled and squeezed her around the waist.

'I have to go. Mike Remfry is going to have his second heart attack unless I can get his new system up and running by the end of the week.'

'See you tomorrow?'

'I won't be late. If it's not done by then he'll probably put out a contract on me. And not the three months on six hundred a day kind, either.'

'I'm going to walk Smokey then I'm off, too. Bollocks! I haven't done anything about his walks while you're away.'

'Happily, I have. Jude's coming round both days to walk him, and Betty's going to pop round a couple of times each day to keep him company.'

'And that, Ivan Ballantyne, is why I love you so much,' she said, planting a lingering kiss on his lips before letting him go and standing up. 'That, and your slinky bedroom moves.'

He grinned. 'Play your cards right and I might show you a few tomorrow night.'

'Ooh, confident, aren't we? Play yours right and I might let you.'

She found Smokey curled up in the sitting room in his bed. He had several, but the one beside the fireplace was his current favourite. The sooty-grey cairn terrier raised his head. He'd had a seizure when he was a puppy that had left him with a droopy right eyelid, so he appeared to be permanently winking.

'Fancy a walk, Smokes?'

He scrabbled into an upright position and jumped out of the bed before racing for the front door, claws skittering across the floorboards.

Kat and Ivan lived in Stocks Green, one of the outlying villages absorbed into Middlehampton over the years. Each retained its distinctive character: Stocks Green was composed of mainly older houses, some dating back to Tudor times. A farm marked its southern border, where the newly married Ballantynes had walked their baby son in his pram, feeding the ducks on the pond when he was older.

From their front door, Kat led Smokey out of the estate, which had been built in the thirties, down Green Lane and then through the farmyard and into the fields beyond. The clear blue sky and warm sun on her back presaged another in the run of unseasonably hot days the south of England had been enjoying recently. Once they were clear of the yard with its array of agricultural machinery, whose purpose Kat could mostly only guess at, she unclipped Smokey.

With a yelp of excitement, the year-old terrier streaked away through the low-growing grass before circling back to the path and then hurtling off after a pair of pheasants he'd flushed out.

Tootling in alarm, their wings clapping the air, the birds easily escaped Smokey's attack. He didn't seem to mind, charging off into the undergrowth before reappearing fifty metres further down.

Kat checked the time. She could be back from their walk and at Jubilee Place cop shop just after eight. Being out here, in uncomplicated nature, gave her time to think.

Her first priority was to identify the dead girl. The fact she was intact and unmarked was a blessing. If you could call any dead person that. Showing people photos wouldn't be too distressing. And when Kat *did* ID her, the family's trauma at having to make a formal identification would be lessened. A little.

She sighed. Right. Because that was like spreading a blanket beneath someone falling off a cliff. It didn't reduce the damage. They still broke. Their lives, as they knew them, were over.

One day you talked about your daughter's plans, what she was up to, where she was going next. And then, bam! She was dead. Going nowhere but the cemetery. You were never going to see each other again. Never going out for a drink and a bop again. Never hanging around the shops again, egging each other on to nick some eyeshadow from Boots, or Haribo from the corner shop on the way to school. Your best friend was cold, and in the ground, and she was never coming back.

A bump against her leg snapped her back to the present. The horrific image of Liv that the killer had sent to the *Echo* faded. Smokey was trotting along beside her, tilting his scruffy little head to knock his cheek against her calf. She placed her memories of Liv back on the high shelf in her mind.

16

'Hey, Smokes. Trying to cheer me up? Thanks, buddy.'

She bent to scratch behind his ear, which made him grunt with pleasure, then straightened as she caught a movement in the corner of her eye.

A lone figure was coming towards her. A man.

For a brief moment, she tensed. But as the figure resolved itself into a recognisable set of features, she relaxed. Permitted herself a guilty smile at the thought she had been preparing to beat up a friend. OK, maybe not a *friend*-friend. But the old geezer now within hailing distance was definitely a dog-walking friend. They met most days. Both on their fixed routines.

She put Barrie's age between seventy and infinity. Old, but ageless, somehow. White hair like thistledown, a deeply lined face, and a twinkle in his eye that made her think he might have been a player in his younger days.

'Hi, Barrie,' she said, when he came to a stop in front of her. 'Where's Lois?'

He turned and waved a hand over towards the hedgerow that separated the path from the next field.

'There, somewhere. She's got the scent of something. Wouldn't come back if I called her. How's tricks with you, Skip?'

She'd asked him to call her Kat a hundred times. But once he'd winkled out of her what she did for a living, the moniker had stuck. He'd been a uniformed copper for thirty years before retiring on a full pension.

'We found a dead body this morning.'

He proffered a crumpled paper bag, spreading the opening with his fingertips.

'Liquorice Allsort?'

'Bit early for sweets, isn't it?' she said, selecting a bobbly pink aniseed jelly all the same.

'A little bit of what you fancy does you good. That's what Mum used to say to us little ones.'

'I didn't think Allsorts had been invented when you were a little one.'

He widened his eyes and let his mouth drop open. 'I'll have you know they were invented in 1899.'

'So you must have been, what, ten?'

'Cheeky mare!' he said, placing an orange, black and white square into his mouth. 'So what's this case you've just landed then? Domestic? Rape-murder? Gang stuff? Drive-by?'

She smiled. Gang stuff? Drive-by? This was Middlehampton, not Manchester.

'A young girl found up in Brearley Woods.'

'Suicide?'

'You know I can't say much, Barrie. Early days.'

'I don't know how you do it, Skip, investigating murders. I really don't. Doesn't it make you despair of human beings?'

'It makes me angry about some of them. The rest, I want to protect.'

'Yeah, but you can't protect them all, can you?'

She shook her head. He was right, she couldn't. But she could try. She heard Smokey's bark, then a deeper sound. Lois. His best friend, although the black and white lurcher towered over him. She came loping up to Kat and nuzzled her right hip.

'You know where I keep the treats, don't you, Lo-Lo? OK, one for you – yes, you too, Smokes. Don't worry, I wasn't going to leave you out.'

Treats dispensed into two greedy mouths, Kat clipped Smokey back on the lead.

'Got to go, Barrie. See you soon.'

'Take care, Skip,' he called over his shoulder, raising a hand in farewell. 'Take care.'

Forty minutes later, Kat turned right out of Union Street into the potholed access road that led to the rear of Jubilee Place police station. She pulled into a spot not too far from the staff entrance. It was 7.51 a.m. She locked her black VW Golf and made her way over to the dirty brickwork of the rear wall of the station. On the way she stopped at the sandwich van to get a black coffee and a bacon roll with brown sauce.

'Morning, Kat, the usual coming up,' the guy said with a smile. 'Loving the lippy today.'

'Flatterer!' she said, grinning, though as she turned away she felt a little lift in her spirits. It was a nice red, but it wasn't her favourite. That would be Chanel Pirate, a vibrant, deep carmine shade she kept for court and nights out.

When she was thirteen, a kind lady who'd lived on their road had told her that 'every young girl should know the importance of having something nice that's just for her'. That same day, she and Liv had caught the bus to the next town over. Two newly teenage firebrands, smart-mouthed, sassy and lairy as hell. Their destination: Skinner & Brown, the big old department store that dominated the High Street.

Pumped up on vodka-laced Fanta that Liv had brought, cigarettes lifted from Kat's dad, and an entire bag of shoplifted Haribo, they'd cruised the make-up counters before spotting the precious black lacquered tubes with that unbearably glamorous white-lettered logo.

CHANEL

Kat almost choked until Liv, noticing her hanging back, hurried over. *Just follow the plan, Thelma. It's going to be fine.* Fearing she might wet herself, but fearing Liv's reaction even more, Kat waited, blood rushing in her ears while Liv distracted the sales lady, then she darted forwards, heart pounding, lifted two lipsticks from the display and slid them into her pocket.

It was a guilty secret she'd never shared with anyone. Now she could afford to buy her own, and she did, as a 'Screw you!' to the world.

She made her way up to the Major Crimes Unit's home on the third floor. Perhaps in 1977, when it was built, the station had been considered modern. State-of-the-art . . . if they'd used the phrase back then. But now, its polished concrete stairwells, with their chipped, white-painted railings, rattling stainless-steel lifts and sticky interior doors with wire-reinforced glass portholes, emanated benign neglect.

She nodded to a couple of uniformed officers on the way up, then pushed through the double doors into MCU. Her bagwoman, DC Leah Hooper, was in already. Leah was a head taller than Kat and angular where Kat was round. Both women wore their hair in practical ponytails, Leah's natural blonde, Kat's dark brown. Leah also possessed, in Kat's opinion, one of the sharpest minds at Jubilee Place. Right now, she was sitting at her desk, chin in cupped hand, staring morosely at her screen.

'Morning, Leah. Everything OK?'

'Just setting up the case files for the new homicide. My computer's on a work-to-rule,' she muttered. 'You know when those scammers ring you and say they've heard your computer's running slow? I wish one'd call me now.' Leah pushed back from her desk with a tut aimed at her non-responsive PC. 'Coffee?'

Kat lifted her takeaway cup. 'Sorted.'

Fifteen minutes later, everyone had arrived. Kat looked around. No sign of Carve-up. Typical. Since his promotion, he'd been making a point of not appearing until 8.45 a.m. A fully paid-up member of the nine o'clock jury, ready to pass instant judgement on whatever had gone down overnight.

I'm senior management, now, he'd told her once, when she'd observed, perhaps slightly more tartly than she meant to, how nice it must be to be keeping office hours at last.

Today, he must have decided an earlier appearance was appropriate, given the events of the previous night.

The doors swung wide and in he strode, in yet another lovely suit. Teal this time, with a faint colour change as it caught the light. No tie, as usual; most of the coppers under fifty seemed to have collectively decided that ties were yesterday's news.

Kat thought he must spend all his disposable income on tailoring. Apart from what he diverted towards the bright red Alfa Romeo Spider convertible he drove into work every day.

The purchase, made just days after his divorce, had aroused considerable conversation in MCU. Admiration from the men and, from the women, reactions ranging from eye-rolls to a particular female gesture involving pinching about three inches of air between thumb and forefinger. Kat wondered how he'd afforded the car, given his incessant griping about the alimony and child support he would now be paying. It wasn't hard to find a plausible explanation: Carve-up was on more than one payroll.

'Morning, everyone,' he called out, his over-loud greeting reaching every corner of the long rectangular open-plan office. 'Got a new DB up at Brearley Woods last night, so I want everyone in the conference room in ten for a briefing.'

Thinking how much she'd like to yell out that a dead teenage girl deserved a little more respect than being called a DB, Kat started pulling information together.

The light dimmed. She looked up. A young guy, maybe mid-twenties, wearing a navy roll-neck jumper and smart black jeans, was standing between her and the window. Floppy dark hair, cheekbones you could use to slice cheese. Large dark eyes. He'd got this far so he was clearly some sort of cop.

'Can I help you?' she asked him.

'I'm new here. It's my first day, actually,' he said, in an accent Kat always associated with the private-school kids she'd played netball against at school. 'Reception said someone could sort me out with a desk once I got up here, and here I am.'

He spread his hands wide and smiled, revealing even, white teeth. Kat smiled back.

'I'm Tom, by the way. Tom Gray.' He held out his hand.

'Kat,' she said, pegging him immediately as a graduate on the fast-track scheme. A Bambi. 'I'm one of the DSs. That's DC Leah Hooper over there. Say hello to Tom, Leah.'

'Hello to Tom, Leah,' she said, grinning.

Kat got up from her desk. 'Any idea who they're pairing you with?'

'Nope.'

'We'll sit you with Craig. He's my oppo, so you'll probably be with him.'

Craig Elders looked up and held out his hand across the desk. The two men shook, and Kat observed the way Tom's body language altered in the presence of his new boss. Less cocky, taking up just a little bit less space than when he'd wandered up to her desk asking for help.

It was funny. Even though one was Black and one white, one nudging forty and one not even thirty, they had that immediate male-bonding thing going on.

She nodded to herself. Craig would soon lick him into shape. He had a degree *and* years of experience to call on.

After ploughing through some overdue paperwork, she looked up at the wall-mounted station clock between two of the windows overlooking the car park. Eight forty.

Time to go.

CHAPTER FOUR

Stuart Carver looked round the room, eyeballing each member of his team in turn. Then the uniformed cops, who brought the total of over-warm bodies in the room to fourteen.

Kat could almost hear the mental countdown he was running before speaking. She sighed. Given that nobody was talking, the 'wait for silence before beginning' trick seemed a bit redundant. But, hey, it was Carve-up's show.

'Morning, everyone.'

Finally!

'OK, big news is, the DB up in Brearley Woods. But before we all get revved up about it,' he said, 'let's not forget there are over twenty – yes, that's right, people, *twenty* – unsolved murders and serious sexual assaults on our books at the mo. So can we please keep everything in proportion? DS Ballantyne, you were duty DS last night; do you want to fill us in?'

It was one of Carve-up's little tricks to keep her in her place. Never calling her Kat. Craig was always Craig. DS Chris Monaghan was always Chris. Leah was always Leah – she didn't get the treatment because, even though she was a woman, she was a DC. Not too much of a threat. Unlike Kat.

Kat cleared her throat. Fine.

'Thanks, Stu,' she said, enjoying the flicker of annoyance on her boss's face. He hated being called Stu. It was childish, but you took your pleasure where you could find it.

'This morning, at approximately 1.55 a.m., a dead girl – a young woman, really – was discovered by two members of the public at the end of the bridleway in Brearley Woods. On the edge of the car park.'

'Dogging, were they?' Carve-up asked, looking round for a smile from someone. Not getting one.

Kat stared at him; giving him one of his own techniques back, with interest.

She took a breath. What she had to say next needed to be convincing. Her heart was racing. She wiped her palms on her thighs then regretted it. Why not just blurt out how nervous she was?

She needed to keep it together.

'The woman appeared to have been asphyxiated. No obvious sign of sexual assault. Obviously we're treating it as suspicious . . .' She stopped. The dam wasn't going to hold. It was coming. The flood of emotion she'd held back for fifteen years was almost upon her.

'Look, there's no point beating about the bush on this. He's back. The Origami Killer is back, and I—'

Carver was holding his hands out, palms out.

'Whoa, whoa, whoa! Rein your horses in, DS Ballantyne. You've got zero evidence for that. Talk about unhelpful. Christ!'

'Really, Stu, you're going with that?' Her breath was coming in gasps but at least the nerves had gone. Replaced with adrenaline-driven determination, turbo-charged by coffee. She counted the points off on her fingers. 'One, the MO. She was asphyxiated using lavender-scented wheat grains. Two, the victim herself. Late teens, slim, brown hair, crudely cut short. Brown eyes. Three, as I said, no sexual assault—'

'You don't know that for sure,' Carver interrupted.

'I do! Four, a pink origami heart tucked into her left bra cup.'

She was aware that everyone was staring at her. New to the team or old hands, everyone knew about her history, how she went tearing off down this rabbit hole every time they caught a whiff of strangeness about a homicide. The rumours about her 'shrine' at home, dedicated to *him*.

Carver slammed his hand down on the table.

'No! We are not doing this again! It's been fifteen years! So how about this? One: every serial-killer obsessive in the world – not just you – knows about the Origami Killer. Meaning, two: a copycat killing is our most likely scenario. Three: she could have just topped herself. We all know what people can do to themselves if they're depressed enough.'

'It's him,' Kat said through clenched jaws. 'We need to gear up.'

Carver's eyes popped wide open.

'Gear up! What do you think this is, bloody Baltimore or something? This is Middlehampton! The chances of another serial killer operating here are a million to one.'

'It's not another one. It's the *same* one! He'll do it again. Quickly. They were days apart at the end, last time. We need to be all over this. Issue a press release. Mobilise a task force.'

Carver shook his head and offered a pitying smile that he beamed around the room. As if to say, *Look what I have to deal with. An obsessive female DS who thinks she's Clarice bloody Starling.*

'Right. For a start, we're not mobilising anything except our arses into gear. In case you don't keep up with either national or local politics, or management memos, our budget has just been cut again.' Groans from the assembled investigators. 'Which means somehow I have to keep producing results on all the crimes crossing my desk every day with less resource than I had last year. You get on with the investigation as per normal, DS Ballantyne. Until we know different, this is an isolated, and obviously tragic, death. Full stop.'

Maybe it was the lack of sleep, her churning stomach or the effects of the shouting match, but suddenly Kat didn't feel like fighting.

'Right. So me and Leah, then?'

'Actually, no.'

'What?'

Kat exchanged a look with Leah. What the hell did Carve-up have planned now?

'Some of the more observant among you may have noticed we have a new member of the MCU family,' Carver said. 'I'd like to formally welcome DC Thomas Gray to the team.'

Tom offered a quick smile and half raised a hand off the notebook he had open in front of him.

'Please,' he said, 'call me Tom.'

'Now, unlike a certain type of old-school copper, I have no problem with university graduates,' Carver said. 'In fact, I welcome them. Times are changing, and the service has to change along with them. So no talk about Bambis or white-glove detectives or anything else, OK? Are we clear? Tom will add some intellectual firepower, and that can only be a good thing, no?' he added, looking straight at Kat.

A chorus of mumblings of 'guv', 'boss' and 'mm-hmm' briefly filled the room.

Kat saw what was coming. No. Anything but that. Babysitting the Bambi was the last thing she needed when the man who'd murdered Liv was back.

'So, Tom, you'll be partnered with DS Ballantyne. She hasn't been to uni like you, but I hope you'll take this opportunity to pick up whatever she can teach you.'

Kat offered Tom a brief smile, then glared at Carver. Imagined pouring wheat grains into that smug mouth of his until he choked. Shocked by her own thoughts, she bent to her notebook and scribbled a few words to dispel the image.

Carver ran through the rest of the active cases and then dismissed everybody back to their desks, their cases, their phones, their personal concerns – worries over the mortgage, rocky marriages, rockier mental health – and retreated to the safety of his office.

At the door, he turned and called out to Kat.

'DS Ballantyne? A word in private, please.'

In his office, she closed the door behind her but didn't take the seat Carver waved at.

'Yes, Stu?'

'What the hell was that?' he asked, glaring at her.

'What?'

His eyes widened. 'That! In my briefing. Jesus! It's like you get one murder that isn't just some Saturday-night special and you're up in the stirrups on your hobby horse and galloping off after your beloved Origami Killer.'

At first she couldn't trust herself to speak. She stared at him. Finally, she managed a brief 'It's not a hobby.'

'No, it isn't. But I'll tell you what it is. It's a bloody obsession. You're obsessed!'

'He murdered my best friend.'

'I know!' Carver said, throwing his hands wide. 'And I'm sorry. But that was fifteen years ago. Get over it. Because I don't want you screwing up my budget or ruining my performance metrics chasing after ghosts.'

She opened her mouth to speak, even though she couldn't trust herself not to start shouting. She didn't get the chance.

'Are we clear?' Carver asked.

'Clear,' she said, fighting down an urge to sweep everything off his desk and launch herself across it.

'Good. Dismissed.'

Breathing heavily, Kat stepped out into the hubbub of a major homicide investigation gathering pace.

She beckoned to Tom. 'Fancy a coffee?'

'Sure.'

'Meet me in the kitchen. I just need a quick word with Leah.'

When she and Leah had the space to themselves, Kat shook her head and sighed. 'That man's a liability. He's putting more women in danger.'

'You're sure it's him, though, Kat?' Leah asked.

'Hundred per cent.'

'But it could be a copycat, couldn't it?'

'No, it couldn't. And you know why?'

'It was before my time. You know that.'

'They never released the details of the lavender scent. They just talked about the chopped-off hair and the origami heart, which was weird enough to keep the media happy.'

'So when all the nutjobs came crawling out of the woodwork confessing to the murders, they gave themselves away.'

'Exactly. And by the way? Thirty-one men came forward to confess. Losers.'

'Don't be too hard on the new boy,' Leah said. 'He seems OK and it's not his fault he sounds posh.'

Kat smiled resignedly. 'I won't be. It's just . . . we'd be more efficient if it was just you and me.'

'On the plus side, at least I won't have to listen to you wittering on about your dog the whole time!'

Kat dropped her mouth open in mock outrage. 'You cheeky bitch! That's my baby you're talking about.'

'Cats, mate. That's the way to go for a copper. Leave them to fend for themselves and they're happy,' Leah said. 'Not like with a dog. I bet poor old Smokey is pining for his mistress right now.' She pouted and made a scarily accurate whining sound.

'Right, one: cats don't have owners, they have staff. Two: Smokey is either asleep or rooting about in the garden for a pig's ear he buried.'

'And three?'

'And three . . . er, haven't you got an unsolved homicide to deal with, *DC* Hooper?'

Leah jumped up and stood to attention, smacking the back of her right hand flat against her forehead.

'Yes, ma'am, Detective Supreme Overlord Ballantyne.'

Still smiling, Kat found Tom in the kitchen, stirring instant coffee granules into two mugs.

'You take yours black, right?' he asked.

'Spot on. You?'

'Milk, no sugar. If you're ever making me one.'

'Let's see how we get on, eh?'

They took the coffees back to Kat's desk. Tom grabbed his swivel chair and scooted back across to her.

'Listen, I hope what DI Carver said in there isn't going to come between us,' Tom said. 'I want to learn from you.'

'Good. Then tell me how we're going to identify our dead girl.'

'Right, right. Well.' Tom brushed a lock of hair out of his eyes. 'We could circulate a photo?'

Kat nodded. 'I see. So we publish a photo of a corpse and say, "Do you recognise this girl?" What if her parents see it?'

Tom's cheeks flushed. 'No, no, of course. I wasn't thinking. I'm a little nervous.'

'Tell me something. Before rocking up here, what exactly were you doing?'

'After graduating, I went straight into Greater Manchester Police as a probationary DC. Passed the national investigators' exam, obviously.'

'Obviously.'

'Then I was on general CID for three months – you know, low-level stuff. Then I was posted down here.'

To this backwater, Kat could all but hear him saying out loud.

'That's a pretty big step up, isn't it?' she asked, genuinely curious. 'General CID to MCU?'

'My aunt's the Police and Crime Commissioner for Hertfordshire, so, you know, it's not what you know, et cetera.'

'Wait, Elaine Forshaw's your *aunt*?'

Tom grinned. Only, now she didn't find it charming, boyishly or otherwise.

'My dad's sister.'

'And she pulled strings?'

Tom shrugged. 'I want to make a difference. Major Crimes is where you can make the biggest one.'

'Right. Well, just as long as you realise we're dealing with real people's lives here, Tom, and not just stepping stones in your glorious career, we'll get on just fine.'

'No, of course. Absolutely. So, what do we do now?'

'Now? You start checking MISPERs—'

'Missing persons, got it.'

'Good. And I'm going to organise door-to-doors around the main entrances to Brearley Woods. Then we'll start looking for any CCTV cameras in the area, and put out an appeal for help – without using any photos, got it?'

'Got it, guv.'

Kat looked at her new bagman.

'One last thing, Tom?'

'Yes?'

'Please don't call me guv. This isn't the 1980s. I prefer Kat.'

He smiled. 'Kat it is, then.'

He wheeled himself back to his desk, and soon his fingers were rattling over the keys as he called up the MISPERs database. He was keen, she'd give him that.

He looked up from his screen after a few seconds.

'The body was quite fresh, wasn't it?'

'Maybe only a day old. Two at most. The post-mortem will tell us more. Ask reception to inform us if anybody comes in to report a girl missing.'

'Because she might have only just been missed. Smart thinking.'

'Thanks,' she said dryly.

He grinned and picked up his phone.

Shaking her head as she listened to Tom sweet-talking the receptionist, even using her first name, Kat jiggled the mouse to wake up her screen, which had dozed off again.

Carve-up might have slapped her down in the briefing and warned her off in his office, but she didn't care. Somewhere out there, a serial killer was preparing to strike again.

With the cursor hovering over the original case file, she raised her finger to click it open, then stopped. Why bother? She knew it by heart anyway.

CHAPTER FIVE

Tom put his phone down and turned to Kat.

'That was reception. A woman's just come in and reported her daughter missing.' He paused. 'She's nineteen, with dark hair.'

'Well go on then!' she said. 'Get her into the friendly interview room. It's number one. I'll meet you there.'

Kat felt it then. That instant blip of adrenaline that always signalled a break in a case. Sometimes it was a report from Forensics, or a tip-off from an informant. And sometimes it was a parent, half-mad with worry, hoping they *were* being silly for going to the police.

As Tom headed downstairs, Kat picked up the phone to the pathologist. Dr Feldman had emailed her to say he'd scheduled the post-mortem for the following Monday. Five days to wait. Even though she knew it was pointless, she asked if there was any way he could speed it up.

'DS Ballantyne,' he replied, with an air of world-weary exasperation, 'do you know how many detectives I get asking me if I can just prioritise their particular body?'

'Is it less than five?'

'That would be "fewer than five", but in any case – no, many, many more than that. And, in case you've forgotten your basic training, I do not merely investigate homicides. *Any* suspicious death falls under my jurisdiction. I also have teaching responsibilities, committee meetings, Home Office-mandated professional development courses . . . Need I go on?'

'No. Sorry, Dr Feldman. I just thought—'

'—that somehow I could wave my magic stainless-steel wand and conjure up four hours out of thin air to conduct your post-mortem by close of play today.'

Kat glanced at an open page of her notebook.

'Well, they do call you the Magus of MGH, the Wizard of the Y-Incision, the Sorcerer of the Stryker Saw . . .'

Was that a dry laugh from the esteemed forensic medicine professor? Or had he just shuffled some papers?

'Did you rehearse those epithets, DS Ballantyne?'

'Did it help?'

He sighed. Theatrically, Kat thought. She held her breath.

'Friday. At 9 a.m. Don't be late.'

'I won't. Thank you.' A beat. 'Oh, Great One.'

She caught the first half of what was definitely a laugh before Feldman ended the call. She closed her notebook.

Kat made her way to the interview room. It smelled of cheap air freshener: a harsh aroma like overripe peaches. Straggly pot plants sat forlornly on the windowsill, the ends of their leaves brown and crispy. The room's main item of furniture was a low, two-seater sofa upholstered in dark grey corduroy, the wales worn smooth on the arms and the edges of the cushions. Along with two mismatched armchairs, one royal blue, one beige, it formed a motley group around a cheap veneered plywood table.

A recently opened box of tissues sat in the centre of the table's coffee-ringed surface. Kat thought whoever had chosen a brand with pretty spring flowers on the packaging should be sent on a witness sensitivity course. Oh, flowers might *seem* to be comforting, but when your son or daughter hadn't come home and you were fighting down panic, they just felt wrong, like whistling at a funeral.

The door opened. Kat stood to greet the witness Tom was ushering inside. Early forties. Her cheeks pale but for two high spots of colour. Her eyes – red, make-up free, and shining as if she had a fever – were unable to settle on Kat's.

Kat motioned with an outstretched arm for her to sit down. Leading her a little, she took the beige armchair, and nodded for Tom to take the blue.

'This is Mrs Hatch,' Tom said. 'Wendy.'

'I'm DS Ballantyne,' Kat said, aiming for a reassuring smile. 'I understand your daughter's not come home. Is that right?'

The woman nodded stiffly, as if the movement caused her pain. She was picking loose bits of skin from the sides of her nails. One finger had already started bleeding.

'Her name's Courtney Anna Hatch. She didn't come home last night and I've spoken to her work and she never came in this morning and I'm really worried because this isn't like her at all. She's never home late on a work night. Never!'

As she always had to, Kat pushed down thoughts of how she'd react if Riley went missing from home.

Kat nodded. Best case: a teenage girl had gone missing when the Origami Killer had just made his return to Middlehampton. Worst case: she'd already turned up in Brearley Woods.

Usually at this point, Kat would be asking backgrounders. *Could she be at a friend's? Staying with a family member? Have you had a row? Does she have a boyfriend?* But this morning, sure in her gut that Courtney was the Origami Killer's latest victim, she had a different set of questions to ask.

'Can you describe Courtney for me, Mrs Hatch?'

'She's quite tall. Taller than me, anyway. Maybe about five-seven, or -eight,' she said. 'Long dark brown hair, like I told you,' she added, looking at Tom.

'How about her eyes. What colour?' Kat asked, trying to draw Mrs Hatch's attention back to her.

'Brown. Lovely they are, specially with a bit of mascara. Such long lashes. Natural, too. None of those fake ones the girls all wear now.'

'Does Courtney have any tattoos, or piercings?'

Mrs Hatch nodded. 'A butterfly. On her collarbone,' she said, pointing at her own, visible above the frayed neckline of what looked like a pyjama top. 'Pink and yellow. I think. No . . . pink and orange.'

Kat glanced at Tom, keeping her face expressionless. *Bet they didn't teach you this at university.*

'Mrs Hatch, this morning we found the body of a young woman in Brearley Woods. Now, she might not be Courtney, but your description does match,' Kat said. 'I'm going to show you a photo of her face. Can you tell me if you think it might be your daughter?'

Mrs Hatch jerked her head up and down, as if performing even this rudimentary movement had to be relearned.

Kat swiped through the crime scene photos she'd taken herself until she found the ones she wanted. The upper half of the dead girl's face. And a second one of the tattoo on her collarbone. She selected the first image and turned her phone round.

The woman – the bereaved mother – stared at the photograph. Her hand fluttered up to cover her mouth. A nearly silent whimper escaped from between her whitened fingers.

'Courtney,' she whispered. Then she stared into Kat's face with eyes already glistening with the first of many tears. 'It's her. What's wrong with her face? Why have you cut off the bottom? He didn't—'

Kat shook her head quickly. 'She's not been marked at all, Mrs Hatch. But I'm afraid she was suffocated. Her nose and mouth were blocked with a substance.'

Tom reached forward and offered the box of tissues to Mrs Hatch. Kat offered him a quick nod.

'Did she suffer?'

How could you answer that? Kat wondered, not for the first time.

Neither truthful option was viable. *I don't know*. Or, given she was murdered: *Yes*.

But that wasn't really what Wendy Hatch was asking. She meant, was she in pain? Bad pain? Prolonged to the point she was screaming for it to end?

Like Liv would have been.

Kat shook her head.

Tom spoke before she could continue. 'It would have been over very quickly. She's at peace now.'

The unwritten rules were pretty clear on detectives venturing into matters of metaphysics. Stick to the facts, offer sympathy, catch the bastards. Kat didn't care. Who could live with the thought of their best friend – or daughter – *not* leaving pain behind? She liked Tom a little more for his compassion.

Mrs Hatch sniffed. 'You never really know, though, do you?' Then, as if each new horror had taken a ticket in the waiting room of her mind until it was their turn, her chin trembled. 'Was she, did he . . .'

This time, Kat did answer promptly, before Tom could step out on to very thin ice.

'I'm afraid we can't say whether she was sexually assaulted until the post-mortem,' she said. 'All I can say is that, from our initial observations, her clothes were not disarrayed and she bore no obvious signs of a physical attack, apart from the substance blocking her airways.'

'Thank you.' A whisper, as if pushing enough air out to form audible speech was failing her.

Kat stretched out a hand and briefly laid it on the grieving mother's knee.

'After we've finished here, DC Gray will arrange for a family liaison officer to be appointed for you, Mrs Hatch,' she said. 'I know this must be such a terrible shock to you, but it would really help me if I could ask you some more questions about Courtney. Would that be all right?'

A nod.

People went into shock straight after getting the worst news possible. It felt cold, callous even, but now was the time to ask the questions that might lead to the killer. Even stretching the definition of the Golden Hour, the timer had barely any grains of sand left to trickle though its tiny waist.

'Would it be OK if I recorded this, Mrs Hatch?'

'Can you call me Wendy, please?'

Kat smiled. 'Of course. So, Wendy, can you tell me about Courtney's routine?'

The interview lasted a further thirty minutes.

According to Wendy, her daughter had been in love with her job as an engineering apprentice at CooperTech, a manufacturing firm on the Springfields industrial estate. It was all she'd ever wanted. She'd got on well with her workmates and socialised with them from time to time, though her closest friends were all from school: Queen Anne's, a comprehensive in the area of the same name on the north side of Middlehampton.

She hadn't had a current boyfriend, although she'd dumped her ex after he slapped her in a club in front of her mates. What was his name? Johnny Hayes.

Was it the first time he'd hit her? Kat wanted to know. Wendy couldn't give her an answer. Kat suspected that meant it was a yes.

She knew Johnny Hayes of old. He'd been one of her first arrests. Nothing serious, just your basic Friday-night drunk and disorderly.

His name would go up on the whiteboard beside Courtney's photo, the caption succinct but freighted with meaning – and investigative potential. Ex-boyfriend. Violent.

As far as Wendy knew, Courtney hadn't had any enemies and she couldn't think of anyone who might have wanted to hurt her daughter. Which was standard fare where members of the public were concerned. It was only gangsters and small-time criminals who knew of *plenty* of people who'd like to hurt or kill their now-dead friend or accomplice. Not that they were always eager to share their names with the cops.

Kat knew she'd have further questions, but these could be handled by the FLO. Although she would be calling round to ask to look at Courtney's room and to ask for her laptop if she had one.

Once Tom had shown Wendy out, Kat called him over, intending to get him started on a deep-dive into Courtney's background. She didn't get the chance.

'What was with all the officialese you used in there?' Tom demanded, hands on hips.

'What do you mean?'

'When she asked if Courtney had been sexually assaulted. You were all, "from our initial observations, her clothes weren't disarrayed" and "she bore no obvious signs of a physical attack". Bit clinical, wasn't it?'

She admired him for taking her to task about her choice of words, if not his tone of voice. But he also needed to understand that it was all about nuance.

'Look, Tom, you're right, OK? Sometimes we ought to use everyday language,' she said. 'Telling a grieving parent their child is "unfortunately deceased" is wrong. You have to just come out with it straight and say they're dead. But—'

'Exactly, so I—'

She spoke over his interruption. 'But when a mother has just asked if the nutter who killed her daughter raped her first, you need to keep it unemotional. That official language is cold, yes. Clinical, too. But it doesn't come with pictures.'

Tom nodded. His hands retreated from his hips to his pockets.

'Oh. So if you say, "We don't think Courtney was raped" . . .'

'Wendy immediately starts picturing it. Yes. That OK with you?'

'Sorry, guv.' He reddened. 'I mean Kat.'

She patted him on the shoulder. 'It's fine. I'd rather you challenged me. It's how you learn.'

He sighed out a breath. 'It's crap, isn't it.'

'What is?'

'Telling people.'

'Yes, Tom. Yes it is. Total weapons-grade crap. But catching the perpetrator and bringing closure to the family? That's not crap. That's what we're in it for. At least, that's what I'm in it for,' she said. 'Now, unless you want to be the one to do the next death-knock, because I guarantee he's already planning his next kill, I suggest we get cracking.'

'What do we do first?'

'Let's go and speak to her boss at CooperTech.'

◆ ◆ ◆

Tom wanted to use the satnav to get to Springfields. Kat insisted he look it up on a map and memorise it.

'Can't have you policing our fine town if you don't know your way around, can we?'

'I'm a detective, not an Uber driver.'

'Exactly. So you're going to *detect* the fastest route from Jubilee Place to CooperTech, and then you're going to drive me there.'

'I thought the DS always wanted to do the driving,' he said with a grin as he accepted the keys she dropped into his palm and opened the doors.

'Where'd you get that? On the *Introduction to Telly Detectives* module?'

He started the engine and pulled away.

'DS Ballantyne, you're not chippy about me having a degree, are you?' he asked, smiling. 'Because I do, actually, respect the fact you chose to gain experience, rather than academic insights into criminology.'

'That's very kind of you, DC Gray,' she said. 'Although, since I joined the police *after* starting university – Nottingham, before you ask – maybe you'd better rein in your snobby assumptions.'

He glanced at her, frowning. 'Starting. But not finishing?'

It was an impressive catch, noticing the story behind the words. 'That's right. Had a change of heart.'

'What happened?'

'You really want to know?'

'Detectives are supposed to be curious, aren't they?' He peered ahead. 'Oh, crap! Which way here? Left.' He flicked on the indicator.

'Sure?'

'No, double crap! It's right, isn't it? On to London Road.'

'Good man.'

Tom switched the signal from left to right and pulled into the correct lane, earning a loud blast from a delivery van bearing down on him.

'So?' he asked, once they were headed in the right direction.

'Fifteen years ago, my best friend was murdered. At the end of that summer, I went off to uni to study law, but I had a breakdown,' she said.

She watched him closely. Wanting to see how he'd react. People could be cruel, despite all the publicity about mental health these days. She remembered overhearing Carve-up once in the canteen, gassing with a couple of other male officers. *To cap it all, they're dumping Ballantyne on me.* Then he'd twirled an index finger at his temple.

She felt her stomach muscles clenching involuntarily.

'Bloody hell, Kat. I'm sorry,' Tom said. 'That must have been awful for you. Did they ever catch who did it?'

She relaxed; Tom wasn't judging her.

'No. But *we're* going to.'

Tom looked round. 'What? You mean—'

'Eyes on the road, please. It's the same guy. The Origami Killer.'

Tom said nothing for a minute. Kat nodded. Good. It meant he liked to think things through before shooting his mouth off. Not like some detective (inspector)s she could think of.

'Is that why you were so—'

'So what?'

'Passionate. In the briefing this morning. Because of your friend?'

'What do you think? Listen, Tom. Forget what Carve-up said. It's him. It can't *not* be him,' she said, swallowing down a lump that had formed in her throat. 'I want you to read the old case files. It'll take you a while, so probably better to take them home with you. I need you up to speed on this.'

'Whatever you say. And, for the record?'

'What?'

'I'm not snobby about cops without degrees and I'm sorry if I came across that way.'

She shook her head. 'It's fine. Just, be aware that this is a dirty old job sometimes, and those of us who've been doing it for a while, well . . .'

'You don't like to see white-glove DCs coming in, acting like they know how everything works because of all that there book-larnin'.'

Tom delivered the last phrase in a comedy backwoods accent that had Kat snorting out a laugh. It felt good, to be bantering with him. Leah was a great cop and he'd never replace her, but Kat thought, with a little time, she could mould him into a half-decent partner.

He pointed at a road sign. They'd arrived at Springfields.

CHAPTER SIX

The engineering manager staggered and had to support himself on a desk when Tom told him his star apprentice had been murdered.

Andy Ferris's shock seemed genuine, but Kat wondered whether he was hiding something, nonetheless. Man in his early fifties plus teenage apprentice equals inappropriate feelings? More? She reproached herself for having an uncharitable thought. Then mentally shook her head. Detective sergeants weren't paid to be charitable. They were paid – in MCU at any rate – to catch murderers.

'Did she say where she was going after work last night?' Tom asked.

'Not to me. Straight home, I assume. She was so hard-working. Diligent, you know.'

'Yes, you said. And you can't think of anyone here at CooperTech who she might have had a falling-out with?'

Ferris shook his head. 'Sorry. No. Everyone loved Courtney.' He looked down. 'Not *loved* loved – but, you know, they liked her.'

'You were her boss, Mr Ferris,' Kat said. 'What was *your* relationship with Courtney like?'

He ran a hand through thick, dark hair. 'What do you mean?'

She shrugged. 'It's a simple question. Was it easy-going? Stress-free? Or was she a handful?'

'A handful?' He cleared his throat. 'Let me tell you something about Courtney Hatch, Detective Sergeant. When Courtney came for her apprenticeship interview, I don't mind admitting, I had a few reservations about her. Cheap suit, skirt on the short side. But within ten minutes I knew I'd found one of that rare breed of teenagers. A born engineer. She was a greatly valued member of the engineering team.'

Kat frowned. That was interesting. Ferris had slipped into some sort of corporate HR jargon. He'd gone from saying how everyone had loved Courtney to describing her as if he were writing a brochure.

Her mind flashed to Tom picking her up earlier on overusing officialese. You did it when you didn't want the witness to form a mental picture. Is that what Ferris was doing? Trying to stop her picturing something?

A memory rose from somewhere deep in her subconscious. Liv and her discussing what went on in children's homes. She heard Liv's mocking tones. Cynical, even at thirteen.

The last one I was in, right? The manager's really old. Thirty at least. And he's perving over this girl who's, like, fourteen! Men're all the same. It's what's between your legs they care about, not your date of birth.

Kat had been shocked at the time. Not so much by Liv's language, which was pretty inoffensive. But by her casual worldliness. How she seemed to just accept this state of affairs. She'd argued, told Liv that she was wrong. Now, twenty years later, she wasn't so sure.

She smiled at Ferris.

'Do you get many office romances here?'

'I beg your pardon?'

'I'm interested in whether Courtney might have been involved with a co-worker. That could be an important line of enquiry for us.'

'Oh, I see. Well, honestly? No.'

44

He was relaxed, hands resting loosely in his lap – no wedding ring. Facial muscles softened. No tightness round the eyes. Maybe she'd misjudged him. Or maybe . . .

She smiled. 'No, there aren't many office romances here, or no she wasn't involved with a co-worker?'

'Well, I'm sure there must be some romances or flings among the staff, but . . . as far as I'm aware, Courtney had a boyfriend outside work. What was his name?' He looked up at the off-white ceiling tiles as if he might find the man's name written there. 'Johnny something. Haynes? Hales?'

It confirmed what Wendy had said about her daughter. Kat made a note. 'We'll look into it. Thank you.'

'Was there anything else?'

'We'd like to take her office PC away, if that's OK? In case she was in email communication with her killer.'

Ferris frowned. 'Ah, I'm not one hundred per cent sure I can authorise that, I'm afraid.'

'Really? Why not?'

'Well, we do store a lot of our stuff in the cloud, but Courtney was working on some highly confidential projects. Worth millions in IP, that's—'

'Intellectual property.'

'Exactly. Well, as you can appreciate, we can't have just anyone poking around in there.'

'This wouldn't be "just anyone", though, Mr Ferris. This would be our digital forensics team,' she said. 'They're hardly likely to run off and start a rival . . .' She paused, realising she had no idea what, precisely, CooperTech manufactured. 'Sorry, what is it you make here?'

'Specialised fuel pump controls for the motor racing industry. Formula One cars, mostly.'

'F1? Cool,' Tom said, his eyes widening like a schoolboy's. 'Do you get to meet the drivers?'

Ferris smiled. 'Occasionally. Last year we had Ramon Sanchez over here on a factory tour. I showed him round personally.'

'Wow! That is—'

'—fantastic,' Kat said. 'Just to be clear, are you refusing to release Courtney's PC to us?'

Ferris's face twisted, as if he'd eaten too many unripe plums and his guts were griping. 'It's not a PC. We're part of the Apple ecosystem at CooperTech.'

'Does that make a difference?'

'Obviously not. But without a warrant, I think I'm going to have to turn down your request.'

'Even though it might help catch your former employee's murderer?'

'I'm sorry.'

He wasn't going to budge, she could see that. 'That's it for now, Mr Ferris. Thank you. Could you point us in the direction of your HR department?'

Ferris escorted them down the corridor from the engineering department and into a small office occupied by two women, one South Asian, one white.

'These are police officers. They'd like to talk to you about Courtney. She's been—'

'Thank you, Mr Ferris,' Tom said, 'we'll take it from here.'

Once the HR managers had dried their tears, Kat established that Courtney hadn't made any complaints about anyone during her time at CooperTech. As far as they knew, she hadn't been in a relationship with anyone, and certainly not Andy Ferris.

Back in the car, Tom turned in his seat.

'Did you not like Ferris or something? Is he a wrong 'un?'

She smiled. 'Nice use of the lingo, Tom. And, no, I didn't like him much. I just got a little vibe off him.'

'He seemed genuinely upset when you told him Courtney had been murdered.'

'*Seemed*, sure. But anyone can fake an emotion if they try hard enough.'

'Is that why you asked if she had any relationships at work? You think they were an item?'

Kat raised her eyebrows. '"An item"? Bit quaint, isn't it?'

'All right, you think they were shagging? Better?'

'Probably more honest. Can you call Wendy Hatch's FLO for me? I want to have a look at Courtney's room later.'

'You need me, too?'

'I can manage. We'll drive back to Jubilee Place. Get yourself those files and make a start.' She thought of something else. 'Does the fast-track cover sending out press releases?'

He nodded. 'I've done quite a few, even press briefings.'

'Have a word with Media Relations. Send out a basic release identifying Courtney Hatch as the victim of murder. Include the shorn-off hair and say she was asphyxiated. Do *not* include the origami heart and *definitely* not the lavender wheat grains. Got it?'

'Yes, *ma'am*!' he said, snapping off a jokey salute.

'Funny boy,' she said, grinning. 'Call to action, anyone see Courtney on her own or with someone between 5.30 p.m. and 2 a.m. on Tuesday night. Anywhere between Springfields and Brearley Woods.'

◆ ◆ ◆

Wendy was round at a neighbour's house, a mug of cold-looking tea beside her.

Apologising for the intrusion, Kat asked her if she could let her in to the house.

Wendy held out her keys. 'I've got no secrets.'

Kat exchanged a look with the neighbour and mouthed *thanks* before letting herself out.

Wendy kept a neat house. Kat poked her head into the sitting room. Knick-knacks covered every available flat surface. Must have taken the poor woman all week to dust them.

The upper floor had two bedrooms and a bathroom. No need for detective skills to work out which one was Courtney's. Mounted on the door to the right was a piece of green circuit board. Components soldered to the shiny silver connectors spelled out 'Courtney's Crib'.

Kat went in. The first thing that hit Kat was the smell of incense, and beneath it, the cloying, slightly sickly aroma of weed. Nothing surprising there. She doubted if there were more than two in ten teenagers in Middlehampton who hadn't tried smoking it at least once. And then there were the uppers, downers, coke and all the rest.

If Courtney's career as an engineer was evident from the sign outside, in here, drugs notwithstanding, was a very different young woman. A double bed was made tidily, with a row of cuddly toys along the wall side.

Make-up and hairbrushes were arranged atop a white-painted dressing table with a tiltable mirror. And on the wall facing the window, Courtney had created a montage of selfies and group shots of her with her friends – in some they were wearing prom dresses, in others beachwear, posing like models.

Donning nitrile gloves, Kat sat at the dressing table and opened the top drawer. Underwear. Nothing too fancy. Just nice-quality bras and knickers. Another drawer held balled-up tights and socks in a variety of bright colours. The third held a hair dryer, its cord wrapped evenly around the handle. Beside the hairdryer was a black velvet bag closed with a drawstring. Kat loosened the cinched cord. Inside was a vibrator and a tube of lubricant. *Good for you*, she thought with a twinge of sadness. *Not relying on your loser boyfriend.*

Where was the laptop? Everyone had one these days, or at least a tablet. Kat thought an engineering apprentice would probably go for the full-fat option and own a nice powerful computer. She found it inside the wardrobe, a modular affair that housed a small desk with a three-drawer credenza underneath.

The laptop was plain black, adorned with a sticker for a band Kat hadn't heard of. She pulled a lightweight office chair over and sat down, opened the lid and tapped a key experimentally.

The machine asked for her password.

Even though she'd expected it, her heart sank. Digital forensics cost money and, worse, time. She ran through a couple of obvious ideas – Courtney's date of birth, then combined with her initials. She flipped the lid closed and looked at the sticker. Opened it again and tapped in 'RedDolphin'. The laptop folded its arms and shook its head. Nu-uh.

'Crap!'

It had been worth a try.

She stowed the laptop in her holdall. If Forensics couldn't do it, it would mean weeks of delays while the manufacturer's legal department did their best to obstruct justice.

On a whim, she returned to the dressing table. Where would a young woman like Courtney Hatch keep a record of her passwords? Because, let's face it, everybody did, didn't they? Even bright young things who could probably *make* a computer. It was too complicated to have the ten or more you needed and keep changing them every month. Most people, Kat reckoned, stuck with one that they used across multiple devices, or else wrote them down and kept the piece of paper somewhere private.

Knicker drawer? No! Too obvious. But at the bottom, where she kept the sex toy? That was far more likely. Kat emptied the drawer out, item by item. She felt around, but there was nothing. Frowning, she reversed her hand and slid it right to the back, palm uppermost. She curled her fingers up until they grazed the underside of the drawer above and felt around.

Her fingertips met a stiff piece of paper that flipped as they passed over it. Getting down on to her hands and knees, she twisted her hand around until she could pincer the sticky square between her index and middle fingers and peel it away.

When she had it the right way up in her hand, she nodded, satisfied that though she was now thirty-three, she could still summon up insight into the mind and habits of a nineteen-year-old version of herself.

Nobody would have been able to guess Courtney's laptop password. It was a random sequence of lower- and upper-case letters, numbers and symbols. No wonder she'd had to write it down; she probably couldn't remember it herself.

Kat hit Return, and the screen refreshed. She was in.

'Speak to me, Liv,' she murmured, before realising what she'd said.

Feeling tears pricking at the backs of her eyes, she opened the email app.

She scrolled through a couple of screens, looking at the From field. Lots of spam, lots from girlfriends, a long and increasingly ill-tempered string with Johnny Hayes, the ex-boyfriend. But that was it. Nothing from Andy Ferris.

She knew she ought to hand the laptop over to Forensics, let the digital team have at it. It was what they were paid to do after all. But she was here, with it right in front of her, and the clock was ticking. She explored her intuition about Andy Ferris.

If he wasn't really sad that Courtney was dead, why was that?

Because she'd been stalking him?

Because she'd been threatening him?

Because she'd been blackmailing him?

Had they been in a relationship, and when he'd come to his senses and ended it, she'd refused to believe him?

Courtney didn't fit the profile for a vengeful ex-lover. She was just too young for the role.

So she wasn't threatening or blackmailing him. But had she had something on him, anyway? Had he suspected as much? Kat launched Word. Pulled up the list of recently opened files. And blinked.

The document heading the list was named 'FerrisThePerv'.

Heart beating faster, she clicked it.

As she started reading, she flashed on what Liv had said about men all those years ago. She felt anger surge through her. After finishing here, she'd be returning to CooperTech and inviting Andy Ferris to attend Jubilee Place police station for an interview under caution.

CHAPTER SEVEN

As Kat walked through the engineering office, Andy Ferris looked up from the tilted drawing board he was hunched over, and frowned. Then he smiled. His features looked as though they were receiving conflicting orders, unsure what expression was being asked of them.

He slid off his stool and came halfway through the office to greet her.

'Back so soon?'

'Could we have a quiet word in your office, please, Andy?'

He smiled and held his arms wide.

'This is my office! We all muck in together at CooperTech. It's the company culture. Anything you want to say to me, you can say out here.'

He couldn't say she hadn't warned him.

'Andy, I'd like to invite you to come to Jubilee Place police station with me, where I will interview you under caution.'

Heads popped up from screens on which the engineers were rotating multicoloured wireframe grids. New product designs, Kat assumed.

'I'm sorry, what?'

'I have some questions I'd like to ask you, and due to their nature, I think it would be best if we did that at the station.'

'But it's the middle of the afternoon! I've got a design team meeting in' – he checked his watch – 'yes, in five minutes. I'm really busy. We *all* are. I told you all I could about Courtney.'

She shrugged. 'These questions don't relate to Courtney directly, Andy. Now, shall we go?'

He folded his arms. 'Am I under arrest?'

Kat shook her head. 'Nothing like that.' *Actually, quite similar to that.* 'You would be attending voluntarily, and you would be free to leave at any time.'

'So I could just not come with you, then? I could refuse.'

Kat smiled. 'You could do that. But then I might feel I had no option but to place you under arrest.'

'But I haven't done anything.'

'It won't take long. And of course, you are entitled to have a solicitor present.'

He stood rooted to the spot. His legs were twitching, though. Kat could sense it in him – that primal need to run, to escape a threat. It didn't mean he was guilty of anything. Most people reacted similarly when asked by a copper to 'come down to the station'.

'Fine,' he said. Then he turned. 'Jack, can you tell Ann I'll have to miss the design meeting, please?'

Kat was not entirely surprised when Ferris requested a solicitor. It was the wise course of action. When the time was right, she intended to sit Riley down and give him 'the talk'. The one all coppers gave their children. The one that basically explained that they never, *ever*, wanted to get a call from a colleague to say their child had been arrested. But if it *did* happen – God forbid! – they were to say nothing without the presence of a solicitor.

But still, the copper in her, not the parent, wondered why an innocent man would feel he needed legal representation.

After a besuited twenty-something solicitor had arrived and been shown in to see Ferris, Kat got them all seated in an interview room. This one was devoid of both soft furnishings and pot plants. No window either. It smelled of sweat and unwashed human skin.

Kat opened the folder, in which she'd inserted a printout of the document from Courtney's laptop. She tapped a pen on the top line, then looked up, inhaled, and smiled at Ferris. She reached over and started the tape recorder. Like fast computers, digital interview recorders were rumoured to exist, but not in Middlehampton.

Once the seven-second screech had ended and everyone had identified themselves, she began with the caution.

'Andy Ferris, you are not under arrest, but you have voluntarily attended an interview at Jubilee Place police station in connection with the murder of Courtney Hatch. You do not have to say anything, but it may harm your defence if you do not mention something when questioned that you later rely on in court. Anything you do say may be given in evidence. Do you understand?'

'Yes, of course I do. But listen, this is a mistake. I had nothing to do with it.'

The solicitor inclined his head towards his client and murmured behind his hand. Ferris bit his lip and nodded.

Probably advising him not to answer unless checking with him first, was Kat's judgement.

'I searched Courtney's bedroom this afternoon, Andy,' Kat said. 'One of the items I found there was her laptop. And on that laptop was a Word document. The title of that document was "FerrisThePerv". Does that title mean anything to you?'

Ferris's cheeks reddened. He twisted in his chair and whispered into his solicitor's ear. The lawyer listened then murmured again, using his hand as a screen once more.

'No comment.'

'Really? Let me read out the first few lines.' She raised the document a little. 'Courtney writes, "The other girls warned me that Ferris is a perv. Apparently he's installed cams somewhere in the ladies and our changing room. I'm going to check them out. If it's true, I'm going to tweak them to send me the IP address of his computer. When I have proof, I will take it to HR."' Kat put the sheet down. 'Have you, Andy? Installed spy-cams in the ladies' loos and the female changing room?'

'No comment.'

'OK. Because, you know, "perv" is a pretty strong word, isn't it? And Courtney was only nineteen. Do you have younger girls than her working at CooperTech, Andy? Did you perv over them as well? That might be leading us towards a very serious conversation indeed.'

'No comment.'

'You see, Andy, what I'm beginning to wonder is, maybe Courtney *did* discover your little cameras. And maybe she did tweak them somehow. She was a clever girl, after all. Did she tell you what she was going to do? Did she blackmail you? Ask for money? Did you decide the best thing to do was to get rid of her before she could expose you?'

'No!' he blurted. 'None of that is true!' The solicitor laid a gentle, professional hand on his arm.

'You deny placing cameras in the ladies?'

'No comment.'

'The changing rooms?'

'No comment.'

'DS Ballantyne,' the solicitor said, mildly. 'My client has already answered your question. Do you have any other questions relevant to the murder of this unfortunate young woman, or are you merely engaged in a fishing expedition?'

Kat said nothing. The lawyer was young, but he was sharp. The words of her mentor, DS Molly Steadman, came back to her. *Don't engage with the brief, Kat. They'll tie you up in more knots than a pervert with a bondage fetish.*

She looked at Ferris. Counted to ten in her head.

'Andy, did you murder Courtney Hatch.'

He folded his arms. And, very calmly, he denied it.

Twenty minutes later, once he and his solicitor were well clear of the building, Kat flopped down behind her desk.

Leah heeled her chair over.

'Long day in which nothing useful happened, a suspect walked because you had insufficient evidence to hold him, and now you need a drink?'

'Something like that. What time is it?'

'Six thirty.'

'Bollocks!' Kat jumped to her feet, knocking a half-full cup of coffee over.

'What is it?'

'I'm supposed to be taking Riley to football practice. He'll kill me if we're late. The coach is threatening to kick him off the team.' She grabbed her bag from under the desk. 'Got to go. See you tomorrow. Bye, Tom,' she called over her shoulder, as she ran for the door.

She met Carver in the corridor.

'Off early, DS Ballantyne?'

'It's not early. I'm taking my son to football.'

Carver smiled. 'That's good. Juggling your many responsibilities. We'll have to call you Supermum, won't we? Tom still in?'

She wanted to punch him. Not for the first time.

'He is. I'll see you in the morning.'

'Of course. After the school run.'

'He takes the bus. I'll be here nice and early. Stu.'

56

Then she left him. Made it to the car park in two minutes. Was swinging out on to Crown Street and accelerating into the tail end of the rush-hour traffic a minute after that.

She turned right at the lights into Roseveare Way and had to slam her brakes on to avoid rear-ending a brand-new, metallic pink Range Rover Evoque. The rear window bore a pink 'Tiny Princess on Board' sign; what appeared to be Swarovski crystals sparkled around the rear light clusters.

Kat imagined the driver. Blonde, fake breasts out to here, fillers, Botox, bling everywhere, and a baby in her car seat with her hair done up in a topknot with a pink ribbon round it, poor little thing. Wife of a Middlehampton FC player and her 'precious little bundle', as she probably put it on Instagram.

Ahead, temporary traffic lights were green, but someone – she craned her neck and could make out the back of a caravan – was making a meal out of pulling around the cones into the contraflow.

'Come on, come on, you could drive a tank through there!' she shouted as the Evoque finally began to roll forwards.

The Evoque jerked to a stop.

'She's stalled it. Perfect!'

After seven agonising seconds, the Evoque moved off, diving for the light, which had just turned amber. The bejewelled rear end disappeared into the narrow lane as the lights switched to red.

Stranded on the wrong side of the contraflow, Kat spent the next three minutes trying to suppress an urge to scream, drive around the obstacle on the pavement, or slam her palms against the steering wheel – a move straight out of Hollywood she'd done once and regretted instantly, as the wheel had bruised the bones in her hands.

Finally, it was her turn. Her tyres screeched as she floored it, drawing a look of the purest contempt from an elderly man walking on the other side of the road.

She was home at five to seven, slewing the car over to park raggedly outside the house.

His face thunderstorm-dark, Riley was sitting on the front garden wall in his kit with the new boots they'd bought him for Christmas, and which, thank God, given the price, still fitted him.

Scowling, he jumped down and climbed in beside her, slamming the door.

'I'm sorry, Riley, I—'

'Can we just go, please. I *told* you what Coach said. If we're late and he drops me from the first team, I'm never speaking to you again.'

She put the car in gear and pulled away. Hoping for at least a nod of approval, she took the circular turnaround at the end of their cul-de-sac at speed. The rear tyres squealed even louder than she'd achieved at the lights, as she corrected the swerve then sped back up to the T-junction at the top of the road.

'I'd like not to die before we get there, if that's not too much to ask,' Riley said.

Somehow, she made it to Middlehampton College's sportsground at only ten past seven. She thought that was pretty good going, and even sought Riley's agreement.

His reply consisted of an even-louder door slam.

She watched as he sprinted, heels kicking up, over to the field, where she could see boys in red and white warming up by jogging round the perimeter.

Maybe she should get out and watch for a bit. Show she was present. Not always dashing off back to her case files. She could always catch up later, after Riley had gone up for the night.

She locked the car and wandered over to the touchline. A few other parents were there, standing around chatting, drinking from reusable coffee cups or checking their phones. She saw Jess Beckett standing on her own and went over to say hi.

They'd known each other since school, and although they'd never been as close as Kat and Liv, they'd both been sporty and had played netball together. They both still played – for a team in the Middlehampton League: the Malbec Mafia.

'Hi, mate,' Kat said.

'You made it, then?' Jess said with an ironic smile.

'Just. I think his place is safe, but my heart might be about to give out.'

'We should go for a drink while they're playing.'

'I'd love to. But I feel duty-bound to stay and watch.'

'Probably best. Soon, though, yeah?'

'Yeah. Soon.'

Being back at the school always produced mixed memories for Kat. She, Liv, and Jess had attended Queen Anne's, the same comprehensive as Courtney Hatch. It was two miles to the west of the College, whose students they'd always despised, calling them 'the nerds'. Probably no more than teenage envy, but kids were so tribal. She worried when Riley complained about the Queen Anne's kids yelling at him across the street. He seemed able to cope, though. He was a tough lad.

The coach had a couple of the boys fetch giant net-bags of footballs. As they kicked them around, Kat's attention drifted back to the day she'd first met Liv.

CHAPTER EIGHT

At twelve, Kat was sporty as well as bright, and had lots of friends. But sometimes she tired of their obsessions with boys or the latest band and would wander off on to the field alone, happy to be by herself.

It was the tail end of lunchtime. Double English to follow, which she normally enjoyed. But they were doing *Macbeth* and it bored her. Ahead, she saw a girl she hadn't noticed before. She wandered over.

'Hi.'

The girl looked at her through long, dark, messy hair. She was pretty. Really nice skin. No spots.

'Hi.'

'Are you new?'

'What's it to you?'

'Nothing. I just haven't seen you around before. What's your name?'

The girl scowled. 'I'm called Why Don't You Mind Your Own Business?'

Kat laughed. 'Bet your mum loved sewing that inside your knickers.'

'I haven't got a mum, OK? So why don't you just piss off and leave me alone? I'm not your charity case and I don't need a friend.'

Kat loved asking people questions about their lives. Her mum told her it was rude, but she disagreed. Couldn't help it, anyway. The urge to ask was always too strong to ignore.

'What happened?'

'What?'

'To your mum. Where is she?'

'How should I know?'

'Doesn't your dad know?'

'No idea. He's gone, too.'

The penny dropped. Kat told herself off for being stupid. 'Oh. Are you in care, then?'

'Don't worry,' the new girl said, scowling, 'it's not catching.'

'Thank God for that! I thought I was going to have to go to the nurse for a decontamination shower. Except she'd probably stare at my tits.'

Finally, a chink in the new girl's armour. A mischievous grin split her face, transforming her. Here was someone Kat could really relate to.

'She a lez, then?'

Kat shrugged. 'Maybe. Maybe not. I just don't want to find out the hard way.'

The new girl chewed her lip. Kat waited.

'Olivia.'

'Huh?'

'My name. It's Olivia. Only I hate it.'

'What shall I call you, then?'

'Liv.'

Kat stuck out her hand and, after a pause, Liv shook it with a hard, bony grip.

'I'm Kathryn, which I also hate. Call me Kat.'

And that was it. 'Inseparable' just about covered it. They sat next to each other, went into town together on the bus after school.

Invented a special wave. They featured so heavily in one another's lives that their teachers began to include jokey little notes in their reports about 'the twins'.

They went right through years seven to thirteen together. Never had a falling out. Even when boyfriends came along. When Liv got transferred to a new children's home, Kat helped her move her stuff. When the Origami Killer started plying his evil trade in Middlehampton, they spooked each other late at night with gory stories about what he did.

On the last day of sixth form – the last day of school ever – Liv asked Kat to meet her on the town side of the school field, so far from the buildings they were invisible behind a line of trees.

'What is it?' Kat asked when she arrived, out of breath, having run all the way after a final meeting with her academic mentor about university.

Liv produced a shiny red penknife from the pocket of her jeans and levered out a short narrow blade that glinted in the sun. Typical Liv. Bringing a knife to school. Literally the one rule you never broke. Not ever. Kat felt the familiar shiver of danger she some-times got when they were together. Liv could take things just that little bit too far.

'What's that for?'

'Let's do a blood oath.'

'A what now?'

'We'll be blood sisters,' Liv said. 'We cut our hands and squeeze them together and our blood mingles. We swear we'll always be there for each other, whatever happens. Always and for ever.'

The idea appealed to Kat's imagination. Their favourite film was *Thelma and Louise*, released the year after they were born. They'd watched Kat's DVD of it so many times they had every line of dialogue off pat.

'Louise, no matter what happens, I'm glad I came with you,' Kat said.

Liv smiled at her.

'Something's, like, crossed over in me and I can't go back.'

Then Liv cut across her left hand, wincing as the blade sliced into her skin.

'Hurts,' she hissed out before passing the knife to Kat.

Hesitating at first, Kat inhaled sharply, then drew the blade across the fleshy mound at the base of her left thumb. It was like being stung by a hundred wasps. She marvelled at the speed with which dark red blood started flowing out and dripping on to the burnt-brown grass.

'Quick,' Liv said. They clasped hands and squeezed. 'Blood sisters. Always and for ever.'

'Blood sisters,' Kat echoed. 'Always and for ever.'

She looked into her friend's eyes, and in that moment, she knew they would always be friends. Always.

◆ ◆ ◆

Three months later, Liv was dead. Suffocated by the Origami Killer. Kat would blame herself. They'd arranged to meet at a wine bar in the town centre. A new place, down by the river on the edge of Fountains Square, with its central stand of trees and bronze sculpture of a couple holding hands. But at the last minute, Kat's boyfriend called her and told her he was dumping her so he could go to university with, as he so charmingly put it, 'a clean slate'.

Distraught, she texted Liv that she wasn't coming, then went home, put her headphones on and cried face down on her bed for three hours. By midnight, she'd consigned him to history – *His loss!* – and was texting Liv again, apologising and suggesting she come round to Kat's for cider and a rewatch of *T&L*, as they called it.

For the next ten minutes she stared at the phone's screen, rubbing the tip of her finger over the fine crack across the top where she'd dropped it, willing a little green speech bubble to appear. Liv didn't reply. Fair enough – Kat had never blown her off before.

As soon as she woke up, she checked her phone, sure Liv would have cooled off enough to send a text, even a snarky one. Nothing. A tiny voice in her head whispered, *What if he's got her? The Origami Killer. Think how bad that would be.*

No. That wasn't funny. Not even a little bit. When they worked themselves up into a frenzy of giggling fear, walking home from the pub in the dark, well, that was fine. That was just joking around. But she'd left Liv on her own this time, hadn't she?

She left a voicemail. Another, ten minutes later. And another five minutes after that. But by 10 a.m., when Liv still hadn't called or texted, the worm of anxiety squirming in her belly had swelled to the size of a snake and crawled into her throat, making her feel short of breath.

She hurried round to the new flat Liv was sharing with another girl who'd just left the care system. But Liv hadn't come home. Kat rang and messaged everyone she knew. Nobody had heard from Liv.

She went to the police only to be given the brush-off. Apparently, someone couldn't be missing – not officially, anyway – for at least two days. Finally, she got them to pay attention. But it was too late. Liv had vanished from Middlehampton.

A week before Kat's parents would be driving her up to Nottingham to start her university course, a police officer, a woman, rang the doorbell. Kat was upstairs, listening to music, when her mum knocked on her door before opening it. She looked terrible. Like she'd got food poisoning.

She told Kat to come downstairs. Called her 'Kat', too, which was totally weird; her mum didn't believe in nicknames, thought they were 'common'. Kat was always Kathryn. Her older sister was always Diana, never Di. And her brother, the baby of the family, was Nathan, never Nate.

'This is PC Harrop,' her mum said. 'She wants to talk to you.'

And then, speaking slowly, as if she were dealing with somebody with learning difficulties, Kat thought, PC Harrop explained that they'd received a letter. It was about Liv. From the man they were looking for who'd been killing young women.

Most of what she said next was a sort of buzz in Kat's ears. But the point was: Liv was dead. They'd found a document on Liv's laptop. A sort of poem-cum-manifesto for the rest of her life. She'd named Kat as her blood sister, next of kin, all-round best mate. PC Harrop was sorry for Kat's loss.

Kat didn't sleep at all that night. Or the one after. Her mother took her to the GP. The doctor gave her some tablets he said would help her. They didn't work. She took twice the dose he'd recommended. Now sleep did come. And with it, nightmares.

When she wasn't poleaxed by the tablets or screaming with night terrors, she walked like a zombie around Middlehampton, fighting the anxiety that made her want to run and run and run and never stop.

Kat drifted through the next few days, feeling as though a thick wad of fluff separated her from the world. She followed her mum around Ikea, numbly agreeing whenever she suggested something would 'look lovely in your flat'.

When the time came, she sat in the back of her father's Range Rover, while he drove, fast, up the M1. Earbuds in, she stared out of the window, seeing nothing but Liv's face hovering over the fields to the side of the motorway.

Kat settled in with her flatmates. Began her law lectures. Drank too much. Smoked a little bit. Then, in the middle of the night just a couple of weeks into her first term, she had the worst nightmare yet. Liv, her mouth stuffed with grains. An origami heart, pulsing pink where her own should be. A man in the shadows, no features. Laughing at her.

And Liv was crying. 'You did this, Kat. You did this. You let him. Why did you leave me?'

CHAPTER NINE

Liv's plaintive cry had never been entirely silent. Even now, fifteen years later, Kat sometimes thought she heard it, in those strange floating moments between sleeping and waking.

She refocused on the pitch.

She could go home and do an hour's work, then be back in time to pick Riley up. Hopefully, playing had diluted the contempt he'd sprayed in her direction on the journey over.

Keeping her head down as she checked her phone, she turned to go and almost bumped into a woman coming in the other direction. She was vaguely familiar. Another football mum. The woman looked as though she wanted to say something, then stood aside to let Kat pass.

Back at home, she took Smokey for a quick walk round the block. As she clipped him on the lead, he looked up at her with that winking expression of his. Gratitude, she decided. Not reproach for leaving him with the dog walker and the neighbour.

'Sorry, Smokes,' she said, as he cocked a leg against a fence post. 'I forgot Daddy was going to be away. We'll go out first thing in the morning, OK? Just you and me.'

Then it was the back bedroom, a glass of red wine and a plunge headlong into the case that had haunted her entire adult life.

Her phone alarm jangled, startling her.

She checked the time. Somehow it had got to 9 p.m. Time to collect Riley.

The traffic had eased off and she was able to cruise through town to the school without any of the tension squeezing her chest that she'd experienced on the way there.

Riley came trotting over to the car almost as soon as she pulled up, waving to his mates and grinning. He climbed in beside her and buckled up.

'How was practice?'

'Great! I scored twice and Coach said I'd shown great improvement compared to last season.'

'That's fantastic!'

She twisted round in her seat and held out a bunched fist. He looked at it, sceptically, then her.

'Really?'

'Please?'

Sighing, and rolling his eyes, he gave her knuckles the briefest of taps with his own, then got his phone out.

Kat put the Golf in gear and reversed out of the space before turning for home. She permitted herself a small smile. You took what you could get, and a fist bump from your previously sulking twelve-year-old son was plenty.

Something told her she might need those small moments of connection with her family over the coming weeks.

That night, she dreamt she was at Courtney's post-mortem. But when Dr Feldman drew the green sheet back, it was Liv lying there, her eyes wide open and milky. She talked all the way through the process, but Kat couldn't understand her. Except for a single phrase.

'Find him.'

CHAPTER TEN

After the morning briefing, Kat went down to Forensics. Darcy Clements had emailed her to say they were releasing the origami heart.

'It's clean,' Darcy said, pushing a strand of greying hair behind her ear. 'He must have used gloves.'

Putting her own pair of gloves on first, Kat took the folded heart from the evidence bag. She intended to check the original evidence bags, but it looked identical to his previous efforts. Same size, same pink paper, same razor-sharp creases. They'd mentioned the hearts fifteen years ago, but not where he'd left them. Carve-up was wrong to say it was a copycat. Nobody but the original Origami Killer would know to leave it tucked into Courtney Hatch's left bra cup.

'What about the cereal grains, Darcy?'

The older woman smiled, bringing crinkles to the corners of her pale blue eyes.

'You were right. Wheat. Specifically, Cotswold wheat.'

'The essential oil?'

'That's where it gets interesting. It's not essential oil. I think it's homemade.'

'How can you tell?'

'The mass spectrometer did detect some essential oil mixed in there. It's made by distilling the natural oils present in lavender flowers. Interested in their scientific name?'

Kat grinned. 'Go on, educate me.'

'*Lavandula angustifolia*. But the lab also found a far larger spike for an inert carrier oil. Looks like it's a nut oil. Probably sweet almond. We'd have to do further checks to narrow it down, which, as you know, has budgetary implications.'

Kat groaned. To her own ears, she sounded just like Riley whenever he was asked to tidy his room.

'We'll hold that in reserve for now. Thanks, Darcy.'

From Forensics, Kat descended to the basement level of Jubilee Place. The minimarket-sized space had been given the official name 'Exhibits Storage and Management'. Which, predictably, nobody used. Even the graduates. Everybody called it, simply, Evidence.

They knew all the detectives down here, of course. But the Evidence staff knew Kat particularly well. And they knew what she tended to want.

Middlehampton had long ago switched to using civilian staff to manage Evidence. The man on duty today was in his late thirties – dressed, despite it being an unusually warm September, in a denim shirt under a sweater.

'How can I help you?' he asked her.

New. Obviously.

She asked for the evidence boxes she needed, and when he'd fetched them from somewhere way back in the room, she thanked him and took them back up to her desk.

The three evidence bags were closed by thick, multi-layered bands of red tape, each layer dated and initialled by the same detective: K. Ballantyne. Clamping her lips together and breathing steadily, if rapidly, through her nose, she slit the tape on the first bag and withdrew the letter. She could make out the text perfectly well through the plastic, but she wanted, needed, to hold the paper in her hands again.

Her eyes refused to focus, jittering across that spidery hand-writing. She coughed, her throat suddenly dry, and tried again.

'Come on, Kat,' she muttered, then took a deep breath, sighing it out with an audible hiss.

Calmer, but only just, she started to read.

> *Dear Detectives of Middlehampton's Mediocre and*
> *Miserable Murder Squad,*
>> *I have done another one.*
>> *Taking her was even easier than last time. Youd*
> *think by now theyd have learnt to be careful but she*
> *got in my car like I was a minicab!*
>> *They are all sluts and whoares who wear their*
> *hair long which as you know is a sin ie Song of*
> *Solomon 6:5 'thy hair is as a flock of goats that*
> *appear from Gilead' and for that reason I have done*
> *this new one as well.*
>> *I choked her out the same way ie with the grains*
> *and I left my trademark which as you know is the*
> *origami heart, it's how I got my name after all so*
> *would be a shame to waste it.*
>> *Maybe you think I am lying, after all, where is*
> *the body? Well I am tired of making life easy for you*
> *so this time I buried her where nobody will ever find*
> *her in a million years.*
>> *See you in hell, because you will never see me*
> *on this earth.*
>> *The Origami Killer*

The original detectives had sent the letter to a handwriting expert, a professor of English at Middlehampton University, and the profiler they'd hired. The last of these turned out to be worse than useless, given that he pointed them in nine different directions, all of which turned out to be dead ends. Although he himself did very well out of his involvement in the case, writing a bestselling book.

Kat knew the graphologist's report almost as well as she did the text of the letter. But again, it seemed to her to be full of bizarrely specific and completely unprovable assertions about the writer's character. Her favourite was: 'Strong in adversity, if initially reluctant to meet difficult challenges.' It managed to cover the author's arse by including two contradictory statements wrapped into one reasonable-sounding claim. What psychologists called 'the rainbow ruse'.

The English professor's report was more interesting. She suggested that the writer of the letter was better educated than they were making themselves out to be. The missed punctuation in words like 'youd', 'theyd' and 'its'; the misspelling of 'whores' as 'whoares' despite correctly spelling an uncommon word, 'mediocre'; the use of commas at the end of sentences instead of full stops: they all suggested someone impersonating a poorly educated writer.

And if that was all they'd been presented with, it was likely the letter-writer would have been dismissed as a crank. But it wasn't, was it?

Because there were two more sentences over the page.

PS. I suppose you want proof I done her so I am sending this lovely polaroid photo. One for you're collection.

From the second evidence bag, Kat took out the faded Polaroid, holding it gently by its lower right corner. Liv lay on her back, eyes wide, head tilted over. Her hair, once so long, and a rich, dark brown, had been sheared off at odd angles. Her mouth and nose were stuffed with wheat grains that spilled down, across her left cheek, on to the mud in which she lay. Her top was pulled up over her breasts, and from the edge of the left bra cup protruded a pink origami heart.

The third evidence bag contained the heart itself.

It took Kat less than a minute to locate the other six hearts. Each bore a small self-adhesive sticky note, numbered in the order the bodies had been discovered.

Hearts 1 through 6 were made from paper in an identical shade of pink. Somewhere between candy and bubblegum. Heart 7, Liv's, differed in that the paper was a little thicker, and a shade darker. Heart 8 – the one Darcy had just released to her – was different again. The same thinness as the first six, but a half-shade lighter.

Did the difference in paper signify anything in particular? Or was he just using what he could get? Maybe he'd had six sheets left from one of those origami sets and then had to buy more. Back in 2008, they'd run all kinds of tests, tracked down suppliers, talked to origami experts. All of that effort for nothing. Dead ends everywhere they looked.

One by one, as she'd done so many times before, she unfolded them, smoothed out the squares, then refolded them.

Each heart was made in an unaltering pattern of folds. In their way, they were perfect. The folds razor-sharp. The corners aligned. The points delicate and never rolled. He'd not written anything on them, inside or out. No cryptic messages, codes or passages from one of the more lurid books of the Bible. She returned to the letter. The profiler had opined that the killer 'no doubt believes him – or her – self to be enacting God's will in some way, as can be seen from the Biblical reference'.

In Kat's opinion, that was a lazy conclusion. The killer had held up a hoop and the obedient little profiling dog had merrily jumped through, no doubt expecting a treat on the other side. The rest of the letter betrayed no evidence of religious mania, and nor, for that matter, did any other aspect of the case.

Kat thought the motive was sexual. The original, all-male investigating team had briefly considered the idea, but then dismissed it out of hand on the grounds that the Origami Killer hadn't inflicted any observable sexual violence on his victims.

Leaving aside a feminist reading that any murder of a woman was sexual by its very nature, what Kat *did* see in each photograph was a dead woman whose hair, a potent sexual stimulus for many men, had been chopped off, and with a paper heart tucked into her bra. Not her jeans pocket. Not her shoe. Or between her fingers. Her *bra*, for God's sake! Of *course* it was sexual.

Kat replaced the hearts in their evidence bags and pinned them to the corkboard she'd screwed to the wall behind the main investigation whiteboard, careful not to pierce the hearts themselves.

Next she pulled up the original forensics reports on the grains. She scanned the first one, looking for the section on the chemical composition. The grains he'd used in 2008 had been buckwheat. The oil was 99 per cent pure essential lavender oil. Same plant: *Lavandula angustifolia*. But no carrier oil, sweet almond or otherwise.

That was interesting.

He'd changed his MO. Not by a lot. But he'd made two significant alterations.

It took less than five minutes online to see what was happening. He must have switched from using the contents of commercially produced wheat pillows to making his own. Distilling essential oils was an expensive, complicated, industrial process. But you could produce less potent but still scented lavender oil in a home kitchen.

The companies who made wheat pillows used buckwheat because it had a predictable moisture content, which was important to comply with fire safety regs. But if he was buying it direct, maybe he didn't realise and had just gone for the cheapest variety. Or maybe he didn't know the difference. Or care.

She visualised a kitchen in a remote house. Somewhere close to Brearley Woods. Maybe on the fringes of the woods themselves, or even inside the perimeter. A man standing at an old-fashioned white butler's sink, steeping lavender flowers in sweet almond oil. Beside him, a sack of wheat grains.

How would he carry them to the kill site? A plastic food bag? A sandwich box? A vacuum flask or reusable metal coffee cup? Hundreds of innocuous-looking containers presented themselves.

Tom knocked his knuckles lightly on the corner of her desk. Startled, she jerked her head up. He placed a steaming mug in front of Kat – 'Black, no sugar' – before sitting opposite her. He took a sip of his own and grimaced.

'Too hot?' she asked.

'Too horrible.'

She grinned. 'This DI when I was in CID had one of those pod machines. The rest of us drank the usual station swill while DI Benwell sipped his lovely cappa-mocha-frocha-ccinos in his office with the blinds down.'

'Popular, was he?'

'As a dose of clap in a convent.'

Tom snorted. 'Is that your background?'

Her eyebrows shot up. 'What?'

He laughed. 'Not the clap, the convent. One of those Ursuline schools. I had an American girlfriend at uni who'd been to one in Dallas.'

Kat shook her head, before taking an exploratory sip of the coffee. Nope, it still tasted bad, even if the new boy had made it.

'I went to one of the comps here. Queen Anne's.'

'That's Northbridge, right?'

Kat was impressed. Showed it. 'Very good. Been studying the town map, have we?'

'Religiously.'

'How about you, Tom. Where did you grow up? I'm guessing not around here.'

He shook his head and took another sip of coffee.

'No, I grew up all over. My parents ran pubs, so we used to move every few years. Longest we stayed was in Kingston upon Thames. Five years. They wanted me to have stability while I did my GCSEs and A levels.'

'Sorry to ask this, but have you had elocution lessons or something? Only, you don't exactly sound like you grew up in pubs.'

He smiled. 'Beware of making assumptions, boss. No elocution lessons needed. Three years hanging around with rich Oxbridge rejects and you end up speaking like them.'

An expression flashed across his face. Something sad. Then it was gone.

'Where did you go to uni, then? York, Durham?'

'Good guess. Durham.'

'So then, Mr Fast-Track, where should we be directing our meagre resources, do you think?'

'Given that the CCTV situation is yielding the square root of bugger all, I think victimology is the way to go.'

'And by that we mean . . .'

'We mean, going over Courtney's life, especially the last year or two, with a fine-tooth comb.'

'Looking for . . .'

'Any men she met or was involved with.'

'Any dodgy men, you mean.'

'No. That would involve making all sorts of assumptions about the man we're looking for. And what we mean by "dodgy".'

Kat was becoming more and more impressed. The Textbook Kid had some smarts of his own.

'Go on,' she said.

'If we limit ourselves to known sex offenders or guys who live alone or have massive porn collections on their PCs, or who just look off, we're excluding, what, ninety-five per cent of the over-eighteen males in Middlehampton? Fred West didn't look weird. He was a smiley guy. The neighbours all loved him. Shipman only looks weird now because we know what he did. It's called confirmation bias. That's when—'

'—people search for evidence to back up their existing beliefs. Once people found out Shipman was a serial killer, they saw a bearded weirdo, whereas actually he was a trusted family GP right up until he was caught.'

'Sorry, Kat.'

'It's fine. I guess we're both finding out what each other knows and doesn't know. Carry on, though, I'm interested.'

He straightened in his chair. 'I've been studying the photos from the crime scene. There are no signs of a scuffle or a fight where she was dumped. So it's possible she went there willingly.'

'Or she was already dead.'

'Yes, but the earth was soft around the site. I didn't see any tyre tracks or extra-deep footprints, so how did he get the body there?'

'Tracks and prints can be brushed away, but let's assume, *for now*, that she met her killer there.'

'If she went there willingly, then she must have known her killer, yes?'

'At least well enough to agree to go there, yes.'

Tom frowned. 'Correct me if I'm wrong, but it would be quite unusual for a teenage girl to meet a man she didn't know well in Brearley Woods after dark.'

'I would say highly unlikely.'

'So either she knew him very well . . .'

'Or trusted him implicitly.'

'. . . or they met in the daytime.'

'Which at this time of year lasts until, what, nine at night?'

Tom nodded. 'If they did meet there in the light, someone might have seen something. Maybe we could put out a request on social media for anyone walking or riding in Brearley Woods the previous day to come forwards.'

'There's already an incident board at the scene, but yes, make a note. We'll do that. Anything else?'

'Yes. Her body.'

'What about it?'

'No defensive wounds.'

'From which you deduce what, exactly?'

'Either he knocked her out before he killed her or it was over before she realised what was happening.'

'Hmm. It could be a blitz kill, but for that to be as fast as you're saying, death would have to be pretty much instantaneous. Shooting, a stab to the heart, a blow to the back of the head,' she said, miming a punch.

Tom flinched at the gesture. He'd have to get used to seeing the results of violence if he was going to make a decent homicide detective.

'You think filling her airways with wheat grains would take too long.'

'I do. As to defensive wounds, I had a quick look at her finger-nails yesterday. They were dirty, so there may be DNA under there,' Kat said. 'We'll know more tomorrow.'

A phone rang. Kat looked over. It was Tom's. She signalled for him to answer.

Was this the call that would unlock the case?

CHAPTER ELEVEN

Tom answered his phone.

'MCU. DC Gray speaking.'

'Am I correct in assuming you're a detective?'

The caller was male, sixty-plus, upper middle class, Tom thought, and probably with too much time on his hands.

'Yes, sir. How can I help you?'

'Name's John Evans. I saw the post on Facebook about the murder. Terrible business.'

'Yes, sir. Do you have some information you believe may be helpful to our investigation?' *Or is this just a social call?*

'That's just it. I don't know, do I? But what I do have is a state-of-the-art security system.'

Tom suddenly found the call a lot more interesting. The man's voice seemed clearer, his words charged with electricity.

Tom reached for a pen and his notebook. 'Where do you live, sir?'

'We're the last house on The Avenue. Braeside. We face Brearley Woods, d'you see, so I thought our cameras might have caught something.'

After establishing that the man would be in for the next thirty minutes, Tom told him to stay put. Kat had left while he was on the phone: time for him to act on his own initiative.

He hit the stairs at a run and was pulling out of the car park on to Crown Street two minutes later. He supposed he could have asked someone else to go – a uniform in a marked car – but this was a solid lead.

Later, with the footage safely copied on to a portable hard drive, Tom raced back to Jubilee Place. On the drive, he allowed himself to fantasise about spotting the killer looking up at the camera.

Headlines floated in front of the car: a head-up display of his forthcoming fame. The *Echo* initially, then the other local Hertfordshire papers, before some stringer for the nationals picked it up. Then there'd be a media frenzy with him at the very centre. He'd be unassuming, reluctant to take credit. He'd emphasise that he was a small cog in a big machine. Part of an excellent team of officers who'd worked round the clock to catch the Origami Killer.

'But you were the one who finally identified him, weren't you?' a beautiful blonde reporter from Sky or the BBC would ask, thrusting her mic under his nose.

And DC Tom Gray would smile, just a little, and nod. 'I was just doing my job. The best in the world.'

The boss would call him in for a congratulatory slap on the back and a glass of single malt. As Tom sipped the mellow spirit, Stuart would lean forwards and say, 'Fast-track means what it says, Tom. Or should I call you DS Gray?'

Three hours later, eyes burning, stomach rebelling against too many cups of station coffee, Tom saw his promotion receding into the distance.

The video quality was superb. Full-colour, HD. Must have cost a fortune. But then, judging from the spacious detached houses separated from the road and each other by vast front gardens, high hedges and barred or wrought-iron gates, the residents of The Avenue probably weren't short of cash.

Broadcast quality it may have been, but it could have been a still image. Only the occasional delivery driver walking up the drive, or a blue tit flying in front of one of the cameras to its nest under the eaves, reminded him he was watching a video. He tried watching at double speed, but after five minutes he started feeling nauseous.

Then he leaned forwards, suddenly wider awake than he had been for hours. A figure in dark clothes and a dark baseball cap walked across the frame, left to right.

He paused the video and rewound so the figure fast-walked backwards across the front of the house and disappeared stage left. He hit Play and froze the image when the figure was halfway across. Despite the video quality, he couldn't make out any features. The dark clothing, which he now saw was jogging gear, gave no clue as to the figure's gender, either. A slim-built man, or a woman with an athletic build.

He played it forwards and back a couple more times. It didn't improve. He printed out a few stills, then let the footage play on.

Half an hour later, the figure returned. As they approached, Tom felt his pulse picking up. Almost directly opposite Braeside, the figure stopped and removed the baseball cap.

Her blonde hair was tied back in a ponytail.

Tom swore, and stabbed his finger on the Pause button.

'What's up, Tom?'

Stuart Carver had stopped by his desk and was looking down with an air of concern. Some of the other male detectives, Tom included, adopted a casual look in the office. Stuart was different. What Tom thought of as an old-school DI. He always wore a suit, always had polished shoes, was always clean-shaven and smelled, not unpleasantly, of aftershave.

Today's suit was a bronze two-piece number in a lightweight fabric that reflected the light with a subtle glow. Tom had never been big on tailored clothing but he could still recognise quality when he saw it. The suit was worthy of a *GQ* front cover. Especially paired, as it was, with a pair of tobacco-brown loafers with gold snaffle bits over the insteps.

'Are those—?'

'Gucci? Yeah, they are. I tell you, Tom. Scrimp on your clothing if you have to, but invest in a decent pair of shoes and you're set, mate. They're the most comfortable pair I've ever worn.'

'Bit outside my budget.'

Stuart grinned. 'Yeah, I know a DC's salary isn't much. But that's what the fast-track's for, isn't it? Won't be long before you're taking your sergeant's exams, and then the sky's the proverbial limit, isn't it?'

Encouraged that the boss's view of his future was as rosy as his own earlier daydream, Tom smiled back.

'That's the plan.'

'Plan? That's the *reality*, Tom. So, why the long face a minute ago?'

Tom jerked his head at the frozen video on his monitor. 'I thought I had a lead. Member of the public handed over his security video. But there's only one person and it's a woman. Doesn't fit our suspect's profile.'

'Welcome to my world,' Stuart said with a sigh. 'Listen, Tom, I know they probably filled your head at uni with a whole bunch of stuff about criminology and forensics and all that glamour-boy stuff. But ninety-nine per cent of policing's just hard work and persistence.'

'That's what Kat says, too.'

Stuart's nose wrinkled. 'Does she? Well, she's not wrong. There's no magic to it. Maybe the odd little piece of luck. But the harder you work, the luckier you get. That's what my old guvnor used to say.'

'Do you think we're going to catch him, then?'

Stuart nodded. 'Course we are. Especially with intelligent DCs on the team.' He looked around the office, where those at their desks were either on the phone or staring at documents. 'So, Tom,' he said in a lower tone, 'do you play sport?'

'Not really, why?'

'Not even golf?'

'I used to play the odd round at uni, but I haven't really had time to find my feet here yet.'

'I play most weekends. As it happens, my usual four are down a man on Saturday. Why don't you come along? I'll introduce you to some people at the club. Don't worry about how good you are. We're a friendly mob.'

Tom smiled. This was how it worked in the real world. Networking. And with the DI and his golfing buddies, too.

'I'd love that! Like it, I mean. To meet them. When. Which club?'

Stuart leaned down and scribbled a note on the corner of Tom's notebook.

'We like to make an early start. Eight OK for you?'

'Perfect.'

Stuart nodded and wandered off, pausing at a few other desks to pat shoulders, ask questions, exchange a joke here and an anecdote there.

There was a name for it – Tom had learned about it on a course. 'Management by Walking Around', they called it. As a senior manager you didn't hide yourself away, relying on reports and statistics. You got out there among your people, found out what was going on through observation, conversation and participation. That was the mantra their lecturer had drilled into them.

In some ways it seemed as old-school as Stuart's liking for fancy tailoring, but it made a kind of sense to Tom. And he would rather a chat over a coffee than a half-hour with a spreadsheet any day.

He saw Kat arriving in the office. She beckoned him over. Time to fill her in on his total non-event of a day.

'I've been reviewing CCTV footage from a property opposite Brearley Woods,' he said. 'So far I've clocked a blue tit and a woman. So, it's a bust, basically.'

'You might as well keep going on the CCTV,' she said. 'The killer could be in the next frame.'

He wasn't. Or the frame after that. Tom finally knocked off at gone seven. Kat had already left for the day. He admired her for the way she kept her life balanced. Children were vaguely in Tom's long-term plan. But right now, his career mattered more than his personal life – which, in any case, was devoid of anyone he could have kids *with*.

As he left the station, a wave of anxiety passed over him like a cloud in front of the sun. Tomorrow's main event. No way to get out of it.

CHAPTER TWELVE

Kat was standing at the stove, making a Bolognese sauce, when Ivan wandered into the kitchen, beer in hand. He cuddled her from behind, nuzzling her neck.

'You smell nice.'

'I smell of a police station, but whatever turns you on,' she said, shoving him back a little with her bottom.

'I've missed you.'

'Yeah, right. I know what *you've* missed.'

'Can I help it if I'm married to the sexiest woman in Middlehampton?'

Riley arrived next. 'Ugh! Get a room, please.'

Ivan turned. 'What? Can't Mum and I even have a cuddle now?'

'Do what you like, just don't make me watch, that's all.'

'How was school today, mate?' Kat asked, freeing herself from Ivan's grasp, though not before giving his groin one last push with her backside.

'"Mate"?'

'It's what Dad calls you, isn't it?'

'Yeah, but he's, you know, Dad. It sounds weird when you say it.'

Kat frowned. Why had nobody told her that one day her little boy would turn, overnight, into this . . . this *mini man*? It was so hard, getting it right when he was so full of attitude. But then she remembered how she and Liv were at his age. Even if Liv had always been the one with more daring, more fearlessness, Kat had often been caught up in the excitement and the thrill of being one of the bad girls.

'You don't like Ri-Ri anymore, which I get. But I can't call you "mate", either. What *can* I call you?'

Riley looked at the ceiling, frowned and put the tip of his index finger to the point of his chin.

'Hmmm. What *is* my mum supposed to call me? Ooh, I know!' His head flopped back to the horizontal. 'Riley! Does Riley work for you? It works for me.'

No way could she manage ten, but she counted to three in her head before answering.

'Fine, *Riley*. How was school today?'

He shrugged. 'OK.'

'OK?'

'Yeah.'

'Well, what did you have?'

'Lessons.'

Seeing where this was going, Kat spotted an escape route. 'Did you talk to anybody?'

Riley's mouth twitched. 'People.'

'What did you have for lunch?'

The twitch extended into a grin. 'Food.'

'Got you! Look, I'm interested, that's all. You're in Year Eight now, and I just want to make sure everything's all right.'

He smiled, and at last she caught a glimpse of the old Riley. The boy not too proud or grown-up to give his mum a hug, or show her a certificate he'd won.

'I'm fine, Mum, really. It's cool.' Then he surprised her. 'How was *your* day?'

'Well, you know we found a dead body yesterday,' she said. 'But we had a bit of good news today, although still sad, because we found out her identity. Who she was, I mean.'

'Who?'

'I can't say yet. But it will be public knowledge soon, then you can ask me more questions.'

'How . . .' he started. 'You know . . .'

'How did she die?'

Riley nodded.

'She was asphyxiated. That means the person who killed her stopped her from breathing.'

Riley was silent for a while. Processing it, she thought. It was so difficult, having these conversations.

From talking to Jess, she knew she wasn't alone in struggling with a preadolescent child. But Jess didn't have to field questions about the methods and motivations of murderers.

She and Ivan had discussed it endlessly. He wanted to shield Riley from all but the barest of administrative details, but Kat had pushed back against that.

'This isn't the eighties, Van,' she'd said one night. 'They've all got phones. They can look up anything. Literally anything. Autopsy photos . . . pictures of dead bodies . . . If we try to protect him, we'll just drive him deeper on to the web looking for answers. At least if I discuss it with him, carefully, we'll know he understands what's going on and that he gets context.'

'Is he a serial killer?' Riley asked now, finally.

Yes! she wanted to answer. *Yes, he is. It's the same twisted bastard who murdered Liv and those other girls three years before you were even born.*

'It's too early to say. All we know is that somebody, proba-bly' – *definitely* – 'a man, murdered a young woman and left her up in Brearley Woods. But I'm going to catch him, Riley. With my team. We're going to catch him and stop him doing it again. I've got a new partner, by the way.'

'What's she called?'

Kat smiled, pleased she'd raised a son who assumed it would be a woman.

'*He* is called Tom.'

'OK. Is he any good?'

'Today was his second day with us, so it's a bit early to say. He seems all right, though – knows how to listen to people. And get this, he went to university.'

Riley rolled his eyes.

'Not this again. I said, I don't want to go to uni. All that debt. Anyway, I'm twelve. I don't have to decide for literally ages.'

'That's true. But it creeps up on you. You can do loads of different things at uni these days. Not just maths or English or physics.'

'Football?'

'Well, I don't think so. But you can do sports science, I'm sure.'

'How about gaming?'

'Riley!'

'Can I learn how to be an influencer? A BMXer? A rapper?'

'A rapper? Give it a rest, mate,' Ivan said. 'Is this because of L-Tox?'

'No,' Riley said indignantly, hands on hips. 'Anyway, he's going to be famous one day. Like, a celebrity. And *he's* not going to uni.'

'Wait a minute,' Kat said, trying to catch up. 'El who?'

Riley rolled his eyes. 'Luke Tockley. In Clarke House. He's going to be a rapper.'

'Unlikely,' Ivan said. 'He's a bad influence, mate. I've said it before. You need to find some friends with their heads screwed on right.'

Riley whirled round, eyes ablaze. 'No, I don't! I like him. He's cool. And he's going to make a load more money than you do.'

He marched off, pausing only to slam the door behind him.

'That went well,' Kat said, drily. 'How come I haven't heard of this L-Tox character before?'

Ivan shrugged. 'He's the new friend I've been trying to tell you about. Remember?'

'Vaguely.'

Ivan sighed. 'I'll show you his YouTube channel later. I think we should speak to Mr Darnley. See if he can suggest Luke sees a bit less of this boy.'

Kat looked down into the pan of bubbling, wine-and-garlic-smelling ragu, stirring it absent-mindedly. Her parents had felt the same about Liv. That she wasn't the right sort of friend for their daughter. Which was a bit much, considering her dad was hardly Middlehampton high society.

'You want the kind of friends whose parents have pools. Tennis courts, even. People who're going places. Who've made something of themselves,' he'd said once. 'I don't know why you want to hang around with Liv. She lives in a bloody children's home, for God's sake. What's wrong with that nice girl we invited to your birthday party? What was her name, Sarah?'

Her mum had smiled that smile that looked like she had trapped wind, and said, 'Cecily Gatehouse.'

Planning her move, Kat was halfway through the sitting room door when she turned and snapped out, sharp as a slap, 'Cecily Gatehouse is a—'

The memory of her mother's freshly lipsticked mouth open in a perfect 'O' as her daughter used an absolutely unforgivable word still made Kat smile.

'Let him have his friendship with the unsuitable L-Tox, eh?' she said. 'Maybe he *will* be famous one day.'

Ivan snorted. 'Yeah, right. I'll be back in a minute. I just need to check my emails.'

Alone in the kitchen, Kat tried to imagine Riley and the mysterious L-Tox hanging out backstage after some arena concert. She saw sultry-eyed women – lots of make-up, skimpy clothes – draping themselves over the star and his entourage. The rapper passing a joint to Riley, or chopping out a line of coke. A young woman leaning over the white powder. Then she saw Courtney Hatch's body, dumped in the woods. The sudden juxtaposition of the images made her shudder.

Maybe Van was right. Maybe they should be keeping Riley on a tighter leash.

Because that had worked for her, hadn't it? The more her parents had tried to keep their rebellious younger daughter away from Liv Arnold, the harder she'd fought to be with her. No. Let Riley make his own mistakes. For now. While they were likely to be small.

She called husband and son five minutes later to collect heaped bowls of spaghetti Bolognese. Smokey trotted in and curled up in his bed by Riley's feet.

After a while, Kat noticed Riley was toying with his food.

'Everything all right, Riley?' she asked.

'Yeah, fine.'

'Then why aren't you eating. It's your favourite.'

Riley glanced at Ivan.

He wrinkled his nose. 'I like it better when Dad makes it.'

Ivan snorted and took a hurried swig of beer.

'Did I make it wrong? I used all fresh ingredients, slow-cooked shin of beef, just like the recipe.'

'It tastes too fancy. Dad uses mince.'

Kat smiled and shook her head. Ivan was grinning across the table at her.

'Oh, Lord, you boys and your fixed little ways. I can't win, can I? How about ice cream for pudding? Don't worry, it's from the shop. I didn't make it myself from passionfruit and double cream.'

'Epic!' Riley said, bumping fists with Ivan. 'What kind?'

'Cookie dough.'

'Yes!'

He jumped up and ran to the utility room where they had a small separate freezer.

'The way to a man's heart . . .' Ivan said, winking.

'Is through the frozen aisle in Tesco.'

They went to bed early, Ivan pushing the bedroom door closed until the latch clicked. He smiled and began, very slowly, to undo his shirt. As the last button came undone, he swivelled round and shrugged it down, giving Kat a wink over his shoulder.

She burst out laughing and lay back against the pillow.

'I am so turned on right now. Get yourself over here, Mr Ballantyne, before I go off pop.'

Afterwards, lying inside Ivan's arm, her head resting against his chest, she listened to his heart tumbling along.

'You smell nice, too,' she said.

'What of? Servers?'

'Man.'

'Ug. Man like woman,' Ivan grunted. 'Like sexing her. Man want sex every day.'

'Man better have a cold shower then, because woman has serial killer to catch.'

'How's the case going?'

'Got the post-mortem tomorrow. That should be fun.'

The following day, at 8.50 a.m., she and Tom were taking the short walk from car park 9 at MGH to the morgue, formally known as the James Frobisher Forensic Medicine Suite.

'Kat, there's something I ought to tell you,' Tom said.

He sounded uncharacteristically nervous. She turned. His skin was pale, and greasy-looking.

'What?'

'I've never actually been inside a morgue before.'

Kat took pity on him. Tom and his fellow university students had probably seen autopsy photos on their course, but nothing prepared you for the three-dimensional – four, if you counted the smell – reality of a dead body being dissected right in front of you.

'Try not to worry. We all have to go through our first PM. Remember, focus on the details, take notes if it helps, and, if you *are* going to throw up, find somewhere away from the body,' she said. 'Feldman doesn't take kindly to cops spewing over his corpses.'

The gallows humour was intended to reassure him. Had it worked? Kat wasn't sure. He looked greener than before, even as he pasted a sickly smile on to his face.

'I'll do my best.'

'You'll be fine,' she said. 'Oh, one more thing. Don't call it "the morgue". Feldman likes us to say "autopsy suite".'

Five minutes later, garbed in green scrubs, they arrived at the door to the autopsy suite. Kat offered him a plastic tube.

'Oil of camphor. It helps with the smell. Rub it on your top lip and around your nose. Careful, though, it can make your eyes water if it gets anywhere sensitive.'

'Best not to have a wank straight afterwards, then.'

She drew her head back. 'Pardon?'

'Too much?' he asked, a blush reddening his cheeks like a schoolboy's.

'*Much* too much. Let's go.'

She drew the surgical mask up over her nose and mouth and went in, Tom behind her.

The pathologist was waiting for them, gowned, booted, masked, and with his face protected from back-spatter by a transparent plastic visor. Beside him, his assistant stood, ready to help his master.

'Good morning, DS Ballantyne,' Feldman said. 'And who do we have here?'

'This is my new bagman. DC Tom Gray.'

'Ever seen a post-mortem before, DC Gray?'

'No, sir.'

Feldman barked out a short laugh.

'Ha! Been a long time since anyone around here called me "sir". Dr Feldman will suffice. So, I only have three rules. One, this is a scientific space. When you enter, you leave your hunches, gut feelings and "copper's intuition" at the door. Two, don't get in my light. And three—'

'Don't throw up over the body.'

'You'll go far, my boy.'

Feldman drew the green sheet down over the dead girl's still-clothed body and dropped it into a bin. Using blue-handled trauma shears, he cut off the girl's clothes for the assistant to bag.

Kat got her first proper look at the Origami Killer's eighth victim. She gasped. The girl looked just like Liv had in that dreadful Polaroid.

The lower part of Courtney's rib cage was bruised. Together with the purple marks on the upper arms, it painted a picture for Kat. The man sitting astride Courtney's torso, his knees pushing her arms into the leaf mould, using his body weight to squeeze the air from her lungs even as he stopped any more from entering.

Feldman held out a gloved hand, into which his assistant slapped a large-bladed scalpel. Emitting a guttural cough, Tom fled to a corner and emptied his stomach into a bin. Kat felt for him. But degree or not, he had to learn.

Two hours later, she led Tom out of the room. She'd seen all she needed to. The dead girl fitted the killer's preferred victim type. Dr Feldman had confirmed what she already knew. She hadn't been raped, or assaulted sexually in any way at all. Cause of death was smothering, with the instrument of choice being approximately five hundred grams of lavender-scented cereal grains that Dr Feldman still insisted needed to be formally identified by Forensics.

Behind them, the door to the autopsy suite hissed on its pneumatic closer. She turned to see Feldman standing in the doorway, his visor up, his mask pulled down.

'DS Ballantyne, a word?'

'I'll meet you at the car,' she said to Tom. Then she walked back to where Feldman was standing.

'What is it, Doc?'

'This is actually my last autopsy.'

'Of the week?'

'Ever. I'm retiring at the end of the month and my time will be taken up with teaching and bringing my replacement on board.'

'Nobody will be able to replace you Doctor Feldman,' she said, suddenly feeling the need for more formal language. 'I mean, I've learned so much working with you over the last couple of years.'

'No need to get all soppy about it,' Feldman said, with a half-smile. 'And I shall still be living in Middlehampton, so who knows, we might bump into each other.'

'Hopefully without the smell of corpses around us.'

'That would be a welcome change, don't you think?'

His smile broadened and he peeled off his right glove before shaking hands.

Kat walked back to her car worrying about Feldman's retirement. Not for the man himself; he'd more than earned it. But for herself.

Feldman might be prickly at times, with the self-assurance bordering on arrogance that came from being so experienced. But he was a superb pathologist. Whoever replaced him would have to be at the top of their game to help her catch the Origami Killer.

CHAPTER THIRTEEN

Tom wasn't daunted by Stuart's invitation to an 8 a.m. Saturday golf game. Even at university, he'd been an early riser. He'd been there to work. To make his parents proud. He was the first in his family to go to university and he wasn't about to let them down by boozing and smoking his way to a poor degree.

In his final year, he'd fallen, hard, for a glorious red-haired Texan, Janis Gibbons. They'd shared a work ethic and spent long days in the university library together.

Only once had he faltered. The memory surfaced now like a bubble of marsh gas emerging from a swamp, bursting and filling the air with its stink.

Tom and his friends had gone for a couple of post-exam drinks in a pub renowned for its popularity among bikers. Supposedly off-limits to students, but in reality perfectly friendly if you went in for a quiet pint and didn't spend your evening waving your college scarf around and talking about postmodernism.

'A couple' turned into 'a skinful' turned into 'too many to count', and then, after one of the bikers made a comment about Janis, it had kicked off.

As the wiry biker's face swam into view, teeth bared, pupils black full-stops in startling turquoise irises, Tom felt a familiar nausea roll upwards from his gut. He squeezed his eyes shut, swallowed his gorge down and shook his head, hard. *No!* He wouldn't remember. He *wouldn't.*

He opened his eyes. Unclenched his fists. Went downstairs and ate a quick breakfast.

Chewing, he thought about the game to come. Why had Carver invited him to play golf? On its face, it was a simple enough question. With a simple answer. Making the new kid feel welcome. And Carver was clearly an arch-manipulator, seeing an advantage in having his own, tame 'Bambi'.

But was there more to it? There had to be, surely? A DI palling around at the weekend with a lowly DC? He shrugged. Time would tell.

◆ ◆ ◆

Tom pulled into the club car park at 7.50 a.m., enjoying the crunch and pop of gravel under the tyres. He knew it was a cheap trick to make members and their guests feel that they had arrived – metaphorically as well as literally – but he didn't mind. None of the pubs he'd grown up in had had drives of any kind, let alone gravel ones.

He retrieved his clubs from the boot and slammed it shut. Looking around, he squinted at the bright sunlight bouncing off gleaming paintwork and sparkling chrome. The cars were a predictable array of status symbols. Jags, of course, Mercs, Beamers, Volvos; even a Bentley, a huge black beast riding on enormous chrome wheels emblazoned with the winged 'B' logo. He smiled. One day. One day.

Stuart met him just inside the clubhouse. He was resplendent in powder-blue trousers, a gleaming white shirt and a sleeveless Pringle sweater. The colours – baby pink, beige and white – reminded Tom of the Neapolitan ice cream that had been his favourite for Sunday tea. That was when his mum could still be bothered to provide a dessert, before the red wine sapped her will as well as her liver.

'Morning, Tom. Got the weather for it, haven't we?'

'It's lovely, boss.'

Stuart frowned. '"Boss"? It's the weekend, Tom. Call me Stuart, OK? In fact, call me Stuart at the station, too. No need to shove my rank down your throat, is there? You'll probably be giving *me* orders before too long.'

He laughed loudly. It wasn't funny, but Tom joined in anyway. It was what the man expected, clearly.

'Are the others here yet?' he asked.

'Let's get you signed in and then I'll introduce you.'

Tom followed Stuart to the back of the clubhouse, where two men were taking turns to mime golf swings.

'Guys,' Stuart called out. 'Here he is! My protégé. He says he used to have the odd game at uni but I reckon he's a hustler. He'll make a double on the first and an eagle after we've all agreed the bets.'

Tom smiled as they joined the other two men – one early sixties, well-preserved, a full head of close-cropped silver hair, the other twenty years younger, shaved head disguising male-pattern baldness. The three exchanged handshakes.

'Colin,' the older man said. 'Morton.'

'Tom Gray. Pleased to meet you.'

'Hi, Tom,' the younger of the pair said. 'Joe Milne.'

'How do you know Stuart?'

'We worked together in CID,' Joe said.

'Are you still in the job?'

'Nah. Got out after ten years. I'm a financial adviser now. Here . . .' He fished a business card from the pocket of his trousers. 'Mates' rates if you ever want some impartial advice on switching your mortgage or whatever.'

Tom pocketed the card. 'I'm renting at the moment, so . . .'

'Keep it anyway, mate. Lifetime offer.'

'Thanks. How about you, Colin?' he asked, turning to the other man. 'Were you a copper, too?'

Colin looked at Stuart, and half smiled. Tom couldn't read the look. They were clearly old friends, but there was something more.

'Nothing so exciting, I'm afraid,' he said. 'Property's my game.'

'Developer?'

Colin nodded. 'In a small way. I have a few things going on in Middlehampton; one or two projects elsewhere in the county.'

Stuart laughed. 'He's being modest, Tom. Colin is one of this town's leading citizens.'

Colin shook his head. 'Oh, come on, Stuart. Tom doesn't want to hear all this.'

'Yes, he does! It's why I brought him up here at this ungodly hour to play with you.' Stuart turned back to Tom. 'Colin's the boss of Morton Land. I'm not talking about some silly little housewife flipping one-bed flats for a ten-K profit. They're Middlehampton's biggest property developers. We're talking office blocks, car parks, even hospitals. Then there's his charity work, his—'

'All right, Stuart, enough,' Colin said. 'I thought we were here to play golf.'

When the tee was free, they strolled over, pulling their trollies. All except Colin.

'Watch this, Tom,' he said, holding up a little black box.

He pressed a button and the electric trolley reversed neatly up to his side.

'As you're our guest, you'll have the honour,' Stuart said.

He presumably meant his wink to the others to be discreet, but Tom still caught it. So that was it. He'd brought Tom out to beat in front of his golfing buddies. Fine, Stuart wanted to play games. Play with this.

Tom pushed his tee into the soft, beautifully maintained grass. He placed his ball on the tee and addressed it. Offered up a little prayer. His swing felt good. He remained motionless, club draped over his left shoulder, as the ball soared into the blue on a perfect parabolic arc.

'Bloody hell,' Stuart breathed from somewhere to his right.

Tom turned and smiled innocently at his new friends. 'Was that all right?'

Colin and Joe erupted into good-natured laughter, which Stuart joined after a few seconds.

Stuart looked slyly at Tom.

'Hey guys, what do graduate DCs have in common with the Origami Killer? They both think a piece of paper makes them God.'

The other two laughed good-naturedly. Tom stared at Stuart, who was smirking. Saw a different side of his character.

Hole by hole, they shared more snippets of background, Middlehampton gossip, the odd remark on this guy's swing or that guy's grip. All good-natured. Until Tom found himself searching for his ball in the long rough, and Stuart suddenly materialised by his right shoulder.

'Thought you might need a helping hand,' he said, poking his club into a clump of couch grass.

Tom spotted his ball almost at that moment, lying, miraculously, in a small patch of close-cropped weeds.

'No, we're good. Here it is,' he said.

Stuart put a hand on Tom's arm as he was lining up his shot. 'A word, before you do that.'

Stuart leaned closer, even though they were completely alone. Tom caught a whiff of his aftershave, expensive and overpowering at the same time. 'Don't get too close to DS Ballantyne. I know it all seems very exciting right now, running around carrying her bags, but you need to think long-term.'

Tom frowned. 'Sorry, Stuart, I'm not sure I understand.'

'I'm saying, if you want to get on, you need to align yourself with the right people. People with influence. Take Colin. Did he get to where he is by waiting for things to happen? No! He went out and bent the world to his way of seeing things. You could do a lot worse than follow his example.'

Tom smiled. 'I'm lost, now. What are you saying – I should go into property development?'

Stuart laughed. It came off as fake. 'No, of course not. I'm saying that, as a DI, I could be much more helpful to you in your career than DS Ballantyne.'

'But you assigned me to her yourself.'

'Yes, I did. So, for example, if you happen to overhear something you think might be helpful to me – you know, as *her* line manager,' he said, 'just, think about sharing it with me.'

'What do you mean, "helpful"?'

'Jesus, do I have to spell it out for you? I thought you lot were supposed to be smart,' he said. 'You're on the fast-track. I can make that track faster still. But I need you to give me something in return.'

Tom opened his mouth to reply but was interrupted.

'Come on, you two!' Colin Morton called over to them. 'Joe and I are growing roots over here.'

'Excuse me, Stuart,' Tom said, then bent over his ball.

Colin turned out to be the best player by far. After Tom's initial drive that had so delighted at least two of his partners, he'd relapsed into his old game. Spotty. More than one excursion into the rough, overcautious on the green, and generally what you might expect from a one-time student golfer.

The quartet reached the eighteenth green; it was 11.30 a.m. and the September sun was bringing a sweat to Tom's forehead. He sank his putt for a birdie, his first of the round.

'Well done, Tom,' Colin said, clapping him on the back. 'Traditionally, the loser buys the first round, but as you're our guest I'll flip that on its head and pay for them myself.'

After the heat of the course, the air-conditioned bar was wonderfully cool.

'What're you drinking, Tom?' Colin asked, after ordering pints of lager for the other two and a gin and tonic for himself.

'Lime and soda, please.'

'Sure?'

'Absolutely. Thirsty work, playing golf. Especially with your boss.'

'Come on, Tom,' Stuart said. 'A little one won't hurt you.'

'It's fine, really.'

'You're not an alcoholic, are you?' he asked, his mouth turning up, just a little, on one side.

There was something behind Stuart's question. More than the obvious banter about men who couldn't hold their booze. Almost as if he knew why Tom didn't drink.

'What, like you, you mean?' Joe put in before Tom could answer.

'I like my drink, there's a difference.'

Ignoring the obviously well-rehearsed chat between the two men, Colin turned back to the barman and ordered Tom's drink.

They found a table by a picture window. The drive from the car park to the main road curved past their corner of the building. Beyond the gravelled strip was a lush green landscape of fairway fringed by weeping willows and flowering shrubs. Taller mature trees stood in dark green clumps, rendered hazy by the sunshine.

'How are you finding the work, Tom?' Colin asked.

'Policing generally, or MCU in particular?'

Colin sipped his gin and tonic. 'I was thinking about MCU. Working for this reprobate here,' he said, nodding at Stuart.

102

Tom shrugged. 'It's early days, but I love it. It's what I always wanted to do.'

'Stuart tells me your line manager is a woman. How do you find that?'

'It's fine. Why wouldn't it be?'

'No reason. What's she called?'

'Kat – Kathryn – Ballantyne.'

'Is that her married name?'

Tom frowned. What an odd question. 'I don't know. I didn't ask.'

Colin smiled. 'Ask her when you next see her.' He checked his watch, a heavy gold number on a matching bracelet. 'Gentlemen, duty – or rather business – calls . . .' He bent to Tom and offered his hand for the second time. 'Good to meet you, Tom. I'm sure our paths will cross again. And when you do decide to take the plunge and get your foot on the property ladder, give me a call, yes?'

Colin handed Tom a business card from a monogrammed silver case.

Tom watched him go. A minute later, the black Bentley cruised past the window.

'What did he mean?' Tom asked Stuart.

'Ask Kat on Monday like Colin said. You'll have your answer,' he said with a soft smile. 'Your round, I think.'

When Tom returned with the drinks, Stuart was alone.

'While Joe's in the little boys' room,' he said, 'I thought we should finish our conversation.'

'What conversation?' Tom asked, knowing exactly what Stuart was talking about.

'Ballantyne thinks just because she's a woman she can cut corners. You probably noticed her and me don't always see eye to eye,' Stuart said. 'So, if you see her taking shortcuts, let me know. No blowback on you. And like Colin, I look after people who do me favours.'

Tom looked across the table at Stuart. All this talk of favours, and bending the world to one's will, made him deeply uncomfortable. He could see all too clearly what was being asked of him. A whisper in Stuart's ear about Kat in return for better assignments, faster progress. Part of him found the idea of a helping hand up the ladder attractive, even if it came from the repellent Stuart Carver. But he wanted to do it on his own. And Kat deserved his loyalty.

'Suppose I don't see her cutting any corners?'

Stuart smiled. 'Well, then. No harm done. DS Ballantyne'll show she *is* capable of following protocol, and you'll stay with her, carrying her bag as usual.'

Tom sat back, processing the veiled threat. For surely that was Stuart's meaning. Betray Kat or spend the rest of his time at Jubilee Place running around after her, rather than running his own investigations.

He'd studied risk analysis at uni.

Was he about to put it into practice?

CHAPTER FOURTEEN

Monday. The start of the second week. Kat bought her usual black coffee and bacon roll on the way in from the car park. Stuart gathered everyone in the conference room, demanding updates on the various cases occupying MCU.

Kat tried to stay focused, but the weekend kept coming back like a bad dream she couldn't shake. She'd spent the two days trying, and failing, to balance three roles: wife, mother and homicide detective.

Van understood the pressures of the job. Mostly. Like she understood his: not the details of his IT consultancy projects, but the stresses and strains of running his own business. She thought it was one of the reasons their marriage worked as well as it did, especially compared to the trainwrecks, car crashes and aircraft disasters that littered Jubilee Place. Sometimes it seemed like the choice was between being a successful divorced cop or a happily married ex-cop.

She'd kept work to a three-hour slot on Sunday morning, getting up early so she could read in peace. At 8.50 a.m., she'd put a pan of sausages on a low heat, brewed a pot of strong tea, and then taken two mugs upstairs to re-join Ivan in bed, after clicking the bedroom door closed behind her with her heel.

She'd been thinking maybe she could encourage Van's caveman side out into the open again. Sunday mornings were often good for both of them. Especially if, as now, Riley was having a sleepover at a friend's house.

'Thanks, mate,' he mumbled, as she slipped in beside him. 'Time?'

'Nine.'

'Been up long?'

'No, not long. Just had some stuff to go over.'

He hauled himself into a sitting position. 'On a Sunday morning? Why?'

Maybe it was the 5.30 a.m. start, or his aggrieved tone of voice, but she reacted more strongly than she meant to. Or at least, that's what she told herself afterwards.

'Because I'm investigating a murder? One that exactly mirrors Liv's?'

Ivan sighed. 'Oh God, not this again, Kat. It's bad enough you have all that . . . stuff . . . in the back bedroom, but now you're up at the crack of dawn raking over it all again.'

She felt the row building, seemingly on its own, like a storm out at sea looking for somewhere to make landfall and cause maximum destruction.

'You were fast asleep. Snoring, by the way, so whatever I was doing wasn't any of your concern, was it?'

'We have a rule, though. No work on Sundays. I stick to it, why can't you?'

She twisted around to look at him. Maybe he was joking. It wouldn't be particularly well judged, but she'd catch the hint of a grin and she'd know. She could forgive him and try to regain the intimate moment currently scurrying away and looking for higher ground to ride out the storm.

But Van wasn't smiling. He picked up his mug of tea and sipped it, looking at her over the rim. Waiting for her to say something. She thought maybe she should say something to mollify him. And then she thought, *No! Absolutely not!* That was her mum's way, not hers.

'I'm not in CID anymore, Van,' she said, trying to keep her voice even, her breathing steady. 'Burglaries and drug deals can wait till Monday, but I'm MCU now. Homicides. Serious sexual assaults. Arson. These people don't keep office hours. Neither can I. And it hasn't eaten into our day, has it? You only just woke up.'

'No, but it's the principle, isn't it?'

She looked at him. Where was this coming from? He'd been delighted when she'd got her promotion. Even after she'd explained the likely impact on their lives, he'd been gung-ho for what he'd called 'your brilliant career'.

He put his mug down and she was able to take in, and recognise, his facial expression. An unmistakable almost-pout.

'Oh my God, this is about sex, isn't it?'

The pout shifted. 'No it isn't!'

'You've got that look you get when I say I'm too tired.'

He folded his arms. 'Well, maybe that's because we haven't been doing it much recently.'

'We did it on Thursday! You did a very seductive striptease, if memory serves.'

'But when was the last time before that, Kat?'

'I don't know,' she said, starting to wish she'd stayed in her office. 'I don't keep a log.'

'Two weeks ago.'

She raised her eyebrows.

'Really? Look, you know things have been a bit busy lately at work.'

'Yeah, I'd noticed. So has Riley. He told me you only just got to football practice in time.'

'Oh, please don't bring Riley into this,' Kat said, suddenly no longer interested in her tea or in Van's caveman side. 'If your libido's giving you gip, that's one thing, but please don't suggest I'm a bad mother.'

'You're not a bad mother,' Ivan said. 'It's just—'

'It's just what?' she said, getting out of bed and grabbing underwear from her drawer.

'Do you think maybe you're making too much of this connection to Liv? Couldn't it just be a copycat?'

'Oh, so now you're a homicide expert as well as an IT consultant? You should hook up with Stuart Carver. He thinks I'm crazy, too,' she said, pulling on her second-favourite pair of jeans.

Ivan got out of bed. He came round to her side, arms wide. 'Nobody thinks you're crazy, love.'

She evaded the incoming embrace. 'There's sausages on the hob. I'm going to walk Smokey.'

Later, they went to watch Riley's team play an away match in Watford. They were thrashed 9-1. The fact that Riley scored Middlehampton College's only goal didn't improve his mood for the drive home.

'We were shit!' he exclaimed as he slammed the car door closed behind him.

'Riley! You were not. You played really well. They were just the better team,' Kat said. 'And, by the way, no swearing, remember?'

'Well, *Mum*, in fact, we totally were sh— rubbish. We should have beaten them easily.'

'Well, I thought you played well. And you did get our only goal, darling.'

'Not that you noticed.'

'Of course I did!' she protested, trying to catch his eye in the rear-view mirror.

'No, you didn't. You were on your phone. Probably checking up on your case.'

Kat bit back her reply, and drove the rest of the way home in silence.

Three words floated between Van and her. *Told you so.*

◆ ◆ ◆

'Earth calling DS Ballantyne?'

Kat started. Stuart was smirking at her. Everyone else was looking her way, too.

'Sorry, Stuart, I missed that.'

'I said' – pause – 'what news on your copycat?'

She thought back to her row with Van. Maybe Carver didn't think she was crazy, but he was happy to play up the notion she was a tunnel-visioned obsessive, too personally involved with the case to see straight or investigate efficiently.

'It's not a copycat. There's no way he could know all the details.'

Carver shrugged. 'Be that as it may, where are we?'

The trouble was, Kat and Tom were precisely nowhere. Andy Ferris might be a perv, although they only had the word of a dead girl on that, but they had nothing to hold him on. The victimology on Courtney was a work in progress. Nothing had leapt out yet. Despite Tom's heroic efforts on CCTV, they hadn't got so much as a single frame that might point to a suspect. Just the blonde woman in the baseball cap.

Was honesty the best policy? Not when Carve-up was asking the questions. In that situation, the best form of defence was attack.

'Tom and I attended the post-mortem on Friday. Feldman recovered what looked like blood from under Courtney's fingernails.

We need to get it to NDNAD for analysis, so I'll need your sign-off on that,' she said, continuing before he could raise objections over budgets. 'We also know the wheat grains were scented in a domestic set-up, not commercially, which will be a great lead when we arrest someone and search his place.'

'And how close do you think you are to arresting someone?'

'I've found some promising leads in the victim's background,' Tom said.

Kat looked at him, half in gratitude, half in surprise. He hadn't told her any of this. But maybe she hadn't asked him. She'd been wrapped up in her own lines of enquiry, after all.

Carver smiled. 'Go on, Tom.'

Tom looked round the room.

'Courtney was a few months out of a relationship with a guy named Johnny Hayes,' Tom said. 'I checked him out over the weekend. He's older than Courtney. Quite a bit older, actually. Twenty-seven. And he's got a record. Minor stuff, mostly, drug possession, threatening behaviour, drunk and disorderly. Kat even arrested him herself once. But there was a domestic abuse complaint a few years back, before he was going out with Courtney.'

The air in the room crackled with electricity as the assembled investigators listened closer to what their newest member was saying.

'Was he arrested?' Craig asked.

'And held in custody for twenty-four hours,' Tom said. 'The victim, his girlfriend at the time, withdrew the complaint and he walked.'

'What did he do to her?' Leah asked. 'A punch? A slap? Coercive control?'

'He choked her until she fainted on the kitchen floor. When she came round, he was kneeling on her holding a pair of kitchen scissors,' Tom said. 'He threatened to cut all her hair off if she ever annoyed him again.'

'Why do they do it?' Leah asked. 'These Neanderthal arseholes. They're just such cowards. I hate them.'

'Ought to give them a taste of their own medicine,' one of the older male cops in the room said. 'Back in the day, you'd have taken him round the back – you know, smokers' corner – and given him a good hiding.'

Leah pulled on her ponytail.

'Yeah, Mike, except "back in the day" nobody would have taken her seriously in the first place,' she said. 'And even if you did batter him, he'd only have gone home and taken it out on her.'

'Much as I'd love to discuss the history of misogyny inside and outside Hertfordshire Police,' Stuart said, 'I have a unit to run. Anything else on Courtney Hatch? No? OK, thanks everyone. Let's get to it.'

Kat caught up with Carver as he was heading back to his office.

'Stuart,' she said to stop him.

He turned. 'Not "Stu"? You must want something.'

'Your sign-off on my NDNAD request.'

'Sure. But standard turnaround, yeah.'

'We have to rush it,' Kat said, biting down on her rising temper. 'We're wasting time. He's going to do it again, you know that.'

'No, I do *not* know that. And if anyone's wasting time, it's you. I know what you're up to. You're still chasing yesterday's demons, aren't you?' He softened his voice. 'Come into my office. Just for a minute.'

Frowning, Kat followed him inside and took the visitor chair.

'What is it?'

'Look, Kat, I'm sorry for what I just said. I know how badly the Origami Killer case shook you up. You were the same age as Courtney, weren't you? When your mate was killed.'

'A year younger, actually. So was Liv.'

Carve-up nodded. 'Exactly. Trauma like that doesn't leave you. It stays with you. Affects everything. Makes you see connections that don't exist.'

'What exactly are you saying?'

'I'm saying, you seem determined to ignore the obvious. That we're looking for a normal bloke who's copying the Origami Killer to muddy the waters,' Carve-up said. 'Why? Because you need it to be a serial so you can lay your own feelings to rest over your friend. It's called "survivor guilt". I read about it on Wikipedia.'

Kat wanted to shout at him. Launch herself over the desk and hit him. But she didn't. Couldn't. Because even though he was just trying to wind her up, the idiot was right, wasn't he? And it was worse than survivor guilt. Because if she hadn't blown Liv off for their drink, *neither* she nor Courtney would be dead.

Carve-up was still talking. '. . . would totally understand if you weren't totally on top of this, on account of some sort of delayed PTSD or whatever. I could put Craig on it, with you assisting, obviously.'

'I'm not suffering from PTSD. Delayed or otherwise. I'm fine,' she snapped. 'And I'm not handing over as lead to Craig or anyone else.'

Carve-up raised his hands. 'Just know the offer's there. I want to support you like I support all my staff.'

Kat glared at him. Presumably not using her first name in meetings was part of that support package.

'Is that it?'

He smiled. 'That's it.'

'Great. Excuse me, I've got a serial killer to catch.'

Back at her desk, she caught Tom looking over at her.

'Everything all right, Kat? You look a bit pale.'

'It's nothing. Just the case,' she sighed.

'You know what you need?'

'Oh, great! Another male cop telling me what I need. Go on then, Tom, what do I need?'

The words, dripping sarcasm like blood off a blade, were out of her mouth before she could stop them. Tom looked stricken. His mouth turned down, and for one horrible moment, Kat thought he was going to cry.

'God, I'm sorry, Tom. That was out of order,' she blurted. 'Come on, tell me.'

'I was going to offer to buy you a decent cup of coffee. There's a new place just opened up on North Street.'

Kat glanced at Carver's office door. 'Yeah, why not? You can tell me where you've got to with looking at the original murders.'

CHAPTER FIFTEEN

The coffee shop was half-full when they pushed through the door and joined the back of a short queue.

'Want something to eat?' Tom asked, pointing at a small glass-fronted display case on the counter, filled with rough-edged pastries and lumpy cookies that had to be home-made.

Kat looked at a willow-pattern plate stacked with cannoli, the crispy pastry tubes overflowing with chocolate or vibrant green pistachio filling. She'd put the wrong trousers on that morning, and with the waistband uncomfortably tight she didn't want to add to the bloated feeling.

'Not for me, but you go ahead. Those cannoli look delicious.'

He grinned. 'They are. I had one this morning on the way in.'

Her eyes widened. 'God, you blokes! Why can you just stuff your faces and not put any weight on?'

Tom moved to the front of the queue and placed his order, a flat white for himself and an Americano for Kat.

'How do you know I don't put weight on?'

She raised an eyebrow. 'You're telling me you've got shapewear on under your jeans, are you?'

He laughed. 'Spanx for men. I like it.'

'Two points for the Bambi,' she said, still smiling. 'You know what shapewear is.'

He shrugged as he accepted the coffees and handed the Americano to Kat. 'I have a friend who swears by them.'

They found a table by the window. Kat took an exploratory sip of her Americano. It was good. Fruity and smooth, where the station swill was dusty and bitter. Outside the window, North Street bustled with shoppers.

'I read all the original case materials,' Tom said, putting his mug down.

'All of them?'

'Skim-read, then.'

'Conclusions?'

'I plotted the body-dumps on a map of Middlehampton. No overall pattern, although three were found in Brearley Woods. Shallow graves or coverings, no real attempt to hide the bodies.'

'And therefore?'

'Either he wanted to get caught, or – more likely – simply didn't believe he would be.' Tom paused for another mouthful of coffee. 'In which case, he was right, of course.'

'Anything else?'

'I know this is a big assumption, but if the murders occurred where the bodies were left, then the sites form a rough circle centred on the Town Hall.'

Kat looked back from the view through the window and into her bagman's face.

'You're suggesting it was the mayor, are you?'

'Stranger things have happened,' he said with a slight grin. 'But, no, I'm not. However, according to the latest developments in profiling, especially what's coming out of Quantico – that's the—'

'FBI training division and the location for their Behavioural Analysis Unit. Thanks for Tomsplaining it, but I do, just, manage to know what's going on beyond the parish borders.'

He blushed. 'Sorry, boss. But they're putting a lot of weight on geographical analysis these days.'

'It's basic policework, Tom. Our killer's a local boy. Serial killers don't travel to commit murder. Not unless they're already moving around, like lorry drivers or travelling salesmen.'

'That would be a reasonable conclusion to draw from the data.'

'So tell me this. In 2008, how many men living in Middlehampton were arrested for a crime serious enough to earn them at least a fifteen-year prison sentence?'

'Er . . .'

'None. Question two from the manual of practical coppering. How many murders have occurred in the UK, *since* 2008, *outside* Hertfordshire, *matching* our boy's MO?'

'Would that be none?'

'Smart boy. Yes, it would.'

'Wow, you really do know this case inside out. So where's he been for the last fifteen years?'

'Is the right question.'

'Could he have just got himself under control. Then, I don't know, been triggered by something and started killing again?'

'If he stopped for fifteen years, it wasn't because he just woke up one day and said to himself, "Oh, you know what? I should just pack it in before I get caught."'

'You almost sound like you know him.'

'I've just been looking for him a long time, that's all.' *And it has nothing to do with the nights I wake up screaming from nightmares where he's taunting me.*

A couple of other customers were looking round at them. She dropped into a conspiratorial murmur.

'The sort of man who is driven to commit crimes like this, he's not in control. Not fully. Oh, he might *think* he is. Especially if he's quote-unquote an *organised* killer. But they're driven by their desires. There's nothing rational about it. Or them.'

'So what *are* we dealing with? And where's he been?'

'My theory? He left the country.'

'So let's put in a request with Interpol then. See if they've got any intel on a serial killer with the same MO as our boy.'

'I've had an open request with those guys since 2017.'

'And?'

'Nothing.'

Tom frowned. 'So he *did* stop.'

She shook her head. 'I think he just went off-grid. Somewhere where he could kill without being noticed. The developing world, maybe. Or somewhere way outside Interpol's reach. Russia, China, bits of Latin America.'

'But if that's true, then why are we even looking at Andy Ferris and Johnny Hayes? As far as we know, they've lived here their whole lives. And no way is Johnny Hayes old enough. He'd only have been eleven or twelve in 2008.'

'Two reasons. Maybe you're right and I'm wrong. I have to consider every possibility, not just my favourites. If it is our original guy, maybe he did find a way to control his urges. And something has got him all fired up again.'

'Or if it's Hayes, or someone like him?'

'There's two of them.'

'Two?'

'Yes, come on Mr Fast-Track! What did your criminology module on serial offenders have to say about types of killer?'

Tom looked at the ceiling. She could practically see the lights and relays flickering in his brain as he went searching for the answer. She stared out of the window while she waited. A woman walking on the far side of North Street stopped and turned towards the cafe. She looked familiar.

'Yes!' Tom said, triumphantly. 'I forgot at first. You mean master-disciple killers, don't you?'

She turned back to him. 'You have the original killer, and somewhere along the line he either picks up an admirer—'

'Or starts grooming a successor.'

'Not so much a successor, not exactly. More like someone he can use when he's not physically up to it anymore.'

The woman outside was looking straight at Kat. The effect was unnerving. Like she ought to have known her.

'You're still convinced it's not a copycat.'

'You've read the files,' she said. 'Sorry, *skim-read* them. How could he know about the lavender? Or the exact placement of the origami heart? It was never released to the media.'

'Coincidence?'

'Really?'

He shrugged. 'It's a possibility.'

'It's an outside possibility. I prefer the chances of you being him to that.'

Tom held his hands out, wrists uppermost. 'It's a fair cop, guv. It was me muvver wot made me do it. She useter 'it me wiv one a them lavender wheat pillers.'

Kat shook her head. 'You kill me.'

She frowned. She'd been watching the woman on the other side of the road during Tom's little bit of playacting. And now she recognised her. She'd been the one Kat had accidentally bumped into at Riley's football practice. Why was she standing there? And why did her expression make Kat feel so uncomfortable?

'There's something I wanted to ask you,' Tom said.

She turned to face him. He looked like he needed the toilet.

'Well, go on then. I think I've proved I won't bite your head off, haven't I?'

'It's not that. It's just . . .'

'Tom, we're in the middle of a murder investigation. I haven't got time to play guessing games with you, too.'

'Stuart invited me to play golf on Saturday with him and a couple of his friends.'

Kat felt an unreasonable suspicion of Tom well up inside her. She chased it away. Why *shouldn't* he play golf with Carve-up? It would be good for his career, if nothing else.

'Go on.'

'One of the other guys was this property developer. Real smooth type.'

Suddenly, without any doubt at all, Kat knew who Carve-up had wanted Tom to meet.

'This property developer. His name wasn't Morton by any chance?'

'Stuart said everybody knew Colin,' Tom said with a nod. 'He asked about you. And when I said your name was Ballantyne, he told me to ask you if that was your married name.'

Brilliant. Carve-up had taken less than a week to get Tom mixed up with his dodgy friendship group. And right at the centre was the dodgiest friend of them all.

How much should she tell Tom? Could she trust him? All the way? She had to. Before Carve-up and his unsavoury friends got their claws into Tom too deeply to pull him free.

'Ballantyne's my married name,' she said. 'My maiden name was Morton.'

Tom's brow furrowed for a second. She saw the light of under-standing flick on behind his eyes.

'Colin's your dad.'

'Yes. And if I can give you a piece of advice . . .'

Tom grinned. 'I must have a look about me. Senior officers queuing up to give me tips.'

'Who do you mean?'

119

Tom bit his lip. 'I think DI Carver has it in for you.'

'You think?'

'Look, Kat, before I say this, I want you to know I'm not going to, but Stuart basically asked me to give him dirt on you. Stuff he could use against you.'

Kat shook her head. It wasn't a surprise. 'Let me guess, his advice was, "Drop DS Ballantyne in it or I'll see you directing traffic."'

Tom pulled a face. 'Not quite, but I'd have excellent upper-arm strength from lugging your bag after you for the rest of my career.'

'Thanks for telling me.'

'You're my guvnor,' he said, shrugging. 'And Stuart's an arsehole.'

Kat laughed. But the anger she felt against her father, and Carve-up, smothered the feeling like a fire blanket.

'My dad's rich, and he's successful. But men like him, in towns like this? Everything comes with a price tag attached.'

'You mean literally, don't you? Is Stuart on the take?'

'I don't know. But I do know my dad. Believe me, he'd think nothing of offering money to a cop if he thought it would get him what he wanted.'

'But that's—'

'Corruption? Yes, it is.'

'Have you talked to him about it?'

'I can't, Tom. I try to avoid my dad as much as possible, to be honest.'

'What if he got investigated?'

She shrugged. 'Then that's on him, not me.'

'But how would you cope? If he was arrested?'

She stared out of the window, searching for an answer that stayed stubbornly out of reach.

The woman she'd bumped into at Riley's football practice was still there. Why was she so familiar? Kat stared, feeling unaccountably anxious, trying to see beyond the uneven home-cut hairdo.

She raised her right hand, fingers in a fist.

And made a quick, flashing movement.

Open-close. Open-close.

Kat gasped. 'No!'

Fear washed over her, making her stomach churn as if she were about to give a speech to the whole station. She felt faint. Nauseous.

That wave.

Only two people in the world knew it. And one of them was dead.

A movers' van trundling down North Street blocked Kat's view of the woman.

It was a hallucination. Brought on by stress. Yes. That was it. Stress. And caffeine. And sleep deprivation. Pulse racing, she waited, eyes glued to the other side of the street. When the van moved, the woman would be gone.

The van parped its horn at a dithering driver in front and then rumbled off.

The woman was still there. A statue among the hurrying pedestrians, like one of those arty images you saw on Instagram where the photographer had used a long exposure.

She looked anxious. Then a small smile crept on to her face.

Kat swallowed. She felt sick.

'Kat, are you all right?' Tom was asking.

She tore her eyes away from the woman.

'Can you look across the street for me, please?'

'What? Why?'

'Just do it!' she snapped. 'Please.'

He turned away from her.

'OK, now what?'

She closed her eyes, unable to look. 'Is there a woman over there. About my age. Blonde hair.'

'Yes. What about her?'

'Oh, Jesus.' Kat opened her eyes. Turned her head on muscles that felt like rusted steel.

The woman was still there. She raised her hand again. Kat's right hand mirrored the movement, though she was unaware of doing it. Years, decades, were dissolving, crumbling. Along with her sanity.

In perfect synchrony, the two women raised fists, then snapped them open-closed, open-closed.

Kat groaned. Dark grey spots were blooming in her vision, crowding in towards the centre. She felt light-headed, dizzy, had to grip the edge of the table to prevent herself toppling sideways.

'I'm going mad, Tom. Oh, Christ, what's happening to me?'

'Look, try and breathe. I think you're having a panic attack,' he said. 'Who is she? Do you know her?'

'I . . . I can't . . .'

'Do you want me to go and talk to her?'

'Would you? I can't feel my legs.'

Tom jumped to his feet, scraping his chair back and banging it into the back of the woman behind him. Apologising, he ran for the door, calling, 'Breathe!' over his shoulder.

'Are you OK?' the woman at the neighbouring table asked. 'You look like you've seen a ghost.'

'I – I think I have,' Kat managed to whisper, before black curtains swung across the edges of her vision, and she had to rest her forehead on the cool surface of the table.

She heard the woman's chair scrape, just like Tom's had. Then, seemingly a moment later, a hand was on her shoulder.

'Here, drink this. It's only water, don't worry.'

She sipped the cool water from the glass the woman had fetched from the counter. It tasted of cucumber.

She heaved in a deep breath and sighed it out.

'Thank you. Did I just faint?'

'I don't think so. But you look awful, to be honest. Did you miss breakfast?'

'No, I'm fine. Thank you so much. Please, I'll be fine.'

The woman's eyes were narrowed with concern. 'I'm a nurse up at MGH, love. I know "fine" when I see it, and believe me, you're not it.'

'I'm a cop,' Kat said, digging her ID out of a pocket. 'Just had a few late nights, that's all. Honestly, I'm OK. Really.' She looked at the door just as Tom pushed back through. 'He's my DC. Go back to your coffee, please. And thanks. That water was just what I needed.'

Tom sat back down again. Kat avoided the window, keeping her eyes pinned on Tom's face.

'Well?'

'She said, "Tell Kat it's me." She wants to talk to you. Who is she, Kat?'

Ignoring him, she stood up, legs shaking. 'I'll see you back at the station, Tom.'

'Are you sure you're all right?'

'I'm fine,' she lied.

She left the coffee shop and waited for a gap in the traffic before crossing to meet her dead best friend.

CHAPTER SIXTEEN

Cars and trucks hooted at Kat as she stumbled across North Street. She flapped a hand at them. Her field of vision telescoped down to a small circle that fitted neatly around the woman's – *Liv's* – face.

She'd tinted her eyebrows blonde, but they looked wrong; too pale for her dark brown eyes. Her straw-coloured hair was still short. But neatly, if amateurishly, cut. Not like that brutal shearing the Origami Killer had given her.

Except he hadn't, had he? Not if she was here.

She reached the kerb and stepped on to the pavement, expecting Liv to vanish at any moment. Her fingertips were tingling; the crawling sensation spread to her hands, then her forearms. What was happening to her?

She took a final step and found herself standing face-to-face with Liv. She stretched out a hand and poked the other woman's shoulder, expecting her to vanish or turn into an ordinary pedestrian. But Liv stayed defiantly solid. Her lower lip was trembling, and this close, Kat could see tears tracking down from her eyes. Regular tears, made of salt water. No blood. No lavender-scented oil.

Kat's breath was coming in quick, short gasps. The tunnel vision had gone, but now she had to peer through a cloud of white sparks that wormed around inside her eyes like she'd stood up too fast.

'Hi, Kat,' Liv said, her voice trembling. 'It's me. I'm so sorry.'

Kat swallowed, shook her head, trying to shove aside the black curtains threatening to swing shut on her vision a second time. If she fainted in the street there'd be an ambulance for sure. She'd be whisked up to A&E, Carve-up would put her on administrative leave, and she'd never catch Liv's killer. Except, wait, how could she if Liv was here, and—

'Liv?' she croaked. Cleared her throat. Tried again. 'Is it really you? Or is this a dream?'

By way of answer, Liv stretched out her left hand and turned it over. A thin white scar ran across the fleshy part at the base of her thumb. She held it up.

Kat turned her own left hand over, revealing a matching scar. She lifted her hand and gasped as flesh met warm flesh.

'Blood sisters.'

Liv smiled. 'Always and for ever.'

She grabbed Liv in a hug right there on the pavement, forcing pedestrians to move around them, tutting, like a river parting around a boulder.

'You're not dead,' Kat said, through her tears, feeling her friend's ribs through her thin top.

'You always were the clever one.'

Kat laughed brokenly, her throat clogged with unshed tears. Held Liv at arm's length. 'I need a drink. A strong one.'

Liv nodded towards a pub a few hundred metres down.

'The King's Head's open.'

'Come on, then.'

The pub was quiet, catering to a few elderly couples eating breakfast at dark, highly polished tables. Liv returned from the bar with two large whiskies.

'Do you still drink Johnnie Walker?'

'Wine mostly, these days. But it'll hit the spot,' Kat said. She sank half the glass in a single gulp; the spirit burned on the way down and she coughed. Her hands were shaking. 'What happened, Liv? Where have you been?'

Such simple questions. But they contained fifteen years of grief, uncertainty and guilt. She'd had to leave her university course because of the trauma of believing herself responsible for her best friend's murder. And now, here she was, back from the dead.

Liv took a sip of her own drink, then put the tumbler down on the tabletop, its coke-coloured varnish ringed white from hot drinks.

'Wales.'

A laugh burst from Kat's quivering lips. She clapped a hand over her mouth.

'Wales? Why?'

'I ran away. I thought the Origami Killer was the guy who ran the home.'

'Shirley House?' Kat asked, still feeling light-headed, but anchoring herself with the simple business of question-answer. Cop-work.

'After the Origami Killer started murdering those girls, I became convinced it was him. I had to have a meeting with him about leaving the home. When I turned eighteen. He made some weird remark about my hair, said it would look nicer if I had it cut short. It freaked me out, you know? Because he, the killer, I mean, he was cutting it off, wasn't he?'

Kat swallowed the rest of her whisky, barely noticing the burn in her throat.

'Why didn't you just go to the police?'

Liv gave Kat a pitying smile. 'Oh, mate, you remember how it was back then, don't you? Any time there was a bit of petty crime, shoplifting, drunkenness, who did they come for? Us! Society's

126

rejects. They'd never have believed me. Anyway,' she continued, her tone becoming more aggrieved, 'I was frightened. I thought he'd just get interviewed and then they'd let him go and he'd know it was me and kill me.'

'So you decided to fake your own death and disappear?'

'It was perfect! Don't you see? I staged the photo and wrote the letters to the newspaper and the police.'

Kat frowned. 'But how did you know the details?'

'It was in the papers, wasn't it?'

Struggling to process what she was hearing, Kat stood on stiff legs and headed to the bar. She ordered two more large whiskies, even though Liv had barely touched hers.

'You haven't answered my question. Where have you been all these years?'

'I was going to tell you when we met for drinks that night,' Liv said. 'I knew this guy, Rhys, who lived in a sort of hippy commune in Wales. I met him when we did this camping trip from Shirley House. I hitchhiked there and he just took me straight in.'

Kat felt more tears pricking at her eyes. A lump had formed in her throat and the whisky didn't seem to be shifting it.

'I thought it was my fault,' she hissed, feeling anger come surging out of nowhere. 'I thought I'd killed you, Liv. Me! And all the time you were just, what, growing vegetables and smoking weed with some middle-class bloody hippies in the Brecon Beacons?'

'It was South Wales, actually. A farm near Newport.'

'I don't care whether it was a farm or a nuclear power station! I tortured myself over it.' Kat finished her whisky and slammed the glass down on the table, drawing apprehensive glances from an elderly couple in a corner. 'Why didn't you reply to my messages? My voicemails?'

'How could I? I was dead, wasn't I?'

Kat swiped a hand across her eyes, then dried it on her trousers. She heaved in a shuddering breath and sighed it out again. Liv was reacting like the arsey teenager from all those years back. She'd never been good at apologising, and the mere threat of punishment, or even disapproval, had her erecting her defences. Which, in Liv's case, were all about attack.

'You really thought it was the manager?'

'Yes! I told you!'

'Why come back now, though? He might still be living here.'

'I never intended to set foot in Middlehampton ever again. Honestly, Kat, you couldn't have paid me enough money to come back,' Liv said, leaning across the table to clasp Kat's hand in a firm, dry grip. Her skin was hard, rough. *Farmwork*, Kat thought randomly. 'Then I read about that poor girl. Courtney Hatch. And I just knew it was him. He's started up again. I knew you were a detective now and I thought I just had to get over my fear and come and tell you about Oldfield. I thought it was my duty.'

'Wait, you knew I was a detective? How?'

Liv smiled shyly. 'I've been following your career. I read the *Echo* online – it's how I found out about Courtney. They did this article about you when you moved to Major Crimes. You remember it, don't you? "Queen Anne's girl joins murder squad".'

Kat nodded. Managed a half-smile. Four shots of Johnnie Walker had calmed her nerves and settled her stomach, which had been threatening to exit her body via her mouth in its entirety.

She looked at Liv. Properly this time. Fans of fine lines bracketed her deep brown eyes, but that old spark still danced there, and behind that, the go-anywhere, do-anything, screw-you attitude that she'd both admired and feared – just a little – all those years ago.

'Why didn't you let me know you were OK?' she asked.

'I wanted to. Truly, I did. But Rhys said it was a bad idea. That Oldfield would get wind of it and come looking for me. Then, as the years went by, I just, I don't know' – she bit her lower lip – 'I just felt you'd be better off believing I was dead for real. I thought you would have moved on.'

Kat grabbed her friend by the shoulders and looked fiercely into her eyes.

'I *never* forgot you. And yeah, I moved on. Out here,' she said, waving her hand around to indicate the outer world. 'But here?' She thumped her chest, over her heart. 'In here? No. I never moved on.'

Now it was Liv who was crying, tears streaming down her cheeks to plop on to the table, splashing off the varnish. She tipped the remains of her first whisky into her mouth and gulped it down noisily.

Kat offered her a tissue. Liv wiped her eyes and screwed it into a ball before pocketing it.

'Can you forgive me?' she asked after a long pause.

'Come here,' Kat said, holding her arms wide. 'Always and for ever, remember?'

The two women hugged awkwardly across the table. Smiling, Kat breathed in her friend's smell from the blonde hair that framed her face. And caught the faint smell of lavender.

She recoiled.

'What *is* that?'

'What?'

'That perfume you're wearing?'

Liv smiled, although she looked nervous, too.

'It's probably incense. I burn it in my room at the farm. I'm really into lavender at the moment,' she said. 'Did you know it has amazing healing properties?'

Kat shook her head. 'I didn't. No. I had no idea.'

Suddenly, she needed to be somewhere else. Anywhere else. Seeing Liv again – and *alive* – after all this time had been a shock, and she still felt a buzz of unreality hanging around her, aided, no doubt, by the whisky. She had one more question to ask.

'Was it you I saw at football the other day?' she asked.

Liv nodded. 'I kept trying to pluck up the courage to talk to you. But I guess I was too nervous. Then just when I was going to, you sort of bumped me and you looked cross and I bottled it. I'm sorry. You must have thought you had a stalker.'

'Look, I want to catch up properly, OK? But I'm literally in the middle of a murder investigation. How long are you in town for?'

Liv glanced at the door.

'I'm going back to Wales today. As soon as we've finished our drinks.'

'You can't stay longer?'

'I don't feel safe. Not with him still out there.'

'Give me your number, then. I'll call you.'

They swapped numbers. It felt so anticlimactic after the shock of meeting again, but what else could Kat do? She had a homicide investigation to run, and Tom would be wondering what the hell had come over his boss.

Kat sleepwalked back to Jubilee Place. How could Liv have just left Middlehampton, and her, without once sending her a message? Yes, it might have blown what she and her hippy friend Rhys apparently thought of as her cover, but Kat would never have gone public with it. Liv would still have been safe from the killer.

And how about Liv's reason for coming back to Middlehampton now? Did Kat believe it? Liv had never struck Kat as the public-spirited type. She couldn't imagine the spiky teenager who'd nicked Chanel lippy from Skinner & Brown talking about her 'duty'. Although Kat would still need to trace Karl Oldfield and interview him.

Then another far more troubling thought made itself heard amid the chaos. Two events bookended the gap in the

Origami Killer's murders. Liv leaving Middlehampton. And Liv returning.

She realised something else. Liv had perverted the course of justice. Kat couldn't let any of her colleagues find out that Liv was still alive. She would be arrested. Charged. Possibly jailed. Kat didn't want that.

And Kat's own investigation would be totally derailed. If one of the Origami Killer's original victims was still alive, they'd have to re-investigate all six of the other murders. The brass would insist on it. It would halve the resources she had available to her. The killer would escape a second time.

No. Liv Arnold had to stay dead. She had to remain the Origami Killer's seventh victim.

Kat's resolve lasted until the moment she got home. Her stomach aflutter, she pushed through the front door, wondering how the hell she was going to keep such a massive secret from Ivan.

He was working at the kitchen table. He looked up, smiled and got to his feet to give her a kiss.

'How was your day?' he asked. Then he stepped back, frowning. 'What's the matter, darling? You look like you've seen a ghost.'

His choice of phrase was so apt she burst out laughing, then found she couldn't stop. She slapped herself, then started crying. Tears coursed down her cheeks, and before she knew it she was enfolded in his arms, sobbing as she hadn't done since Liv had disappeared all those years ago.

Finally able to step back and gulp in a deep breath, she slumped into a chair, Ivan kneeling beside her, his face creased with concern.

'She's alive, Van,' she hiccupped. 'Liv's not dead. I saw her today.'

His eyes flashbulbed. 'You did *what?*'

Over the next twenty minutes, Kat laid out the story of her meeting with Liv, from the accidental contact at football practice to the drinks in the King's Head. She answered each of Ivan's questions patiently, even when he repeated one or expressed disbelief or outrage at how Liv had behaved.

'There's just one thing,' she said.

'What?'

'You can't tell anyone about her. She needs to stay dead. Well, hidden away on her commune, anyway. It would raise too many difficult questions and set my investigation back so far I might never catch the Origami Killer.'

'Fine by me. I hope she does stay there. Don't let her back into your life, Kat. Not after what she did to you.'

Kat smiled at her husband's loyalty and nodded. How could she tell him it wasn't that simple?

CHAPTER SEVENTEEN

The following day, Kat returned from an interview to find MCU vibrating with energy. People were moving faster. Voices were louder. Phones were ringing constantly.

She saw Leah and was about to ask her what was going on, when the big boss, DCI Linda Ockenden, spotted Kat from across the open-plan space.

'Kat! My office.' She scanned the room. 'Stuart, you too, if you please.'

'What's going on?' Kat asked Leah.

'They found another body in Brearley Woods.'

'Was she . . .'

'Youngish. Brown hair, origami heart, lavender wheat grains. It's him.'

'DS Ballantyne!' It was the boss, standing in her doorway, scowling. 'Any time today is good.'

Middlehampton HQ boasted three DCIs: overt, covert and MCU. Keeping any of them waiting was suboptimal, to put it politely. But you'd run fastest when Linda Ockenden was shouting your name.

Kat made it to her office a few paces ahead of Carver, who followed her in and pulled up a second chair. Ockenden leaned forwards, clasping her pudgy hands on her desk. Her mouth, a thin-lipped red slash, was set in a line. She regarded them both over the top of her heavy-framed black glasses. As always, Kat felt like she was in front of the headmistress.

'Bastard's done it again,' Linda said. 'This changes everything.'

'I told you it wasn't a copycat,' Kat said out of the corner of her mouth.

'Sorry, are we still at school?' Ockenden snapped. 'I'd remind you there are two dead girls in the morgue and the media are sniffing around like cadaver dogs. This case is about to go national.'

'Sorry, ma'am.'

'Yes, well. I'm switching things around. Stuart, I'm taking over as SIO. And Kat, I want you as my deputy as well as the case officer. Think you can handle it?'

'Of course, ma'am.'

'But, boss,' Carver said. 'She's not passed her SIO exam.'

'No, but she's on the path. And I trust her. She knows this case better than anyone—'

'But that's the point, isn't it?' Carver interrupted. 'She's *too* close. Personally involved. It isn't appropriate.'

Linda narrowed her eyes at Carver. Kat savoured the way his expression changed. He'd chased a suspect into the middle of a motorway and turned to find himself in the path of an onrushing eighteen-wheeler.

'Next time you think about interrupting me, DI Carver,' Linda said, a terrifyingly peaceful smile on her face, 'I advise you to think a little bit harder, if you can manage it. Because, one: it's rude. Two: it's disrespectful to my rank. And three: I don't appreciate having my judgement about what's *appropriate*' – air quotes – 'called into question by a man who drives a motorised dildo. So, Kat's my deputy and you're going to work on those other unsolveds, yes?'

Kat said nothing. But inside she was rejoicing. Carve-up had turned a fine shade of puce. With him out of her hair she could start making real progress. And working directly under DCI Ockenden would be a fantastic opportunity.

Kat had just got back to MCU when her desk phone rang.

'DS Ballantyne.'

'Kat, it's Polly. There's a guy down here wants to talk to you. Says it's about the Courtney Hatch case.'

'Name?'

'One of your regulars. Ethan Metcalfe.'

Kat sighed. 'Could you tell him I'm in a meeting, please, Polly?'

'I expect it's going to go on all day, isn't it?'

'Definitely,' she said, grateful for the receptionist's insight.

'Who was that? You look like you just ate a bad prawn,' Tom said, coming to stand by her desk.

'It's a guy I was at school with. Ethan has this podcast called *Home Counties Homicide*. Every time there's a murder in Middlehampton, he's on the phone as soon as the news gets out, wanting to offer me his help. Once, he wanted me to go round to his place to inspect his murder map.'

'And?'

'I told him I was a little busy with my own murder map, thanks very much.'

'You don't think it could be helpful this time? Given we don't really have a suspect, yet.'

She looked up at him, seeing a way to appease him and also show him how much time well-meaning members of the public could waste when they really set their minds to it.

She held up a hand and used the other to call Polly back.

'Polly, is Ethan Metcalfe still there?'

'Yes. He's making a phone call. Either that, or faking it to hang around here.'

'Good. Get him to wait. I'm sending Tom down.' She looked back at Tom, smiling. 'Off you go, then.'

No sooner had Tom disappeared than Carver was striding across the office towards her. No academic experts needed in order to interpret his body language. He had a bug up his arse the size of a housecat.

'I suppose you think you've hit the big time now,' was his opening salvo.

She wrinkled her brow. A portrait of her at this precise instant would be titled *Innocence*.

'Sorry, Stu, what do you mean?'

'It's DI Carver to you, Ballantyne, for a start.'

'Yeah? Well, it's DS Ballantyne to you,' she shot back. 'Seeing as you can't bring yourself to use my first name like everybody else.'

Her heart was thumping. Carve-up was so rank-conscious he even made the receptionists call him by his official title. Jabbing at his pride was a high-risk move, but she couldn't stop herself.

'OK, *Kat*,' he said. 'You might be deputy SIO but remember, you still report to me. I want to know everything you're doing on the Origami Killer case from now on.'

Kat saw DCI Ockenden approaching from behind Carve-up. Said nothing. Kept her gaze fixed on his face.

'So you've come round to my way of thinking, then?' she asked.

'What?'

'Not a copycat. It's a serial killer. It's *the* serial killer.'

He scowled. 'Just watch your step.'

Ockenden's expression was hard to read. Part amusement, part fury was Kat's assessment. Those eyes weren't so much twinkling as glittering behind her glasses.

'If you've quite finished trying to intimidate my deputy, Stuart, I need to talk to her,' Ockenden said. 'Alone.'

Carver's switch from bullying a subordinate to cowering before the alpha female was impressive to watch. He swivelled towards

Ockenden, but not fast enough to deny Kat the sight of his fury at being caught out.

'We were just discussing reporting lines, boss,' he said.

'Bollocks you were. Kat, with me, please.'

Kat didn't even need to shoot a final one-liner at Carver. She knew her departing back would speak on her behalf.

She followed Ockenden into her office. 'Door open or closed, ma'am?'

'Closed.'

Ockenden motioned for Kat to sit at the round table by the window.

'You want a coffee?'

'Yes, please, ma'am.'

Ockenden nodded, returned to her desk and pressed a button on her desk phone.

'Annie, can we get two coffees in here, please?' She raised her eyebrows at Kat, who mouthed, *Black, please.* 'My usual, and an Americano for DS Ballantyne.'

Ockenden sat down at the table, puffing a little as she got herself comfortable. She patted her stomach. 'Need to go on a diet.' A beat. 'Not going to happen. Anyway, before we get down to details, while you're my deputy we'll forget all the "ma'am" bit, OK? I'm Linda and you're Kat, yes?'

'Yes, Ma – Linda.'

Ockenden chuckled throatily. Kat heard her boss's high-tar habit in the liquid sound. 'You'll get used to it. I called my first guvnor Ma-Tina so many times, it stuck.'

Kat smiled. She'd only ever observed DCI Ockenden from afar or listened to her in the occasional briefing. But here she was, sitting opposite the Head of Crime, calling her – trying to, anyway – by her first name.

'How do you want to run things, Linda?' she asked. 'Given we now have two murders committed by the same man.'

'How do *you* want to, you mean? I'm SIO on three investigations at the moment, so it's your call. You're my eyes and ears on this one.'

The reality dawned on Kat. All the responsibility for directing the investigation. All the glory, if it went right. All the accountability if it didn't. Well, it had just better go right then, hadn't it?

How *did* she want to run it? Best get her thoughts in order before answering. A knock at the door bought her a little time. Linda's PA appeared with a tray containing coffees, a sugar bowl, and a plate with two chocolate digestives.

With the room to themselves again, Kat took a sip of the coffee. It was delicious.

'Mmm, that's really good.'

'Annie gets it for me. I'd tell you where from but then I'd have to kill you,' Linda said, spooning sugar into her coffee.

Kat was expecting another nicotine-infused chuckle. None came. The effect was disconcerting.

Now Linda did laugh. 'Got you! Sorry, Kat, I couldn't resist. It's just M&S.'

Wrong-footed again, Kat smiled nervously.

'The killer's a bloke who lives in Middlehampton,' she said. 'He's going to be at least mid-thirties. I think we should put out a public announcement for women between the ages of seventeen and twenty-five to be extra vigilant. I could do with some additional help, so I wondered whether we could move DC Hooper back over to my team?'

'No problem. What else?'

'From what I've seen so far, he's got basic forensic awareness. And I don't think he's impulsive,' Kat said, picturing the killer as

138

she spoke, bringing him into a sketchy reality. 'We're not going to catch him fleeing a scene with scratches on his face or anything.'

'So how are we going to catch the twisted little sod?'

'Even if he's not making any overt sexual attack, I'm sure this is about sex for him. I want to put out an appeal for information. Maybe there's a previous girlfriend or a wife in the picture. Maybe he's into something kinky in bed.'

Linda pursed her lips. 'You want to ask the good ladies of Middlehampton if their old man likes a bit of erotic asphyxiation? Not sure how well that would work, to be honest. Seriously, Kat, you need to clear this one up fast. You and I both know he's not going to stop at two. This force caught a bucketload of flak last time around. I don't want that to happen on my watch. Are we clear?'

'Yes, Ma-Linda.'

Linda smiled. 'Told you.'

'I'm going to go up to the new crime scene,' Kat said. 'Then we need to ID her. I want to fast-track the post-mortem, as well. There's a new pathologist, apparently.'

'So I hear.'

'You mentioned the media before. I think we should hold a press conference. Get in front of it. There's too much speculation on social media, too.'

Linda agreed, with a caveat.

'But let's *try* to keep a lid on it. I don't want a full-blown panic. When I was in Manchester, we had a nutter up there slashing the backs of women's thighs,' Linda said, rolling her eyes. 'My Chief Super did a briefing, OK? Literally the next day, some bloke tripped on a loose paving slab and bumped into a woman and got the crap beaten out of him by a bunch of United supporters. Turned out he was a vicar, too. Poor sod.'

Kat grinned. Not at the vicar's plight, which was terrible. But her boss's comic timing.

'So, stick to the facts, and don't air my personal belief that the Origami Killer's back.'

Linda nodded. 'Smart girl.'

'About the budget,' Kat said.

'Look, just stick to the basics, if you can. But this is Cat A stuff. If you need something extra, come and see me.'

Kat nodded, grateful that Linda was the variety of brass who knew the realities of sharp-end policing. You could achieve results, but sometimes that meant getting up in the penpushers' faces.

'Will do. Thanks.'

Kat put her hands on the arms of the chair, ready to go.

'One more thing, Kat.'

She tensed. 'Yes?'

'You haven't talked about a profile.'

'I've told you what I think's going on with him.'

'I know that. And between us? I agree with you. He knows the area. He wants to be close to home for afterwards,' Linda said. 'He's old enough to have done the original six and young enough to still be doing the physical side of it.'

'Why do I sense a "but" coming?'

Linda twitched her mouth to one side. A quarter of a smile.

'But, if this case turns into a runner – more deaths, time dragging on – the press will ask about it. Then people will be all over social media asking why haven't we done it,' Linda said. 'Then I'll have Detective Superintendent Deerfield on the phone asking me what the problem is. And the ACC Crime and then the Chief Con himself. And when the dust finally settles and, God forbid, we don't catch him, or we do but only after he's killed another two or three or five, it'll be asked at the case review and your next annual appraisal. And you really don't want Stuart Carver holding that over you, do you?'

Kat shook her head. She could just imagine how that particular conversation would go. It would probably end with her punching Carve-up. Not good.

'Can I speak frankly, please? And off the record?'

'Sounds like you're about to anyway.'

Kat hesitated. What she was about to ask was, to paraphrase Linda, disrespectful to a superior officer's rank. Then she remembered Linda's scathing put-down of Carve-up and decided to risk it.

'Why is DI Carver such a dick? He's had it in for me ever since I transferred into MCU. I've never given him any cause,' she said, hearing the note of complaint in her voice and unable to banish it. 'He won't even call me Kat. It's always DS Ballantyne.'

'Yeah, I heard that this morning. Listen, Kat, I've been a copper for twenty-two years. In that time, most of the senior officers I've served under have been fine,' Linda said. 'You get the odd dinosaur, but they're mostly harmless. With Stuart, my best guess? He feels threatened by you. You're younger than him, you're smarter than him and, quite honestly, you're a better detective than him. Off the record, of course.'

'Of course.'

'You're deputy SIO on this one. That gives you considerable leeway. Just avoid him. If he tries to give you any grief, tell him to come and talk to me. I think I scare him. You can see his balls shrinking into prunes,' Linda finished with a wink. 'So, profiler.'

'Do I have to?'

'You don't *have* to,' Linda said. 'I'm just *advising* you to.'

Kat nodded. It made sense. Not the hiring of a profiler. Just doing what Ma-Linda advised her to. If only she'd advised her to avoid talking to the media at all costs.

CHAPTER EIGHTEEN

Kat sat in a cubicle in the ladies, head in her hands, trying to rationalise her fears. She'd read somewhere that public speaking was in most people's top three phobias. She thought whichever psychologist had compiled the list ought to have made that speaking in public *to the media*.

After washing her hands and giving herself a bracing pep talk in the mirror over the sinks, she went to see her media support officer about organising the press conference. Freddie Tippett had the wide-eyed gaze and smooth chin of a choirboy, but was renowned for telling the filthiest jokes in Jubilee Place.

'Good idea,' he said. 'I've been fielding calls from the local papers and websites individually, but we're starting to get a few nibbles from the big boys.'

'When can we do it?'

'Shall we say 9 a.m. tomorrow? That'll make sure we have time to get the nationals down here.'

Kat swallowed. Nodded. Said, 'Perfect.' Didn't mean it.

After the meeting with Freddie, Kat went to see Craig Elders. She found him at his desk, paging through a report.

'Craig, got a minute?'

He ran a hand over his close-cut hair. A scar a couple of shades lighter than the rest of his dark brown scalp curved above his left ear. The result of a knife attack during a drugs bust that had become the stuff of station legend.

'Sure,' he said with a smile. 'Anything that stops me having to read this garbage.'

'I just got out of a meeting with Linda Ockenden.'

'Yeah, I heard that. Deputy SIO. Kudos.'

'Thanks. So, she asked me what I needed and I said I wanted Leah back working with me. I hope that's not going to leave you short-handed.'

He shook his head. 'It's fine. We just closed a case so she was at a loose end anyway. She'll be delighted to be back with you. I don't think she shares my enthusiasm for the fortunes of Middlehampton FC.'

'Nobody does, Craig. You're a fanatic.'

He grinned. 'Hey! We're in with a shot at the Premier League next season.'

She grabbed Leah and Tom and found an empty meeting room.

'Welcome back, Leah,' Kat said.

'Thanks. Craig was driving me crazy with his footie talk.'

'Not a fan, then?' Tom asked with a smile.

'Don't get me wrong. I'm an Eels fan. I used to go with my dad,' Leah said. 'But Craig's obsessed.'

'Eels?' Tom questioned.

'Eel fishing was Middlehampton's big industry in the seventeenth century.'

'Noted.'

'Let's focus, shall we?' Kat said, suddenly aware of the massive responsibility she'd just been handed. The buck might stop at Linda, but it would make a lengthy detour across Kat's desk on the way. 'Tom, what did Ethan Metcalfe want?'

At the mention of his name, Leah rolled her eyes. 'A date with Kat probably. He's what you might call a fan.'

'We went to school together,' Kat said, recalling the way Ethan would stare at her from across the canteen, or turn up to watch her play netball.

'He says he's got a theory about the killer's identity,' Tom said. 'I asked him what it was but he literally said, "It's for DS Ballantyne's ears only." I tried to get it out of him, but he just clammed up. He's a fantasist.'

'Oh, he's a fantasist all right,' Leah said. 'Kat in sexy undies, mainly.'

'Leah, please!' Kat felt her cheeks heating up. She'd done everything she could think of to discourage Ethan at school, even arranging to snog another boy when she knew he'd be passing. 'Do you want me to send you back to Mr Football?'

'Anything but that, please!' Leah wailed.

'Then can you start looking at local suppliers of essential oils, massage supplies, all that? He's probably buying the lavender online, but you never know, maybe he likes to shop local.'

'What about me?' Tom asked.

'We're going up to the crime scene. I want you to focus on identifying the second victim. As soon as we have an ID we can start mapping their lives against each other. I want to know what they had in common,' she said. 'Then we're going to pay a visit to Johnny Hayes.' She turned to Leah. 'Courtney Hatch's violent ex-boyfriend.'

They agreed to meet up at the end of the day.

Twenty minutes later, Kat pulled up at the entrance to Brearley Woods nearest to the site where the second girl had been found. A CSI van was already parked in the roughly circular clearing, along with two marked cars.

It took her and Tom ten minutes to walk into the woods and find the site. Sun streamed through the brilliant green beech leaves overhead, lighting up the tiny white wildflowers that dotted the forest floor. Somewhere overhead, a woodpecker was rapping his way to a new home.

Tom put a voice to her thoughts. 'Seems too beautiful to be the scene of a murder.'

After giving the cordon guard their collar numbers, she and Tom ducked under the fluttering tape. Darcy was already taking photos, logging actions and recording exhibits. She nodded to Kat. 'Morning.'

'Hi, Darcy. What have we got?'

'She's young. Eighteen to twenty, maybe? Brown hair crudely cut short. Origami heart in left bra cup. Choked on wheat grains.'

'Lavender?'

'Yup. Poor thing. She's really pretty, too. Was, I mean.'

Kat knew the case was hard on Darcy. Her daughters were sixteen and eighteen. Blondes not brunettes, but still. If you were a mother, this kind of thing could make you both fiercely protective and simultaneously terrified you might lose your child. Or that they might lose a best friend.

'Who found her?' Kat said, looking around for some old geezer with a dog.

'Couple of lads on mountain bikes. They're only young. They've been sent home. The scene guard's got their contact details.'

'We'll drop in after this, then,' Kat said. 'Let's go and take a look, Tom.'

They entered the white forensics tent. Inside, a couple of CSIs were taking samples from around the body. One was pouring liquid plaster of Paris into a shallow impression in the soil.

Kat squatted down a metre back from the corpse.

'Who did this to you?' she murmured.

The girl's arms were positioned at her sides. The smell of lavender wormed its way into Kat's nostrils and made her think of Liv. She shuddered. *Not now, Kat. Not now.*

She saw a bruise on the dead girl's throat. *He held you down. Probably sitting on your chest like Courtney.* The obscene tide of wheat grains flowed over her mouth and top lip and trickled down the right side of her face, to form a drift in the angle between her neck and her collarbone. *You and Courtney could be sisters. And Liv. And the other dead girls.* It wasn't just the hair. The face shape, the build, the height: they were all the same.

'Penny for them,' Tom said, startling her out of her reverie.

She stood up, knees clicking. 'He's a psychopath, yes?'

'Probably.'

'Definitely.'

'OK.'

'Trust me. Common factors when they turn to murder include a dysfunctional childhood and a screwed-up relationship with their mother,' Kat said. 'This relationship often contains deviant or abusive sexual elements.'

'And therefore?'

'And therefore . . . I think these girls could represent his mother.'

'Not an ex-wife or girlfriend?'

'It's possible. But my gut's telling me this boy has mummy issues.'

'Why?'

'It's the lack of violence. Correction,' she said immediately, 'the lack of sadistic violence. To me, it looks like he needs to kill them but subconsciously he wants it to be . . . respectful? I know it's not quite the right word.'

'I get it. The heart, the lavender, the pose. It's like he wants her to be perfect.' He switched to an off-key voice, halfway between a whine and a growl. 'My mum never loved me.'

'Something like that. Seen enough?'

'More than.'

146

The two boys who'd discovered the dead girl lived a few houses apart on the north side of the woods. Kat parked between them and walked up the path of the nearest house. A plastic deer grazed the Astroturfed lawn.

'He's never going to get full on that,' Tom said.

Kat rolled her eyes. 'Why don't you take the lead on these?' she said, ringing the doorbell.

The woman who answered the door gave their IDs the barest of glances. Her eyes flicked from Kat to Tom and back again.

'I'm DC Gray. This is DS Ballantyne,' Tom said. 'Are you Mrs Gough? Billy's mum?'

'Yes. He's in a terrible state.'

'We just need to ask him a few questions. May we come in?'

'He's already told the officers in the woods everything.'

'It won't take long. He's not in any trouble.'

The woman turned her back and walked down the hallway. They followed her into a bright sitting room that gave on to the road. A boy a few years older than Riley sat in the centre of a squashy powder-blue sofa, head bowed over a phone on which his thumbs danced.

There goes the story, Kat thought.

'Billy. It's two police officers to talk to you,' his mum said. Then, when he didn't look up: 'Put that down, love. You'll get eye strain.'

Tom sat in an armchair. Kat stood in the corner, knowing she'd fade into the background as the boy focused on the man asking the questions. Mrs Gough hovered in the doorway before finally offering tea.

Kat shook her head. With obvious relief, the woman sat beside her son, reaching out without looking down to hold his hand. He jerked it away as her fingers found his. Would that be Riley in a few years' time? Allergic even to Kat's touch?

'Hi, Billy. My name's Tom. That's my boss over there. Her name's Kat. Can you tell me what happened?'

'I know her!' the boy blurted out.

'Pardon?'

'Her! The dead girl. In the woods. I know her!'

'OK, Billy. Listen, that's going to be really helpful. What's her name?'

'I don't know. But she lives round here. On Windemere Close,' he said. 'I know because I go through the cut-through there on my way to school and I see her getting into her car. It's the house at the end. With the yellow front door. A bunch of girls share it.'

Tom made a note then looked up. 'Did you tell the other officer?'

Billy shook his head. 'I was shaking. It was awful, man. I had to get away. I wasn't thinking straight. Am I in trouble? Like, wasting police time or something?'

'No, you're not in trouble,' Tom said. 'What matters is you're telling us now. And you're sure it was the same girl?'

'Yeah, man! I – you know, she . . .' His cheeks reddened.

'You fancied her,' Tom said gently.

'Yeah. She was, like, hot. And now she's dead.' He burst into tears. His mother gathered him into her arms, and this time he didn't flinch but allowed her to enfold him in a hug.

Tom stood without Kat having to prompt him.

'Thank you, Billy,' he said, 'and you, Mrs Gough. We'll see ourselves out.'

On the pavement, Kat nodded to Tom.

'You were good in there.'

'Thanks, boss.' He consulted his phone. 'Windemere Close is just over there.'

They began the short journey to Kat's second death-knock of the week.

CHAPTER NINETEEN

The house at the end of the close had a buttercup-yellow front door with an Art Deco stained-glass insert depicting a sunrise. The front path was tiled in a black-and-white geometric pattern – diamonds edged with chequerboard – and wide enough to walk up side by side. At the front door, Kat paused.

'First death-knock, I'm guessing?'

'Yes. Been a week for firsts.'

'Everybody hates it. But my advice? Give it to them straight. Not brutal, but don't try to dance around it either,' she said.

Tom nodded. She watched his Adam's apple bob in his throat.

He rang the bell, a digital unit with a little screen inset above the button. Kat counted off the seconds. She'd reached five when a young woman appeared on the screen. Huge glasses magnifying dark eyes.

'Hello?'

'Police, madam,' Tom said. 'Could you come to the door, please?'

'Well done,' Kat murmured.

Tom nodded. His lips were a taut line.

The door opened. A young woman of perhaps twenty-two or -three stood there, wearing an oversized grey T-shirt printed with

#TooHotForYou in neon pink text. She tugged at the hem, which sat mid-thigh. 'Working from home,' she said with a guilty smile.

Tom held out his ID and introduced them, as he'd done a few minutes earlier at the Goughs.

'Is everything OK?' the woman asked, a frown on her otherwise mirror-smooth brow.

'Can we come in, please?'

She led them into a small lounge, and sat down in an armchair with her legs folded under her.

'Can I ask your name?' Tom said.

'Mae Fisher. Look, what's this all about? I'm really worried now.'

Tom drew in a breath. Kat held hers.

'Earlier today the body of a woman was found in Brearley Woods. I'm really sorry to have to tell you this, but we have reason to believe it might be your housemate.'

Behind the oversized glasses, Mae's eyes welled with tears.

'Oh my God. Which one?'

This seemed to flummox Tom. He looked to Kat, panic in his eyes. She nodded her encouragement. He'd started now. Best to let him finish it.

'How many do you have?' he asked finally.

'Three. There's Suzie, Millie and Jade.'

'Do any of your friends have dark brown hair? They'd be about five foot four, maybe a little taller.'

'Oh, no, nooo,' she moaned. 'That's Jade. Suzie just dyed hers red and Millie's blonde like me.'

'Could I show you a photo on my phone?' Tom asked. 'Just the top half of her face. Maybe you could tell me if it's Jade.'

She nodded, without speaking.

Tom tapped his screen, scrolled and tapped again, then rotated the phone towards Mae.

She glanced down, away, then back again for longer.

A fat tear rolled from underneath her glasses and dripped into her lap, turning the pale grey T-shirt the colour of charcoal.

'That's her,' she whispered. 'That's Jade.'

'I'm so sorry for your loss,' Tom said, managing to make the standard phrase sound like he meant it.

Maybe he did. Kat would try to make sure he held on to his compassion for as long as possible, like she had.

'Mae, can you tell us Jade's surname, too, please?' Kat asked. 'And do you know who her next of kin is?'

'It's Root. Her mum and dad live over in Cherryville.'

'Do you know their names?'

'Tim and Anita. They're so lovely. Oh God, this is going to kill them,' she wailed. 'Her mum only just got over breast cancer this year.'

After a few more minutes consoling the bereft young woman, Kat stood, signalling for Tom to follow her.

'We have to go. I'm so sorry,' she said. 'Is there someone you can call? Maybe one of your housemates could come to sit with you?'

Mae nodded. 'Millie's at the gym. She'll be back soon.'

Once Mae had closed the front door, Tom exhaled noisily.

'I really messed that up, didn't I?'

'Why do you say that? You did really well.'

'When she asked "Which one?" and I froze.'

'Oh, Tom. If that's all you're worrying about, forget it,' Kat said. 'It was fine. *You* were fine. Come on, we're going to the dark side now. Mr Johnny Hayes.'

◆ ◆ ◆

Hayes lived a couple of miles away, in the end house of a red-brick terrace. Two storeys, bay windows with white-painted frames, wooden still – unlike those of most of his neighbours, who'd opted to replace the originals with uPVC.

Tom stuck out a finger and rang the doorbell.

Now he wasn't delivering the death-knock, Kat thought, Tom had recovered a little of his confidence. He waited five seconds then rang again, adding a loud triple-knock and a call of 'Police, Mr Hayes' for good measure.

Kat was about to suggest they give up when the door swung inwards.

'Johnny Hayes?' Tom asked the whip-thin man, who regarded them with an amused smile. He was dressed in a gleaming white T-shirt and expensive-looking ripped jeans, and his feet were bare.

'It's John Hayes, actually. What do you want?'

'We'd like to ask you a few questions about Courtney Hatch. Can we come in?'

'Who?'

'Courtney Hatch, Mr Hayes. You may have read she was murdered last week.'

Hayes shook his head. 'I don't read the papers.'

'But you remember Courtney?'

'No. Should I?'

Not wanting to either conduct the interview on the doorstep or have Hayes run rings about her bagman, Kat stepped forwards, ID out.

'Can we come in, Mr Hayes? Please?'

Hayes shrugged. It was odd, he seemed not to recognise her. The amused smile didn't shift by a millimetre.

'Fine, but it'll have to be quick, I've got a meeting in half an hour.'

Hayes led them into a tidy kitchen overlooking a garden laid mostly to lawn.

He took a chair and nodded towards the others – the nearest to an offer of a seat they were going to get, Kat decided. She pulled out a chair adjacent to Hayes. Tom took the seat directly opposite him.

'Courtney Hatch,' Tom said. 'Ring any bells?'

'Should it?'

'You went out with her a few months back.'

'If you say so,' Hayes said with a smile.

Tom furrowed his brow. 'This isn't a joke, Mr Hayes. She's been murdered.'

'No, yeah. I mean, I get it. I totally do. Thing is, if it was a few months ago, that was before my accident.'

'What accident?'

'Well, it was more of a medical emergency, really,' he said. 'I suffered an' – he scanned the ceiling again, as if he had prompts scrawled across its combed plaster surface – 'subarachnoid haemorrhage leading to partial but irreversible amnesia. You can check my medical records, too, if you like.'

Kat looked at Hayes. The smirk hadn't left his face. If it was a lie, it was unusually specific, and he was right, the hospital would have a record.

'So you don't remember your ex-girlfriend, but you do remember what you were doing last week?' Tom asked. 'Bit convenient, isn't it?'

Hayes shrugged. 'You'd have to ask my neurologist.'

'Where were you on Monday night, Mr Hayes?' Tom asked. 'Between the hours of 6 p.m. and 6 a.m.?'

Hayes looked back at Tom. 'Here.'

'Can anyone confirm that?'

Hayes shook his head. 'Nope. Sorry.'

'How about the Tuesday before? Can you account for your movements?'

'Out all night with some mates: couple of pubs then a club. Back about 3 a.m. Bed.' He spread his hands. 'If these girls have been murdered, I'm sorry, but it wasn't me.'

'Why did you say that?' Kat asked. 'Why did you say "girls" plural?'

For the first time since they'd arrived, his smile faltered. He pointed at Tom.

'He asked me where I was when two girls were murdered.'

'No,' Kat said patiently. 'My colleague only asked you where you were on Monday and the Tuesday before.'

'Well, I must have put two and two together, then, mustn't I? Two different times, two different murders.'

'Yeah,' she said, 'I suppose you must. If you can just give my colleague details of the people you say you were with, we'll leave you to prepare for your meeting.'

Five minutes later, Tom pulled away from the kerb. 'That was impressive. Catching him out like that,' he said.

'It might be something. It might be nothing,' Kat said.

'You think he did it?'

'I didn't feel it off him, did you?'

'Not sure I did, but any pointers you could give me would be gratefully received.'

'No effort to be charming, or helpful. Snotty attitude. No obvious concern for the victims. No offers to help us with the investigation. And he didn't look at me like he was visualising me naked, chopped into pieces, or otherwise inconvenienced.'

'Noted.'

After dropping Tom off at Jubilee Place, Kat drove herself to the university. If Linda wanted a profiler, she'd have one, if only because it was Kat's arse on the line. But she had a plan; it was risky, but she thought it might – if only just – deliver results.

CHAPTER TWENTY

Kat left her Golf in the main university car park and headed towards the psychology department, passing between two modern buildings faced in bronze-tinted glass. Students wandered the landscaped grounds, checking their social media or chatting with each other, phones still held loosely in dangling hands.

The department was run by a professor who, on his personal website, styled himself as a 'certified' – *meaningless term* – criminal profiler. Kat had seen his work on the original case, and the man himself on TV. He was a shameless purveyor of the sort of cookie-cutter profiles that were about as useful to a working homicide cop as an inflatable baton.

Kat had no intention of paying his exorbitant fees.

She walked down a gently inclined path lined with sword-leaved Mediterranean plants, and pushed through the psychology department's double glass doors. To the left was a staircase and a single lift; to the right, a cafe. Kat turned right.

She ordered herself an Americano then stood facing away from the counter, scanning the room. She spotted two girls sitting at a table separated a little from the others by a square pillar posted with colourful gig flyers and notices about mental health awareness.

Assuming an open expression, she walked over to their table. One of the girls had spiral ringlets of coppery hair, while the other wore her dark hair in a ponytail. Kat's heart flipped. The second girl was a dead ringer for Courtney Hatch.

'Hi, girls!' she said brightly. 'Mind if I sit with you? I have a question I need to ask you about the psychology department. It's my goddaughter. She wants to study here.'

'Sure,' the red-haired girl said, her ringlets swaying as she lifted her head. 'What's the question?'

'Well, she's really interested in criminology, and I just wondered whether you have any lecturers you really rate, you know? She's very keen to study under someone who knows their stuff.'

'Dr Capstick,' they said in unison, then giggled, turning to each other. 'Jinx! Mega-jinx!'

Kat smiled. So they still said that? She and Liv used to, delighting in inventing ever-more complex variants when 'jinx' was said in unison.

'She's the best,' said Ringlets.

'Yeah, she really understands what makes people tick,' Ponytail added. She dropped her voice to a murmur. 'Like, for instance, we're not really supposed to say "deviant" anymore? We have to say—'

'—atypical morality.'

And they finished each other's sentences. *Just like we used to*. Kat swallowed, trying to shift the lump that had formed in her throat.

'But Doctor Capstick—' Ponytail said.

'Clare,' Ringlets corrected.

'Yeah, Clare. She says it can hinder our efforts to understand the criminal mind unless we acknowledge that the way they think isn't just different, it's wrong.'

'Dangerous,' Ringlets added.

'Have you seen the news about the girl who was murdered?' Kat asked, wanting to ensure the ponytailed girl wouldn't fall prey to the Origami Killer's decidedly deviant urges.

'Yeah, it's awful,' Ringlets said.

'But you girls look out for each other, right?' Kat asked.

'Of course, but, I mean, it's not like he'd come for one of us, is it? She – the girl, I mean – worked in a factory, didn't she? So, like, that's his type. Working-class. We're students?' Ringlets added, as if Kat might have failed to notice.

Kat shook her head. 'No. Not at all. His last set of victims came from all walks of life,' she said, instantly fearing her use of cop-speak would give her away. 'Some were working, but one was a student, just like you. Another was a trainee solicitor. And, I don't want to worry you,' she said, looking at Ponytail, 'but you do have a resemblance to those girls.'

Her eyes widened. 'You don't think I'm, like, a target, do you?'

'No, I just think you should be extra vigilant. Don't meet any man you don't know. Especially if he's not from the university.'

She turned to find herself pinned by Ringlets's stony stare. 'You're not here about your goddaughter at all, are you? You're a detective.' The girl looked closer. 'I think I saw you on the telly last year.'

Kat briefly considered denying it and leaving, but if the girl was sharp enough to figure out her minor subterfuge, she deserved the truth.

'Sorry. I didn't want you to clam up.'

'Because we're students, you mean. Defund the police, all that?'

Kat felt a blush of shame heating her cheeks. 'Don't hate me. Please?'

Ringlets sighed. 'We believe in the justice system, OK? We just want to make it better.'

'Well, you're certainly smart enough,' Kat said. 'But I meant what I said. Take care of each other, all right?'

Ten minutes later, having phoned to introduce herself, she was knocking on a door bearing a simple aluminium plaque: *Dr. C. Capstick*.

The woman rounding the desk to shake Kat's hand was about her age. Annoyingly skinny, model-tall. Sharp features that gave her a bird of prey's piercing look.

'DS Ballantyne, a pleasure. Please have a seat. Can I get you a coffee?'

'I just had one, thanks,' Kat said, 'and I appreciate you seeing me without an appointment.'

She sat. The woman opposite her leaned forwards, her wide-set eyes bright with curiosity. 'This is about the Origami Killer case, I'm guessing? I know you're not calling it that officially. Not yet, anyway. But social media is all over it.'

Kat nodded. It suited her just fine if the public were ahead of the brass on this one.

'My boss thinks it would be a good idea to get a profiler involved.'

Clare's mouth twitched. A smile hidden in plain sight. 'And you don't?'

'If I thought it would deliver genuine insights, I might.'

'A bit of arse-covering, then. I do have other responsibilities, if all you want is a box ticking,' she said, spreading her arms as if to encompass a world of unseen tasks of which Kat could have no conception. 'In any case, Professor Halpin is the profiler round here, not me.'

Kat shook her head. 'I'm sorry if I offended you. But it's not Professor Halpin I want. It's you. In fact, I found my way here by a back route.'

Clare smiled properly this time, an expression that Kat could imagine loving if she were one of her students. Or a partner. She glanced at the other woman's ring finger. Bare.

'I'm intrigued. Tell me.'

Kat explained how she'd solicited the students' opinions before asking to speak to Clare.

'And now I'm flattered. Ringlets and ponytail, yes? That would be Amber Jones and Michelle O'Malley. They're joined at the hip. So, how can I help?'

'Once we've caught him, I'll be looking for an admission. It might help me with the interview if I had some clue as to what makes him tick.'

She watched as Clare wrinkled her nose, twirling a silver pen around in her fingers.

'I'd need to see your file, if that's the right word?'

'It is, and yes, of course. I'd give you full access. You'd just need to sign a couple of things.'

Clare paused for a second. 'When can we start?'

'Now, if you like. I've got everything I need on my laptop.'

Kat spent a few minutes locating the files she needed and printing out the forms for Clare to sign. Once that was done, she sent everything to a printer in the corner of the office.

'I read about the first case in last week's *Echo*,' Clare said, while the printer whirred. 'It said there was a previous series of killings.'

'Yes, fifteen years ago.'

'I was living in Brighton then, looking forward to university. And those girls – I'm assuming they were girls?' Kat nodded, and Clare continued speaking. 'They bore a strong physical resemblance to each other and these two new victims, yes?'

'They did. He's got a type.'

'How is he killing them?'

'Chokes them to death with wheat grains. They're lavender-scented. We never disclosed that detail to the media, and we haven't this time round either.'

'Anything sexual about the attacks, overt or otherwise?'

'If you hadn't added the last bit, I'd have said no.'

'But . . .'

'His signature. He tucks an origami heart into their left bra cup.'

'That's interesting. The *Echo* was a little vague on that point. Maybe they felt it wasn't suitable for a family newspaper. It just said "amongst her clothing". Is there anything else you can give me as a steer?'

'You'll see when you read the file, but the attacks don't look frenzied. And there's minimal signs of struggle, either on the ground or on the body.'

'You think they meet him willingly? Maybe where the bodies are deposited?'

'It's my working hypothesis, yes.'

'When do you need something in writing?'

'You're pretty hot on human motivation . . . why don't you tell me?' Kat said with a smile.

Clare flicked her eyebrows up briefly. 'Oh, I see. Today would be good, yesterday would be better, last week would be ideal. I'd like a couple of days, so, Thursday?'

'Honestly? That would be great,' Kat said. 'I'd rather have it done well than rushed.'

'Fine. And thanks for trusting me. I hope I can do more than just tick a box for you.'

'I hope so, too,' Kat said feelingly. 'I really do. About your fee . . .'

Clare looked surprised.

'I wasn't actually thinking I'd get paid.'

'If you knew what your boss charges for one of his profiles, I think you might.'

Clare leaned forwards and a sly grin spread across her face. 'Tell me.'

It was breaking a confidence. Probably some procurement rule, too. But Kat felt a real bond with Clare. She leaned forwards, mirroring the psychologist's pose.

'I had some bad news this morning. My car needs a new clutch. The garage quoted me fifteen hundred pounds.'

She passed the open-mouthed lecturer a business card and left without another word.

CHAPTER TWENTY-ONE

That evening, Kat arrived home to the sound of Ivan and Riley arguing. She dropped her stuff on the sofa on her way past the sitting room, then opened the kitchen door.

Ivan was standing with his back to the French doors, backlit by brilliant sunshine. He was jabbing a finger at Riley.

'What's going on?' Kat asked.

Riley's cheeks were aflame and his eyes glistened with tears. Ivan's cramped expression signalled anger mixed with that deeper concern that couldn't always be expressed in words.

'Dad grounded me for a week! For nothing!' Riley shouted.

Ivan inhaled deeply then sighed it out. 'He's in a WhatsApp group—'

'I've left it!' Riley interrupted. 'I'm going to, anyway.'

'—that was sharing images of a girl in her underwear.'

A cold weight dropped into the pit of Kat's stomach. She sat down in a hard chair and looked into her son's eyes. He was only twelve. How could this be happening? Images flashed through her mind, of pictures she'd seen on a brief rotation in the Sexual Crimes Unit at Jubilee Place. Of uniformed officers coming to arrest Riley. A courtroom. A judge, staring down at her son.

He's only twelve! she heard herself screaming. Then another, darker, thought intruded. *How old are serial killers when they start?* She pushed it down.

'Is this true, Riley?' she said, heart thumping.

'I didn't post them. They were just there. I looked by accident.'

'Is it *true*?'

A tear rolled down his scarlet cheek. He nodded.

'I caught sight of one when I was making tea,' Ivan said, coming to sit beside Kat. 'I asked him to show me the thread and there were a couple more.'

'Can I see, please,' Kat said, holding out her hand towards Riley.

But it was Ivan who placed the unlocked phone in her palm.

She found the pictures easily. The girl appeared to be in her late teens. The background suggested a real bedroom – band posters, photos and inspirational quotes Blu-Tacked to the wall. It looked a little like Courtney's.

'Riley, who is she? This is so, so important. Do you understand?'

'It's Luke's big sister.'

The courtroom images faded. 'And how old is Luke's sister.' *Please let her be in Year Thirteen. Better yet, at university, or working.*

'I don't know. I mean, not for sure,' Riley said. 'She left school last year.'

Kat shuddered with relief. Oh, thank God. Not a minor. Big trouble out of the way. Which just left the regular kind.

'Come here, sweetie,' she said.

He complied meekly, standing in front of her, head down.

'I didn't ask for them, or anything,' he said, his voice thick with snot and tears. 'They just came, you know?'

She gently placed her finger under his chin and lifted his head up so they were eye to eye.

'Who else is in this WhatsApp group?'

'You can't go and tell their parents!' he blurted out. 'They'll never speak to me again.'

'I need to know.'

He listed off half a dozen first names, all of whom she recognised.

'How did Luke get these photos of his sister?' Ivan asked.

Riley shrugged. 'Don't know. Maybe he, like, hacked her phone, or something? They look like selfies.'

Kat took another look at the images. They did have that aura about them: knowingness mixed with innocence. As if to say, *Look at me, but not if you're a weirdo.* Maybe the girl had never meant the images to be shared. Or maybe she'd shared them with her boyfriend. Either way, how could she explain to a young woman she'd never met that the world was *full* of weirdos? And that if . . . *if* . . . pictures of you in your undies – however private you thought they were – escaped your phone and made it on to social media, you'd just become a target for half of them. The bad half. The *evil* half. The men who learned early to see women as objects before graduating to—

She shuddered. She couldn't let the Origami Killer infect her family any more than he already had.

She hugged Riley tightly, then released him and looked into his eyes. 'I think you should leave the group and delete all the threads and photos from your phone,' she said. 'If anyone asks, you can say Dad and I decided you were wasting too much time when you should be doing your schoolwork or practising your football skills, OK? Would that work?'

He nodded, sniffed. 'I s'pose so.'

'Good. Now, I think we need to talk about those photos, don't we? Why girls take them and why boys like to look at them.'

'Oh God, Mum, please! I know, OK? We did it with Mr Boone in sex ed.'

He wriggled out of her arms and scooted round the kitchen table to sit opposite her.

'Well, Mr Boone's not a police officer. But I am,' Kat said. 'What if Luke's sister was only sixteen, not eighteen? That would make her a minor. If she'd found out and complained, or one of the other boys' parents had, Luke would have been arrested. Probably charged with distributing indecent images of a child. You could have been in real trouble. *All* of you. Not just him.'

Riley's face crumpled. Kat hated seeing him like this, but she needed him to understand. She glanced at Ivan, looking for support. His eyebrows lowered by a millimetre and his lips tightened. A warning. *Don't be too hard on him. He's only a boy.*

She flashed him a look she hoped he'd interpret correctly. *Better he learns here, and now, than by sitting in an interview room facing a detective. An* on-duty *detective.*

'Riley?' He looked up at her. 'This case I'm working on. The two girls he's killed aren't much older than Luke's sister. Now, I don't know why he's doing it, but one thing I *do* know is, he doesn't think of them as people. Not really. When you just have pictures of young women, or girls, like in your WhatsApp group, that's a little step towards feeling that *they're* not real people either.'

'But, Mum, I told you. He just sent them,' Riley said. 'You can't *not* see them. They're just there.'

She nodded. It was true. And adults – including, recently, a serving police officer – had been caught out in exactly the same way.

'I know, darling. I do, really. I trust you. But I – we – need you to understand that this isn't just some Mum-and-Dad thing. There are some very bad men out there and—' A tiny crack and a sharp pain at the end of her finger broke her train of thought.

She looked down. Found she was clutching the edge of the table hard enough to drive the edges of her nails into the soft pine. One had just broken off at the quick.

Riley nodded, sniffing. 'I'm sorry, Mum. And Dad. Really.'

Kat took a breath. Forced herself to smile. Her cheeks felt tight. 'Then let's leave it there, yes?'

'But am I still grounded? Only it's football practice tomorrow.'

Kat exchanged a look with Ivan. He'd put the punishment in place. It was up to him to lift it.

'Maybe I overreacted,' he said, after a pause. 'But I want you to promise me something. If anyone sends you any more images like that, you come and tell me or Mum immediately, yes?'

'Yes.'

'Promise?'

'Promise. Can I go now?'

'Of course. I'm sure you've got homework to do.'

The beginnings of a groan passed Riley's lips – then, thinking better of it, he nodded meekly and headed upstairs.

'Well, that was something to come home to,' Kat said. 'Do we need to discuss it?'

'Not specifically. I'm fairly sure Riley got the picture,' Ivan said. Then, looking serious: 'Don't you think you went in a bit heavy?'

Kat frowned. 'What do you mean? You were the one shouting when I got home.'

'Yeah, but you practically accused him of being a sex offender or a bloody serial killer, for God's sake.'

'Yes, and you know why, Van? Because every word I said was true. This is how they start. They *do* see women as objects. Men, too, come to that. I just worry, you know? I mean, what if' – she dropped her voice to a murmur – 'what if *he* did something really bad? How the hell would we cope?'

Ivan put his hands on his hips. 'OK, now you're being ridiculous. Riley saw a few saucy bedroom selfies and now you're worried he's the next Fred West?'

Kat felt her confusion as a physical ache located behind her breastbone. She rubbed the spot but the pain didn't ease.

'No, of course not.'

Ivan nodded. 'Good, because otherwise I think we'd have some serious talking to do, don't you?'

She shrugged, feeling like a young girl again, being told off by one of her teachers. She hated it. Something about the name of the boy who'd shared the pictures jolted her mind into a different gear.

'Wait. This Luke. It's not the wannabe rapper, is it? Luke Tockley? What was he calling himself? L-Tox?'

'The very same. I told you we should speak to Mr Darnley.'

'OK, and I said let Riley have his dangerous friend. Fine, but can you do it, Van? I'm up to my ears in the case. I really don't have time to go into school.'

Ivan shrugged. 'Looks like I'll have to, doesn't it? Just try and remember you have a family as well as a case, Kat.'

He was being unreasonable. Of *course* she remembered! *You try hunting a serial killer*, she wanted to shout. *It's a lot harder than they make it look on the telly. And it's a damn sight harder than wiring computers together.*

She settled for a bald statement of fact. 'He killed another girl.'

The four words flipped a switch in their conversation. She felt it as a mercy, even though the cause was so horrific.

'Oh God,' Ivan said. 'Same as the first one?'

She nodded. 'I have to stop him, Van. He's leaving hardly any gap between them. Last time it was months at the beginning. Now it's not even a week. I'm deputy SIO now. It's all on me.'

'Which is good news, right? Apart from the circumstances, I mean. It's a step-up. It's what you've always wanted. Ever since Liv.'

'Who basically strolled back into my life like a ghost, dropped a bombshell that she faked her own death, and now she's disappeared back to her hippy friends on some Welsh farm.'

'You said she was frightened it was the children's home manager.'

'We're checking him out.'

'So it's understandable if he's still at large. It could actually be him, couldn't it?'

'I don't know. A bloke makes a weird remark about her hair so Liv pegs him as a serial killer? It's a bit thin, don't you think?'

'That's your department, not mine,' he said, shrugging. 'Drink?'

'Just a small one. I want to take Smokes for a walk before we eat.'

After a glass of red wine that only the most charitable of alcohol counsellors would dub 'small', Kat went upstairs to change. She found Smokey curled into a fluffy grey ball on their bed.

'You cheeky monkey!' she said, scruffling him under the chin as he raised his head to give her a sleepy-eyed wink. 'You'll be getting under the covers soon, and then where will we be?'

Smokey yawned widely, his pink tongue curling back on itself. Shaking her head, Kat pulled out a pair of jeans. She threw her shirt in the laundry basket, had a quick sniff under her arms, then put on an old T-shirt.

'Come on, you,' she said, clicking her fingers at Smokey.

With a yip of excitement, he scrambled to his feet and jumped down off the bed, before nosing the bedroom door open and hurtling down the stairs so fast she worried, as she always did, that he'd break his neck at the bottom.

They were halfway round the big field before they met Barrie and Lois. Kat shared as much as she could, and finally asked him the question that had been bugging her. Did he think it could be a woman? It was unlikely, he said, but he'd once worked on a case where a woman from the next town over had hacked up four men for, as she said in court, 'the pleasure of it'.

As an answer, she found it less than reassuring. It merely added to the pressure she was feeling about the following day's press conference.

◆ ◆ ◆

In the end, the press conference wasn't as bad as she'd been expecting. Between them, she, Linda and Freddie managed to downplay the idea they were hunting a serial killer. Especially one who'd last been active in Middlehampton fifteen years earlier.

But the moment they started taking questions, Kat had to fight down her reservations about the direction they'd decided to take. In her gut she knew it was a serial killer. When a journalist asked a question that gave her an opening, it took all her self-control, aided by the fear of the bollocking she'd get from Linda, not to blurt it all out.

Somehow she got through it, her underarms hot with sweat and her stomach burning with stress-induced indigestion.

What she wanted now, more than anything else, was a handle on the Origami Killer's psychology. She wanted Clare Capstick's report.

CHAPTER TWENTY-TWO

The psychologist, Clare Capstick, was as good as her word. Kat arrived at work on Thursday morning to find an email waiting in her inbox. She downloaded the attached report, and knew, after reading the first sentence of decidedly un-academic language, that she'd made the right pick.

> When you catch this deviant killer, don't waste your breath trying to get him to feel anything for his victims or their loved ones. He is almost certainly a psychopath and, as such, will have little to no empathy, and no interest at all in developing any.
>
> For men like him, the world is simply a mirror of their desires. At the moment, his killings lack any sadistic sexual element. However, given he could choose literally anywhere on the body or at the deposition site to leave the origami heart, placing it inside the left bra cup suggests to me a strong sexual element.
>
> The lavender seems to me to be particularly significant. It will mean something to him. It's not a

scent you would typically associate with young girls; their grandmothers perhaps, but not them. He is turning them into another woman. One who wronged him in some way. Almost certainly the woman who raised him i.e. his mother, or if she was in prison, absent or murdered by a partner, an aunt or grandmother.

The cutting off of the hair also points to a sexual component in his relationship to his victims. Women's hair has always been associated with their sexual power. Read the Bible for plenty of examples. In removing it, the killer may believe he is robbing this wounding mother-figure of her power over him.

I think he has conflicted attitudes to sex. On the one hand, he finds it frightening, as it reminds him of being a powerless, possibly abused, child. On the other, he is in all likelihood a heterosexual man and, as such, will desire women sexually.

When you catch him, I suggest exploring this conflict in interview. The suggestion that he has 'mummy issues', possibly incestuous ones, may infuriate him and lead him into errors or admissions he would prefer not to make.

The final sentence of the introduction echoed Kat's own thoughts, even down to referencing 'mummy issues'.

At 10.45 a.m., an alarm went off on her phone. She glanced down. *Jade Root PM.* She grabbed her bag and headed down to the car park. No need to take Tom along this time.

◆ ◆ ◆

Kat found the new pathologist alone in the autopsy suite. He was sitting at one of the benches along the wall, typing notes into a template. For the post-mortem, she assumed.

She cleared her throat. 'Hi.'

He swivelled round.

Her belly, not normally troubled by nerves at post-mortems – she'd already seen too many – flipped.

The new guy at MGH – the *good-looking* new guy – had deep-set brown eyes, dark stubble on his cheeks, and wore an expression that might have been a smile if he had just a little more to be happy about.

He came towards her, and now he did smile.

'Jack Beale. Pleased to meet you, DS Ballantyne.'

'Call me Kat,' she said as they shook hands. His was deliciously cool, and dry to the touch. No wet fish in the autopsy suite.

'I shall, then. And you should call me Dr Beale.'

'Oh.'

'Joking. Jack's fine. Only my students call me Dr Beale, however much I try to discourage them.'

'You have students?'

He grinned sheepishly. 'I know, I know. I look like I only graduated from medical school the day before yesterday.'

Kat frowned, aware she was looking him up and down and apparently unable to do anything about it.

'Sorry, how old are you, exactly?'

His grin widened. 'Straight-talker, aren't you? I'm thirty-seven. And a half, since you want to know exactly,' he said, the humour evident in his voice. 'I started my degree at eighteen and trained full-time for the next sixteen years. I've been practising, as it were, since 2021.'

Kat felt her cheeks heating up, despite the air conditioning in the dissection room.

'I am so sorry. That was just rude of me,' she said. 'I didn't mean to suggest you weren't qualified.'

'The hospital authorities would take a dim view of my wandering around down here if I wasn't, I assure you,' he said. 'And how about you, Kat? You're a bit young to be a DS on MCU, aren't you? Or do you pay monthly visits to some secret clinic in the Swiss Alps for an off-books monkey-gland treatment?'

She laughed. 'Touché. Like you, I've worked hard. Obviously policework is better for my skin than expensive non-human-primate youth serums.'

'Shall we get started, then?'

Kat looked back at the door. 'Shouldn't we wait for your assistant?'

'Might be a long wait. He called in sick this morning. Spot of D&V. I thought, if you had time, I might get you to handle the photography, too. Someone who sits on a higher branch than I do has made a complete bollocks-up this week, and both snappers are off at the same time. I did call round, but I only have so much time to spend leaving voicemails. Essentially, it's austerity with knobs on.'

Kat shrugged. It was the same everywhere. 'I'm happy if you are. Evidentially, it's fine.'

'Good. I'll tell you which shots I want, and I guess you'll take any *you* want without being asked, yes?'

'Works for me.'

173

Once they were both gowned and masked, Jack whisked the green drape back from the body.

They worked side by side for two hours, him speaking into the overhead mic, directing Kat to take photos at each stage of the dissection; her trying to keep out of his way while still observing closely.

Somehow, being so intimately involved with the reduction of a human body to its constituent parts lessened, rather than increased, the sense of barely-held-in-check horror she usually felt at post-mortems.

Not nausea. That was for rookies. Or those poor souls whom Mother Nature had decreed should always have a weak stomach. Rather, a sense that evil lurked just below the surface of normality, one millimetre below the depth normal people's vision could perceive. Like some huge, pewter-scaled predator cruising in murky water, waiting for the unwary to venture down from the surface into its own dark domain.

Then it was done. Jade's torso bore a Y of spidery black sutures and Jack was pulling off his gloves.

'I'll have my report to you by close of play,' he said.

'Which means what in your world?' Kat asked. Dr Feldman was brilliant, but his sense of time had been elastic, to put it kindly.

Jack smiled. 'Well, normally anywhere between 6 p.m. and midnight, depending on my workload. But I could hand it to you in person, if you fancied a drink after work. Say half past six?'

Kat looked at him as he waited for her reply. She wanted to say, *Yes, of course.* Why shouldn't she? Two colleagues meeting for an after-work drink to discuss a key piece of evidence. Yet there was the small matter of that little gymnastics routine her stomach had performed when she first clapped eyes on Jack Beale. And she couldn't deny it, there had been something charged in the air between them as they'd worked – *Flirted!* an inner voice shouted – like ozone after a lightning strike.

No. She was imagining things.

His lips curved upwards a little more. They were red, and somehow she found herself imagining how they would feel against her own.

Cops and doctors. It was such a cliché. But those relationships worked because they understood each other better than cops and IT consultants ever could. The stresses of the job. The weird hours. The gallows humour. It might be nice not to be judged if you came home talking about dismembered bodies and smelling of blood. Or if you did a little work on a Sunday morning before your husband was even awake.

'So, a drink?' Jack asked again, smiling.

He'd removed his gloves and shucked off the top half of his scrubs to reveal a navy T-shirt. He had lovely forearms, she thought. Strong, but not too muscly. Just enough hair.

She gulped in a breath. 'I can't. I'm sorry.'

Pulse bumping uncomfortably in her throat, she extricated herself from Jack Beale's brown-eyed gaze, and her scrubs, which she tossed into a bin before smiling awkwardly and retreating to the other side of the swing doors.

Once safe inside her car, she let out a breath. What the hell had just happened? She'd nearly agreed to go for a drink – *A date!* her prissy inner voice piped up – with Jack Beale, knowing with total certainty what lay behind that irresistible grin of his.

But she *had* resisted. Not him, with his tousled hair and too-too-kissable lips. But her own flash of adolescent desire that had bloomed like a speeded-up film of a flower opening.

Jack emailed his report at 6.30 p.m. along with a short covering note.

I enjoyed working together today.

'Time spent with cats is never wasted.' –
Sigmund Freud

Jack

PS I saw your wedding ring. Mr Ballantyne
(assuming you took his name) is a lucky man.

Now there was a mile or so of Middlehampton streets between
her and Jack Beale, she permitted herself a small smile.

'Coming to the Archers, Kat?' Leah asked. 'Me and Tom are
going.'

'Yeah, go on, then.'

On the walk to the pub, which sat just around the corner from
Jubilee Place, whatever brief electricity had sparked between her
and Jack Beale earthed itself through the soles of her feet. Outside,
drinkers stood in groups, where they could smoke and enjoy their
condensation-beaded pints of lager and glasses of wine in the sun.

Leah found a table in a quiet corner, and Kat gave Tom a
twenty.

'Pint of lager for Leah, and a small Pinot Grigio for me, please.'

He returned with their drinks and a Coke for himself.

'You not a drinker, then, Tom?' Kat asked, taking a sip of her
wine.

He wrinkled his nose. 'Used to be. Gave it up.'

'Bit young to go on the wagon, aren't you?' Leah asked, wiping
a skim of froth from her top lip.

He frowned, and in that brief expression, Kat read pain, and
something else. Shame perhaps? He opened his mouth, then closed

it tight, as if he wanted to prevent words spilling out. He didn't have to explain himself.

'Listen, Leah,' she said, 'if it stops Tom getting a gut like half the blokes at Jubilee Place, that's got to be a good thing, right?'

Leah rolled her eyes. 'Yeah, it's a talent wasteland.'

'Er, hello? Sexist talk!' Tom said, smiling again, to Kat's relief. 'Do I need to find myself a safe space?'

'Nah, you're all right, mate,' Leah said. 'Kat and I don't bite, do we, Kat? I mean, not unless bitten first.'

They laughed, although Kat noticed another flicker of sadness cross Tom's face at Leah's quip. The talk turned, inevitably, to the case. Twenty minutes later, Kat finished the last of her wine and got up.

'You guys stay. Enjoy the downtime,' she said. 'I have a feeling we won't be getting much more of it until this case is closed.'

CHAPTER TWENTY-THREE

The following morning, Kat gathered her team – larger now, and including a couple of civilian investigators.

'Leah, where are we with local retailers of herbal oils and all the massage stuff?'

Leah nodded, consulting her notebook. 'I've been in to see all the ones I could find,' she said. 'They all stock lavender oil and a fair few sell dried lavender flowers as well. But they sell loads of it to dozens of different people. Nobody remembered any males who stood out as being odd in any way.'

Kat made a note. 'Tom, how about you?'

'I tracked down the guy who was running Shirley House in 2008 like you asked,' he said. 'Karl, with a K, Oldfield.'

'Do we have an address?'

'It's 28 Pitt Street, in Northbridge.'

'Is he working?'

'Sorry, I don't know.'

'No, it's fine. That's good work, Tom. We'll go and see him after this.'

'What's the plan, Kat,' Leah said. 'Now you're deputy SIO. Which is great, by the way.'

Kat nodded her thanks. 'We have nine victims in total. Seven from before, who I'm calling "the originals", and two current, who

I'm calling "the new girls". I want to know how their lives intersected. Within each group and across them,' she said. 'What are the things they have in common.'

After the meeting, Kat collected Tom from his desk.

'Ready to go and see if Karl-with-a-K Oldfield's accepting callers?'

The traffic in the centre of town was heavy. At one point they managed to travel fifty metres in five minutes. As they inched closer to the obstruction, Kat sighed with frustration. The council had blocked off the northbound side of South Street. Free of the contra-flow, she put her foot down in frustration, only for Tom to caution her against speeding.

'Wouldn't do to get a ticket on our way to interview a suspect.'

'Yeah, I think I could probably talk my way out of it, Tom, but thanks anyway. And while we're on the subject, let's stick to "person of interest" for Mr Oldfield. Call him a suspect and we're duty-bound to arrest him, as I imagine you know.'

'Sorry. Just a turn of phrase. Everybody says it. Even Carve-up.'

Kat had to bite her tongue. Why didn't that surprise her?

'At the risk of sounding like your mum, I'm not everybody. It's a good habit to get into. You call someone a suspect in court when they were only a person of interest at the time, and their brief will be on you like a starving dog on a bone. I've seen it happen.'

'Sounds like it might have been up close and personal,' Tom said.

'Let's just say a young DC learned a valuable lesson.'

She took a left at the Central Library's magnificent carved terracotta frontage, into Hempstead Street. London Road was the more direct route but it meandered right through the Bramalls, Middlehampton's permanent market. It drew shoppers from surrounding villages as well as the town itself, and negotiating the buses, traders' vans, mobility scooters and the press of pedestrians called for more patience than Kat could draw upon right now.

Northbridge was a largely residential area on the north bank of the River Lea. It had once been home to the town's well-to-do merchants, and their legacy took the form of grand Victorian red-brick houses, many now converted into flats.

Like so many other roads in Middlehampton, Pitt Street – which ran east to west – contained mainly terraced houses. Each distinguished from its neighbour by the colour of the front door, the flowers in the window boxes, or the subtle variations in replacement uPVC windows.

Plane trees lined the sides of the road, although their scaly bark was upstaged by a magnificent magnolia in a front garden a third of the way down the street. Kat parked beneath its broad canopy.

'We're just going to interview him, but we're going in prepared,' she said. 'That means we each take an extendo with us. They're in the boot. Ever use one in anger before?'

He grimaced. 'Sorry. You can add that to autopsies and death-knocks.'

'What exactly *do* they have you doing on the fast-track?'

'Oh, you know, getting fitted for chief inspectors' suits, filling out expense forms for lunches with the PCC, that kind of thing.'

'Yeah, and the tragic thing is, you think you're joking, don't you?'

He shook his head, grinning. 'No. The real tragedy is *you* think I am.'

She sighed. 'Come on, then.'

Kat opened the boot and unzipped the black holdall she'd loaded in when they'd left Jubilee Place. She handed Tom an extendo – officially an ASP-21 extendible baton – and took one for herself. The squat black tube sat easily in a pocket or even a small bag but could be flicked out and locked by friction to a very handy twenty-one inches.

'If for any reason he looks like he's going to pull something, you deploy it and yell at him to back away, yes?'

'Got it.'

'Anything more than that, we both go in with approved strikes. If he's right-handed, that's your primary target area.'

'Do you think it'll come to that?' Tom asked.

'Who knows. I've had multiple murderers come along as quiet as lambs, and I've had nursery nurses lose it big-time and go for me with a bread knife,' Kat said. 'Just be a good Boy Scout.'

'Be prepared.'

'Yes. That. And give him a good hard smack if he looks like causing a ruckus.'

Number 28's path was weed-free, and the slate paving slabs gleamed in the sun, as if polished. At the front door, painted a deep glossy green, Kat looked at Tom. 'Shall we?'

She rang the doorbell and took a step back, hand already closed around her ID.

CHAPTER TWENTY-FOUR

The man who opened the door was fiftyish, his greying hair receding from a high, lined forehead. A long, elegant nose gave him a somewhat imperious look, as if he might be more important than his humble dwelling suggested.

He was wearing a soft, beige cardigan in which moths had nibbled multiple holes, and cotton chinos. The knees were muddy. He wore walking boots, also encrusted with earth. An image flashed through Kat's mind. A murderer, scraping soil aside to dump a dead girl into a shallow grave.

He smiled. A pleasant, open expression. 'Can I help you?' He followed Kat's gaze. 'I was gardening. Sorry, I wasn't expecting visitors.'

Gardening on a workday? He looked a little young to be retired. 'Karl Oldfield?'

'Yes, that's right. If this is about my party membership, I'm afraid I don't really have the funds at the moment. That's why I cancelled, you see?'

So they didn't look like Jehovah's Witnesses, but apparently they did look like canvassers from a political party.

She held out her ID. 'We're with Middlehampton Police, Mr Oldfield. DS Ballantyne and DC Gray. May we come in, please?'

Oldfield stood back. 'Of course. Would you like to follow me?'

Kat glanced at Tom, raised her eyebrows. What did he think? He shrugged. Not reaching for his baton, at least.

They followed Oldfield along a narrow hallway and into a spacious modern kitchen, decked out in gleaming white units.

'I was just about to make myself some tea,' he said, gesturing at a fat-bellied, brown china teapot with its lid off. 'Would you like some? Best thing for cooling down on a hot day.'

'That would be nice – yes, please,' Kat said, nodding to Tom while Oldfield's back was turned.

'For me, too, please,' he said.

'I usually drink Assam in the afternoons – seems appropriate for an Indian summer – but I could make it with English Breakfast?'

'Assam's fine,' Kat said. 'Thank you.'

While Oldfield pottered about, getting cups and saucers out of the dishwasher and pouring milk from an old-fashioned glass bottle into a white china jug, Kat looked around the kitchen.

On one wall, she saw an untidy vertical ladder of pencilled height marks that started at about 40 centimetres and continued to 188. She wandered over to the wall and peered at the names.

'Edward and Leanne,' she said.

Oldfield turned. Smiled.

'My kids. Both flown the nest now, I'm afraid. Eddie's at Bristol studying neuroscience and Leanne's working in London as an actuary,' he said with a smile. 'Beats me where they get their brains from. Certainly not from me.'

'From Mrs Oldfield, perhaps?' Kat asked.

The smiled twitched, faltered, then slid off his face altogether. 'Probably. Helen was brilliant.'

'"Was"?' Kat asked.

She'd seen colleagues shy away from such simple questions, taking the use of past tense as a clear sign not to stray on to someone's grief, or resentment at an unwanted divorce. Kat liked to ignore signs. *Keep Off the Grass. Residents' Parking Only. Don't Ask Me About That.*

'She died,' Oldfield said, pouring boiling water on to the leaves he'd just spooned into the teapot from a battered Union Jack tin. 'Five years ago, now.'

'I'm sorry,' Kat said, looking past him to the lush back garden, thick with roses and herbaceous borders. The soil in this part of Middlehampton was a gardener's dream. Crumbly, rich in nutrients from when the Lea had been a much wider river. Deep, too.

'It was rather ridiculous, really. We were cycling in Gademere – the wetlands, you know?' Kat nodded. 'Helen had a heart attack. Dropped dead on the spot. I was thirty or forty metres ahead of her. Didn't even notice. Another cyclist came racing after me and told me he'd seen her fall off her bike. By the time I reached her she was already dead. She was a gifted botanist. At the university. She'd just landed a big research contract with a pharmaceutical company.'

The story sounded rehearsed. And Oldfield's voice was flat. Maybe he'd used it to insulate himself from the pain of his wife's death.

'What sort of research?'

'Helen and her team had identified a couple of new active ingredients in common herbs with the potential to manage anxiety disorders. They were quite far along but they hit a stumbling block. Then the Big Pharma boys turned up offering research funding. They were grappling with side effects, you see. Including high blood pressure. I've always wondered whether she might have been testing it on herself. You know what scientists are like. Perhaps that caused the heart attack. I suggested it and they held an inquest, but the coroner recorded a verdict of death by natural causes.'

'And when you say "common herbs"?' Kat prompted.

He frowned. 'Ginseng, guarana, I think. And lavender. Or, to give it its scientific name, which Helen drilled into us all—'

'*Lavandula angustifolia*,' Kat said, sliding a hand into her back pocket to check on her baton.

He smiled. 'A fellow botanist. Shall we take the tea out to the garden? It's such a lovely day.'

The garden was even more beautiful than it had looked through the kitchen window. The sweet, peachy smell of old roses hung in the air.

'Your garden's lovely,' Tom said.

'Thank you. It keeps me busy.'

'So you're retired then?'

Kat was impressed. Again. Tom had made the same logical jump she had.

'I used to run a children's home, but I left that all behind years ago,' he said.

'Must be nice to have all your time to yourself.'

'It does have its compensations, certainly.'

Once he'd ushered them to a teak seating group centred on a table with brass-hinged top, Kat felt it was time to get to the point of their visit. Oldfield was clearly in no hurry. Perhaps he was simply lonely. Wife dead, children gone. *Nobody to observe his comings and goings*, a small, cynical voice cut in.

'We're investigating two murders, Mr Oldfield.'

'Call me Karl, please. Less formal. Otherwise I feel like you're about to arrest me,' he added with a grin.

'Karl, then. These murders are linked to each other, and, we believe, to a series of seven more that occurred in 2007 and 2008.'

He was pouring tea into three cups as she said this. The flow from the spout wavered and he splashed a little into the saucer. His lips twitched in irritation. Then he smiled, nodded, and topped up the cup before offering milk and pointing out the sugar cubes in a little silver bowl.

'You're talking about the Origami Killer, aren't you?'

'Why do say that?' Kat asked.

'I was living in Middlehampton back then, too. Is that why you're here? Do you want to speak to me about my time at Shirley House?'

'Why do you ask?'

He took an unhurried sip of tea then replaced the cup in the saucer with a quiet *chink*.

'It's tragic, but we had a connection to two of his victims. Sally Robb and Liv Arnold had both been residents,' he said calmly. 'I loved those girls as if they were my own. I was devastated when the news came out. We all were.'

Knowing all about Liv, Kat focused on the second Shirley House girl.

'Tell me about Sally. What was she like?'

Oldfield ran a palm over his face, which was sheened with sweat.

'Like a lot of the children we cared for – all of them, really – she had her good days and her bad days. You must have met kids like her before,' he said. 'They don't end up in a children's home as a lifestyle choice. They've been through trauma of one sort or another. You can't blame them for acting out occasionally.'

Kat nodded. 'While she was with you, can you remember if she had any boyfriends? Especially older boys? Maybe even a young man?'

Oldfield pulled his mouth to one side. He looked away from her.

'There was one lad who she seemed keen on,' he said in a faraway voice. 'He used to wait for her at the gate. He was older than her.'

'Did he have a name, this boy?'

'I'm sorry – if she told me, I've forgotten. It was a long time ago.'

Kat nodded. 'Of course. But you saw him? At the gate?'

'Yes, once or twice. He looked pleasant enough. I mean, no leather jacket and tattoos, no oily motorbike roaring up and down the street waking the neighbours when he brought her back from wherever they'd been. Oh, wait. I do remember his name. It was Evan. No, Steven. I'm ninety per cent sure it was Steven. Or maybe she called him Steve.'

'Was he white? Black?'

'Oh, white. Yes.'

This was going nowhere. She wasn't getting a vibe off him to suggest he was a 'wrong 'un'. Then Dr Feldman's words floated back to her from Courtney Hatch's post-mortem. Maybe it was time for an old-fashioned tactic instead of relying on what the pathologist had referred to, dismissively, as 'hunches, gut feelings and "copper's intuition"'.

'Could I use your loo, please?'

'Of course. Must be all the coffee I expect you detectives drink,' he said with another smile. 'It's upstairs. First door on the left.'

'Thanks. Tom, perhaps you could ask Karl what else he remembers about the events of 2008.'

Leaving Tom running Oldfield through a series of detailed questions, she headed inside. The interior of the house was dark, and she had to blink until her eyes had adjusted after the bright sunlight.

Upstairs, she bypassed the bathroom and pushed open each of the other three matching stripped-pine doors off the hallway. The first room – neat, orderly – contained a double bed, wardrobe and dressing table. Nothing leapt out at her. The second was a smaller bedroom. Equipped for guests, down to a little wicker basket on the chest of drawers containing miniature bottles of shampoo and conditioner. She'd need a search warrant to find anything in such a tidy space.

Feeling that she had very little time left before even the most capacious copper's bladder could reasonably have been expected to empty itself, she opened the third door.

The room was fitted out as a study: an antique writing desk beneath the window, books lining the walls. It smelled musty.

She scanned the crowded shelves, which were packed with hundreds if not thousands of paperbacks. The narrow space in front of the spines was host to dozens of little objects. What an NYPD detective she'd met once had called 'tchotchkes'. 'It's Yiddish,' he'd said in his crow-squawk Brooklyn accent. 'Meaningless crap people collect and can't throw out.'

Sitting between a red-painted model Mercedes, one gullwing door open, and a tiny phrenologist's head with personality traits marked out in black glaze, sat an origami model.

Kat stared at the little piece of folded paper.

Not a heart, admittedly. That would have been too much of a gift. A frog, rendered in beautifully precise folds.

Kat turned to the desk. At this angle, she could see into the numerous cubbyholes above the writing surface. Each contained another origami model.

Her pulse racing, seeming to narrow her throat so she had to gasp for breath, she stooped to examine them.

A penguin. A crane. A bull. An elephant. A basket.

A heart.

CHAPTER TWENTY-FIVE

Kat marched out of the room and took the stairs two at a time, sliding her hand along the banister to ensure she didn't break her neck.

She ran through the kitchen, willing her pulse to settle but unable to stop the sensation of blood waiting to burst free of her ears.

Into the garden, where she saw Tom nodding, jotting something down in his notebook.

Round the table so that she was standing over Oldfield, making him twist in his seat so that he could look up at her. She kept her hands behind her back, the right curled around the handle of her baton.

'Karl, I'd like to invite you to come with us back to Jubilee Place police station to continue this conversation there.'

At this, Tom rose from his chair and stood on Oldfield's other side. Kat was pleased he'd read her body language. Doubly so when she saw the way his right hand had slid nonchalantly into the pocket containing his own baton.

Oldfield merely smiled. An expression Kat suddenly loathed.

'Is that really necessary? I thought we were doing so well here. Your assistant . . .' He turned to look up at Tom. 'I'm sorry, is that the correct term? Anyway, Tom here was just asking me for my whereabouts on the night poor Courtney Hatch was murdered. I was telling him, too, wasn't I, Tom?'

'This would be purely voluntary,' Kat continued, trying to ignore the painful bump of her pulse in her throat. 'You'd be free to leave at any time.'

'But that would be under caution, yes?' He smiled apologetically. 'Sorry. I had to know a little law when I was managing Shirley House. Sadly, some of the kids used to run afoul of it on occasion. I was often asked to act as an appropriate adult.'

Kat was quivering with adrenaline, primed for the slightest aggressive move, which would end up with Oldfield on the floor nursing a severely bruised arm at the very least. He was either buying time or playing with them, she couldn't tell which.

'It would be under caution, and you would be entitled to have legal representation.'

He shook his head. 'No, no. There's no need. If you're sure we can't finish off here?'

'I really do think it would be better if we talked in a slightly more formal setting,' she said, tightly.

He shrugged. 'Could I at least change first?' he asked, gesturing at his mud-stained trousers.

'No need,' she said. 'We don't mind a little dirt, do we, Tom?'

'OK, then. I suppose we should go,' he said, rising to his feet.

Rigid with tension, Kat took a step back to allow him to round the table, and then followed him through the kitchen. She paused while he locked the French doors, then tracked him along the narrow hallway, ready for him to either whirl round and attack or make a run for it. Out the front door and, finally, into the back seat of the car. Tom slid in next to him, keeping his body half turned towards Oldfield.

As Kat pulled out of the parking spot, she wondered whether she was wasting time chasing a lead only Liv seemed sure of. Too late for that, now. They'd embarked on a course of action, and they needed to either arrest Oldfield or eliminate him.

Should she be thinking about Liv in the same way? Maybe, as deputy SIO and case officer, she should apply the same level of scrutiny to her best friend – who had faked her own death for reasons Kat still wasn't sure she understood – as to the man who'd run the children's home where she'd spent her teenage years.

Thinking about Liv, rather than concentrating on the route back to the station, she ended up mired in the traffic pulsing through the Bramalls like blood corpuscles squeezing through a fat-clogged artery.

By the time they reached the car park at the back of Jubilee Place, she had added several more items to the mental copy of her policy book. Top of that list was a trip to Wales, just to eliminate any doubt that everything Liv had told her was true.

Once Kat, Tom and Oldfield were seated in the interview room, she started the tape recorder, introduced everyone, then gave Oldfield the caution.

'And could you also confirm, again for the tape, that you do not want a lawyer with you for this interview?'

This was always a tricky moment. People were often all smiles and jokes in the car but then, faced with the hard, right-angled reality of a sweat-scented, harshly lit interview room, started yelling for a lawyer as loudly as they could.

'That's correct,' Oldfield said, with a small smile. 'I have nothing to hide.'

Personally, Kat thought anyone who allowed detectives to interview them under caution without a lawyer present was a fool. Apart from anything else, *everyone* had *something* to hide. And that guilt could manifest itself in surprising ways.

Professionally, she was always delighted. It made her job easier.

'Let's begin, then, shall we? Karl, tell me about the origami.'

'The what?'

'The origami. In your study. Who makes it?'

His eyes narrowed to slits and the edges of his nostrils whitened. 'You had no right.'

'It was an honest mistake, Karl,' she said. 'I was looking for the lavatory. I opened the wrong door.'

'But I gave you clear instructions! It's the first door on the left at the top of the stairs.'

'The origami, Karl?'

'It's not a crime, is it?' he added, folding his arms.

'Of course not. Lots of people make folded-paper models. Frogs. Boats. Hats. You did a heart, didn't you? A pretty, pink heart.'

His faced changed from a hostile glare to an open smile. The man seemed to have a new emotion for every question. Or perhaps none, trying on expressions like other people – *normal people*, Kat's subconscious supplied – tried on outfits.

'I can see where you're going with this, DS Ballantyne. But I'm afraid you've rather got the wrong end of the stick. Leanne makes them for me.'

'Your daughter.'

'Yes. Remember? I said she worked in London.'

'As an actuary. And you're saying your adult daughter, presumably busy with a demanding professional job and . . . a family?'

'A husband. No children as yet, but I'm hopeful I may soon have my first grandchild.'

'So, a busy professional woman with a marriage and possibly a new family on the horizon, has time to make complicated origami models and, what, posts them to you?'

'Yes! It's a little tradition of ours. She did it through university as well. I taught her, you see. When she was a little girl.'

'When you were manager of Shirley House?'

He nodded, eager now to agree with her.

'Yes! And before. It was a hobby of mine. Silly, I know, really. I was busy myself,' he said. 'You wouldn't think I had time for it, either, but it was relaxing. Like some people do yoga. I do – did – origami. Then, when the papers started calling that awful man the Origami Killer, well, it sort of took the shine off my hobby. I stopped after that. But Leanne, bless her, sends me one every now and again in a letter. It's sweet, really. I wouldn't mind if she stopped but she just does it. I think maybe it's a de-stresser for her, too.'

Tom, who'd been taking notes, leaned forwards across the table, and looked briefly at Kat, eyebrows raised. She nodded her permission. *Go ahead.*

'Can I ask you, Karl, when exactly you stopped making origami models?'

Oldfield looked up at the ceiling. Smoking had long been banned at Jubilee Place but the nicotine stains of old remained stubbornly present, the shades of suspects past.

'Well,' he said slowly, 'that would have been, I suppose, about January 2008. January or February. That's when the media started calling him the Origami Killer.'

Tom made a note. Kat knew he'd be checking the media archives as soon as he left the interview room.

'And what about the models you'd already made?'

'I threw them all away, of course,' Oldfield said. 'Can you imagine the impact they would have had on a vulnerable child coming to see me? They'd have been terrified. It wasn't as if the nickname was a big secret, after all. Everybody was talking about him back then. You're a little young to remember, but Middlehampton was in the grip of terror. A sort of community-wide panic attack.'

Tom leaned back.

'Is your mother still alive, Karl?' Kat asked.

'She is – why?'

'Where does she live?'

'Why do you ask?'

'Could you answer the question, please?'

'You won't get any sense out of her. She has Alzheimer's. She's lived in a care home since my father died.'

'Which care home?'

'I'd really rather you left her out of this. Ask me all the questions you like. I have nothing to hide. But my mother has nothing to do with this.'

'Nobody's going to upset your mum,' Kat said. 'I promise. Now, which care home is she living in?'

He looked at her, and for the first time since they'd brought him in, she saw something she didn't like. A defiance behind the eyes. A hardness. And something that worried her more. Something sly. He was hiding something. But was it his guilt? Or something else?

'I'd like to go now, please.'

Kat felt like an angler with no barb on her hook, desperate to keep this big fish on the line. Could he be the Origami Killer? He'd fit right in on her murder wall in her room at home. Right sex, old enough, a connection to one of the victims, his wife's research into lavender, a room stuffed with origami models, including a heart. He'd claimed his daughter made them, but he'd also admitted to making origami models himself before destroying them all back in '08. But it wasn't enough. She needed a little longer with him.

'Which of course would be your right, Karl,' she said, forcing a smile. 'But can we just clear up your whereabouts for two dates first, please?'

'The dates of the two murders, I suppose,' he said with a sneer. 'Or are you going to try to pin the original seven on me, too? I don't want to answer any more questions, thank you.'

Kat looked at him for a long moment. Thinking about what he'd just said. She tasted bitter disappointment. Oldfield had just dropped to the bottom of her list of potential suspects.

She closed her file and switched off the tape recorder.

'Thanks for your time, Mr Oldfield.'

'What?'

'DC Gray will show you to the front desk.'

Tom looked at her in mute enquiry. She gave him nothing back.

They had to keep looking, before the Origami Killer claimed a new victim.

CHAPTER TWENTY-SIX

Kat was at her desk when Tom returned.

He pulled up a chair. 'What just happened?' he asked as he sat down, his face betraying doubt and confusion, and maybe, in the tight lips and combative stare, even a hint of irritation.

'It's not him.'

'You can't possibly know that. We didn't even get as far as his alibis.'

Kat looked at her bagman. She had to think fast. Karl had said seven girls were murdered back in '08, whereas the actual total was one less. No way would the real killer take credit for a murder that never happened. He'd see it as beneath him. How could she tell Tom she knew it wasn't Karl? She couldn't. Not without revealing that Liv was still alive.

'Call it a hunch.' It sounded pathetic, even as she said it.

'A hunch,' he repeated, clearly taking the same view.

It would mean wasting Tom's time on a lead she knew wouldn't pan out, but she couldn't see any other option.

'You're right. We need to go by the book. Give it an hour or so, then go back and talk to him at his place again. Apologise for bringing him in, if you like. He seems to like you, so blame me if you think it will help. And get his alibis for the current two. I saw you noting the dates when he said he stopped doing origami. Check the *Echo* and see if you can find the first time anyone referred to the Origami Killer.'

'What are you doing next?'

'Got a lead I need to follow up.'

She left him sitting there before he could ask her what sort of lead.

Finding a quiet space, she gave herself a few minutes to think. If Oldfield ticked five boxes, Liv ticked at least four. Old enough. Knowledge of the killer's MO. Lavender. A fifteen-year absence. Was *she* hiding something, just like Oldfield? The thought made Kat feel sick. Her gut told her neither was guilty; her copper's brain told her to follow the evidence.

She phoned Liv, who answered and began speaking in the same breath. 'Hey! How's the case going? Did you track Oldfield down yet? Oh my God, is that why you're calling? I knew it! Did you arrest him. Has he confessed?'

Kat had to smile. The girl she'd been drawn to on that long-ago school day flashed into brilliant photographic clarity.

'Slow down! I want to come and see you. You just rushed off before. I thought we could have a proper catch-up.'

'I'd love that! But I guess it'll have to be after the case is closed. You guys work all the hours God sends, don't you?'

'Actually, I thought I'd come now.'

'What, today-now, you mean?'

'Yeah, today-now,' Kat said, smiling. 'Are you in? At your commune or whatever you call it?'

'We call it a "community", but yes, I'm here. It's my turn to cook tonight. If you could see me, I'm peeling about a hundred potatoes into a metal bucket,' Liv said.

'Send me the address. I'll see you in a few hours.'

'Hurry up. You can help me with these spuds. Stay for dinner, even. Or for the night. There's lots of room.'

On the basement level, Kat snagged the keys to a big maroon BMW tuned for fast pursuits and stuck her phone in the holder on the windscreen. The satnav app thought she'd make it to Bryn Glas Farm, Summerleaze, in two hours and thirty-one minutes.

An hour and fifty minutes later, limbs buzzing with adrenaline, she parked the BMW on the edge of a concrete farmyard, where chickens pecked for scraps and a duck waddled between a barn and a pond. Kat climbed out and drew in a deep breath. Her lungs filled with the smells of livestock and fertiliser – and, below those, a trace of diesel oil.

Stretching, she looked across the yard at a rambling farmhouse in bricks glazed gold by the sun. It was like something out of Riley's favourite book when he was little. The story of the Little Red Hen.

'*Who will help me catch the serial killer?*' Kat asked.

'*Not I,*' said the detective inspector.

'*Not I,*' said the profiler.

'*Not I,*' said the children's home manager.

'Then I'll just have to catch him myself,' Kat muttered under her breath as she reached the farmhouse.

The door, silvery-grey weathered wood studded with black iron nails, stood wide open, revealing an empty kitchen dominated by a huge, scrubbed table.

Curled up on a rag rug by an Aga, a black-and-white border collie raised its head and regarded her with one blue eye and one brown. She squatted and smiled.

'Hey,' she crooned. 'Anyone about?'

The collie unfolded itself from the bed and padded across the floor, its claws clicking on the dark slate tiles. Kat held her hand out, knuckles uppermost, for the dog – very much a boy, she saw as she peered under his belly – to sniff. He emitted a strong, almost musky, scent.

'Can you smell *my* dog?' she asked him, before giving him a scratch behind the ears. 'Because he can probably smell *you* from here.'

After a few more seconds, he gave a mighty shake, sending his ears snapping like flags in a high wind, before returning to his berth by the range.

'Hi,' a plump middle-aged woman said, entering the kitchen from a door at the rear of the dim room. 'You've met Duffle, I see.'

The woman's accent wasn't Welsh. More of a countrified version of Tom's acquired drawl. She wore a floaty maxi-dress and, judging by the way her body moved inside it, very little else. From beneath the hem of her dress, dirty, bare feet festooned with silver toe-rings peeped out. Large silver earrings dangled against her neck.

'He's lovely.'

'He is. Who are you exactly?' It wasn't an aggressive question. More one of puzzlement.

'I'm a friend of Liv's. Is she around, do you know?'

The woman smiled, revealing slightly crooked teeth.

'She had to pop into Newport. We've run out of garam masala. Who knew?' she added, holding her hands wide.

'I guess even self-sufficiency has its limits.'

'Got that right. Do you want some tea?'

Kat nodded and took a seat at the table while the woman, who introduced herself as Tamara, busied herself making tea. Unlike Karl Oldfield's fussy, single-man ritual, Tamara just slung a couple of teabags into mugs.

With the tea made, she sat opposite Kat at the table.

'You're the detective, aren't you?'

Kat pulled a face. 'That obvious, huh?'

Tamara put her head to one side, making one of her earrings brush against her shoulder, and gave Kat an appraising look.

'I suppose *someone* here might have a nice crisp white shirt like that, but I doubt it,' she said. 'Anyway, no, that's not it. Liv told us all about you.'

'She came to see me in Middlehampton.'

'Yes. That cost her, you know. I had to give her something to calm her down for the trip. Just a Xanax, before you ask.'

Kat smiled. 'It wouldn't bother me whatever you'd given her. I'm homicide.'

'That dreadful man's back. It's why she wanted to go and see you.'

Kat saw an opportunity to check Liv's whereabouts without having to ask her directly.

'And apart from that, has she been here the whole time? Safe, I mean?'

Tamara nodded. 'Pretty much. The locals have accepted us for the most part, but we tend to keep ourselves to ourselves.'

'How about last week?' Kat asked. 'Tuesday.'

Tamara took a sip of her tea.

'Yes, she was here. All day.'

Kat nodded vigorously, then eased off, feeling she was over-cooking the act.

'Good, good, that's reassuring. I wouldn't have wanted her to be anywhere near Middlehampton then,' she said. 'Too traumatic, given everything she went through.'

Tamara put her mug down and stared at Kat, fingering her left earring.

'You're checking she has an alibi, aren't you? My God, you drove all this way because you think your friend – your *best* friend, I should add – is a serial killer! And people wonder why we don't trust the police.'

'People also wonder why other people fake their own deaths,' Kat snapped back, unable to stop herself.

The light dimmed as someone filled the doorway from the yard.

'Who doesn't trust the police?'

Dreading the conversation she knew was coming in the next few minutes, Kat turned in her chair. 'Hi, Liv.'

'You're here!' Liv put her shopping bag down and swept Kat into a hug so tight it stopped her breathing. 'Thanks for coming all this way. I feel so much safer here.'

'Yeah, well, you'll have to put me down or I'm going to faint,' Kat said.

Tamara stood up. 'I'll leave you two to it, then,' she said, arching one eyebrow.

When the older woman had gone, Liv made herself a cup of instant coffee and sat beside Kat, her eyes shining.

'You look great,' Kat said, meaning it.

Away from Middlehampton, Liv looked more relaxed. Even without Tamara's sedative.

'Thanks! You too. I love this,' she said, taking a fold of Kat's shirt between thumb and forefinger.

'It's only H&M. I think it was a tenner.'

'Yeah, but you always knew how to make cheap clothes look good. Remember when we used to go round the charity shops? I'd come out of the changing room looking like a bag lady and you'd be all, "I'm Avril Lavigne."'

Kat nodded as a memory from school surfaced. A boy teasing Liv about her clothes. *Which charity shop d'you get them from, then?*

Liv had smiled sweetly and walked back to the boy. She'd lashed out with both hands, scoring deep bloody scratches across his cheeks, and damaging his right eye so badly he was off school

201

for a week. He'd finally reappeared with a thick pad of gauze taped over the wound.

Kat had been both shocked and exhilarated by the violence. At the time it had seemed like Liv meting out some righteous justice to a prick in designer jeans and a branded polo shirt. Worth the suspension it had earned her. But now . . . she wondered about that darkness in Liv that, even then, had sometimes frightened her.

Liv took a quick slurp of her coffee. 'What did Tamara mean, about not trusting the police?'

Kat sighed. No way was she going to lie to Liv. What would be the point, when the hippy-dippy mother hen, or whoever she was, would only spill the beans later?

'I need to ask you a couple of questions. And I want you to just . . .' She hesitated. No, she couldn't see an easy way of saying it. 'Just hear me out.'

'OK, but why the amateur-dramatic face?'

'When you faked that photo, how did you get all the details of the crime scene right?'

Liv grinned. 'This girl I knew back then was going out with a copper. He told her and she told me.'

Kat shook her head. Brilliant. Some dimwit bigging himself up to his girlfriend by sharing the spicy details of a homicide case.

'Did he have a name, this copper?'

Liv closed her eyes for a moment. 'Stewie, I think. I didn't know his surname.'

Kat was suddenly sure *she* did. Another charge on Carve-up's rap sheet.

'What about the letter? I didn't recognise your handwriting.'

'Rhys did it for me.'

'You had it all figured out, didn't you?'

Liv nodded. 'Pretty much, yeah.'

'Liv, where did you go after we went to the King's Head?'

'You know where. I went to get my car – it's one of the ones here, we're all insured to drive it. And I drove back to the farm.'

'Did you stop anywhere?'

'No. I went straight through.' The light of understanding dawned in Liv's eyes, just like it had in Tamara's. 'Wait, you want me to give you an alibi, don't you? Oh my God, Kat, how could you?'

Kat was in too deep now to back out.

'How about last Monday and the Tuesday before that? Where were you then?'

Liv's mouth dropped open. 'This is literally crazy! I was here,' she said. 'This is why Tamara was in a mood, isn't it? You're investigating *me*, aren't you?'

'No! I'm not *investigating* you. I came all the way out here to *eliminate* you. To rule you out, not in. It's how we work,' Kat said.

'But why would I kill anyone at all, let alone those girls? I can't believe this, Kat, I really can't.' Liv's eyes had filled with tears and she swiped at them with her hand. 'How could you even ask me those questions, after everything I went through?'

'But you didn't go through *anything*, did you? That's the whole point,' Kat said. 'You faked it. Right down to the letter with the bad grammar.'

'I had to! I told you.'

Suddenly, Kat had had enough of Liv's histrionics. 'Listen! After you disappeared, I lasted about a fortnight at university. I had a breakdown, Liv. A proper nervous breakdown! Nightmares, panic attacks, depression, binge-eating, the works! The grief almost destroyed me. I thought he'd ended my life as well as yours. Little by little, I built myself a new life, and then, fifteen years later – fifteen! – you just come waltzing back into Middlehampton expecting to just, what, pick up where we left off? I mean . . . you know that's why I joined the police, right? So I could stop more girls getting murdered.'

Kat was crying. For the girl who'd lost her best and dearest friend. Who'd never been able to fully grieve because they'd never found her body. Who'd suppressed so much pain in order to move on.

'I thought he was going to kill me,' Liv said quietly.

'Oldfield? We interviewed him,' Kat said, blotting her own eyes with a tissue. 'It's not him. I'd bet my life on it.'

Liv shook her head. 'No,' she whispered. 'Not him.'

'What?'

'Not Karl. I lied to you when we met. I'm sorry, Kat, I really am.'

'Who, then? Who did you think was going to kill you?'

'It was an older boy. Steven, that was his name.'

'Wait. Steven, as in the boy Sally Robb was going out with?'

Liv nodded, sniffing. 'He asked me out, but I said no. I got this weird feeling off him. He frightened me.'

'So why did you send me after Oldfield if you knew he wasn't dodgy? Jesus, Liv, do you have any idea how much time you've wasted as a result of that? Not to mention making me drag some innocent widower into an interview room under caution.'

Liv's eyes flashed. There it was again: that old defiance. 'Maybe he's not the killer, but he was dodgy all right. If you interviewed him, you must have been able to tell. That's what you do, isn't it? Detectives, I mean. You smell guilt on people.'

Liv had a point. Oldfield *had* emitted weird vibes. Just not serial killer vibes.

'Maybe,' Kat said.

'Definitely.' Liv looked away, then continued in a small, far-away voice. 'I thought if I pointed you at Oldfield, it would frighten Steven off when he saw you closing in on Shirley House. I'm still terrified Steven'll track me down and kill me. Because they never stop, do they? Not until they're caught. Or killed.'

Kat scratched at the back of her neck, feeling the conversation slipping away from her. Liv's reasoning sounded just about believable, but there were so many holes in her story, so many places where it just didn't stand up to scrutiny. Ever since Liv's return, she'd been wondering whether her friend had some sort of mental health problem. Was that why Tamara had a supply of Xanax ready to dish out?

'No, they don't,' she said.

'But a first name isn't enough, is it? Not a common one like Steven. He'd just lie low then come looking for me.'

Kat sighed. Whatever the rights and wrongs of Liv's explanation about Steven, her witness testimony had put an innocent – albeit dodgy – man into a police interview room.

'Liv, you realise what you've done, don't you?'

Liv was rotating the mug between her palms until Kat shot out a hand and stopped it physically.

'Yes, and I'm sorry. I know wasting police time is an offence. But can't you see why I did it? Why I *had* to do it?'

'It's worse than that. This isn't just wasting police time. You literally perverted the course of justice. For the second time. That's a really serious crime. I can't believe this.'

Liv shook her head. 'You've got it wrong. We looked it up first. Me and Tamara. It's fine, because I didn't *intend* to pervert the course of justice. Wikipedia,' she added triumphantly.

'Oh, you and the earth mother looked it up, did you? Well, newsflash, Liv, you looked it up in the wrong place,' Kat said, trying to manage her breath, which was coming in short gasps. 'If you make a false allegation that risks an innocent person getting arrested, that passes the threshold. Crown Prosecution Service.'

Liv's tears, so recently stemmed, burst free again. 'You're not going to arrest me, are you?'

'No, I'm not going to arrest you,' Kat said. 'Although part of me wants to. Instead, I want you to tell me everything you remember about this Steven character.'

Kat took notes as Liv spoke almost without a pause for ten minutes, her fingers knotting and unknotting on the scarred table-top between them. Finally, she stopped.

'I think that's everything. I know it's not much, but I hope it helps you catch him.'

Kat nodded briefly. 'I hope so too, Liv, I really do. Listen, I have to go.'

Liv nodded, sniffed. Kat realised she'd been close to tears the whole time. Then, as Kat started to rise from her chair, Liv grabbed her wrist, hard enough to hurt, pulling her back down again.

'Wait!'

She looked away from Kat, over at the collie, out the window. Finally, she raised tear-filled eyes to lock on to Kat's. The words came out in a rush.

'You can't go yet. I have to tell you something. It's important. It's everything!' She took a deep breath and spoke in a great torrent of words. 'After I ran away, I wanted to see you so badly, Kat, it was like an ache. Always there, deep down in my belly, in my heart, everywhere, ever since I left Middlehampton. I felt so guilty about leaving you like that. It was eating me up. I mean, you were the one person who loved me unconditionally, whatever I did, whatever I was like. The only one who never hurt me or dissed me for being poor or in care or a skank or whatever. And I betrayed that love. Flushed it down the toilet. I was so frightened. But I should never have let that stop me letting you know I was safe. I just—'

She looked away again, swiped the back of her hand under her nose, where transparent mucus was dripping in a fine string. Kat felt her throat thickening, as the years fell away and her old friend, her Liv, was back. Properly, this time.

'It's OK,' she said softly. 'It's OK.'

Liv shook her head. 'It's not. I wasn't strong enough back then, but when he started up again, I knew I had to come back to see you. To *tell* you. I know I let you down, pretending to be dead, but then, when I read about how he'd killed Courtney Hatch, I couldn't bear it any longer. Because she really *was* dead, and she couldn't tell her best friend how much she loved her. I couldn't do it a second time, Kat. I just couldn't lose you a second time.'

Kat got to her feet and this time Liv let her. She came round to Liv and knelt on the hard slate floor beside her, folding her into an awkward hug. A corner of the table dug painfully into her chest. She ignored it.

'Why didn't you just tell me all this in the pub when you came back?'

'I was going to. But I was so nervous, and then you had to go and the moment passed. Please don't be angry with me.'

'I'm not angry with you, Liv. I promise. We'll get together again, OK? Soon. When the case is finished.' She stood. 'I really do have to go, though.'

Liv looked up at her. 'I'll come to see you off.'

Outside, the September sun was blazing down, making Kat wonder about climate change. The smell of manure was stronger than ever. They hugged again, then Kat climbed into the BMW's stiflingly hot interior. She switched on the ignition and turned the air conditioning to full power. Before closing the door, she leaned out a little.

'I need to make a call. Don't wait out in the sun.'

Liv nodded, smiled and raised a hand in farewell. Fist then finger flash: open-closed, open-closed. Kat watched Liv until she disappeared into the gloom of the kitchen, then called Tom.

'Remember Oldfield mentioned a boyfriend of Sally Robb's? Steven something?'

'Yes.'

'My informant confirmed it. So Steven's now a suspect. We've only got a first name and an old description but we're on to him, Tom. I'll call you tonight.'

Kat ended the call, feeling as if she'd just put down a heavy weight she'd been carrying for far too long. She pulled out of the farmyard, scattering squawking chickens before the BMW's front wheels.

A mile down the lane, she came up behind a tractor lumbering along the narrow road. Edged out into the middle. The gap was just wide enough. She flicked on the signal and jammed her foot down hard.

With a roar the BMW surged forward, rounding the tractor, which delivered a brutally loud blast from its air horn. Given what was going on around her, she thought she could manage the driver's disgust.

She called Ivan on hands-free and told him she'd be home in a few hours.

CHAPTER TWENTY-SEVEN

Kat pushed through the front door to be greeted by Ivan carrying two glasses of champagne. Adele's 'Make You Feel My Love' was playing in the background.

'What's all this in aid of?' she asked, as he ushered her into the kitchen.

'Riley's having a sleepover with Harry and Joe, so I thought we might have a nice night in,' he said.

The table was laid for two, with multiple sets of cutlery, and two candles, which Ivan now lit. The kitchen was suffused with the smell of Indian spices and frying onions.

'Are you cooking what I think you are?' she asked, smiling at him and then taking a sip of the champagne.

He grinned. 'We have vegetable pakoras to start, then beef madras, Kashmiri greens and mustard-seed rice.'

'And for pudding?'

'Fresh mango.'

'Our engagement-night dinner,' she said with a widening smile.

'I thought we could recreate it.'

She took another sip of the champagne, loving the way the bubbles intensified the hit of the alcohol on her empty stomach.

'*All* of it?'

'Well,' he said, enfolding her in his arms and kissing her lightly on the lips, 'as much as we can manage.'

'In that case, Mr Ballantyne, I'm going to take a shower. Give me five, then come upstairs,' she said, her voice thickening, suddenly wanting her husband of twelve years very much indeed.

Later, they sat opposite each other at the table, Ivan in striped cotton pyjama trousers, Kat in a teal silk slip. The food was delicious, but not, Kat reflected, as delicious as the hour she'd just spent in bed. Yes, they'd argued the other day about her working on Sundays, and the business with Luke Tockley and those damn WhatsApp photos of his sister. But they'd got through it, and that was what mattered.

Jack Beale's PS came back to her. *Mr Ballantyne is a lucky man.*

She frowned at the memory. What had she been thinking, flirting with him? In the autopsy suite for heaven's sake!

'What?' Ivan asked.

'Nothing. I'm just a very lucky woman, that's all.'

His expression changed. Clouds obscuring the sun. 'Look, Kat, about the other day. I was just frustrated that we're seeing less of you since your promotion. But I was out of order. I'm sorry for all those things I said. I love you.'

She reached over the dishes of curry and beckoned for his hand. She squeezed it tight.

'I love you, too.'

He grinned. 'Does that mean we can do it again after dinner?'

'I don't think I'll need to for at least a week after that one,' she said with a smile. 'Seriously, Van, I do love you so much. I mean, you have this great career, but you're here, so you've always looked after Riley, too.'

'It's how we work it, isn't it? And your folks have been fantastic. I don't think I could have coped otherwise. Especially when he was little.'

She didn't want to think about her parents. Not this evening.

'Do you think we did the right thing?'

'Letting them look after him, you mean?'

'No. You know, that WhatsApp business.'

'Yeah, I think we did. It put the fear of God into him, and I genuinely believe he didn't know the pictures were coming.'

She nodded and topped up their glasses. 'I suppose he's probably googling "boobs" by now anyway.'

'If that's all he's looking for, I'd be very surprised.'

'I suppose you and your mates were giggling over porn then, were you, at his age?'

'And you weren't?'

'We looked, of course we did,' she said. 'Jess stole one of her dad's magazines once. But it's different for girls, you know that. I just worry for him, Van.'

'I know you do. I do, too. But he's going to be fine,' Ivan said. 'We keep the comms channels open, don't we? Nothing's off limits.'

'You're right. It's been a hell of a week, that's all. It's a nasty case.'

'Have you got any leads?'

'Finally, I think we do.'

'You want to talk about it?'

'Not the details, but when I was with Liv she told me she'd lied about why she ran away.'

Ivan put his spoon down with a loud clink.

'She really dumped on you, you know that, right? I mean, how can she just waltz back into your life as if nothing happened? She faked her own death and left you behind to suffer. It's even why you do the job you do.'

'Don't you think I know that?' she asked gently.

He passed a hand over his eyes. 'Sorry, darling, of course I do. It's just, she's unreliable. I don't want her hurting you again.'

'She won't. We're different people now. I'm married, happily, and she's knitting her own bras on some commune in Wales.'

Ivan didn't smile. In truth she didn't think much of the gag herself. He sighed deeply.

'All this time, you've had your room upstairs. All those news-paper clippings, the photos. For nothing. She was alive the whole time.'

Kat nodded. Scooped the last hedgehog-spike of fragrant mango pulp into her mouth.

'I know. When the case is over, I'm taking it all down.'

◆ ◆ ◆

Kat woke early the next morning and was reading case documents when Ivan came down at eight to find her.

He kissed the back of her neck and put the kettle on.

'You working today?'

'At home, but yeah. We've got to start hunting down this sus-pect. It's the best lead we've got.'

Two hours later, she was striding through the centre of town with Smokey trotting along beside her. She'd called up all the herb-alism shops Leah had visited and decided to re-canvass those in the centre of Middlehampton.

She looked down at Smokey. Sensing his mistress's interest, he glanced up at her, lazy eye winking.

'Can't hurt to double-check, can it, Smokes?' she said.

The first three couldn't help her. They all seemed to sell hun-dreds of bottles of lavender oil. But the fourth shop she entered was different. Leah had only spoken to a part-timer, but Kat found herself talking to the owner. The woman did remember a customer who'd bought three kilos of wheat grains, saying he wanted to start making his own scented pillows to sell online. But Kat's hopes foundered on the rocks of her description.

A thirty-something man. Which could mean between twenty-five and forty-five in reality. Average height, average build. Clean-shaven, neat haircut. Oh, and the killer detail – he might have had a tattoo on one arm, or the other. Of a skull. Or maybe a girl made up to look like a skull.

Just as Kat was thanking her and leaving the shop, the woman called her back.

'Wait! There was one more thing. As he was leaving, a woman came in and said hello to him. She called him Steve.'

Three was the charm: Oldfield, Liv and now the retailer had all identified a man called Steve-slash-Steven.

As she walked home with Smokey, she wondered how many adult men registered as living within a Middlehampton postcode were called Steven, or Stephen.

By the end of the following day, as well as a thumping head-ache, she had her answer: 617, according to census data. Then there were those men who weren't on the electoral roll. Those who went by Steven, even though it wasn't their given name. And those who had changed their name by deed poll.

And a fifth category.

Men who told everyone their name was Steven when it wasn't. Because they were serial killers of the cunning kind, at the very least intelligent enough to realise using their own first name might be career-limiting. Would their Steven be a member of that group? She hoped not.

What could she do with the information? Release it to the media? Yes, because *that* would work. The producers of *Crimewatch* would be all over Kat, begging her to come on the show. *We're looking for an average-looking man calling himself Steven who lives in or around Middlehampton. Call* Crimestoppers *if you think you might know him.*

Never mind serial confessors, they'd have a tsunami of calls to field. Everyone from concerned citizens to vengeful ex-partners, mischief-makers to podcasters, all jamming the switchboard for months.

No. She needed a different strategy. Fast. Before any more girls were murdered.

CHAPTER TWENTY-EIGHT

Dispatch called Kat out at 9.23 p.m.

A woman foraging for wild mushrooms in Brearley Woods had seen a hooded man acting suspiciously. She'd shouted a warning and the stranger had taken to his heels. Fearing the worst, she'd approached the spot where the stranger had been squatting. When she saw what the stranger had been lingering over, she'd stumbled backwards, thrown up, then called 999.

Had she been more alert as the night wore on, she might have noticed the glint of the scene-lights reflecting off a camera lens in the trees beyond the cordon. A man dressed in dark clothing, his face smeared with black make-up, taking notes. Smiling to himself. Jogging away.

In fairness to Kat, she was focused entirely on the corpse of the young woman who lay on the ground in front of her. A single word raced around in her brain like a dog chasing its own tail.

Escalation.

It was in the textbooks. And now she was seeing it with her own eyes.

The girl's face was bruised. And there appeared to be a lot of blood on the back of her scalp, matting the short-cropped brown hair.

Her clothing was disturbed, too. Her miniskirt was pulled up her thighs to reveal pale pink knickers. He'd yanked her top down, snapping the spaghetti straps to reveal her bra with its folded paper heart. The bra was white cotton embroidered with tiny pink flowers, so achingly innocent that Kat had to wipe away tears.

A purse lay nearby. No cash, but a handful of credit cards. They had a name. Corinne Gregory.

◆ ◆ ◆

The next morning, back at Jubilee Place, she gathered her team around her. She pointed at the crime scene photos she'd just finished mounting on the whiteboard.

'Here's what we know. His name is Steven, or at least that's what he's calling himself. He's probably in his thirties. He's got some sort of charm. Enough to persuade young girls to go out with him in the middle of a panic about a serial killer,' she said. 'So far, he hasn't left DNA at the scene, but I've asked Darcy to lean on the forensics lab to fast-track our samples from last night. Any word on that, Darce?'

'They said they'll do what they can. But with all the cuts that could still mean a few days.'

'Keep the pressure on, OK?'

'There's one more thing. The samples Dr Feldman collected from under Courtney's nails. They got misfiled somewhere between MGH and here. But they finally turned up yesterday, and when I ran the basic tests, they were dirt, not blood.'

'Brilliant. What else have we got?'

The answer was as depressing as in all the other briefings she'd held: the square root of bugger all. After urging them all to keep looking – and if that failed, re-looking – she went to make herself a coffee. She came out of the kitchen to see Leah beckoning her over.

'What is it?'

'The big boss wants to see you in her office. She doesn't look happy.'

'Great. Do you think I should stick a book down the back of my trousers?'

'I'd go with *Blackstone's Crime*. Nice and thick.'

Dry-mouthed, Kat took her coffee along the corridor to Linda Ockenden's office. She knocked.

'Come!'

As she took in the other visitor, her heart sank. Detective Superintendent David Deerfield's nickname was 'The Undertaker', because he'd buried so many promising detectives' careers. With his lugubrious expression, dark, conservatively cut suit, snowy-white shirt and navy tie, he could easily have passed for a mortician.

'Good morning, sir,' she said.

'Take a seat, Kat,' Linda said. 'You know Detective Superintendent Deerfield.'

'Yes, ma'am.' She turned to Deerfield. To Kat, his long upper lip with its deep groove reminded her of some sort of hyper-intelligent rodent. 'By reputation, mostly.'

'As an assassin of detectives' aspirations, presumably.'

She shook her head. 'No, sir. Not at all. I mean as a brilliant SIO.'

Oh God, had she really just said that out loud? From his amused smile, it seemed she had.

'Let's get down to business, shall we?' Linda said. 'Before DS Ballantyne starts a David Deerfield fan club.'

Feeling a blush creeping over her cheeks and powerless to prevent it, Kat nodded. 'Of course, ma'am. You've heard the latest.'

'You mean the third Middlehampton girl this twisted bastard has choked to death with bloody aromatherapy supplies? Yes, that little snippet had crossed my transom.'

'I'm concerned to know what progress you've made, DS Ballantyne,' Deerfield said. 'I understand from Linda you're deputy

SIO. Brilliant or otherwise, that role calls for a certain level of control. *Are* you in control?'

'Yes, sir. I am,' Kat said, hearing the distant *clop-clop* of black horses walking ahead of a black, glass-sided hearse bearing a floral tribute: KAT'S CAREER. 'We have identified a suspect.'

'Really,' he said, turning to look at her face-on. 'Who?'

'His name's Steven. He's been seen buying large quantities of wheat grains in one of the health shops in town,' she said. 'Two witnesses have identified a man known to them as Steven who was going out with one of the original murder victims, Sally Robb, in 2008.'

'Does this Steven have a surname?' Linda asked.

'Not yet, ma'am. But I've identified six hundred and seventeen men over the age of eighteen in Middlehampton called Steven, with a "v" or a "ph".'

Linda snorted. 'I can cut that down by one for you. My husband's name is Steven, with a "v", and I'm fairly sure he's not a psychopath. Mind you, sometimes I feel like strangling him, but that's another story.'

'I'm starting operations to get them all TIE'ed,' Kat said, hoping Linda's dark humour meant all was not lost. 'On which subject, if I had more resources, it would really cut down the time it's going to take.'

She held her breath. It always came down to money. But to trace, interview and eliminate over six hundred people was going to be a bank-buster unless they wanted to spend years doing it.

'I think we should be able to manage that, Linda, don't you think?' Deerfield said, before turning to Kat. 'You may feel I'm breathing down your neck, DS Ballantyne, but I have ACC Crime Andrew Chilworth breathing down the back of mine. Oh, and our esteemed Police and Crime Commissioner, Elaine Forshaw, who – need I remind you? – is up for re-election this year.'

'Honestly, sir, I get it. And thank you.'

'Careful, DS Ballantyne, you haven't caught him yet. And you must. There's already speculation in the media that the Origami Killer's back. When they find out – which they will – that he's claimed a third victim, whatever heat you're feeling now will seem like a pleasant spring day. Middlehampton will be serial killer central.'

'I understand, sir.'

'Very well. I assume you have work to do.'

She nodded, and got to her feet. She knew a dismissal when she heard one. She also knew it was time to hold another press conference. The big one. The one where she finally got to tell the story the way it *ought* to be told.

CHAPTER TWENTY-NINE

Kat managed a fitful night's sleep, interrupted by several trips to the loo and a dream in which she couldn't find the press conference room, only to suddenly arrive, naked.

On the way in to work, she passed several outside broadcast vans bearing the familiar logos of Sky, ITV and the BBC.

The media room normally appeared overly roomy for the ten or so local hacks who turned up to briefings. This morning it was abuzz with excited chatter from the two dozen or more journalists currently sitting, standing and crouching in front of the Hertfordshire Police-branded table where Kat sat between Elaine Forshaw and Linda.

Kat was sweating from the glare of the TV lights, and her own hyperactive nervous system.

'Good morning, ladies and gentlemen,' Linda said, in a commanding voice that brought the room to an immediate stillness so complete Kat heard the vibration of somebody's mobile phone.

'I am Detective Chief Inspector Linda Ockenden and I'm the senior investigating officer on this case. To my right is Elaine Forshaw, the Police and Crime Commissioner for Hertfordshire. To my left is my deputy, and the case officer for this investigation, Detective Sergeant Kathryn Ballantyne.

'Mrs Forshaw and DS Ballantyne will give short statements, and then we'll open it up to questions. Please don't interrupt. You'll all get your turn.'

Miraculously, not a single journalist barked out a question. Kat felt renewed respect for her boss. Mind you, she thought anyone foolhardy enough to go against Linda's wishes might find themselves sent to wait outside her office on a hard chair.

Elaine Forshaw cleared her throat.

'Middlehampton is a good town. A hard-working town. A peaceful town. And yet we face the terrible fact that a monster walks among us. Worse still, a monster known to those of us with long-enough memories. And yet I say to the people of Middlehampton, be wary, yes. Be cautious, yes. Be alert, yes. But be afraid? No. We are bigger than him. We are better than him. And, in our police officers, led by DCI Ockenden and her deputy' – she turned briefly to Kat and nodded – 'we have a team of dedicated, determined and dogged detectives who, I am sure, will track him down and arrest him.'

A barrage of digital flashes sparkled blue-white in Kat's face. Blinking, she realised it was her turn to speak.

She stared out, trying to find a friendly face. But suddenly, all the journalists blended into one multi-headed creature, mobiles or digital recorders held aloft, furry grey boom mikes hovering overhead like the antennae of moths.

Her heart was racing, and she suddenly needed, very badly, to pee. Her mouth was dry, and she swallowed. Kat looked out at the rows of expectant faces, and froze.

At the back of the room, leaning against the wall with his arms folded, stood Stuart Carver, wearing a sober navy two-piece suit. He was looking straight at her, a smirk on his lips.

Beneath the table, Linda's knee nudged her own. Pulse pounding in her ears, Kat opened her mouth, unaware what she was going to say next.

'This man, this *monster*, as Mrs Forshaw rightly called him, has brutally murdered three young women,' Kat said.

She could hear her own voice as if it were coming from a separate person. Beneath the table she pinched the web of skin between her left thumb and forefinger hard, with her nails. The pain banished the floaty out-of-body experience. She cleared her throat. Felt in control again.

'I know you call him the Origami Killer, which is catchy. But he's not some sort of criminal mastermind. All he is, is a vicious murderer. The three girls whose families are now deep in their grief were called Courtney Hatch, Jade Root and Corinne Gregory. Please remember their names.

'Mrs Forshaw is right to say that the women of Middlehampton shouldn't live their lives in fear. But this man is dangerous. And he does choose victims who have certain physical characteristics. Therefore, I want to urge young women between the ages of seventeen and thirty to be extra-vigilant as they go about their daily lives. Especially if they have long brown hair and brown eyes.

'I would say to these young women, don't agree to meet men you've not met before. However charming, however nice they seem. Make sure somebody knows where you'll be if you have to go out on your own.

'And to members of the public in general: Courtney, Jade and Corinne were found in Brearley Woods. If you've used the area to walk your dog or go hiking, or birdwatching, or even if you were just passing through, please call Jubilee Place switchboard or Crimestoppers if you have noticed anyone acting suspiciously over the last two weeks.

'OK. I'm sure you have questions.'

Bedlam ensued as every single journalist shouted out at once. Freddie appeared at Kat's side and selected a female reporter in the middle row.

'Alexa Robinson, Sky News. DS Ballantyne, you said you're working on the assumption that this is the same man who murdered seven young women in 2008.' Kat noticed the reporter glancing at Carve-up. What the hell? Had he just nodded at her? 'Is it also true that his last victim was your best friend?'

To Kat it felt as though all the oxygen had just been sucked out of the room. Nobody moved. Nobody made a sound. If she tried to breathe in, would anything happen, or would she just choke? She heard a faint ringing in her ears.

She inhaled, and the ambient noises – the wall clock ticking, distant traffic noise from Crown Street, people coughing and clearing their throats – returned in a rush.

Where the hell had the journalist got hold of that fact? It had never been made public at the time. She realised in a flash. Carver's smirk had disappeared, but he was watching her closely.

But now she was faced with a dilemma. Agree with the assertion, and she was also agreeing that Liv was dead. A lie that then made her complicit in Liv's perverting the course of justice. Deny it, and she risked exposing herself and Liv to two very different kinds of investigation.

She made a decision. The lesser of two evils.

'It is, yes.'

'Well, don't you think that your relationship with one of the previous victims might be clouding your judgement? Are you even the right officer to be leading this investigation?'

Kat opened her mouth, but she couldn't think what to say. Carve-up and his pet reporter had stitched her up. Linda had warned him off when he'd first tried to have Kat removed from the case. Now he'd made a second attempt, using the Sky reporter as his proxy.

Before Kat could answer, Linda broke in.

'Thank you very much, everyone. That's it.'

She turned to Kat, ignoring the welter of questions raining down on them.

'Let's go.'

◆ ◆ ◆

Linda closed her office door. Kat slumped into a chair.

'I'm sorry, Linda. I just couldn't think how to answer.'

'Not your fault. In case you're thinking of taking what that bitch from Sky said to heart? You *are* the right officer to lead this investigation. If you weren't, guess what? You wouldn't be leading it.'

'Thanks.'

What she wanted to say was that her judgement couldn't be clouded because Liv wasn't one of the Origami Killer's victims. Great. So now she was lying to her SIO as well.

'Look, Kat, it's a game, right, with the media,' Linda said. 'They want a story, we want help with catching a killer. They give a little, we give a little less. Or we try to,' she added wryly. 'Any idea how she got that little titbit about your friend?'

'No.'

Yes.

After leaving Linda's office, she marched straight back to MCU, her anger deepening with every step.

'Everything OK, Kat?' Leah asked.

Kat barely heard her. Carried on in a straight line towards Carve-up's office.

The door was closed. She almost wrenched the handle off as she burst through. He looked up, wearing an unconvincing look of puzzlement.

'You bastard!' she shouted.

'What's the matter, Kat?' he asked with a smile.

224

'You leaked that detail to the woman from Sky to embarrass me. You probably suggested to her I was unfit to run the case, didn't you?'

He came out from behind his desk, hands held out wide.

'Now look, I know we haven't always seen eye to eye, but I would never—'

'Liar!' she shouted.

'Listen, *DS* Ballantyne. You just crossed a line. You do *not* accuse a senior officer of leaking and then call him a liar when he denies it.' He grabbed her by the right arm. 'Not ever!' he hissed into her face.

She didn't mean to hit him. That's what she told herself immediately afterwards, while he was tilting his head back and trying to avoid getting any more blood on his shirt front.

Tom rushed in. 'What the hell?'

'Bitch hit me,' Carver said nasally. 'You saw, right? Oh, you are so burned, Ballantyne.'

Kat looked at Tom, incredulous that, all of a sudden, she was in the wrong. Tom returned the look.

'Sorry, Stuart. I just heard shouting. I didn't see anything.'

'What?' Carver's eyes were wide above the scarlet-blotched handkerchief he was using to staunch the bleeding. 'You must have.'

'I didn't. Shall I get the first-aid kit?'

'Leave it. I'm going to see Linda.'

Carver staggered past Tom, giving Kat a hard shove with his shoulder on the way out of his office.

She looked at Tom.

'Did you really not see?'

He held her gaze. 'Must've had something in my eye. Come on, let's get you a glass of water. It might be worth getting some ice for that hand, too.'

If Kat thought swollen knuckles would be the only conse-quence of her altercation with Carver, the illusion didn't persist very long. Ten minutes later, she was sitting opposite Linda in her office.

Her hand was throbbing. But that was nothing compared to the painful thumping of her pulse in her throat. Dissipating anger, shame and anxiety combined to make her feel physically sick.

Linda sighed. 'Is it true, Kat? Did you assault DI Carver in his office just now?'

Kat nodded, fighting back tears.

'Why?'

She wanted to lay it all out for Linda there and then. How Liv had miraculously risen from the dead. How she'd only kept it secret so it wouldn't torpedo the live investigation. How Carver had leaked the detail about their friendship to the Sky journalist. How he'd provoked her. Asked for it.

That last phrase made her shudder. It sounded a little too close to the pathetic excuses abusers offered up in interview.

No! She was a good cop. Alive or dead, Liv made no difference to Kat's will to catch the Origami Killer. She'd build a case that wouldn't rely on Liv in any way. Liv just had to stay out of sight on her farm and all would be well.

Kat said none of that. Because an escape route presented itself.

'He grabbed me,' she said. 'I reacted instinctively. In self-defence.'

Linda narrowed her eyes. 'Grabbed you where?'

'My arm. Hard.'

'And that's the truth, is it?'

'Yes. I admit I shouted at him. I was frustrated at his constant efforts to undermine me, culminating in what I believed to be his leaking of a personal detail to the media. Then he took hold of me, and I reacted instinctively to defend myself.'

Linda offered a tight smile.

'Relax, Kat, you're not in the dock. Yet. So, what you're telling me is this: whilst in no way unfit to continue leading this investigation, nevertheless you unwisely let your emotions get the better of you. And, in the heat of the moment, after physical provocation from DI Carver' – she paused – 'you lamped him.'

'Yes.'

Linda clasped her hands on the desk.

'Stuart's all for having you charged with assault. Or at the very least investigated by Professional Standards.'

'They should investigate *him*,' Kat said.

'Look, Kat, I haven't forgotten our earlier conversation about Stuart. Leave him to me. I'll see he doesn't make a complaint.'

'Thanks, Linda, I really appreciate that. It won't happen again.'

'It better bloody not,' Linda said. 'I can't have my management team scrapping with each other when there's a bloody serial killer on the loose.'

Kat got up to go. 'I'll get straight back to it.'

Linda shook her head.

'No, you won't. Take a couple of days off. Get your head straight. Walk the dog, spend some time with your family,' she said, not unkindly. 'It's not a suspension. It's not even official. Call it my concern for your welfare.'

'But I can't!'

'Yes, you can. I need to give Stuart something to salve his wounded pride. I'll take a hands-on role for a day or so.'

'But—'

'Back here on Thursday morning, Kat.'

Kat shut her mouth. Her mother's advice on arguing with Riley over minor points came back to her. She had to pick her battles.

'Yes, boss.'

Linda nodded. 'Better. Although' – she paused – 'I suppose if you worked on it from home, I wouldn't know, let alone be able to stop you, would I?'

Kat collected her laptop and headed home.

◆ ◆ ◆

She'd just taken Ivan a coffee, surprising him with a kiss on the back of the neck as he was hunched over his own laptop, when her phone rang.

'Oh God, it's my mother,' she said.

He grinned. 'See you later, then. Give Sarah my love.'

She rolled her eyes.

'Hi, Mum,' she said, descending the stairs and heading back to the kitchen and her own mug of coffee. 'What do you want?'

'Can't I call my daughter without wanting something?'

'You can. You just never do.'

Her mum ignored Kat's barb, as she always did. She'd raised aloofness to an art form.

'I suppose you must be terribly busy with this awful murder thing, Kathryn,' she said. 'I saw you got your name in the paper. Just a pity it couldn't have been for something a little more . . .'

'More what, Mum?'

'Well, it's not very nice, is it? Paddling around in all that blood and whatnot,' she said. 'Look at Diana. She's in the paper, too, from time to time. But that's because she's opened a new office or taken on another accountant to help manage the clients.'

Kat's older sister was everything Kat was not, as far as her mother was concerned. Well groomed, in a starchy way, a white-collar professional, and, of course, a Conservative voter. Kat had never disclosed her political views to her mother, but it hadn't stopped Sarah Morton from reaching her own conclusions. If Kat was everything her sister wasn't, then it followed, logically, that she must be 'one of those awful socialists'.

In fact, Kat usually voted for the independent candidate, but she wasn't going to give her mother the satisfaction of knowing.

'Ah, yes, Diana's clients,' she said. 'I see one of them was up before the beak last month. What was it again? Oh, yes, I remember. Over-trading and VAT fraud.'

'That was nothing to do with Diana, darling. She was as shocked as everybody else.'

'Of course she was, Mum. You keep telling yourself that. And how's my baby brother? Still in the building trade?'

'As you well know, Nathan is a property developer, like your father. In fact, that's why I was ringing.'

'So you *do* want something.'

'Well, maybe,' she said coquettishly. 'Daddy has some rather exciting news he wants to share with you all. I don't suppose you might have an hour free this evening?'

Kat was about to cite the pressure of work – anything to avoid spending time with her family – when her conversation with Tom in the coffee shop last week came back to her. If her dad was trying to corrupt her new bagman, maybe she could use this opportunity to warn him off.

'Actually, yes. What time?'

'Oh, that's wonderful, darling. Say, eight?'

Her mother ended the call, explaining she needed to call her other two children now she had 'the difficult one' on board. Just like her to slip the knife in, even as she did something as supposedly innocent as arranging a family get-together.

CHAPTER THIRTY

At 8.05 p.m., Kat turned into Gadelands, a long, tree-lined private road widely considered to be Middlehampton's most prestigious address.

Her parents lived in the last house: a six-bedroomed mock-Tudor mansion in an acre and a half of land.

A gravelled drive looped around a grassy island, on which stood a full-sized, gilded reproduction of the statue of Eros in London's Piccadilly Circus. In front of a half-timbered wall groaning with wisteria were parked the rest of her family's cars. In matching black, her dad's Bentley and her mum's Range Rover; Diana's white Audi A5 convertible; and Nathan's scarlet Porsche 911.

She parked the Golf and got out, patting its dusty bonnet.

'Don't let the mean kids bully you,' she whispered with a smile.

Her shoes crunching on the gravel, she approached the front door, half intrigued, half dreading whatever news her father had to impart.

'Darling!' her mother cried as she opened the door, resplendent in a turquoise silk dress that shimmered in the light cast by the carriage lamp above the door.

She kissed Kat on both cheeks then thrust a glass of champagne into Kat's hand. 'We're all in the drawing room.'

'You look nice, Mum,' she said. 'New dress?'

Sarah kicked up her trailing foot like a 1920s flapper. 'Balenciaga. Daddy bought it for me last time we were in town.'

'Middlehampton or London?' Kat asked mischievously.

Sarah laughed; a tinkly sound like a chandelier being dusted. 'Cheeky! London, naturally. Bond Street.'

She led Kat into the huge sitting room. Kat picked her way between antique chairs, feeling her boot heels sinking into the thick pile of the Turkish rug. A Steinway grand piano gleamed in one corner, a piece of sheet music open on its stand. She ran a finger along the keys and plunked out a basic chord. Pulled a face.

'Your piano needs tuning,' she said.

Her mother ignored her. 'Here she is, everyone!'

Kat kissed her sister – suit, heels, perpetually pinched expression as if she were constipated – and brother – gelled hair, goatee, a teenager's spotty complexion still, despite his twenty-six years.

Neither embrace felt anything more than perfunctory. She kept a three-seater leather sofa between herself and her dad, who was standing by mullioned French doors that gave on to a striped lawn at least four times the size of the MCU main office.

Colin Morton turned towards his younger daughter and smiled. He was dressed less showily than his wife, but Kat knew his tastes. The white shirt, blue trousers and boat shoe combo appeared studiedly casual, but he'd have chosen each for its cachet as much as its fit.

'Hello, Kat,' he said with a smile. 'Glad you made it.' The *finally* was unspoken, but audible to everyone in the room.

'What's the big news then, Dad?' she asked.

'No need to dress it up with a big speech. Not when we're all family. You all know Nathan's made quite a decent showing for himself as a property developer. Like I told him when he left school, there are no free rides in the Morton family. But now, I've made him an offer he can't refuse,' he said, trying for, and missing, Marlon

231

Brando's garbled Italian-American accent from *The Godfather*. 'I'm buying him out and putting him on the board of Morton Land. So, raise your glasses to the new era in the Morton dynasty!'

Reflexively, Kat raised her glass, though she barely sipped the champagne.

Nathan fixed her with a triumphant look. She stared back, feeling like the wrong child had been saddled with the black-sheep label. Her prim and proper older sister kept the books for people Kat personally would cross the street to avoid, unless she was arresting them. And now her little brother was going into business with her dad.

She managed to stay for another twenty minutes, then touched her father on the elbow.

'I have to go. Can I have a quick word? In private?'

He took her into a wood-panelled room dominated by a mahogany desk with an inset red leather top. He closed the door behind him.

'What's on your mind, Kitty-Kat?'

'Don't call me that. You know I hate it.'

He frowned. 'It's a perfectly nice nickname. I always called you that.'

'Yes, you did. And I always hated it.'

He smiled magnanimously. 'As you wish.'

She tried to wrong-foot him with a change of subject. The reason she'd asked to speak to him in private.

'How was your golf game?'

His eyes twinkled. 'Which one? I play twice a week.'

'The one where your *friend* Stuart Carver brought my new bagman along.'

'Fine. Tom's a good lad. Rubbish golfer but nice enough for all that.'

'Why did you tell him to ask me about my name?'

'Come on, Kitty-Kat, I just wanted to make sure Tom knew the lie of the land, that's all. Can't your old man have a bit of fun?'

'Fun? Listen, Dad, I know how you operate. I've always known. Whatever you've got going on with Carver, that's your business. But leave Tom out of it.'

Colin furrowed his brow. 'I don't know what you mean. I haven't got anything "going on" with Stuart. Apart from playing golf, of course. And you'll forgive me, but I can't really dictate who Stuart brings along to make up the four.'

Kat sneered. 'Oh, and I suppose you didn't offer to do him a favour? What was it, a discount on a new flat? Help pay his mortgage?'

'You've got me all wrong, daughter-mine. You always have. I think it's those student politics of yours. Not that you were there long enough to really pick up any, but you know what I mean. You don't really trust the free market, do you?'

'Oh, I trust the free market, Dad,' she said, angered by his casual write-off of her brief time at university. 'It's *you* who doesn't. That's why you try to rig the game so Colin Morton always wins. There's nothing free about that.'

Maybe her jab struck home. Suddenly his good humour disappeared, like the wisp of vapour from the neck of the second bottle of champagne he'd opened.

'Listen,' he said, pushing his face towards hers. 'I run a legitimate business. Yes, I play golf with people who might be in a position to do me favours. But that's how the real world works. It's not illegal. It's called networking. That's all. If you think I'm dodgy, why don't you dob me in to your mates in the fraud squad or whatever it's called? Let them take a look at me. Because they'll be wasting their time, darling.'

Kat stood her ground, even though she was so close to him she could smell his subtle, spicy aftershave.

233

'You know why. I have to keep you separate from my professional life. If they ever do come calling, I want there to be an air-gap between me and you. Unless you've murdered someone, I'll keep out of your hair. And you' – she stuck a finger in his chest – 'keep out of mine. And my bagman's. OK?'

He held his hands up.

'Whatever you say, Kitty-Kat. Whatever you say.'

Feeling her rage boiling up like an unwatched soup pan, she left him there and strode back to her car, shouting a goodbye to the rest of her family from the front door.

At 3.30 p.m. the following day, while she was on the home stretch of a walk with Smokey, Tom called Kat. He sounded like he was in shock.

'He's done it again. DCI Ockenden wants you back pronto. I'm texting you a location.'

She reached the site in the woods where the Origami Killer had dumped – and that was absolutely the right word for it – his latest victim thirty minutes later.

Kat reeled back from the body. He was losing control.

Compared to the neat, almost formal way he'd posed Courtney, this girl had been flung aside like a rag doll. She lay across an ancient oak tree's web of gnarled, mossy surface roots. Her limbs were splayed at unnatural angles; they looked broken to Kat.

A purse lay nearby. She picked it up and opened it. No cash, but a handful of credit cards. She peered down at one: she had a name. Ruby Spence.

Still no overt sexual assault, but Kat was prey to a black fear at the edge of her perception. If she couldn't catch him soon, that would change. She recalled Detective Superintendent Deerfield's words about feeling the heat. It was like carrying her own personal Saharan sun with her everywhere she went.

The pressure from the media, she could handle. Even Stuart wasn't really a problem. He'd glare at her across MCU, but he was keeping out of her way. Whatever Linda had said to him had obviously sunk in.

No. The pressure came from within.

The original girls and the new victims formed a chilling chorus inside Kat's head.

Find him, they whispered. *For us. For the new girls. Find him.*

CHAPTER THIRTY-ONE

At the end of the day, she was standing in front of the murder wall in MCU. It was 7.45 p.m. and the building was virtually deserted.

She stared at the large-scale map of Middlehampton stuck to the wall, straining to understand the pattern she felt had to be there.

They'd plotted the home addresses and places of work of the originals, including Liv, and the new girls. Twenty-two coloured dots. Blue for the originals' homes, red for their workplaces. Green for the new girls' homes, orange for *their* workplaces.

Their homes were in different neighbourhoods but they formed a rough crescent that curved between the suburb of Hartsbury, in the north, to Sheepton, a village a couple of miles south-east of the town boundary. Nothing to suggest that the Origami Killer was locating them based on where they lived. Or where he did, for that matter.

No two girls worked for the same employer. The odd manager turned up in more than one place, but each was discounted. The wrong sex, the wrong age, newcomers to the town, alibied: throw an allegation their way and it slid off like a fried egg on a brand-new Teflon pan.

She traced the rough pentagon that linked the industrial estates and business parks where the girls had been working at the times of their deaths.

Springfields

Morton Fields Business Park

The Campus

Middlehampton Technology Park

Blackthorn Way Industrial Estate

This was the connection. It had to be. He was hunting them through their places of work. But how?

She squeezed her eyes closed against the tears of frustration that threatened to burst free.

'How, you sod?' she shouted.

Her voice bounced back off the whiteboard, reinforcing the feeling that she was alone in the world, not just MCU.

She looked up at the station clock on the wall, its red sweep-second hand smoothly wiping away each preceding, fruitless minute.

'Hell!'

She was supposed to be watching Riley's team play football. She'd been working hard at being around for him more, wanting to steer him away from bad influences like Luke Tockley. But their relationship still felt delicate, fragile: like a cracked porcelain vase glued together. She grabbed her things and ran downstairs.

Preferring to think of her drive from Jubilee Place to the sports-ground as determined rather than reckless, she arrived only ten minutes late.

Out of breath, she joined the other parents on the touchline. She saw Riley, making a run down the left wing before breaking off into a trot and turning to wait for a pass, hand aloft. He looked in her direction. She raised a hand in a half-wave. Had he seen her? The scowl suggested that he had, and he was angry she'd missed kick-off.

As the play continued, her thoughts returned to the dead girls. The players moved across her field of vision but it was like watching TV with the sound turned down. She saw their mouths working, calling for the ball, and she could see the ref raising the whistle to his lips. But the soundtrack was of muffled screams, whimpers, and finally, the rustle of a body tumbling down into a thick bed of dried leaves.

What were the commonalities between the girls? What did they all do?

Cheers erupted from the adults around her, mixed with the triumphant, cracking yells of eleven pubescent boys. Someone touched her elbow, making her jump.

It was Jess. 'Hi, Kat. Did you see? Riley just scored.'

Kat realised she'd drifted away from the match and reproached herself. She was supposed to be here for Riley. 'I was miles away.'

'Header from the far post off Alfie's chip.' Jess grinned. 'You can tell him you saw it now.'

'Thanks, mate. He'd never have forgiven me if I said I'd missed it.'

The match ended in a victory for the opposing team. After a post-match debrief, Riley trotted over with Alfie, Jess's son.

'Hey, Riley,' Jess said. 'Fab goal there.'

'Thanks.'

'You were great, Riley,' Kat said. 'Such a good header off Alfie's chip.'

He looked at her through narrowed eyes. She held her breath: had their little ruse worked, or could Riley tell she was parroting the line Jess had supplied. The moment passed. He smiled.

'It *was* good, wasn't it?'

'Epic,' she said, smiling over his head at Jess.

As the two boys trotted back to the car park, phones already out, Kat turned to Jess.

'You're a lifesaver!'

Kat had been thinking about heading back into work. But maybe the case could wait for a while longer. She really needed a break, however brief.

'Do you fancy a drink later?' she asked Jess.

'Why don't you come back to mine? I can give the boys pizza and we can have a drink without having to queue in the pub.'

'I'd love that. Hey, Riley! Pizza at Alfie's suit you?'

'Awesome,' he said, bumping fists with Alfie.

Kat smiled, pleased that Riley had at least one friend who wasn't rapping about 'hoes' on YouTube.

The boys wolfed down a whole pizza each, chased them with ice cream, then headed upstairs to Alfie's room.

Jess poured more wine, a delicious off-dry rosé. They clinked glasses.

Kat gestured at her friend's sleek bob. 'That looks amazing.'

Jess ran her fingers through silky auburn hair that swung back into place like a curtain. She smiled.

'Bit of an extravagance, actually, but I got a little pay rise this month. I went to Toni and Guy instead of my normal place.'

'It suits you.'

'Thanks. So how's your big case going. It's been a bit of a worry, actually.'

'Because of Erin, you mean?'

'Yeah. I mean, she's blonde and she's younger than those poor girls, from what the *Echo* said, but you still worry, don't you? I've told her she's not to meet anyone she doesn't already know and only to go out in a group. That's enough, isn't it? I mean, you can't ground them at their age, they just ignore you.'

Her eyes had filled with tears and she swiped them away with a finger.

'Hey, hey,' Kat said, patting Jess's shoulder. 'Erin'll be fine. What you said is exactly the right advice,' she said. 'Listen, I've been trying to think. Do you remember when we had that summer job at the packaging factory?'

'The one on Springfields? Of course. God, that was such a laugh.'

'What did we do?'

'Folded boxes as far as I can remember, why?'

'No, sorry. I mean, in our breaks. Before work, after, lunchtimes.'

Jess frowned and looked away towards the town.

'Well, we used to hang around outside smoking quite a lot. And we'd get lunch.'

'Was that all?'

Jess grinned. 'Well, we used to drool over the hunky delivery guys.'

Kat felt something, then, the stirrings of an idea.

'Go on.'

Eyes bright, Jess said, 'Do you remember Janelle Butler?'

Kat narrowed her eyes. Rummaged around in sixteen-year-old memories. 'I do! Dyed blonde hair, legs up to here, always wore those micro-mini skirts. The men on the line couldn't keep their eyes off her.'

'That's her. She got off with that guy, remember? The courier? He was at least ten years older than her. We called her a tart behind her back, but I think secretly we were jealous.'

Kat nodded. The idea that had been stirring began to solidify.

At 3 a.m. the following morning, after lying immobile for two hours beside Ivan – who was snoring, loudly – Kat climbed out of bed, got dressed and drove back into Jubilee Place.

She made herself a coffee and then went to sit in the incident room, alone, in the pool of yellow light cast by a dented and chipped Anglepoise lamp. For perhaps the first time since seeing Courtney Hatch's body, she felt optimistic.

Jess had given her the idea.

The killer – Steven, as he called himself – was meeting his victims *at* work, but not *in* work. She could imagine a colleague committing one murder, or even multiple murders at the same company. But the theory broke down when all the girls worked at different firms, on different industrial estates.

Steven was someone who turned up every week. Maybe every day. Someone everybody interacted with, but nobody noticed. The same way they did with the chair they sat on, the locker where they stored their personal stuff, or the office water cooler. He was just there. Part of the furniture.

He was a regular visitor to all of the dead girls' workplaces. So regular that he was invisible. Just another face among the hundreds that came and went during the day. Then, like the courier who'd charmed his way into Janelle Butler's knickers, he made his move.

He was average-looking. Maybe he was *good*-looking. But in a Jack Beale sort of way. Not unattainably handsome, but charming nonetheless. He wasn't abducting them. He was inviting them. He was asking them out. And they were agreeing, despite all the publicity.

She grabbed a pen and started scrawling up ideas.

Courier

Window cleaner

241

Delivery driver

Taxi

Stationery supplier

Refuse collector

Bus driver? Is there some sort of shuttle service?

Office cleaner

What else, what else?

'Come on,' she said. 'There have to be more.'

But her mind refused to yield further ideas. She threw the pen across the room. It hit the wall, leaving a slash of black. Sighing, she trudged over to retrieve it.

Her optimism, fanned into life by the caffeine coursing through her system, evaporated just as quickly. They were two weeks into the investigation and what did they have to show for it? Really? Nothing. Andy Ferris, Johnny Hayes and Karl Oldfield all had definite 'off' factors, but none looked good for the murders. Either *they* had alibis or *she* didn't have enough evidence to hold them. She made a note for Tom and Leah to re-interview all three men.

She yawned mightily, cracking her jaw. Maybe she could grab a quick twenty-minute kip and awake refreshed with the insight that would lead to the killer waiting for her.

She curled up on the dark grey corduroy sofa in the friendly interview room and closed her eyes. Sleep wouldn't come. She rolled over, trying to get comfortable, then, sighing, struggled into an upright position.

'You're not going to find him in here, now, are you?'

A woman was sitting opposite her, her right leg slung over the arm of the armchair. Kat knew she was Liv, even though her face was in shadow. She was tipping wheat grains from one hand into the other. The stench of lavender made Kat want to retch. She tried to rise but her elbows were pointing the wrong way. Slowly, sinuously, a serpent of fear shifted in the pit of her belly, paralysing her as it slithered upwards before settling in a cold coil around her throat.

She couldn't breathe. Her eyes widened as Liv walked over, still letting the wheat trickle through one fist but now into Kat's open mouth. She shook her head. Tried to shout, but only felt the tiny hard grains bounce and scuttle down her throat.

'No!'

Kat sat bolt upright. Sun was streaming through the window. Gasping, she held the neck of her shirt open. Heat and the humid stink of fear rose from her chest. Though she knew it was just the dream, she could still smell that cloying lavender scent. She went to the window, threw it wide, and leaned out to drag in deep lungfuls of fresh air.

Five minutes later, after she'd made some coffee and bought a bar of chocolate from a vending machine, she was sitting at her desk. It was 6.45 a.m. Silently, she spoke to the man whose victim Liv had pretended to be.

— *You've been at this a long time, haven't you?*

— *You know I have. Fifteen years minimum.*

— *Maybe longer.*

— *Maybe.*

— *You like to kill women.*

— *Liking doesn't come into it. I* have *to.*

— *Did they all look like Courtney? Like Liv?*

— *They did. It's my type.*

– You're a psychopath. What if you're lying?

– What if I am?

– Then there'll be others who don't fit the victim profile.

As she supplied the last answer, she opened her eyes. Sent an email to Tom, then hurried out. She needed a shower and a change of clothes. And she had the basis of a new theory that needed working out while she drove.

CHAPTER THIRTY-TWO

By the time people began drifting into MCU, Kat was sitting cross-legged on the floor of the big conference room.

Around her, the files of every unsolved stranger-murder of females older than sixteen that had occurred within twenty miles of Middlehampton since 2005. A total of thirty-two. Twenty-seven of the victims were white. Three were mixed-race. Two were Black. Not wanting to add unnecessary bias into her work, she'd sorted the victims alphabetically.

Tom popped his head round the door. 'Morning. Coffee?'

Kat looked up from the file she was reading. Ginnie Fasuba was a Nigerian office cleaner. Her partially burnt body had been found by a couple of meth addicts in the Meadows, the glass-strewn park at the centre of the Vale, a rough neighbourhood on the south side of Middlehampton.

'Please,' she said, holding up her mug. 'Did you get my email?'

'Sorry, haven't logged in yet.'

'I want you and Leah to re-interview Andy Ferris, Johnny Hayes and Karl Oldfield. Not under caution, just a friendly chat.'

'What if they're not feeling friendly?'

She looked at him levelly. 'Tell them the alternative is arrest on suspicion of murder.'

When he returned with her coffee, she'd closed Ginnie Fasuba's file and picked up the next. *Pulford, Candace J.* – aka Kandy aka Bobbi aka Mitzi.

Candace had worked at one of the factories on the Springfields industrial estate through the early 2000s. That was a point of commonality with Courtney Hatch. She'd supplemented her wages with occasional sex work and had several arrests for loitering for the purposes of prostitution, the earliest when she was sixteen. Her battered body had been discovered at the back of the factory.

She'd been strangled, some of her hair pulled out by the roots. No sexual assault, but the pathologist had commented that the degree of violence was severe. He'd speculated, 'though I am aware it is outside my remit', that the perpetrator had entertained 'a peculiar degree of hatred for the victim'.

Kat looked at the arrest photo. She sat back and held it up in front of her eyes.

'My God!' she murmured.

The woman staring out of the glossy paper at her could have been Liv. Or, at least, Liv with a decade's hard living behind her and possibly some sort of habit to keep her demons at bay.

Dark brown hair, held back in a ponytail. A rounded face. A hint of defiance behind the dark eyes.

Not just Liv, either. The originals and the new girls. Was this the Origami Killer's first victim? Why was she older, though?

She read on, hunched over the documents that constituted Candace Pulford's relationship with the criminal justice system, first as an offender, then as a victim. She'd been thirty-four when she was murdered in 2006. So born in 1972.

According to the report from Social Services, she'd had a child in 1988, when she was sixteen. A son. Stefan. No father named on the birth certificate. Child looked after well, despite her occasionally chaotic lifestyle and problems with drugs and alcohol. No concerns for his welfare. *No concerns?* Kat shook her head. Wow.

Kat wiped a hand across her mouth. Was this it? The break in the case? Not a forensic break, but the other kind. The kind of break that all cops hoped for. Luck. The luck you generated for yourself by coming into work at three in the morning and wrestling a problem into submission?

Stefan/Steven. A boy ashamed of his mother's occupation, who could easily have tweaked his given name.

Wait . . . How old had he been in 2006? Eighteen. Had his first victim been his own *mother*? It made a horrible kind of sense. He'd killed her, then, unsatisfied, kept returning to the act, each time selecting a girl who resembled his original victim.

She went to the door and looked around for Tom or Leah. Then cursed herself. She'd sent them off to re-interview Ferris, Hayes and Oldfield. One of the civilian investigators, a retired DI from Thames Valley, was at her desk.

'Rosie, could I see you in here for a minute, please?'

Kat showed her the file.

'I need you to find Stefan, aka Steven, Pulford.'

'Person of interest?'

'Suspect.'

Kat ran across MCU and knocked on Linda's door.

'Come!'

Kat went in and closed the door behind her. Linda looked up.

'Bloody hell, have you been nicking speed from Evidence?'

'Sorry Ma-Linda,' Kat said, swallowing and taking a deep breath. 'I think I've found him.'

Linda leaned forwards. 'Sit down, breathe, then tell me everything. Who he is, what you need, yes?'

'Yes,' Kat said, sitting down and wiping her palms on her trousers. 'His name's Stefan Pulford, but we know he goes by Steven now and his mum was a part-time prossy. Sorry, I mean—'

'Sex worker, yes. I know the terminology, Kat. Get on with it, but for Pete's sake slow down or you'll give me a heart attack.'

'Right. Yes. So, back in 2006, this woman called Candace Pulford was found murdered. Strangled, beaten, clumps of hair torn out. She's a dead ringer ... sorry ...' Linda glared at her. Kat smiled nervously. 'She looks just like the other victims.'

'What are you saying, she was his first?'

Kat nodded excitedly. 'I think he killed his mother, and that's what gave him the taste for it. It set the pattern.'

Linda made a note. 'We need another press conference. Today, if possible. Get Freddie on to it. I'll lead but you make the appeal, yes? Anybody knows this man, utmost importance, extremely dangerous, blah blah blah.'

'I've put Rosie Gifford on to locating him.'

'Are you cross-referencing him with the list of Stevens you created?'

'About to.'

'Good. Anything else?'

'Not right now. But when we find him, we should have a firearms team on standby. He's a strangler not a shooter but, given how many he's killed, we've got to regard him as a deadly threat.'

'Agreed. Get on to that, then. I'll take care of the budget.'

Kat left Linda making calls and, at her desk, started on her own list of actions, beginning with the firearms squad commander.

By the end of the day, her initial excitement had damped down into something more familiar, and more dispiriting. The sense of a lead fizzling out like a wet firework.

She met Tom and Leah at 6 p.m., briefing them on her research into Candace Pulford and the search for Steven.

'How'd you get on with Ferris, Hayes and Oldfield?'

'We got nowhere,' Tom said.

'Not *nowhere*, nowhere,' Leah chipped in. 'Andy Ferris finally admitted to having a spy-cam in the ladies at CooperTech. We handed him off to CID.'

'Nice one. That's one less perv we have to worry about. But what about *our* man?'

'It was the same with the other two,' Tom said. 'They just gave us the same answers as before. And I know we're not supposed to go with our guts, like Dr Feldman said, but I honestly didn't get a bad feeling off either of them. You didn't either, did you, Leah?'

Leah shook her head. 'Hayes is a smug so-and-so but he's not a serial killer. And Oldfield just needs a good shag, if you ask me.'

Kat smiled. 'Trust you, Leah.'

'What?' Leah exclaimed, eyes wide. 'I'm just saying he's lonely, that's all.'

'He did seem very interested in your chest,' Tom said, grinning.

'All right, you two, let's keep some focus here. So those three are in the clear?'

'Yes,' they chorused.

'So what now?' Tom asked.

'This all started at Springfields,' Kat said. 'That's where his mum was murdered. And it's where he found Courtney Hatch. Leah, I want you to work with Rosie on tracking down Steven Pulford – I suspect he's not using his own surname. Tom, you're coming with me tomorrow.'

'To do what?'

'A stakeout.'

'Sounds exciting.'

Kat caught Leah's eye. A look passed between them.

'Yeah,' Kat said. 'It does, doesn't it? Right, I need to see my family and I really need a good night's sleep. You two finish up and get home, too. There's plenty of people working on this now, so don't feel you have to be here all night. It's not healthy.'

Tom left at once, though Leah lingered behind. She pulled something out of her pocket and held it out.

'I found these in the friendly interview room between the sofa cushions.'

Kat looked down. Leah was holding out Kat's house keys on their distinctive fob with the laminated picture of her, Ivan, Riley and Smokey. Kat took them gratefully.

'Thanks, mate.'

'Not healthy, eh? Maybe you should practise what you preach,' she said with a smile.

Kat sighed. 'I know, but—'

'We'll get him, Kat.'

'Yeah, we will,' Kat said, nodding her agreement. Wishing she could believe herself.

CHAPTER THIRTY-THREE

Tom beside her, Kat pulled out of the Jubilee Place car park at 6.30 a.m. the following morning.

For cross-country blue-light runs, Kat preferred the maroon BMW with its leather seats and powerful engine. For this operation, she wanted something lower key. They didn't get much lower than the dirty grey, high-mileage surveillance transit van in which she and Tom rattled through the early-morning traffic. The footwells were awash with fast-food cartons, crushed cardboard takeaway cups and sweet wrappers. It smelled of sweat, farts and frustration. She wrinkled her nose.

'Still think it's exciting, Tom?'

'If we catch the Origami Killer, yes, definitely.'

'Let's keep our fingers crossed, then. I'd hate to disappoint you.'

'Where are we going?'

'Springfields, assuming this pile of junk makes it that far.'

'Any special reason?'

'I think what you *meant* to say was, "Can you explain your tactical reasoning, boss, as I am as keen to learn today as I was when I first rocked up in Middlehampton with the ink still wet on my degree certificate."'

He laughed. 'Yeah. That's exactly what I meant to say.'

'Springfields was where Candace Pulford worked. Also where her body was found. It was also, as we know, where the first of the new girls worked. I had a summer job up there. There's something about the symmetry that intrigues me,' she said, signalling to enter Springfields. 'Rosie Gifford's trying to trace Steven via the databases, but he might have changed his name, so this is about as old-school as it gets.'

She pulled up on one side of the central area, around which the factories and industrial units clustered. An island in the centre was planted with the sort of stiff-leaved, vaguely Mediterranean plants the council seemed to love. Drought- and pollution-tolerant, Kat supposed. Low-maintenance, too.

'Now what?' Tom asked.

'Now we sit here and make a note of every single vehicle that arrives that isn't a private car. Buses, minicabs, delivery drivers, couriers, whatever. I've got teams at the other four places the girls worked and we're going to tabulate and cross-check our results. Anyone who turns up at all five is a person of interest.'

By 10.45 a.m. Tom had recorded thirty-seven vehicles coming and going from Springfields. The majority were couriers or goods vehicles delivering supplies or being loaded with pallets. Five had been driven by women. Kat instructed him to mark those entries in his log with a 'W'.

'It probably won't be them.'

At 11.05 a.m., a raucous blare of 'La Cucaracha' played on discordant air horns.

Kat had only been half-awake, and snapped upright. 'What the hell is that?'

'Snack van,' Tom said. 'Looks like the one at the station.'

He sounded bored. So much for the exciting world of stake-outs. The high hadn't even lasted until coffee time.

'Want one?'

'Yes, please. A latte . . . with an extra shot, if he can do that?'

252

'Okaaay. That might translate into an extra spoonful of instant, but I'll ask,' Kat said, straightening up and grimacing as her hip joint cracked. 'Anything to eat?'

'Could you run to a Kit Kat?'

She smiled. 'I think we could probably manage that.'

She climbed out and went over to join the queue.

Behind her, she heard a distant shout. A man's voice. Calling her name. He sounded edgy, aggressive even. She spun round, almost bumping into a girl standing behind her, head bent over her phone.

'Hey!'

'Sorry.'

The man shouted again. Kat's pulse picked up. She touched the back of her waistband, but the extendo was in the van.

Then she groaned. The overweight figure puffing towards her with a messenger bag slung over one shoulder was Ethan Metcalfe.

She stepped out of the queue.

'Why are you ignoring me?' he demanded. 'I have vital intelligence on the case.'

'I'm not ignoring you, Ethan. I've just been in the middle of an extensive and very high-pressure investigation.'

His face was pale, and he kept biting at his lower lip. His hands were opening and closing convulsively.

'Actually, you *are* ignoring me,' he said prissily. 'I have left seventeen phone messages with reception and sent thirty-three emails. I haven't received a reply to any of them.'

'We're getting a lot of emails from the public, Ethan,' she said, pulse picking up a little. 'Thousands. And hundreds of calls, too. It's nothing personal.'

'But, Kat, we were at school together. You know me,' he said, his voice taking on a whiny tone. 'I'm not just "the public", I have a podcast: *Home Counties Homicide*. I've investigated every murder in Middlehampton since 2000.'

253

'No, Ethan, you really haven't,' she said, impatient to be shot of him now and cross she'd had to give up her place in the queue. 'You've basically just read out Wikipedia pages to . . . How many listeners do you actually have, anyway?'

He stared at her defiantly. 'It's not about how many, Kat. It's about the depth of involvement. My listeners are deeply engaged with my show. They'll want to know why MCU in general, and you in particular, is spurning my offer of assistance.'

She shook her head. This was ridiculous. She was trying to track and arrest a serial killer and Ethan was just wasting her time, trying to get a foot in the door of her investigation. Her thoughts juddered like a train crossing a set of points. He was trying to *insert* himself into her investigation.

She took a half-step back.

'Is that a threat, Ethan?' she asked, sounding calmer than she felt.

'No, it's not a threat. But you have to understand something, Kat,' he said, taking a step towards her. 'I know how serial killers think. I know how *this* serial killer thinks. I could be of real value to you.'

Kat took a breath. Trying to think. Two instincts fought for primacy inside her. To put as much distance between her and Ethan as possible, and to stay close with him until she could twist his arm up behind his back and arrest him.

'I don't think you could,' she said. 'Now, I need a coffee, so I'm going to ask you, please, to back up a little. You're making me uncomfortable.'

'*I'm* making *you* uncomfortable?' he shouted, making the other people in the queue turn to see who was losing it. 'How do you think you're making *me* feel? I just want to help you!'

With that, he grabbed her by both shoulders and pushed his face into hers.

'You knew I fancied you at school and you just laughed at me,' he moaned. 'And you're still laughing at me behind my back, even now.'

She was too shocked to move, and found, in any case, that she was held fast in a surprisingly strong grip. Ethan's breath smelled of bad teeth and cigarettes.

Then the guy from the sandwich van was behind Ethan.

'Let her go, arsehole!' he yelled, before breaking Ethan's grip, spinning him round and landing a solid punch on the point of his chin.

Ethan toppled sideways, collapsing into the girl who'd taken Kat's place in the queue. She screamed and jumped back, so that Ethan's head smacked into the concrete.

Tom arrived, out of breath, just as Kat was sending the sandwich guy back inside his van.

'But I should stay here to keep an eye on that loser,' he protested.

'Thank you, but I'm fine. Really,' she said.

'Kat, are you OK?' Tom asked. 'I was watching him, just keeping an eye, then he just went for you. I'm sorry.'

She smiled, though she was shaking. 'I'm fine, Tom, really. Call an ambulance and go with him to MGH. Get him checked out. He might have a concussion.'

'Then arrest him?'

She considered it.

'Yes. Assaulting a police officer.' She drew Tom aside. 'Just hold him for a couple of hours. Give him a good scare and a better talking-to, then let him go.'

'But, Kat . . .'

'He's harmless.'

'He grabbed you. That didn't look harmless to me.'

'Tom! I'm fine, OK? I'm fine. Ethan's a sad little man looking for some excitement. Just make him understand he's not going to get it pestering the police. If it happens again, we'll charge him with wasting police time. Tell him to stick to his podcast.'

'You're sure?'

'Yes, I'm sure. I'm also the boss. Do it, please.'

She looked down. Ethan was leaning on his elbows, looking dazed. A bruise was already forming on his jaw.

'What happened?' he asked.

'I'll explain in the ambulance,' Tom said, getting him to his feet and walking him off to a nearby bench. 'Ethan Metcalfe, I'm arresting you . . .'

'Are you all right?' the girl in front asked Kat.

'Occupational hazard,' Kat said with a wry grin.

'You're the one after the Origami Killer, aren't you?'

'One of them, yes.'

The girl smiled, revealing transparent braces on teeth that looked perfectly straight to Kat. 'Yeah, but, like, you're the main one, aren't you? I saw you on the telly the other night.'

Kat nodded. 'Guilty as charged.'

The girl snickered. 'Funny.' Then her face fell. 'But, you are going to get him, right? I mean before he kills any more?'

'We're doing our best, yes.'

'I wish we still had the death penalty.'

Kat kept her opinions on that score to herself. She nudged her. 'Your turn.'

'Oh, right.' The girl turned and bought a sandwich, a cold drink and a banana.

Kat recognised the coffee guy who'd laid Ethan out. Tom had spotted it first: he did the breakfast run at Jubilee Place. He even had a poster stuck up on the side of the serving hatch. Photos of the dead girls with a headline: *Can you help find their killer?* Then an instruction to call Kat, and the main switchboard number at Jubilee Place.

'Good luck,' the girl said, as she walked over to a bench among the sword-leaved plants on the central island.

Kat smiled at the coffee guy. 'Thanks for that,' she said. 'You're a star.'

'Can't have some weirdo assaulting my customers, can I? Especially not a regular.' He frowned. 'I won't get into trouble, will I? You know, for punching him? If he makes a complaint, I mean?'

'No. You acted proportionately to prevent a crime, i.e. an assault on a police officer. If you do get any blowback, come to Jubilee Place and ask for DS Ballantyne. I'll sort it for you.'

He puffed out a breath. 'Thanks. I didn't know your surname before, just Kat. What can I get you?'

'A latte with an extra shot, an Americano, no milk, and two Kit Kats, please.'

'Sure.'

He turned away to prepare the coffees. A siren wailed and blue lights flickered off the windows of the industrial unit behind her. She watched as two green-uniformed paramedics climbed out of the ambulance and went over to where Tom and Ethan were sitting.

'Here we go,' the coffee guy said with a smile, putting two takeaway cups on the counter.

'How much?' she asked, reaching into her pocket.

'On the house.'

'There's no need.'

'Please. After what just happened, you know . . .' He seemed almost embarrassed to have been caught out in an act of generosity. Then his eyes widened. 'Oh! I forgot the Kit Kats.'

He stretched out a hand for a box to one side of the window, picked out two of the chocolate bars and placed them on the counter beside the coffees.

Something fell out of his cuff and landed on the counter. A pip? Kat followed its skittering progress as it spun towards her.

No. Not a pip. A cereal grain.

A wheat grain.

CHAPTER THIRTY-FOUR

Trying to appear nonchalant, despite her skittering pulse, Kat reached for it. But he tutted and swept it back inside the van, on to the floor.

Heart racing, she managed to thank him for the coffees, then gathered them up along with the Kit Kats. He pointed at the poster.

'Not sure it'll help, but you have to do your bit, don't you? I mean, if you don't catch him soon, he might just leave the country or something.'

She mumbled a response then turned, intending to tell Tom to leave Ethan with the paramedics, only to see the ambulance pulling away.

Still clutching the coffees and Kit Kats, she walked, on legs that were suddenly trembling from hip to ankle, back towards the van. She passed the girl who'd chatted to her.

'What do you think of him?' the girl asked her with a grin.

'Who?'

'The coffee guy! He's fit, isn't he?'

'He's very—'

'All the girls at my work like Sandwich Steve. Steve the Stud, that's what we call him. He's been out with at least three of us.'

'OK. Excuse me. I have to go.'

Kat strode back to the surveillance van, dropping the coffees into a bin on the way.

Inside, heart pounding, eyes fixed on the sandwich van, she considered her options. Could she make an arrest? What evidence did she have? She didn't want to go too early and then have to release him immediately.

She phoned Linda Ockenden. That was what SIOs were for, after all.

'Make it quick. I'm just going into a meeting.'

'I've found him! I've found the Origami Killer, I'm looking straight at him,' she gabbled.

'Slow down. Say again?'

Kat took a breath. 'I'm sitting in a surveillance van at Springfields industrial estate. I have eyes on the suspect. I want to arrest him.'

'What have you got on him?'

'The name for a start. It's Steve.'

'So is my husband's, as I think I mentioned. And at least 616 other men in Middlehampton. What else?'

'He drives a sandwich van and he calls at Courtney Hatch's workplace.'

'Does he call at the others?'

'I don't know yet. But he fits the description we've got.'

'He's average, you mean. Average height, average build, average looks. You do know what "average" means, don't you, Kat? I can't let you arrest some random Mr Average because he sits in that particular demographic, can I?'

'He's got a poster of the dead girls, asking people to call me if they know anything. It's a classic tell.'

'Or just someone who genuinely wants to help you.'

'I see where you're coming from, but that's not the best bit.'

'What is?'

'A grain of wheat just fell out of his sleeve.'

'That's better. Does it smell of lavender?'

'I don't know.'

'Sniff it, then! I take it your detection skills extend to identifying the scent of lavender.'

'I can't.'

'Why? Have you got hay fever or something?'

'I couldn't pick it up.'

The silence on the other end stretched out to five seconds.

'Where is it, then?'

'On the floor of his van.'

'Right. And you're sure it was wheat? This little grain that you don't actually have.'

'Yes!'

'How sure? Could it have been barley? Or oats? Was it a toast crumb? A Rice Krispie?'

'I'm sure it was wheat.'

'No, Kat. You *want* it to be wheat,' Linda said. 'You haven't got anything that gets us anywhere *near* the threshold for an arrest. We'd have his solicitor advising him to sue us for wrongful arrest before you'd even booked him in. Then he's away on his toes, and if he is our man, he goes into hiding and we've got a full-scale nation-bloody-wide manhunt on our hands.'

'Then let me go after him. Give me a search warrant. I'll get the grain and then we'll have him.'

'That's your plan, is it? You know what his lawyer would say? "My client makes wholemeal bread sandwiches for his clients. This grain – if it even *is* a grain – probably just fell off a slice of bread." No, Kat. No warrant,' Linda said. 'Find another way to catch him if you think he's your guy. But no searching, no flimsy arrests. There's too much riding on this. That meeting I just mentioned? It's with the Undertaker, the mayor and the bloody ACC Crime. I want this done by the book. In fact, I want the book to look like sloppy policework compared to how you're going to do things. Understood?'

'Yes, ma'am.'

The line went dead. Linda hadn't even bothered correcting Kat's use of her honorific.

As she jammed the key in the ignition with trembling fingers, the sandwich van's own engine fired up. She twisted the key. The engine turned over with a rattly wheeze but refused to catch.

'You are *joking*! Seriously?'

The sandwich van passed her on its way out.

She tried again. It sounded as if someone had emptied a bag of ironmongery into a tumble dryer.

Again.

The nails, screws, nuts and bolts came to a stop in the bottom of the drum. Silence followed.

She picked up her phone to call it in, then hesitated. As Linda had said, she really didn't have enough evidence to arrest Steven. Yet. She resolved to go it alone for now.

By the time she got the ancient engine to catch, it was too late for a pursuit. But not too late to track him. It took most of the rest of the day, but using ANPR cameras and CCTV, Kat traced the white van from Springfields all the way back to the Saint Mark's area of Middlehampton. Saint Mark's was an older neighbourhood, mainly occupied by families who could trace their roots in the town back generations. A smattering of newer immigrants from eastern Europe and a few asylum-seekers gave the area a more diverse feel than its determinedly bourgeois neighbour, Northbridge, or the rougher but less diverse neighbourhood of Grove Park.

She lost him when he turned off the main road into a quiet residential street called Canada Road. It was enough. She drove straight over, parked a couple of streets away and walked to Canada Road. The sandwich van was parked halfway along.

She called Rosie Gifford.

'Hey, Rosie, have you got an address for Steven Pulford yet?'

'There are three possibilities – a few differences in spellings and initials. Just trying to narrow it down.'

'Have you got one on Canada Road?'

'Yes. Number 31.'

'OK, that's it. I've got him. Talk later.'

On the drive back to Jubilee Place, she debated whether she could – or should – rope Tom into her plan. Decided against it. She still wasn't entirely sure where his loyalties lay. Yes, he'd got her off the hook after she'd punched Carve-up. But he'd also gone off to play golf with him and her dad.

Fine. So it would be down to her favourite three coppers: *me, myself and I.*

CHAPTER THIRTY-FIVE

At 1 a.m., Kat slipped out of bed and got dressed in the dark. Black jeans, black T-shirt, black trainers.

Ivan stirred.

'You get a call?' he mumbled.

'Yeah. Go back to sleep. I love you,' she whispered, bending to place a kiss on his forehead.

'Love you, too.'

She could hear his snores as she left the house, clutching her car keys tightly to stop them jingling.

The air outside was still warm. But she shrugged on a black puffer jacket just the same. She'd pushed a folded navy-blue base-ball cap into one of the pockets.

She drove carefully, never breaking the speed limit, from Stocks Green, round the ring road, then cutting in down London Road towards Saint Mark's. Apart from a couple of night buses, and the odd minicab, the roads were quiet.

One of the advantages of being a police officer was that you knew where the CCTV cameras were. Avoiding them all, she made her way along back streets, taking little-known cut-throughs, until she reached the end of Canada Road at 1.27 a.m.

She parked one street over, on Australia Road, and climbed out. Pulled the cap free of her pocket and settled it low over her eyes.

Hands in pockets, head down, she knew she looked suspicious, but being unidentifiable was more important. She walked the length of the road, keeping to the centre where, hopefully, doorbell cams wouldn't pick her up. She turned left into Kenya Road and then left again into Canada Road.

'Sandwich Steve' had parked his plain white van right outside his house. She approached it cautiously, passing on the other side of the road, and looked up at the first-floor windows. None showed so much as a chink of light, and she was grateful for the sober habits of the street's residents.

She crossed to the van at its rear. A sticker on the left-hand door read, in a wonky font, *No sandwiches left in this van overnight!* She hoped the same didn't apply to wheat grains. From her puffer's left pocket, she took out a set of lock picks. Ten seconds later, she was pulling the door open and slipping inside.

With the door relocked and the torch's beam part-shielded by her fist, she checked every corner. The interior of the van had been fitted out with stainless-steel cabinets, a fridge, a coffee machine, a two-ring burner, a microwave and a sink. She was amazed at how much kit he'd managed to cram in.

A machine-turned partition at the front of the compartment divided off the kitchen area from the front seat. No light could escape. She adjusted her grip on the torch and doubled the amount of light.

Everything was spotless. Steven might be a serial killer, but he obviously didn't want any trouble with Middlehampton Council's food-safety inspectors. Jack Beale's autopsy suite wasn't any cleaner.

She frowned in irritation. Why was she thinking about Jack Beale now? She was in the middle of a borderline illegal search, not lying in bed, enjoying a little pre-sleep fantasy.

She got down on to her hands and knees and started a methodical sweep of the floor, shining the torch under the units, around their locked-off rubber casters and behind square-section legs bolted to the steel plating. Plenty of dust. A tiny triangle of shiny red plastic that might have come from a sachet of tomato ketchup. But as for cereal grains, wheat or otherwise, not a sign.

Trying to stay calm, she crawled towards the partition, working up the left-hand side and down the right. Beneath the sink, pipes sheathed in braided steel mesh disappeared through holes in the floor. With a surge of anxiety she saw that the holes weren't perfect. At least one had enough space for a wheat grain to fall through.

Whatever lay beneath – a sump, the chassis, metal channels – she knew she'd never be able to find it down there. Not without some serious cutting equipment. And she wouldn't be allowed anywhere near a set of Jaws of Life without a seizure warrant.

She flicked the torch back towards the front of the van and her heart caught in her mouth. There it was! A white oval lying in the shadow where a rubber caster met the shining steel floor.

She lay on her belly and stretched out her hand. Managed to get the tip of her index finger on it and slid it towards her. Something changed in the texture under her fingertip; it seemed to soften. She dragged it closer then looked at whatever was sticking to the end of her finger. It was a grain of cooked rice.

She sighed. Maybe Steve hadn't swept the wheat grain to the floor at all. It might have lodged between two units or bounced into the sink.

Flicking the rice off, she got to her feet, cracking her head against the extractor hood over the gas burners. The clang inside the hard-surfaced box was loud. Her heart stuttered in her chest. Had it been audible outside? Of course it had! She had to work fast.

The sink was clean. If the grain had gone down the plughole, she'd need a wrench to undo the trap. Forget it. Where else? The units were butted tight up against each other. The gaps were all too narrow, maybe half a millimetre at most.

'Come on, come on,' she murmured, urging herself on, ignoring the fear turning her guts to water.

She heard a front door open and then slam shut. Christ! It was him. He was coming back to the van!

A man's voice called out. A voice she recognised.

'Hello? Who's there? If you're looking for cash like last time, you can forget it. It's safe and sound where you'll never get it, you little sods!'

She held her breath. Got down on to her belly and squeezed herself in behind the fridge. If he came in through the rear doors, there was a chance he'd miss her.

Footsteps approached the van. Her stomach flipped. Oh God, what was she doing? She was an MCU DS. A deputy SIO. On the telly every week trying to reassure the good people of Middlehampton that she was in control. How would it look if Steven gave them phone footage of her, cowering inside an innocent man's sandwich van, face bleached white by the flash? Easy answer. Like a woman applying for a minimum-wage job in a warehouse, that's how.

The bang from the rear door had her biting her lip in shock. But it didn't open. He must have thumped it. The handle mechanism clicked a couple of times.

More footsteps circling the van. The roller shutter rattled. Then the driver's door handle clacked. Followed by the passenger door.

She felt sick with fear. All she could do was keep her head down, staring at her feet and praying he'd give up. Content that he'd scared whoever it was off before they'd broken into the van.

'I'll get you next time,' he said, though clearly to himself. 'Bloody tomcat. I'll cut your balls off and feed them to you.'

Kat let out the air trapped in her lungs in a long, slow, controlled breath. *Tomcat. Tom. Kat. Funny.* If only he knew.

She waited, perfectly still, until she heard the front door open and close again. She leant her head back against the cool steel wall of the van. That had been too close. Despite the gravity of the situation, she felt a laugh bubbling up from her gut. Just nerves. There really wasn't anything remotely funny about this.

The bang right behind her head was enormous. She stifled a scream.

'You in there, you little bastards? I could kill you and claim self-defence, you know.'

He'd come back. Opened and closed the front door to lull whichever neighbourhood bad boy he suspected of robbing him into a false sense of security. Well, it had almost worked, hadn't it?

Kat tried to squeeze herself into an even smaller space. She pulled her knees up to her chest and wrapped her arms around her shins. Her pulse roared in her ears, rushing like the surf in a seashell.

But that was it. The rear door didn't open. Steven didn't come at her, eyes glaring, teeth bared. She listened as his footsteps receded for a second time. The front door opened and, straining her ears, she heard his feet slapping on the hallway floor. A long pause, she counted to nine, and then the door closed, quietly, and she heard the latch click home.

Shakily, she unfolded herself, putting her hands down flat on the floor to push herself upright. Something dug into her right palm, just at the base of her thumb.

She turned her hand over. She couldn't believe it. Denting her flesh, stuck there by her sweat, was a tiny grain. Not rice this time. Caramel-coloured, with a crease running between its two pointed ends.

Not oats. Not barley. Not a toast crumb. Or a Rice Krispie.

Wheat.

CHAPTER THIRTY-SIX

Kat climbed out of her car with little awareness of how she'd got home.

She knew she'd left the sandwich van in a state halfway between terror and amped-up readiness, convinced she'd find Steven waiting for her.

But he hadn't been there.

It was 4.10 a.m., now. Too wired to sleep, she went into the kitchen. Smokey raised his head off his bed, gave her a dozy one-eyed look, then flopped back down again. She sat at the table and looked at the minute piece of evidence she hoped would convict Steven of multiple murders. Cases had turned on less. OK, she had the small problem of explaining how she'd acquired it, but surely there'd be a solution.

'What's that, Mum?'

She turned to see Riley standing there in his Middlehampton FC pyjamas, rubbing his eyes.

'What are you doing down here, sweetheart? It's ever so early.'

'I needed a wee, then I heard someone come in. I thought it would be you so I came down to say hello.'

'Oh, Riley, that's nice of you,' she said. 'Come here. Are you too old to sit on my lap?'

Yawning, he shook his head. He shuffled into the kitchen and into her waiting arms. Kat felt the weight of him, the imprint of his sharp little seat-bones on the tops of her thighs. She hugged him close.

'I love you, Riley.'

'I love you, too.'

'You know, whatever you do, I'll always love you. And I'll always be there for you.'

'I know,' he mumbled, 'because you're my mum.'

'That's right. And what is my only job?'

'To keep me safe,' he mumbled, sounding as if sleep was already pulling him away from her.

He sagged against her shoulder and she bent to kiss the top of his head. He smelled of sleep and, just beneath it, the unmistakable scent of boy-sweat. He was growing up fast. She wanted to hold him for a little longer, but if she didn't release him now she'd end up carrying all six stone four of him up the stairs.

'Hey,' she whispered. 'Kiss night-night, then off you go, OK?'

''Kay.'

He kissed her on the cheek then slid off her lap and stumbled away from her.

She sat up for a long while after sending Riley back to bed. Thinking about sons and mothers. The relationship had been the stuff of sitcoms and stand-up routines since the dawn of time. Sons loved their mothers but needed to pull themselves free. Mothers had to let them, but still wanted to keep their sons safe. Unless they abused their offspring so severely they became serial killers like Steven Pulford, who returned the favour by making them their first victims.

Riley wasn't like that. He was just a normal boy who was starting to be interested in girls, even if the pictures of Luke Tockley's older sister were entirely inappropriate.

269

Oh, God, why was it so difficult? And, while she was on the subject of difficult relationships, why couldn't Liv see how much she'd complicated Kat's life? She was glad Liv was alive, of course she was, but Liv didn't really seem to realise the devastation she'd left in her wake.

Finally, having drunk a cup of tea laced with a shot of whisky, she headed upstairs.

After a couple of hours' sleep, she took Smokey for a brisk walk around Stocks Green. She nodded to a few people she recognised, out with their own dogs before the heat of the day made walking uncomfortable. Perhaps sensing her eagerness to get to work, Smokey trotted along beside her without stopping to sniff every lamp post.

'I've got him, Smokes,' she said, looking down at the little grey dog.

But she hadn't.

Kat was talking to Darcy Clements.

'I'll do my best, Kat, but you know what the lab's like.'

'Tell them I have budget. *Lots* of budget. I want it back today. I *need* it. I can't tell if it smells of lavender anymore. Maybe it's from his supplies before he soaks them. I don't know. But this is the break we've been looking for.'

Darcy nodded. 'There's someone there I can call. He keeps asking me out, so I'll just have to play the femme fatale, won't I?'

'Darcy Clements, you're a married woman!'

Darcy chuckled. 'So are you. But from what I hear, that doesn't stop you using your feminine charms to get what you want.'

'Sorry, what?'

'Our new pathologist?'

'Jack Beale?'

'Unless we have another one.'

'He was flirting with *me*!'

Kat felt herself blushing. Hospitals and cop shops. Both subject to all kinds of rules about privacy and confidentiality, yet swirling with more gossip than a hairdresser's salon.

Darcy held her hands up, smiling. 'Whatever you say.' She paused. 'He is fit, though, don't you think?'

Kat pictured the pathologist in his scrubs, smiling at her. Remembered the not entirely unpleasant squirming sensation in the pit of her belly. His nice arms, strong hands.

'He's all right, I suppose. A bit cocksure.'

Darcy raised an eyebrow. 'Interesting word to use. Sure we're not having a little Freudian-slip moment?'

Kat's mouth dropped open. 'Darce!'

'I mean, I wouldn't kick him out of bed for eating Doritos, that's all I'm saying,' Darcy said with a wink.

'Just get me my analysis, please,' Kat said, grinning broadly.

The moment Kat re-entered MCU, Leah hurried over, a triumphant smile on her face.

'I found a connection between the new girls,' she said.

Kat followed Leah to her desk. The DC pointed at a document open on her screen.

'They all got their jobs through the same employment agency. Prime Personnel on Ropemaker Street.'

'I know it. The MD plays for one of the teams in my netball league.'

'Viv Wellesley, yeah, she said she knew you. Well, they use temps to match CVs to jobs using some software they developed,' Leah said. 'They all work at home, and guess who processed our four dead girls?'

Kat saw it before Leah could tell her. Saw who it wasn't, rather. Sandwich Steve. Oh, Christ, had she made the biggest mistake of her career?

'Please tell me it was Steven Pulford.'

Leah shook her head. 'Karl Oldfield.'

'But he's retired!'

Leah shrugged. 'Steven drives a sandwich van for a living.'

Then Kat recalled Oldfield's answer to Tom's gentle enquiry when they'd sat in his garden. He'd said he'd left the care system behind. Something like that, anyway. And they'd assumed he meant he wasn't working. But he had a home office. A home office that Kat had snooped around in. A home office full of bloody origami models.

'Maybe officially, but he's on their books. Viv showed me,' Leah said. 'He would've had access to their photos, Kat. He could have just sat at home and picked them out, like off Tinder.'

'Right. Bring him in. Preferably voluntarily.'

'Kat!'

She turned at the shout. What did Tom want now?

Eyes wide, he hurried over.

'You're not going to believe this,' he said. 'I've been doing a deep dive on Ruby Spence. She just had a restraining order granted by the court. It was gummed up in the works, which is why it didn't show up earlier. Guess who's not allowed within five hundred metres of her home? Johnny Hayes.'

'What?'

'He's connected to two of the victims. He's got a conviction for domestic violence and now this.'

'He's also got an alibi for Jade's murder.'

'But what if he was really only after Ruby, and he murdered the other girls to throw us off the scent?'

'Then we need to pick his alibi apart.'

'Leave it to me,' he said and practically ran back to his desk.

Her force mobile rang. The third interruption to Kat's day didn't blow another hole in her already ragged theory, but made her heart sink all the same.

'It's John in R&P, Kat. Member of the public found a body in the middle of Brearley Woods. Thought you'd want to know.'

'Where exactly?'

'You got what3words on your phone?'

'Yes.'

'Put in participated-dot-melon-dot-drips. The nearest entrance is a bridleway that starts about half a mile along the St Albans Road. On the west side, you know it?'

'Yep. Thanks, tell them I'm on my way.'

◆ ◆ ◆

Another secluded spot, sun streaming down through the canopy.

Another dead girl, limbs outflung, head twisted so the choking grains spilled on to the ground. Her flesh was mottling, already turning purplish green. So she'd been there for a day at least.

Another family whose lives were about to be torn apart by grief and shock.

Kat looked down at the corpse of the Origami Killer's fifth new victim. And nodded. Whatever control he had once exerted over his impulses was almost gone. He'd delivered a heavy blow to the back of her head with a blunt object. Maybe the bloodied section of tree branch the size of a cricket bat that lay near the body, half hidden in the nettles.

And as well as choking her with the wheat grains, he'd strangled her. An ugly necklace of dark bruises encircled her throat.

But it wasn't the wound to the head, or the manual strangulation, that gave her an oddly perverse sense of satisfaction, even as she grieved inwardly for another life lost to a psychopath.

He'd pulled her top off so violently it had ripped. And, five or six centimetres above the lace edging of her left bra cup, a deep, double row of bloody punctures disfigured her otherwise-smooth pale skin.

'He bit her,' one of the CSIs said, quite unnecessarily in Kat's opinion. 'We'll be able to get DNA.'

'Fast-track it, yes? I want it on tonight's run.'

'It'll cost.'

'I don't care!' she snapped. 'Sorry. Just get it done, please. Inform whoever you have to. I've got authorisation to spend whatever's necessary.'

Not quite true. She'd still have to clear it with Linda, but she didn't anticipate any objections from the woman leaning on her for results.

'You're the boss,' the CSI said.

'And check for semen in the surrounding area,' she added. 'Even if he didn't rape her, he may have masturbated.'

'Into stinging nettles? Seems unlikely.'

'Just look, would you?'

She left the CSI to it and went over to where Darcy was briefing two more. All trace of their earlier banter had been left far behind. This was business. And a dirty, unpleasant business it was.

Darcy held up an evidence bag with a mobile phone inside it.

'He didn't even bother taking her phone. She had her details on the lock screen. Her name's Shannon Hollister.'

'That's something, I suppose. I'll get someone to locate her next of kin. What else have we got?'

'The usual, basically. Origami heart, lavender-scented wheat grains.'

'Do you think that bit of wood is the murder weapon?'

'Looks like it. We'll need to run the blood. It might not even be hers.'

Kat frowned. 'If we get a match on the DNA, that might not matter.'

She called Leah and asked her to check whether Shannon was on Prime Personnel's database. Leah called back five minutes later to confirm that she was.

Kat drove back to Jubilee Place to find Leah and Tom in conversation.

'We've got Karl Oldfield in interview room three,' Tom said.

'Yeah, and he wouldn't come voluntarily, either,' Leah added. 'We arrested him on suspicion of murder. That wiped the smile right off his face. Smarmy little git.'

'Lawyer or no lawyer?'

'Lawyer.'

Kat frowned. That was interesting. Oldfield hadn't wanted representation last time. Now he did. Had she missed something? She'd sensed he was hiding *something*, but not a string of murders. Had she been wrong?

Kat took Tom with her and stepped into the interview room.

CHAPTER THIRTY-SEVEN

Suddenly, Karl Oldfield didn't look quite so harmless as he had the first time they'd met.

Kat saw musculature beneath his grey cardigan she hadn't noticed before. His hands, which were spread out on the table, were large, heavy-knuckled. She was having trouble imagining those stubby fingers folding origami paper, but none at all picturing them encircling Shannon Hollister's slender neck and choking her to death, breaking the hyoid bone and stopping the blood in her carotid arteries reaching her brain.

She uttered the official caution. Karl nodded and answered 'Yes' when she asked him if he understood.

'Karl, last time we spoke, you said you had your gardening to keep you busy. Is that all you do to occupy your time?'

'Well, I do some driving for an old folks' home. You know, to the shops, the Central Library, that sort of thing,' he said. 'We went over to Dunstable Downs last week. The weather was glorious.'

'Very commendable. I was thinking more of an actual job. Paid, I mean.'

'I left the world of full-time employment behind me years ago, DS Ballantyne, as I think I told you before.'

Kat nodded. 'Yes, you did. How about a part-time job? Maybe a customer assistant in a DIY store? Uber? Deliveroo?'

He smiled. 'I think I'm a bit old to be riding a bike around Middlehampton with a box of pizzas on my back, don't you?'

She smiled. 'How about something clerical? PC-based? You're not too old for that, are you?'

'No, but I have my pension to rely on, and my father left me some money.'

'So you're saying you don't undertake any paid work?'

'That's correct.'

'I see.' Kat selected a sheet of paper from the file she'd brought with her. 'For the tape, I am showing the suspect a copy of an invoice submitted to Prime Personnel on 20th September 2022 and paid by them three weeks later. The item listed is "CV data entry". The amount is three hundred and ten pounds. The name of the contractor is Karl Oldfield.' She passed the sheet across to him. 'Could you explain that to us, please, Karl?'

He glanced down at the paper and nodded. 'Of course. A simple lapse of memory. That was last year. I'd forgotten. It was just some casual work I took on because it sounded interesting. Nothing sinister, I assure you.'

'Transferring information from CVs on to a database sounded interesting?'

He shrugged. 'I enjoy a challenge.'

She nodded. 'Here's a challenge you might also enjoy, then, Karl. For the tape, I am showing the suspect a list of names of candidates that he processed during the project he completed for Prime Personnel.' She slid the sheet towards him with the tip of her finger, withdrawing her hand before he reached for the document.

He paid more attention to this one. Then he looked up at her. She sensed a change in his demeanour. A wariness that hadn't been there before.

'What am I supposed to do with this?' he asked.

'Have a look at the names highlighted in yellow, Karl. In fact, could you read them out, please?'

He turned to his solicitor. 'Do I have to?'

'No.'

'I'd prefer not to,' he said.

'Why is that, Karl?'

'It's them, isn't it?'

'Who, Karl? Who is it?'

'The dead girls,' he said in a quiet voice.

'That's right. Including a new one. I've just come from where her body was dumped,' she said. 'I'll read them for *you*, then.' She picked up her own copy. 'Courtney Hatch. Jade Root. Corinne Gregory. Ruby Spence. Shannon Hollister. They were pretty girls, too. Look.'

She spread out five full-colour photos, blown up to A4 on the table before him, then gave another, 'for the tape', recitation of the evidence.

He kept his eyes fixed on hers.

'Look, Karl!' she said sharply.

His head dropped down and he scanned the photos quickly before returning his gaze to hers.

She placed a second set of photos on top of the first.

'Not so pretty after they were murdered, were they?'

'Please,' he said, flinching. 'It wasn't me. I had nothing to do with those girls.'

'But that's not true, is it, Karl? You saw their CVs. You knew where they lived. You knew where they worked. You knew what they looked like. And they all look alike, don't they? Did you notice that just now? Did you notice it back then? Do they remind you of someone? Is that why you killed them?'

'No!'

278

'DS Ballantyne, you're badgering my client,' the solicitor said sharply.

'Your client is under arrest for the murders of five women. Maybe more.'

'You have arrested him on *suspicion* of those crimes, nothing more. He has denied carrying them out. Do you have any actual evidence?'

Kat placed a pink origami heart on the table.

'You said your daughter made it for you, Karl. Are you still sticking to that story?'

'Yes! I told you. It's a little tradition of ours.'

'I've sent an officer to London to interview Leanne. She's going to ask her whether she can remember sending you all those origami models.'

'Good. Because she'll say yes, and then where will you be?'

'Maybe you asked her to make you a batch of hearts. It'll be easy enough to find out.' She passed a third sheet of paper across the table towards him. 'For the tape, I am showing the suspect a list of dates. Karl, these are the dates when the first four victims were murdered. Can you account for your whereabouts on each of them, please?'

Karl picked up the sheet of paper and scrutinised it. Kat waited him out. The quartz wall clock ticked twenty-three times before Karl replaced the sheet of paper on the table. He turned to his solicitor and murmured something behind his hand. The solicitor shook his head and murmured a response. Karl rotated in his chair to look at Kat.

'On the advice of my solicitor, I have no comment to make in response to that question.'

'Really? I have to confess, Karl, that does surprise me. Up to now you've seemed so eager to help us. What's changed?'

'On the advice of my solicitor, I have no comment to make in response to that question.'

'Do you deny murdering Courtney Hatch, Jade Root, Corinne Gregory, Ruby Spence and Shannon Hollister?'

'On the advice of my solicitor, I have no comment to make in response to that question.'

Kat nodded, surprised that it had taken him this long to shut his trap.

'Interview ended at 5.31 p.m.'

She nodded to Tom, who switched off the tape recorder. Then she gathered her papers and photos and got to her feet.

Outside the interview room, Tom was all smiles. 'That was brilliant. Literally brilliant. I've never seen anyone handle an interview like that before.'

'Thank you. I've had a lot of training.'

'Yes, but it's not just that, is it? You got right under his skin.'

She shrugged the flattery off. He'd gone 'no comment', hadn't he, so what had she really achieved?

'We'll have another go at him later.'

'Ready when you are, boss.'

She smiled. 'OK, puppy dog, buzz off and do something useful before you wag your tail clean off.'

She pulled her phone out and called Ivan.

'Hey, how's it going?' he asked.

'Good. We've got someone in custody. But it's going to be a long night. Can you walk Smokey tonight and handle tea?'

'No probs. Do you think it's him?'

'I hope so, but there are two more guys in the frame too. It has to be one of them, Van, it just *has* to.'

'You'll get him, love. I know you will.'

'Thanks, mate. Got to go. Love you.'

'Love you, too.'

Kat went to find Darcy, hoping the lab had done their thing with the wheat grain.

When she found her, the older woman was beaming.

'Just the person. You're going to love this,' she said.

'What is it?'

'I just had an email from the lab,' Darcy said, holding up a red-taped evidence bag. 'They finished testing the grain you brought me. This is the remaining half.'

'And?'

'It's Cotswold wheat, and they found traces of sweet almond oil and *Lavandula angustifolia*. We've got him.'

Kat hugged her forensic coordinator. 'You're a star!'

Then she marched over to Linda's office. Time for that difficult conversation.

Kat closed the door behind her and came to sit opposite her SIO. She inhaled. No time like the present. Felt a nervous smile quivering on her lips.

'What's up, Kat? You look like you won the lottery and then pissed your knickers.'

'That wheat grain I saw in the sandwich van? I recovered it and it tested positive for the exact same ingredients as he's been using to choke his victims.'

Linda frowned.

'Hold on a second. Recovered it how?'

Kat took a steadying breath. Found it didn't work. Confession time.

'I traced his address, and I searched his van.'

The look Linda bestowed on Kat made her feel thirteen years old again, hauled up before the headteacher to explain why she and Liv had been seen in town during lesson time.

'You conducted an illegal search.'

'I had no choice.'

Linda slapped her palms down on her desk. 'Of *course* you had a choice! You could have done what I told you, for a start, and run this investigation by the book. Oh, wait, that's not what I said at all, is it? I said, make the book feel like a grubby piece of pornography in comparison, didn't I?'

'Words to that effect, yes. I'm sorry.'

'You've dropped me right in it, now, haven't you? As SIO there's no way I can un-know this,' she said. 'And there's absolutely no way I'm going to allow you to ask for a retrospective search warrant so you can "find" it legally. That would be corruption, and I don't care how many serial killers we could catch as a result. I'm not going to flush my career down the toilet for you or anyone else.'

'I know. And I wouldn't ask you to. But—'

'As evidence, it's burned. If you say this Steven character's your guy, fine. Prove it. But do it with something legal that we can use.'

'I can, Linda. That's the whole point.'

'Feel like sharing, or is this another little secret you intend to keep from me?'

'You know he bit the fifth girl?'

'Yes.'

'So he'll have left DNA. All I need's a sample from him and it's over.'

'Which you can't get until you arrest him. And you can't arrest him until you have something new, as I think I just mentioned. Anyway, what about this Oldfield character you've already arrested?'

'We're going to have another go at him later tonight. He's guilty of something. I just don't think it's murder. I still think Steven's the one we should be going after.'

'Look, Kat. I know you want to put him away. But it might be Oldfield. In which case you already have a DNA sample. Rule him out before you start chasing another suspect, yes?'

'Linda, please.'

Linda shook her head.

'No. You do this my way, Kat – or not at all.'

◆ ◆ ◆

Kat restarted the interview at 9.45 p.m.

'How are you doing, Karl? Have they given you something to eat?'

'Yes. A ham sandwich and some very poor-quality tea. I could barely finish it.'

She grimaced in sympathy. 'Yes, I'm sorry about that. Station tea isn't known for its quality. Did you murder those girls, Karl?'

The lurch in direction didn't take him by surprise as she'd hoped. Perhaps his solicitor had warned him. Instead he simply looked at her.

His chest rose and fell steadily, no heaving breaths, no quick little gasps. Nothing, in short, that indicated he was even mildly anxious. Instead he appeared resigned. His shoulders were slumped and there was a dead look behind his eyes. Not the cold blackness of a psychopath's gaze, either. Just . . . What was it? Resignation. Yes. He looked like a man who'd given up.

Her own pulse quickened. This was it.

'My client wishes to make a statement,' the solicitor said.

Kat sat forward. 'Go on then, Karl, let's hear it.'

The solicitor passed a sheet of paper to Karl. Swallowing noisily, he picked it up, and now Kat did see a sign of his inner emotions. His cheeks were aflame and he was sweating.

The top edge of the paper trembled as if disturbed by the tail end of a distant breeze.

CHAPTER THIRTY-EIGHT

Karl cleared his throat, loud in the otherwise silent room.

'Since the death of my beloved wife, Helen, in 2018, I have been in the habit of regularly visiting' – he gulped – 'a prostitute, for sexual and emotional release. On two of the nights when I have been asked for an alibi, I was, in fact, with this young lady. Although I cannot provide alibis for the dates I have been asked about, I hope that, given the linked nature of the murders for which I have been, ah, arrested, my inability to commit two can be taken as my inability to commit any. That is all I have to say.'

Karl's statement had the undeniable ring of truth about it, even though she detected his solicitor's voice behind the precise phrasing. In any case, all she had to do was check with the sex worker, and he would be home free. That would leave Steven Pulford as her prime suspect with Johnny Hayes trailing a distant second.

'I see,' she said. 'Can you give us the name of this young lady?'

He glanced at the solicitor, who nodded minutely. 'She calls herself Scarlet.'

Kat made a note, assuming that Karl's 'young lady' used a *nom de guerre* like most of the working girls in Middlehampton.

'How do you get in touch with Scarlet?' she asked.

'Er, I call her.'

'Do you have her number?'

The solicitor slid a second sheet of paper across to Kat. It bore a mobile phone number beside the name, which was in speech marks. Clearly, he was no more convinced by the name than Kat was.

Kat suspended the interview and stepped outside into the corridor. She called the number. After seven rings, it was answered.

'Hi, this is Scarlet,' a young woman purred. 'Who's feeling lonely today?'

'One of your clients is,' Kat said. 'He's in custody on suspicion of murder.'

'Who is this?' The seductress voice had vanished, replaced by a solidly Middlehampton accent.

'DS Ballantyne, Hertfordshire Police. This man, Karl Oldfield, has given us your name as his alibi.'

Scarlet, or whatever her name was, laughed. 'Oh no, you haven't given Karl a tug for them Origami murders, have you? Poor old sod can barely get it up to give *me* a seeing-to. He mostly wants to talk about his dead wife, poor love.'

'If I give you some dates, can you confirm that he was with you?'

'Yeah, of course. But not now. Got a client coming round in a couple of minutes and I need to finish changing.'

'When will you be free for a quick chat, then?'

'He's booked me for the night. Tomorrow morning?'

'This is quite urgent. I'm investigating five murders.'

'Yeah, and that's awful. But I've got to go to work. Ten all right for you?'

'Can you come to Jubilee Place?'

'Why don't we meet somewhere public? Not great for my image to be seen getting too friendly with you lot, if you know what I mean.'

'Fair enough. How about the Bramalls? I could meet you by the Butter Cross.'

'Yeah, that'd work.'

The line went dead.

And so, the following morning, did Kat's case against Karl Oldfield. In a brief, fact-packed exchange under the wind-smoothed sandstone cross where dairy farmers had once sold their produce, Scarlet, real name Abi Smith, confirmed Karl Oldfield's alibi. She added, unasked, that he was gentle, kind, and about as far from her idea of a man who'd hurt women as it was possible to get.

A thought occurred to Kat.

'If you don't mind me asking, how old are you?'

'Old enough, if that's what's worrying you,' came the sharp rejoinder.

'No, that's not what I meant at all.'

'I usually tell clients I'm nineteen,' Abi said, fluttering a pair of oversized false eyelashes. 'You know what men are like.' Kat did, and smiled her understanding. 'But I'm actually twenty-seven.'

'You look good,' Kat said.

'Yeah, well, it's a hard life if you're on the street,' Abi said. 'Girls out here look fifty by the time they're thirty, if they last that long. It's why I changed to escort work. Also, no drugs. Kill your looks, they do.'

Kat frowned. 'Can I ask you a personal question?'

'Depends on what it is.'

'Why do you do it? If you're not hooked, I mean?'

Abi's lip curled. She leaned away from Kat and folded her arms. 'What, you mean why do I *demean* myself like this?'

'No, I—' Kat stopped mid-denial, because Abi was right. That *was* what she'd been thinking. Or partly. 'Sorry. But it's dangerous. Even escort work. I have a friend in CID who's working on a case right now, a suspect accused of violence against one of your, well, your co-workers.'

'You mean Nita, don't you? Bastard messed her up good and proper. She tell your friend why?'

'I'm sure she did.'

'She asked him – *asked*, mind, not told – to use a condom,' Abi said, eyes flashing. 'Next thing she knows, he's battering the life out of her. It was only because her flatmate had a job cancelled and came home early that she survived.'

'I'm sorry. Molly's a good detective. I know she'll do whatever it takes to get him convicted.'

'Yeah, well, to answer your question, ever hear of austerity? Five years ago, I lost my job up on Castle Hill, the business park, you know? I've got a kiddie to feed and clothe and send on school trips. And there's not a lot of nice, cushy jobs around at the moment for a woman like me with no qualifications.

'My mum looks after him and I do what I do to survive. And, by the way? I make decent money, too. Sometimes, like with poor old Karl, I feel more like a bloody social worker than a prossy. Know what I mean?'

Something Abi had said sparked a connection in Kat's brain. About sex workers and their children. Because Candace had had Stefan, hadn't she?

'Abi, I need some information from you, and it goes beyond simply providing an alibi for a suspect. Could I give you a little something for your time? Maybe you could put it towards the next school trip?'

She fished a twenty from her purse and held it low in the space between them.

Abi looked down, then at Kat.

'You got kids, too? You look like you have.'

'A son, Riley. He's twelve. What's your son's name?'

Abi bit her lip. Kat could see it, the delicate trade-off she was working on. Sharing confidences with a cop meant crossing a line.

287

But it might also mean a level of protection unavailable to her friend Nita.

'Justin.' The banknote vanished. 'What kind of information?'

'Do you know if any of the working girls here were around in 2006?'

Abi smiled. 'Blimey! Seventeen years ago? This isn't exactly a long-term career choice, you know.' Then her eyes sparkled. 'Actually, you know what? I lied. It is! At least for one of us, anyway. You want to talk to Theresa Leonard. Everyone calls her Terrie. She's what you'd call an escort. A very high-class one, too.'

'I know Terrie. Do you have her contact details?'

Abi gave Kat an address in Canalside and extracted from her a promise not to let Terrie know who'd provided it.

On the way to see Terrie Leonard, Kat called Tom and told him to de-arrest Karl Oldfield.

CHAPTER THIRTY-NINE

Kat drew up outside a converted warehouse that backed on to the canal. The original golden brickwork glowed in the sun, which glinted back at her off a brushed-steel door. She pressed the buzzer for Flat 7 and stared into the black eye of the entrycam.

'Hello?'

'Hi, Terrie. It's Kat Ballantyne. Can I come in?'

After a three-second pause, the latch buzzed.

The stylish woman who answered the door made Kat feel distinctly underdressed, if not underpaid. Nothing flashy: forest-green linen trousers from beneath which a pair of burnt-orange loafers peeped, a cream silk blouse that flowed over her curves in soft folds, as though sculpted from marble. Discreet silver drop-earrings and a matching pendant in the notch of her throat.

'Thanks for seeing me, Terrie,' Kat said.

She followed her host into a large white sitting room, furnished with turquoise sofas and hung with a large oil painting of a flower meadow. A picture window gave a view of the canal and more converted warehouses on the opposite bank.

'It's been a while, Kat. Last time you and I chatted, you were rocking a rather fetching little cap with a chequered band. Funny, because I was working down there' – she pointed at the towpath – 'and now I live up here. Drink?'

'I could murder a coffee.'

Terrie grinned wryly. 'Unfortunate turn of phrase for someone in your line of work.'

'But relevant. I want to ask you about Candace Pulford.'

'Coffee first.'

With two white mugs resting on a glass-topped coffee table, Terrie crossed one long leg over the other, revealing more of the burnt-orange loafer on her right foot.

She caught Kat looking.

'Nice, aren't they?'

'Nice? They're bloody gorgeous.'

'Prada. Gift from an appreciative client. He's a big wheel in the chamber of commerce, and the council.'

Kat nodded. How very unsurprising. 'Good for you,' she said with a smile.

Terrie took a sip of coffee. 'How did you get my address? The flat's not in my name.'

Kat had been expecting the question. 'It was on file.'

'I doubt it. I've never been in trouble with the law, despite your best efforts,' Terrie said. 'Lie to me again and I'll ask you to leave, Candace or no Candace.'

Kat inhaled. She couldn't break Abi's confidence, but she needed to find some sort of truthful answer.

'One of the girls in town gave it to me.' She felt more was called for. 'Listen, Terrie, how you and she make your living? I couldn't care less, as long as you're safe. I asked her because I think there's a link between Candace Pulford's murder and the Origami Killer, and I think you can help.'

She waited, feeling sure that a financial inducement would produce the opposite effect on Terrie to the one it had had on Abi. Terrie uncrossed her legs and planted her feet square on the soft, cream carpet. She leaned forward and Kat caught a whiff of the other woman's perfume, a light, floral scent.

'Nobody cared when Candace was murdered, you know. Not really. The *Echo* did this little article, but you can imagine the angle,' she said, pulling her lips to one side. '"Tart's ill-judged career choice finally catches up with her." You lot were no better. You know what one of the detectives said to me? God, I can remember it as if it were yesterday. He said, "Stick to looking at the mirror on the ceiling, love, and leave me to look for the murderer." Can you believe it?'

Kat found, with a pang of shame, that she could. Very easily.

'The girl I spoke to said you thought half the cops in Middlehampton were on freebies back then. Anyone in particular?'

Terrie frowned. 'Sounds like you're investigating corruption, not murders.'

'Just following an idea,' Kat said. 'Seeing where it leads me.'

'There were three of them back then. Called themselves – with, I might add, a distinct lack of imagination – the Three Musketeers,' Terrie said. 'You know, swordsmen? Although the one who seemed to like me had more of a stiletto than a sabre. Proper pencil-prick, he was. It was all I could do not to ask if it was in yet.'

Kat let out a short burst of a laugh. Recovered herself.

'Did this D'Artagnan have a name?'

Terrie nodded. 'Stu Carver.'

Kat swallowed. 'I'm sorry, could you say that again, Terrie, please?'

'Stu Carver. I hear he's ascended to the heights of DI these days. He was a PC back then. Cocky little sod, too. Not afraid of delivering the odd slap, either. You know, nowhere it would show. A proper expert. Just to make you feel things could get worse if you didn't go along with him.'

Kat's mind was spinning. She had witness testimony that Stuart Carver, *Detective Inspector* Stuart Carver, was, or at least had been, corrupt in the early 2000s, using violence and intimidation to secure sexual favours from prostitutes. Not to mention Liv telling her he'd leaked details of the original crime scenes. He'd deny it, of course, if she confronted him. But it was information. And information was power.

All that was for another day. She had a killer to catch and the clock was ticking. He'd been escalating the violence and taking less time between kills, and she had no idea how long she had before he'd claim a new victim. Then a worse thought struck her.

'Do you think it could have been him who killed Candace?' she asked.

Terrie shrugged. 'It's possible. Any man's capable of murder if you ask me. But honestly? No. I don't.'

Kat felt a weird sense of relief. Tackling a corrupt colleague was one thing, arresting him for being a serial killer took things into a much, *much* darker place.

'Did you ever suspect anyone at the time?'

Terrie nodded. 'I did.'

'Who was it?'

'This is going to sound really peculiar. But it was her son, Stefan.'

Kat's heart rate tripled. She felt the shock as a physical change in her body, as her muscles tried to propel her up and off the sofa and back to the station to issue a warrant for Steven Pulford's arrest. She forced herself to stay calm.

'Why did you suspect Stefan of his mum's murder?'

'God, I need a drink if we're going to go back over all that,' Terrie said. 'Join me?'

'It's a bit early for me.'

'Suit yourself.'

Terrie crossed to a pale wooden drinks cabinet and returned a few moments later with a tumbler of brandy. She took a slug and then looked at Kat.

'You know how she was killed, right? You've read the file?'

'Strangled. Some of her hair pulled out. The pathologist's report said the violence was extreme.'

Terrie nodded, took another swig of her brandy. When she put the glass down, the bottom clanked against the glass tabletop. It was the first sign of anything other than perfect composure she'd shown since Kat had arrived.

'We all knew Stefan. He used to hang around, try and chat us up. You know, practising his lines on the working girls like it wouldn't matter if he failed. Then this one day, he came up to me – I was working in the Meadows back then – and said he wanted to do business. He said it was his eighteenth birthday and he wanted to lose his virginity.'

'What did you do?'

'What do you think I did? Took him back to mine. He was a bit of a loner and I thought he probably deserved a break.'

'Then what?'

'I got undressed, and that's when he produced this wig. Dark, long. He wanted me to wear it. Well, as kinks go it was pretty low down the list, so I said, "Sure, if that's what you'd like, love," or words like that. I mean, a lad's first time, you want it to go well. It's probably not going to last longer than a few seconds anyway, is it?'

Kat had a feeling she knew what was coming.

'Go on,' she said.

'That's when he got this bottle of perfume out. He wanted me to cover myself in it. And it was really old-fashioned. It was—'

'Lavender. It was lavender, wasn't it?'

'Yeah. How did you know? Oh my God, *he* uses it, doesn't he?'

Kat could only nod.

'I said something like, "Isn't that a bit old-fashioned? Like something your granny might wear?" And he just asked me, very politely, to put it on. So I did.'

293

Then a surprising thing happened. A tear rolled out of Terrie's left eye, down her smoothly powdered cheek. It dropped on to her wrist and she looked down at it, frowning, as if she didn't know where it had come from.

'What happened, Terrie?' Kat asked in a gentle voice.

'He told me to turn around,' Terrie said. 'To just stand there with my back to him. I felt him close to me. He held me by my arms, and he started sniffing my neck. Really inhaling deeply, you know? Like a dog or something. And then . . .' Her voice cracked. 'And then he grabbed the wig off my head and put it around my neck. He was strangling me. I thought I was going to die. So I fought back. I elbowed him in the gut, and he sort of fell off me and then I kicked him right where it hurts. He hadn't even got undressed yet. I screamed at him to get out and he just ran. Candace was murdered the very next day. When I read in the *Echo* how she'd been killed, it was like a connection in my head. I could join the dots.'

Terrie was crying properly now, her perfectly powdered cheeks runnelled with tears. Kat offered her a tissue from a little cellophane packet she always kept handy.

'You went to the police, didn't you? You told them about Stefan, and that's when the detective told you to stick to what you did best.'

Terrie dabbed at her nose before dropping the damp tissue in a discreet wastepaper basket. She nodded.

'After that I decided to stay well clear of all of it. When he started killing more girls, I just took extra care about my clients. And I advised my friends to do the same.'

'I'm so sorry for making you relive that, Terrie,' Kat said. 'And I'm sorry nobody took you seriously at the police station, too. But *I'm* taking you seriously. And I'm going to stop him.'

Looking at Terrie, she wondered whether the older woman believed her. After all, she had good reason not to.

CHAPTER FORTY

Kat arrived back at Jubilee Place to learn from Darcy that the DNA recovered from the bite mark on Shannon Hollister didn't match Karl Oldfield's sample. Even without his alibi, he was in the clear.

Entering MCU, she saw Tom, head in hands, staring morosely at his computer.

'What's up?' she asked him.

'Johnny Hayes. It's not him. His alibis – plural – are watertight.'

'That's still good policework, Tom. You've eliminated him.'

That just left Steven Pulford. She went to see Linda.

'I want to run a familial DNA test on the sample from the fifth victim. If it comes back a match to Candace, who we know had a conviction for soliciting, then that'll point to her only child, Stefan.'

'You want me to give you an extra twenty-five thousand? That's a big chunk of money I don't have to spend on a single throw of the dice, Kat.'

Kat's heart was pounding. She knew what she was about to say would shove her squarely into career-damaging territory, but she had no choice.

'What about all those families who are grieving right now? Do you really want to add another one? I'm running out of FLOs as it is.'

Linda's eyes narrowed to slits. 'Now, look here, Kat—'

Kat couldn't stop now. She had to ride it all the way to its conclusion.

'He's going to do it again, Linda,' she said, trying to speak calmly despite her raging emotions. 'You know he is. We have to do something to stop him before it's too late. I don't know about you, but I couldn't live with myself if we didn't run it and he murdered another young girl, all because I couldn't get my nice piece of legal evidence in time.'

She stopped talking, clamping a hand to her throat as if to physically prevent any more words erupting. She'd already raised the stakes way beyond what she could afford.

'Is that what you think I'm asking you for, Kat?' Linda asked, finally. 'A "nice piece of legal evidence"?'

Kat felt wretched. Sick with worry that she'd just torpedoed not just the case but her own career.

'No. I'm sorry, that's not what I meant at all. I just can't bear the thought that even though I've got enough to take him off the street before he murders anyone else, I can't. You have to see it, Linda, the wheat grain *proves* it's him.'

'You know it proves nothing of the sort, Kat,' Linda said in a voice all the more upsetting for being so calm. 'He could just sit there in the interview room and say, "Must have come from my wheat pillow. I have terrible neck pain in the mornings, and it really helps." Bang! He walks, and you're left looking like you're playing with a My First Detective kit. Everything else is just conjecture and circumstantial evidence.'

'Which is precisely why I want the familial DNA test. Juries love DNA, you know that. And it's what you've been asking me for: hard evidence.'

'A familial DNA test won't provide it though, will it? All you'll get is a probability. It's *likely* that this person is related to that person.

And what if there are hundreds of families in Middlehampton who light up the boffins' machines, never mind the rest of the country? Then what?'

'Fine. Then let me arrest Steven for his mother's murder,' Kat said. 'We take a swab, blue-light it to Birmingham, get it on the 8 p.m. run and have the results back while he's still in custody. His DNA matches the DNA in the bite mark and we're home and dry.'

'His mother's murder?'

'I have a witness who says he employed three elements of the Origami Killer's MO on her in 2006: choking, lavender and a thing about long brown hair. And that links him to Candace's murder. Please, Linda, this is enough, surely?'

Linda gave Kat a long stare.

Then she nodded.

'Before you arrest him, I want a written-up risk analysis. If you're right, he's murdered at least thirteen women. That means he must be considered extremely dangerous. Like you said before, get a firearms team sorted.'

Kat left Linda's office planning a different type of approach altogether. The risk analysis would have to wait. Because the biggest threat she could see was that Steven might feel the heat, just like he had in 2008, and simply disappear. He'd practically told her that's what he was planning at Springfields.

She had no intention of letting that happen.

◆ ◆ ◆

It was just before 4 p.m. Kat had set a surveillance team monitoring Steven's house on Canada Road, and after leaving Linda's office she checked in. Steven was at home. She went to find Tom and a couple of uniforms.

Before the four officers climbed into the cars, she turned to face Tom.

'Ready?'

'Yeah.'

'Nervous.'

'A bit.'

'Try again.'

'OK, I'm bricking it.'

'That's better. If we're going to be partners, we need to be honest with each other.'

'So how are *you* feeling?'

'Like I might throw up at any moment.'

He grinned. 'Got any sick bags in your pockets?'

'Get in, Bambi.'

She drove fast through the town centre, blue lights on, sirens off, the marked car following, until they reached Canada Road. Two minutes later, backed by the uniforms, Kat stood at Steven's front door. She nodded at Tom, who unsheathed his extendo, then stepped forward and rang the doorbell, long and hard.

After a wait of two seconds, she hammered on the wood with her fist, then returned to the bell push. Heart pounding, she stood back and waited. After what felt like an eternity but was probably only a minute or so, a light went on in the hallway.

The door opened.

Steven stood there in jeans and a black T-shirt. His hair was wet, and he held a towel loosely in his right hand.

'Steven Pulford, you are under arrest on suspicion of murder.'

'My sandwiches aren't that bad, Kat,' he said, smiling. 'My food hygiene certificate's up to date.'

Pulse racing, Kat held up her cuffs. 'Turn around, please, and put your hands behind your back.'

He complied and she snapped them home with a satisfyingly loud noise from the steel ratchets.

Once she'd finished reciting the caution, she nodded to the uniformed PCs.

'Get him back to the station and booked in on a charge of murder.'

And try to avoid Linda Ockenden, she wanted to add.

They took an elbow each and marched him down the path and into the back of the marked car.

Kat called the custody sergeant. 'It's Kat here. You've got a Steven Pulford on his way in. I want him swabbed the moment he's inside the door and the sample biking up to the lab on a blue light, please.'

Then she called Darcy and made the necessary arrangements for the sample to be fast-tracked and the results sent back to her the moment they were in.

'Oh, and Darcy? I want the full work-up. Direct and familial matches, please.'

She turned to Tom. 'Now we turn this place upside down.'

'Shouldn't we call in a search team, a POLSA?'

'We will. And the CSIs. But we're going in first.'

Assigning Tom the ground floor, Kat headed up the narrow staircase, pulling on a pair of nitrile gloves. She found the master bedroom and stood on the narrow strip of carpet between the double bed, which was flanked by matching pine nightstands, and the window.

To her left was a built-in wardrobe with two sliding doors. To her right, a pine chest of drawers and a wicker laundry basket. The walls were bare, not a single print, photograph or poster. It was a curiously impersonal room, as if a clean-up team had already been through it, scrubbing away the owner's personality.

The nightstands contained nothing out of the ordinary. The sort of random collection of items she'd seen in dozens of other houses. Underwear, socks, phone chargers, half-used packets of paracetamol.

She turned to the wardrobe and slid the right-hand door across to the left. Some shirts on wire hangers, a couple of pairs of trousers, a single, pale grey suit made of some lightweight fabric.

The left-hand door revealed built-in shelves on which folded sweaters rested, along with T-shirts and running gear. Beneath the lowest shelf, which sat at waist height, were six shallow drawers faced in wood-patterned vinyl, each perhaps ten centimetres deep. Expecting to find rolled ties, or possibly coiled belts, she hooked her index finger into the topmost drawer and pulled.

The interior of the drawer had been subdivided into nine square compartments. They were all empty. She frowned. Pulled the next drawer open. And this time, drew in a sharp breath. Four of the compartments were empty. Each of the others held a plait of dark brown hair, secured at each end by a red rubber band.

'Tom!' she shouted. 'Get your arse up here, now!'

Tom's feet thundered on the thinly carpeted stairs, and he burst into the room, extendo flicked out and held in the ready position.

'What is it?'

Wordlessly, she pointed at the open drawer. Tom rounded the bed and stood in front of her, staring down into the drawer.

'Bloody hell,' he murmured, closing the baton.

On to each plait was tied a small brown card label. Kat lifted the nearest out and turned the label around. It bore two initials in neat, black capitals.

S.H.

'Shannon Hollister,' Tom said.

Kat opened the other four drawers, one after the other. Each had been subdivided into the same nine compartments. And every single one held a hank of plaited brown hair.

White-faced, Tom was muttering under his breath. 'Four nines are thirty-four, no, six. Plus five is, is . . .'

'Forty-one,' Kat supplied. 'He's killed forty-one girls, Tom.'

She went back to the second drawer and, one by one, turned over the other four plaits.

Even if she had been playing with a My First Detective kit, she thought she would have been able to work out the significance of the other sets of initials.

C.H.

J.R.

C.G.

R.S.

Courtney Hatch, Jade Root, Corinne Gregory, Ruby Spence.

She knelt in front of the array of trophies and repeated the process with the bottom drawer. The first three sets of initials meant nothing to her. But the other six sent her mind flying back to that terrible year when she thought she'd lost her best friend.

G.C.

T.B.

S.R.

E.L.

S.W.

F.C.

'Gretchen Smith, Tonia Buchanan, Sally Robb, Erica Lincoln, Shelley Waghorn, Faye Cates,' Tom intoned, as if reciting a prayer.

She looked round and up at him.

'You learned their names? Good man.'

Tom frowned. 'Where's LA?'

'What?'

'Your friend.' Tom said, sounding shocked. 'Liv Arnold. I can't see her initials.'

Heat flashed across Kat's face and she felt sweat break out on her chest. She needed a convincing explanation and she needed it now.

'She probably didn't tell him her real name. She did that with boys,' she said, realising with a stab of shame that she'd just lied to her bagman. Again. 'Or else he misfiled it.'

'Pity it didn't help her,' he said, nodding. 'So who are the others, do you think?'

'I don't know,' Kat said, trying to tamp down the panic she'd been feeling moments earlier. 'But wherever he's been for the last fifteen years, it's obvious he carried on killing.'

'I found something else,' he said. 'In the kitchen. I was going to come and find you when you yelled out.'

As she followed Tom downstairs, Kat felt a surge of anger at herself. She should have foreseen that by protecting Liv she'd be caught out every time the subject of her murder came up. And what would Steven say when they interviewed him? She had no time to think of that now. There was evidence to gather.

Arriving in the neat kitchen, what struck her was the total absence of anything visible that suggested anyone actually cooked in there. Not a jar of pasta, a bowl of apples, a box of teabags near the kettle. It was like a show home designed to appeal to people who might regard colour or decoration of any type as offensive.

Tom squatted by the sink and opened the cupboard. A half-empty bag of grains sat like a squat, fat toad, wedged in beside the sink trap. A box of freezer bags rested beside it. On the other side stood a plastic bottle three-quarters full of a clear liquid. She unscrewed the cap and sniffed: lavender.

'All we need now is the origami paper,' Tom said.

Leaving Tom to continue his search of the kitchen, Kat went into the through-lounge. At one end of the room, which was as devoid of pictures and signs of a human occupant as the rest of the house, stood a simple MDF desk on chromed legs like oversized hairpins. A cheap office chair was pushed in beneath it.

It bore, on its otherwise spotless surface, a cardboard packet of pink paper squares. Dead-centre lay a folded heart. Swallowing the saliva that had suddenly flooded her mouth, she looked up. Mounted on the wall above the desk was a shallow white box, half a metre to a side and maybe eight centimetres deep. Two doors met in the centre, secured by a little brass cabin hook. She flipped the hook over and opened the doors.

'Oh God.'

She felt nauseous, and gripped the back of the chair for support as she looked at the contents of the cabinet.

Where the manufacturer had intended a dartboard to sit, and on the insides of the doors, were mounted dozens of photos. Every single one bore the image of the same young woman, even though they were all different. Long, dark brown hair. A certain spark behind the eyes, also brown. A curve to the jawline.

Around the edge of each photo was the same shadowy frame. It came to her as she stared at them. It was the inside of the serving hatch of Steven's van. As her eyes skittered over the array of images of the girls who, she was now sure, represented his mother, Candace Pulford, she gasped and took an involuntary step back.

She was looking at her own face. The background was the staff entrance of Jubilee Place. She was smiling, looking just below the line of the camera.

Of course she was. Because she was smiling at *Steven*. She knew exactly which day it was. She'd been wearing her red lippy and he'd complimented her on it. And she had smiled and felt just that little bit better about herself for the rest of the morning.

She felt as though she were addressing the dead girls personally as she worked through the insight.

That's how he hunted you, wasn't it? He wasn't super-hot. Not threateningly sexy. But nice-looking. Just with a bit of added charm. He flattered you, he complimented. He remembered your order and probably asked your name and then used it. He was a bit older, but not a lech. And when he asked you out, probably shyly, as if he thought you'd say no, you were only too happy to agree.

Tom came in and stood by her side.

'Bloody hell.'

She turned to him.

'Come on. We'll let the professionals finish the search. You and I have an appointment with the Origami Killer.'

The only available duty solicitor didn't arrive at Jubilee Place until 9.25 p.m. Thirty minutes later, Kat settled herself into a seat facing

Steven. Beside her, Tom faced the duty solicitor, a tired-looking young woman in a suit that looked like it needed a good press.

Kat felt sorry for her. They weren't paid a great deal, they were on call in the depths of the night, and, from time to time, they had to sit beside people who had committed the most awful crimes imaginable. And sometimes beyond even that.

Kat looked at Steven first, then the solicitor, then back at Steven. His black T-shirt revealed a tattoo on his left bicep: a girl's face painted like a Mexican Day of the Dead skull.

CHAPTER FORTY-ONE

Kat switched on the tape recorder.

'Steven Pulford, you have been arrested on suspicion of the murder of the following people.'

She read out the names of the original girls, noting with a flash of anxiety his fleeting frown when she reached Liv's, and the new girls. She held back Shannon Hollister's name. For now. She added the official caution.

'I do understand, but you've got the wrong man,' he said. 'It's like I've been saying since you arrested me. I haven't murdered anyone.'

'I think we both know you've murdered a lot of people, Steven, starting with your mum,' she said. 'That's why they all look like her, isn't it? Right up to Shannon Hollister.'

Kat leaned on the dead girl's name, just a little. And she got her reward. Steven's left eyelid flickered. Just the once. But it was enough. He knew her. He'd killed her.

'I'm sorry to disappoint you, but I really have nothing to do with any of these awful crimes.'

'So you're telling me you have absolutely no knowledge of a young woman named Shannon Hollister?'

'I'm certain,' he said with a smile. 'It's quite an unusual name. I think I'd have remembered.'

'You've never met her?'

'No.'

'And you didn't murder her?'

'No.'

'Let's move on,' Kat said, recalling Clare Capstick's words about the killer's mummy issues. 'Did your mum abuse you, Steven?'

He had been confidently holding her gaze. But now, his eyes slid away.

'No.'

'No? Did you fantasise about having sex with her?'

He shifted his weight from hip to hip. 'Horrible suggestion, but no.'

'Did you rape her, then?'

This time, he shuddered visibly. Disgust rippled across his face. He shook his head; a smile appeared, as false as a plastic police badge. 'Again, no.'

Wrong! she wanted to shout at him. Nobody smiles when a detective accuses them of that.

'Either way, one day you snapped and you murdered her. You left her body behind her workplace at Springfields.'

He folded his arms. His pupils were dilated. A passage towards the end of Clare Capstick's report came back to Kat. *Under enough stress, psychopaths can start to come apart. We call it decompensating. It means the wall of psychological defences they've erected to protect themselves starts to crumble. They can become vulnerable at that point. But dangerous, too.*

'I did not. Nobody knows who killed Mum,' he said. 'Maybe if she'd been more respectable, you lot would have put more effort into finding her killer.'

Kat nodded thoughtfully, letting him think he'd just made a devastating critique of police priorities.

'"Respectable"?'

His top lip curled back like a dog's. A fleeting expression.

'She was a whore. I'm sure you found that in your files.'

'That's an unpleasant word, isn't it? For a son to use about his mother? From what I've heard she was trying to earn a little extra money to look after her son. After little Stefan.'

This time he was unable to control his facial expression. '*Unpleasant?*' he sneered. 'Which term would you prefer, DS Ballantyne? Sex worker, I suppose. But why not be a little creative. Ooh, I know! How about physical therapist? Or leisure consultant? Stress relief coach?'

The solicitor laid a cautionary hand on Steven's left wrist. He looked down, then at the lawyer, as if seeing her for the first time.

'I think I'd like you to remove your hand, please,' he said in a quiet voice. 'Right. This. Second.'

Kat felt goosebumps break out on her arms. She was glad she had a long-sleeved shirt on.

The solicitor lifted her hand away and looked at Kat. A child could have interpreted her expression. She'd just realised that she was sitting on the wrong side of the table. Ten centimetres from a man who would think nothing of snapping her neck as if it were a breadstick. She swallowed audibly.

The menace that had inflected Steven's voice and subtly altered his features just a moment ago had gone. In its place, the open, smiling countenance he'd maintained throughout the interview.

'Sorry, where were we?'

'Can you tell us about the hair we found in your wardrobe?' she asked.

'Oh, that.'

'Yes, that. You know, the forty-one plaits, each labelled with initials, twelve of which match those of the twelve murder victims attributed to the man known as the Origami Killer.'

'I've been thinking of diversifying. I want to start a wig business. Those are samples from India. Real human hair. I think they get it off women who sell it. There's such terrible poverty there.'

'How do you explain the initials?'

'I had to name them somehow, to keep them separate. I just thought I might as well use the initials of the murder victims I read in the papers. I can see how it might look a bit odd, but they are dead after all, so it's not like I'm hurting anyone.'

'You also have a dartboard cabinet in your lounge filled with photos of the dead girls, and others,' Kat said. 'Plus origami paper.'

'It's true, I have been following the case quite closely, Kat,' he said, smiling. 'But that's because I live here. I did the origami so I could understand what makes him tick, that's all. I thought, if I could recreate aspects of his MO, it might be helpful one day if you hadn't caught him. And I do know the police quite well. I sell you your morning coffee and bacon roll, don't I?'

'Yes, you do, Steven. But it's a bit strange, isn't it? Replicating the killer's signature in your home. Weren't you worried how it might look if anyone found your' – she paused – '*recreations?*'

He shrugged. 'I suppose so. But as I didn't do it, I can't see why that would matter.'

There was a knock at the door. Kat turned. Leah's expression – barely suppressed smile, sparkling eyes – said it all. She held a single sheet of paper in her hand. Gave it to Kat without a word.

Kat looked down. One of the results delighted her. The other came as a total shock.

She nodded.

'Thanks, Leah. See you shortly.'

She returned to her chair. Gazed at the murderer sitting before her.

'Steven, at 8 p.m. this evening, the DNA lab in Birmingham performed a test on the sample you supplied when you were arrested,' she said. 'It is a match, an *exact* match, to the sample we recovered from Shannon Hollister's body. Would you like to explain to me how your saliva ended up in a bite mark on the left breast of a murder victim? A murder victim you have denied, while under caution, of knowing?'

'It must be a mistake. The testing equipment must have been faulty. They probably haven't calibrated it this month.'

If he was rattled, he didn't show it. It was as if his house, with its unreadable outward appearance, were a mirror of its occupant, neither of them giving away anything. Until you dug a little deeper.

Kat smiled, suddenly feeling she could afford to. She was about to dig a lot deeper.

'Steven, we're talking about millions of pounds' worth of highly sophisticated laboratory equipment, not an in-car speed camera,' she said. 'However, I'm sure at your trial, unless you decide to plead guilty and avoid all the stress, the Crown Prosecution Service barrister will be happy to confirm that the equipment was all tested, certified, checked, and generally in tip-top legal shape.'

He shrugged. 'Maybe a technician made a mistake.'

'Fair enough,' Kat said with a smile. 'How are your teeth?'

He pulled his head back. 'Pardon?'

'Visit the dentist regularly? Go for your twice-yearly check-up? Get the old scale-and-polish from the attractive young hygienist?'

'How is this relevant?' the solicitor asked, suddenly finding her voice again.

'When you murdered Shannon Hollister, Steven, when you *bit* her, you left an impression in that poor young girl's flesh that's as clear as anything you'd give to an orthodontist,' she said. 'Bite marks are as individual as fingerprints. Did you know that? From your frown, I'd say you didn't. So, the amazing thing, the actually, truly, *brilliant* thing, is that even if the DNA lab mixed your sample up with the Yorkshire Ripper's, we'd still have you. Now, I've requested that a forensic periodontist attend this police station tomorrow morning first thing. She's going to bring with her a state-of-the-art camera and we're going to take 3-D images of the inside of your mouth. If they match the bite mark, we won't even need the DNA evidence.'

Steven turned to his solicitor. 'Can they do that?'

The solicitor frowned.

'Yes, we can,' Kat said before the woman could answer. 'I have the legal authority to compel you to submit. If you refuse, I am also authorised to use such force as is necessary to secure your cooperation.'

'Well, I *do* refuse. This is outrageous. What about my rights. My *human* rights?'

'Your human rights will be fully respected at all times,' she said. 'But the taking of a dental image doesn't infringe them in any case, so you needn't worry. This is England, Steven, not some dodgy dictatorship. Interview suspended,' she said with a pleasant smile. 'Get some rest, Steven. It's your right. We'll see you in the morning. Sleep tight.'

◆ ◆ ◆

The forensic periodontist arrived at 9.15 a.m. the following day. She was a petite woman with a high, soft voice like a schoolgirl's that belied her thirty years' experience in the field.

In the end, Steven complied with her requests meekly, opening wide like a child on his first visit to the dentist. That didn't stop her from inserting a frame to hold his jaws apart.

'I'll need an hour or two to compare the two images,' she said, packing her equipment away.

The periodontist's email arrived at 11.35 a.m. Kat read it, scrutinised the annotated 3-D images, and smiled, satisfied. Half an hour later, tape machine running, she restarted the interview.

'The forensic periodontist sent us her results, Steven,' she said. 'They're conclusive. You bit Shannon Hollister. I can show you the photos if you like. They're fascinating. Incredible detail.'

'Do you have a question for my client?' the solicitor asked. From her tone, it was clear she just wanted to be out of the interview room, putting as much distance between her and her client as was possible without leaving Middlehampton.

'I do, yes,' Kat said. 'Can you explain how a bite mark that exactly matches your teeth, down to tenths of a millimetre, including the missing second premolar in your upper left jaw, found its way on to the left breast of a murder victim?'

Steven turned his emotionless gaze on Tom. Then Kat. She felt the hairs on the back of her neck erecting again. Her stomach clenched. It was like looking at a snake. Or a crocodile. Something predatory that could no more fathom the feelings of a human being than it could solve mathematical equations.

Slowly, Steven straightened in his chair and leaned towards her. 'No' – a pause – 'comment.'

She pursed her lips and nodded. She looked down at the NDNAD report. And the line that had shocked her before. 'I've seen your birth certificate,' she said. 'Under "Father's name" it says "unknown".'

He shrugged. 'One of the world's great mysteries.'

'*I* know who he is.'

The effect on him was instant. He reared back in the chair, gripping the arms, face blanching. 'What? You can't. Nobody knows. He was just one of my mother's tricks.'

She nodded. 'I know you questioned the accuracy of our DNA equipment last night. But I think we both know that was just for effect. Here's the thing, Steven. When the lab ran your DNA, it returned not one, but two matches,' she said, watching the changes to his skin tone and the increasingly random movements

312

of his eyes. 'The first was a perfect match to the saliva we found on Shannon Hollister's body. The second was a familial match to another recently submitted sample from Jubilee Place.'

His eyes flickered. His jaw muscle moved under the skin of his cheek.

'Who is it? Tell me. I have a right to know.'

Kat stared back at him. He was losing his cool. That could work in her favour.

'Why don't you tell me what I want to know first?'

Silence stretched out between them like a taut steel wire threaded with forty-one beads, each representing a dead girl.

CHAPTER FORTY-TWO

Steven turned to Tom.

'I'll explain it. But not to you, you smug little git. You can leave. I'll talk to Kat and nobody else.'

Tom's mouth dropped open.

'Interview suspended,' Kat said, snapping off the recorder.

She got to her feet.

Outside, in the corridor, Tom turned on her. 'You're not seriously going to let that arsehole order me out of the interview, are you?'

'If he's going to make an admission, Tom, yes, I am.'

'He's playing you. Can't you see that? He probably just wants to get off on talking you through how he killed them all.'

'And if that's what he starts doing, I'll terminate the interview. We've already got him,' she said. 'This is about saving time, money and pain. Remember, we've got dozens of grieving families out there, all looking for closure.'

He sighed. 'I just wanted to be in at the finish.'

'I know. But when he resorted to insults, *that* was the finish.'

She left Tom to watch the final act from the observation room and went back inside.

Steven turned to the solicitor. 'I won't be needing you anymore, Beth. You can go, too.'

Without so much as a sideways glance at her client, the solicitor gathered her things and left, shooting Kat a look. *Good luck.*

Steven started speaking the moment Kat finished reminding him he was still under caution. 'I was two the first time she did it to me,' he said in a quiet voice. 'She used to put me in the airing cupboard while she entertained her tricks. Can you imagine that, Kat? Growing up listening to your mother rutting in the next room?'

'No. I can't. What was it like?'

He smiled. 'Actually, it wasn't too bad. It was warm, and there was a big space behind the tank where I could snuggle down while I waited. It had a light, too. For my fourth birthday, she found this origami book in some charity shop and bought it for me. It came with a packet of paper. I could only make simple models to begin with. Dog. Fish. Hat. Baby stuff, really. The first one I mastered was the heart. I did loads of them. I sat cross-legged, warm next to the tank, folding, folding, folding. Smelling these lavender bags she stuck everywhere because she thought the smell was, quote-unquote, *ladylike.*

'She'd let me out when they were finished. She wasn't a complete psycho. I'd hold up my little folded heart and she'd take it from me. If she was in a good mood, she'd smile and say, "Pretty", and tuck it into her bra. If not, she'd crumple it up and fling it in my face.'

'When did you kill your mum, Steven?'

'I was eighteen. She was still plying her trade. I'd just had enough. Even when she wasn't turning tricks, her boyfriends were disgusting. They looked at me like I was some kind of simpleton. So I just waited outside the factory where she worked. When she was on lates, she finished at two in the morning, so it was pretty quiet. I strangled her and I dumped her there.'

'Is that when you started killing the others?'

'Not straightaway, but yes, pretty much. Everywhere I went I saw girls who reminded me of her. I just had this need to kill them.'

'And you just gave in to it, like needing a cigarette,' she said, feeling a surge of disgust so powerful it left a metallic taste in her mouth.

He shrugged. 'Like I said. I needed to.'

'So you admit to murdering Candace Pulford and the other women back in 2008?'

He sighed. 'I do, yes.'

'How did you find them, Steven? Did you have a snack van back then, too?'

He shook his head. 'No. I was working as a driver's mate. For a stationery supplier. Geoff did the driving, and I lugged the boxes into the offices. I used to chat to the receptionists, hang about waiting to get stuff signed, you know? It was an easy way to meet girls. You're sort of there but not there, if you know what I mean?'

'Invisible until you step out of the shadows.'

He grinned. 'Exactly! Just a guy in a uniform. And one thing I knew was, girls love a good listener. I worked out this method, you know? I'd be a perfect gentleman. Offer a compliment, but nothing obvious. Never about their figures or anything. Ask them about themselves, their jobs, what their ambitions were. I could tell they weren't used to it. Honestly, I ought to write a book about it. You know, *Pulford's Pickups: The Complete Guide to Attracting Women*.'

Inwardly Kat shuddered. Steven's sudden willingness to talk wasn't matched by even a shred of insight into his own behaviour. She'd leave that side of things to the judge.

'Why didn't you try to hide the bodies?'

He shrugged. 'I didn't really think I needed to. You know, because I wasn't interfering with them. I wasn't leaving any evidence behind me.'

'What about the hearts?'

'I made them with gloves on. And I wore gloves to put them, you know, with the girls.'

'I see.'

'Do you, Kat? Do you understand me? I hope you do.'

'Why did you stop killing in 2008, Steven?'

A smile ghosted across Steven's face. 'Well, after I killed Faye, they brought in a new detective to head the investigation. You probably know that already. He seemed to be taking it more seriously. I thought I'd better make myself scarce. I went to Europe. Travelled around. I'd never been out of Middlehampton, so you can imagine it was quite an eye-opener.'

'And you carried on killing, didn't you? You killed at least twenty-nine more girls.'

'That many? I lost count, to be honest. It's partly why I keep the hair.'

Kat frowned. 'What I don't understand, Steven, is why you came back?'

He sighed. 'Brexit. Without freedom of movement, I was a bit stuck. I returned two years ago.'

'But you didn't start killing again until last month. Why?'

He smiled. 'Katya.'

Kat shuddered. 'Please don't call me that, Steven.'

'Not you, silly! My wife. Katya's Polish. I met her the day I got back, if you can believe it. She's a freelance translator. She didn't have many friends. And I thought, well, Steven my boy, here's your chance. You can marry her, get her pregnant and settle down and maybe, just maybe, you'll be able to stop this time.'

'Did it work?' Kat asked dryly.

'For two years, yes, it did. Although there was something wrong with her. We never did get a child. Then she left me. Just upped sticks and went back to Poland. Said I, quote-unquote, *frightened* her.'

317

'Why? What did you do?'

'She has short blonde hair, so I asked her to wear a wig. You can probably guess what kind. In bed, I mean. And I wanted us to play with my special grains.'

Kat felt her gorge rising. '"Play".'

'Yes.'

'And she left you because of that?' *Sensible woman.*

'Yes, if you can believe it. I'm afraid to say that without Katya as an outlet for my urges, things just sort of slid a bit. I killed Courtney about two weeks after Katya flew back to Warsaw. It's really not my fault, Kat. I'm the real victim here.'

Was he baiting her or did he genuinely believe what had just emerged from his lips? It didn't matter. She needed one more word from him.

'Did you murder Courtney Hatch, Jade Root, Ruby Spence, Corinne Gregory and Shannon Hollister?'

He held her gaze for a second. Then he smiled. 'Yes. Yes, I did.'

'Thank you, Steven.'

He bit his lip. 'So who is he? You said you'd tell me who my father was.'

She glanced at the DNA report again. Obviously, Karl Oldfield had been visiting prostitutes for a lot longer than since his wife's death. In fact, as far back as February 1988. Candace Pulford had been sixteen; he'd been twenty. She gave birth to Stefan in November of that year.

She briefly considered withholding the information. No. She'd made a promise, and promises, even to serial killers, needed to be kept.

'Your father is a man named Karl Oldfield.'

His eyes flashed. 'I want to see him. I *demand* to see him.'

Kat looked at Steven across the table and saw him for what he was. Not a disturbed genius. Not a highly intelligent, cultured, gentleman-murderer. Just an average-looking man in ill-fitting prison sweats. A self-pitying psychopath with zero awareness of what he was. No snarling countenance. No ranting about Satan or Jesus or talking dogs. He had urges and he acted on them. That was it. A repulsive killer who talked about his victims the way other men talked about their favourite Netflix show, or their toy car collection.

She got to her feet.

'Stay in your seat, please, Steven,' she said, half hoping he'd lunge at her so she could beat him to the ground. But he just sat there, arms loose by his sides, smiling at her. She crossed to the door and opened it. 'You can come back in now,' she told the uniformed PC standing outside the door. 'Take him down to the cells. We're done.'

But as she was about to leave, Steven called out to her.

'Kat?'

She turned, slowly.

'That last one in 2008? Olivia Arnold? That wasn't me. I was going to,' he said, with another repellent smile. 'I asked her out, but she turned me down flat. I think she might have sensed I wasn't quite as charming as I made myself out to be.'

'Tell it to the judge, Steven,' she said.

He was done. He could protest all he wanted that he hadn't killed Liv but who would believe him?

Feeling suddenly nauseous, she spun round and left the room.

CHAPTER FORTY-THREE

Kat's life returned to normal.

Not normal-people normal.

She was still up to her armpits in post-mortem reports, forensics, witness statements, and slack-jawed male murder suspects, slumped with their legs so far apart she wanted to kick them in the nuts and shout at them to show some respect. But normal-for-Kat normal.

Even Linda's bollocking for ignoring her instructions for the arrest had only been delivered at half-strength.

A couple of weeks later, she was heading home after clearing the last of the Origami Killer paperwork for the Crown Prosecution Service. Just as the lift doors were closing, a hand snaked in between them. They slid open and Carve-up stepped inside, resplendent in a shimmering silver-grey suit. Kat tensed, but all he did was press the button for the ground floor.

On the way down, he turned to her.

'Something felt off when that Sky tart asked you about Liv Arnold in the press conference,' he said.

'I don't know what you mean,' she said.

'Don't you? You see, you're not the only star detective in MCU. I might be senior management now, but I do know how to follow up lines of enquiry.'

She shrugged, acting breezier than she felt. 'Whatever.'

He grinned evilly. '"Whatever." Yeah, OK, we're teenagers again. Anyhoo, funny thing is, a few weeks ago, Tom mentioned you met some woman in the street when you two went out for coffee. Said you came back white as a sheet.' He leaned closer. 'Like you'd seen a ghost.'

Kat glanced at the floor indicator. She was trapped. Nowhere to hide, nowhere to run. One floor to go then she could be free of him. His hand slammed the red button labelled EMERG STOP. The lift shuddered to a halt, cables twanging somewhere over their heads.

Carver turned to face her full-on.

'I started wondering who this mystery woman might be. Couldn't be a friend, could it? You don't turn white when you meet a mate in the street, do you? Or not a current one, anyway.'

'What are you getting at?' she said, hoping that speculating was as far as he'd got, fearing it wasn't. Her palms felt damp and her fingertips were tingling.

'What I'm getting at, *DS Ballantyne*, is that it would be really weird, you know, practically *ghostly*, if you saw an old friend who you thought was dead. That would really spook you, wouldn't it?'

She opened her mouth to reply. To defend herself. Then closed it slowly. He didn't know it was Liv. Not for sure. And without evidence, he had nothing.

'Amazing though it might seem, Stu, I think you've been working too hard. You're imagining things. Maybe you should take a couple of days' leave.'

He nodded. 'You know what? Maybe I should. Although I'm a terror for working on my days off. Like, I'll be all set to sit down to watch the football and I'll find myself ringing the council to request CCTV footage from North Street on the day you were there.'

Carve-up thought he was being clever. In reality his moves were as predictable as any low-level thug she'd gone up against in

321

the interview rooms. *You scratch my back, DS Ballantyne . . .* they'd say, as if they'd just coined this brilliant phrase.

'What do you want, Stu?'

He stepped back and let his hand drift up to the emergency stop button.

'I know you've been poking your nose into my business,' he said. 'Well, maybe you should poke it all the way back out again. I'm sure if you did that, I could spend my time off watching Middlehampton and not hours of CCTV.'

So that was it. Blackmail. Leave Carve-up's corruption alone and he'd not report her for professional malpractice. But she had another card to play in this unpleasant little game he'd started.

'Maybe instead of watching football, you could watch a movie, Stu,' she said, making him frown. 'You know, one of those oldies. How about *The Three Musketeers*?'

The frown turned into a scowl. He opened his mouth. Then closed it again. She could see his mind working beneath his thin-skinned forehead, wondering whether this was an innocent riposte or whether she actually knew something. Kat smiled at him. Waited.

He jabbed the button and the lift jerked into motion again. Ten seconds later, they reached the ground floor and the doors opened. Kat stepped out. From behind her, Carve-up threw out a final insult she only heard half of.

'—you, Kitty-Kat.'

Shaking with anger, she headed for the car park. She called her dad.

'Hello, daughter-mine, nice to hear from you.'

'Stuart Carver just called me Kitty-Kat,' she said, suddenly short of breath.

'Sounds like things are thawing between you, then. That's good.'

'Cut the crap, Dad! The only person in the entire world who calls me that is you. And you know I hate it.'

'I may have let it slip during a golf game.'

'Really. Well your golfing *buddy* just threatened me. And now I'm wondering whether my nickname is all you let slip.'

'What do you mean?'

'I mean, maybe you told your tame DI to put the screws on me so I wouldn't look too closely at his relationship with you.'

'Kat, darling, this must be stress talking. I know how much that case took out of you,' he said, sounding infuriatingly reason-able. One of his conversational tricks. 'Anyway, I thought we'd agreed that you'd leave any potential investigation of my business affairs to your colleagues. Not, of course, that there's anything *to* investigate, but you get my drift. What was it you said? "Unless you've murdered someone, I'll keep out of your hair."'

She swallowed hard, but the lump in her throat refused to budge. It felt like she'd swallowed one of Colin Morton's damned golf balls.

Unable to speak, she stabbed the End Call button and climbed into the car.

◆　◆　◆

Kat spent most of the following Saturday clearing out the spare bedroom and burning everything, including her copies of the police files, in the incinerator at the end of the garden.

As she poked at the fire with a stick, her phone rang. She answered without checking caller ID.

'Kat, it's me. It's Liv. After you left the farm I realised what an idiot I'd been,' she said. 'I thought we could go out for a few wines and catch up properly, you know?'

Kat's mood, so relaxed just a moment ago, shifted. She felt resentment rearing up out of nowhere. Fifteen years with literally zero contact and now Liv wanted to go for a drink? Carve-up's threats echoed in her head as she answered.

'I'm still pretty busy with work, Liv. And it's a fair old drive to Wales.'

'I could come over to Middlehampton. It might be fun to hang out now that you've caught Steven.'

'No!' Kat said, almost shouting, then again, at a normal volume, 'No. I want to see where you've made your new home. There must be some fantastic pubs on the coast near you.'

'Well, there are a few. Hey! You could stay over this time.' She laughed. 'We could have a midnight feast. It'd be just like old times.'

Kat's heart sank. Had Liv always been like this? Impulsive? Expecting Kat to drop everything whenever she called?

'Let me check my diary, OK? I'll text you some dates.'

Five minutes later, as the files burned down, Ivan came out to stand beside her. He put his arm around her waist, and they stood together, hip to hip, inhaling the smell of burning paper.

ACKNOWLEDGEMENTS

I want to thank you for buying this book. I hope you enjoyed it. As an author is only part of the team of people who make a book the best it can be, this is my chance to thank the people on *my* team.

For sharing their knowledge and experience of The Job, former and current police officers Andy Booth, Ross Coombs, Jen Gibbons, Neil Lancaster, Sean Memory, Trevor Morgan, Olly Royston, Chris Saunby, Ty Tapper, Sarah Warner and Sam Yeo.

For their patience, professionalism and friendship, the fabulous publishing team at Thomas & Mercer: commissioning editors Leodora Darlington (now moved on to pastures new) and Victoria Haslam; development editor Russel McLean; copyeditor Gemma Wain; and proofreader Jill Sawyer. Plus the wonderful marketing team including Hatty Stiles and Nicole Wagner. And Dominic Forbes, who really delivered on the brief with a fantastic cover design.

The members of my Facebook Group, The Wolfe Pack, are an incredibly supportive and also helpful bunch of people. Thank you to them, also.

And for being an inspiration and source of love and laughter, and making it all worthwhile, my family: Jo, Rory and Jacob.

The responsibility for any and all mistakes in this book remains mine. I assure you, they were unintentional.

Andy Maslen, Salisbury, 2023

ABOUT THE AUTHOR

Photo © 2021, Kin Ho

Andy Maslen was born in Nottingham, England. After leaving university with a degree in psychology, he worked in business for thirty years as a copywriter. In his spare time, he plays blues guitar. He lives in Wiltshire.

Follow the Author on Amazon

If you enjoyed this book, follow Andy Maslen on Amazon to be notified when the author releases a new book!
To do this, please follow these instructions:

Desktop:

1) Search for the author's name on Amazon or in the Amazon App.
2) Click on the author's name to arrive on their Amazon page.
3) Click the 'Follow' button.

Mobile and Tablet:

1) Search for the author's name on Amazon or in the Amazon App.
2) Click on one of the author's books.
3) Click on the author's name to arrive on their Amazon page.
4) Click the 'Follow' button.

Kindle eReader and Kindle App:

If you enjoyed this book on a Kindle eReader or in the Kindle App, you will find the author 'Follow' button after the last page.